Only the
River Runs Free

A NOVEL

ONLY THE RIVER RUNS FREE

A NOVEL

BODIE & BROCK THOENE

THOMAS NELSON PUBLISHERS

Nashville • Atlanta • London • Vancouver

Published in association with the literary agency of Alive Communications, 1465
Kelly Johnson Blvd., Suite #320, Colorado Springs, CO 80920.

Published in Nashville, Tennessee, by Thomas Nelson, Inc., and distributed in
Canada by Word Communications, Ltd., Richmond, British Columbia, and in the
United Kingdom by Word (UK), Ltd., Milton Keynes, England.

Library of Congress information
Thoene, Bodie, 1951–
    Only the river runs free / Bodie and Brock Thoene.
        p.   cm.
    ISBN 0-7852-8067-7
    I. Thoene, Brock, 1952– . II. Title.
PS3570.H46054   1997
813'.54—dc21   97-29671
                                              CIP

Printed in the United States of America

1 2 3 4 5 6 7 - 03 02 01 00 99 98 97

For Chance and Jessie; the joy grows daily . . .
and for Maria Lanakila, with thanks.

Other Books by Bodie and Brock Thoene

Shiloh Autumn

The Twilight of Courage

Hope Valley War

The Legend of Storey County

The Zion Convenant Series

The Zion Chronicles Series

The Shiloh Legacy Series

The Saga of the Sierras

Prologue

For he comes, the human child
To the waters and the wild
With a faery, hand in hand,
From a world more full of weeping than he can understand.

—W. B. Yeats from the "The Stolen Child"

It was late afternoon of a cold, raw day in February 1827. The Galway mail coach threaded a slow course across the long barren plain that led west toward Lough Corrib and Castletown and the mountains that lay beyond.

Rain fell heavily throughout the day. Thick black mud obscured the yellow side panels of the coach, clung to the wheels and traces, and added to the burden of the exhausted horses. Dripping umbrellas hung down from every side of the vehicle. A dozen passengers were crammed within. Flannel nightcaps and shared blankets offered some warmth as they peered out through the dirty glass at the landscape.

Conversation had trailed away hours before. Some of the travelers dozed while others sank back in moody thought, wondering if the journey would ever end. These were the lucky passengers who had cash enough for the best seats, the inside seats.

Outside, hats firmly pressed down and lashed in place with scarves, heads tucked against the biting wind, were seven additional travelers. These could not afford the comfort of full-fare accommodations.

In the back rumble with the guard sat a burly, cheerful man who seemed untroubled by the weather. He called himself Daniel and offered no other name, first or last. Appearing to be in his mid-forties, the wayfarer was clean-shaven, broad of face, and handsome. The wind had stung his cheeks to ruddy red and his eyes were bright blue. An oiled foraging cap was tied beneath his chin. He held one wing of a wide cloak around a boy of not more than eight years of age who slept snuggled against him.

Daniel glanced down at the child's fair complexion and blond hair. "Poor little fellow. He's sleepin' it out well. For such a great house, they certainly don't take over-much thought of him or they'd never have sent him out on top of a coach in such weather, without so much as a coat." The man plucked at the sleeve of the boy's thin jacket. "I have heard his father was once a member of the Irish Parliament in Dublin before it was dissolved."

The guard, who gathered up every shred of gossip along the roads of Galway, nodded curtly and returned, "Aye, that he was. The Burke stood for Castletown at our Parliament in Dublin. Then after the Act of Union he gave his fortune fightin' for the Emancipation. The English said he conspired, though they could prove naught. 'Twas years in an English prison that near broke him, that and her ladyship's death, God rest her soul. The brother-in-law, Marlowe, took charge of affairs then and this lad was sent away to school. Now The Burke is dyin', if he's not dead already. Me second cousin is a stablehand in those great ruined stables of the great ruined manor. He says the great House of Burke cannot afford so much as a greatcoat for the heir."

"Is Marlowe the lad's guardian then?"

"Aye. By English law. Who can say what will come of the boy? Old Marlowe has a son Connor's age. William is the pretty creature's name. No extravagance is too good for him. They say William treats the servants like . . . servants. While Connor calls all by name and sits at the hearth among even the lowliest. William was sent to school in England, to Eton among the sons of the English lords; Connor to Dublin, to some boarding school. I cannot recollect the name of it. Marlowe holds the reins in this matter and would not mind if little Connor Burke was to follow shortly after his father. Then they might have a free hand with the estate. Marlowe'll let the cold weather do his dirty work. Aye. The boy has no coat, nor will he from the grace of Marlowe."

At this Daniel tucked the child's hand protectively beneath the hem of the cloak and pondered what he had heard. A long hour of silence passed as the traveler gazed sadly at small Connor Burke and then at the misty landscape of Galway.

Horses straining at the harness, the coach climbed upward through the wild beauty of rocky, undulating hills. Like the tweed of a rough woolen cloth, the countryside of Connaught was a mix of brown and green patches stitched together by the slim gray threads of stone walls. Here and there along the way were dilapidated cottages and meager lean-tos for livestock. The poverty of western Ireland was evident everywhere. Hovels amid the thin soil made clear the meaning of the words of the defeated Irish lords when they said they were "banished by the English to hell or Connaught."

"How far now to Burke Park?" Daniel asked the guard.

"Over the crest of the hill. Perhaps a mile. Castletown a bit farther."

Leaning down, Daniel said softly to the boy, "Connor, my lad, wake up. You're not far from home now. Are you dreamin' of the fire and the stew and the warm bed—eh?"

The guard cocked an eyebrow at the stirring child. "A bit of bread if he's lucky and a roof over his head if those who have charge over his father's affairs are moved by pity."

At this Daniel's blue eyes flashed anger, as though he knew some terrible secret about the men who managed the affairs of the once mighty family of Burke. But he held himself from comment, regained a look of detached interest, and nudged the boy as the gate of Burke Park rose into view. To the guard Daniel remarked, "No need to blow the horn for this stop." The coachman looked puzzled, but obligingly put by his brass trumpet.

Connor Burke sat up stiffly and shuddered. Glancing at the gray sky he squinted and inquired of Daniel, "Home, sir?"

Careful not to let the guard hear him, the big man nodded once, then bent low to whisper in Connor's ear, "Tell your father that Daniel came this far with you. Tell none other in the house but Molly. I'll be at Ballynockanor with the priest if you have need." Then in a loud voice he remarked, "Here you are, little Master Burke! I hope you find your father in better health." He swung the boy down to the ground and gave him a solemn nod of farewell as the coach started on to the Castletown Inn.

Connor Burke stood in the center of the road watching after the coach until it disappeared over the rise. A thin, frail, old man hobbled out of the dilapidated gatehouse, peered suspiciously at Connor, then with a cry of recognition rushed to him.

"Bless me, 'tis the young master! God be praised you've come in time!" The aged porter struggled to open the gate, which hung on a rusted hinge.

"Hullo, Liam. How's my father then?"

The elderly servant replied with a gloomy nod. "I daren't go near the house. When your father took ill a month ago, your uncle had me served notice. They tell the master I've gone, though I'm still here as you can see. Molly Fahey brings me news from the great house and supper from the kitchen each day so I haven't starved. Ah, what's to become of us all?"

Connor did not respond to Liam's question. He could not. "Father will get well and everything will be as it was," he said, then walked past the gate and into the grounds. Connor had only heard of the *good* times. Honor and fortune were bedtime stories that had sweetened his dreams till his mother had died and left him alone with his broken father.

Evening was fast approaching. Connor looked up into the swollen clouds, the gloom of the day reflecting the foreboding in his heart. The avenue that led to the manor house was nearly obliterated from disuse and neglect. Fences had long ago been broken up for burning. Ancient trees that had once canopied above the road had shared the same fate. Cattle grazed in unkempt fields that had been the broad lawns of the estate in better days. His eyes traced the distinct outline of the old stone mansion, with high pitched roof and tall pointed gables beneath the sky. With an indefinable sense of fear, Connor kept his eyes fixed on the solitary light that twinkled from the upper window where his father lay. The rest of the house remained in darkness.

Daylight was nearly gone when Connor mounted the long flight of slate steps that led to the terrace. The balustrades were broken now by time and weather; the heavy granite stone was cracked and crumbling. The massive oak doors were left wide open to the cold, giving the mansion an utterly deserted feel. Connor stepped over the threshold and into the hall. A small peat fire flickered in the center of the massive hearth. The walls about the boy were lined with grim portraits of Connor's grandfathers who had ruled the House of Burke for generations. What must those old men think of their kingdom now? Stern, dark eyes seemed to follow the boy as he shuddered and moved toward the fire.

Above him the sweeping staircase vanished into shadow. The sound of men's voices drifted down to him as he stretched out his hands to warm them. Uncle Marlowe was here and some other man whose voice Connor could not recognize. He longed to see his father but waited, hating the thought of Marlowe seeing him cry. And Connor knew he would cry when he saw his da again, perhaps for the last time.

Behind him footsteps sounded on the paving, then stopped abruptly. Connor turned to see who had entered the hall. After a long moment the voice of Molly Fahey cried, "Is it you, Connor? Mary and Joseph! Have you come then?" She did not wait for

Connor to reply, but rushed to him and pulled the boy into her arms. Relief flooded him, and he began to cry as he had not let himself since her letter and the meager coach fare had arrived at school in Dublin.

"Molly! Am I too late? Can I see him?"

Brushing back his damp hair and wiping his tears and her own with her apron she whispered, "Marlowe's up there with him and John Stone as well. Your father called for the priest, but they've sent for the vicar, Master Hodge, the Protestant. Small comfort to your poor dear father . . . ah, but when he sees your face, Connor Burke! Well, then!"

"Daniel said to say he came with me. He's at the priest's house in Ballynockanor, he is."

She had no time to reply, but crossed herself in silent gratitude.

The voices of Marlowe, Stone, and Vicar Hodge moved from the bedchamber onto the balcony that overlooked the hall. Molly gasped and pulled Connor into the shadow beside the grimy fireplace. Placing a finger to her lips she warned Connor to silence. Her mouth against his ear she whispered in a barely audible tone, "They do not know I sent for ye. After they've gone we'll go to your da."

Marlowe's words were distinct, echoing in the great chamber. "The boy will be no problem, I assure you. Fetch him at school in Dublin and then apprentice him to . . . well, to some trade or other."

Connor leaned his head in despair against Molly, and she held him tighter.

John Stone, steward of the Burke estate, replied, "My wife's brother is a merchant captain who sails out of Belfast. He'll be glad to take the boy."

The vicar blew his nose loudly and said, "The will is witnessed. Aye, it's witnessed. No one will dispute my word."

It was then that Marlowe caught sight of Molly's white cap and apron in the shadow. "Who's there?" he called from the balcony.

Pushing Connor back against the wall, Molly called up, "Only me, sir. Only Molly. The fire's low, sir." She moved into the light as if she had not heard a word of their conspiracy. The maid snatched up the iron and jabbed at the pitiful mound of peat bricks, sending a few sparks crackling up the chimney. "And a poor fire it is, too, against the cold that comes through that open door, sir. Like a barn it will be until the hinges are repaired. We'll need more fuel if there's to be any warmth at all in this great drafty house, sir! Donovan the dairyman has cut a fine mound of black, heavy turf up at Ballynockanor. Say the word and I'll send to him for . . ."

Her cheerful babbling was cut off by an oath from Marlowe. "Clear off with you! Let the fire die and get back to your kitchen!"

Molly replaced the poker. Connor caught the gleam of fury in her eyes, but still she smiled vaguely up at the trio as if she had paid the rebuke no mind. "And would you be havin' a cuppa tay, good sirs?"

Marlowe roared, "Get back to the kitchen, or you'll be given notice and turned out like the rest. I'll not have some half-witted charwoman eavesdropping about!"

Molly curtsied low and whispered to Connor, "Stay put." With that she waved brightly at the faceless figures above her and rustled away toward the kitchen.

The men waited until Molly's footsteps receded, then proceeded slowly down the stairs.

Marlowe said, "His Majesty's government knows me for a loyal fellow. There will be no question. When we collect the rents my brother-in-law so kindly forgave . . ."

"And the tithes," replied the vicar, rubbing his hand across his chin. "Don't forget the tithes."

"We'll be putting the estate back on the map again." Marlowe finished the thought and summed up the plans for his future. "New beginnings, eh? Marlowe Park we shall rename it, so no one misses the point. With your help there will be light and fire in this hall once again, when Burke is dead and buried. I promise you that, gentlemen!"

They passed, unseeing, close to Connor, who crouched into a ball beside the peat bricks. The boy smelled the scent of stale cigar smoke and whiskey on his uncle's clothes. *When Burke is dead?* Marlowe's cheerful voice burned in Connor's mind. The boy fought the impulse to fly at his uncle and pound the protruding belly that strained the buttons of a soiled silk waistcoat. The child peered out at the lean-shanked legs as they sauntered toward the open door and heard them call for the carriage.

In a businesslike tone the vicar remarked, "The funeral ought to be on a Sunday. There'll be no getting people to come on any other day."

Marlowe's voice echoed back, "It won't be long now, gentlemen. I'll send word when he's dead."

Pity and grief constricted Connor's throat. He would not cry! He must be a man! Who would mourn his father when he was gone? Who would care that a great patriot had sacrificed everything for the people of the land and for Ireland? Connor remained huddled between the peat and the cold stones for nearly three-quarters of an hour. His stomach rumbled with hunger. He had not eaten since early morning, and it was past nine o'clock.

At last, when Marlowe had made his way back to his own room and the light from the flames was little more than a glow against the pavement, Molly returned. She held the stub of a candle, which she lit at the hearth. In the roomy pockets of her apron she carried two thick slices of soda bread and a roasted potato.

"Have you eaten Connor, lad?" She offered him the morsels of food, which he crammed into his mouth and the pockets of his jacket. "I thought you might be hungry." She raised her eyes to the landing. "Well, then. Monster Marlowe is gone to his bed. Come along. Your poor dear father will be glad to see you, child."

She led him down the corridor to the servants' stairs, then up a narrow spiral staircase to the second floor and the back entrance to the bedroom. Afraid to speak, Connor followed in silence and dread. He knew well this would be the last hour on earth he would spend with his father.

Mindful of unoiled hinges, Molly opened the door of the bedroom slowly. With a quick, uneasy glance she warned Connor, "Do not expect that he will look as he once did. . . ." Her words trailed off as they entered the sickroom. A pile of documents and papers was heaped on a small round table between two chairs by the fire.

Molly bolted the door to the front hallway and left the back entry slightly ajar for a quick escape.

The peat burned low and Molly, clucking her tongue at the chill, tended the blaze. Connor waited at the foot of his father's bed. Labored wheezing emanated from behind the curtains of the four-poster. He knew he stood in the presence of death, and yet he could think of no one now but his mother.

Closing his eyes he pictured her lying on the sofa of the drawing room. *The window was open; the blinds drawn. Sunlight streamed in with a June breeze. The scent of flowers filled the room and she smiled at him and asked him to sing for her. . . .*

Unbidden, Connor muttered the word, "Mama?"

Molly put her hand on his shoulder and led him to the side of the bed. Drawing back the heavy curtain she spoke, "Master Burke, the son is come home from Dublin to be with you. It's himself, sir, Connor."

A faint sigh and some unintelligible words replied. Connor stepped closer, shaking his head as if there were some terrible mistake. The old frail man before him could not be his father! His beard had grown and grayed so much, and he had wasted away so much that Connor could barely recognize him. He was lying on his back, his arms outside the blankets. Connor fixed his gaze on the hands. *The hands were unchanged!*

Connor groaned and slipped his small fist beneath the large, strong fingers of his father. There was a momentary closing of the grip and then a release.

"Da!" Connor choked on the word. "I've come home to you, Da!"

Now the large head of The Burke pivoted slightly on the pillow. Eyes attempted to define the dim shape of the child. "Conn? Is it yourself, lad?"

Connor sank to his knees and laid his head down beside his father. "It's me, Da. Your own Connor. I've come home to you."

Molly added gently, "The boy traveled the whole long way from Dublin. . . ."

With a startling energy Burke attempted to sit up and whispered fiercely, "You must get him away, Molly! If Marlowe knows he's here!" He began to cough. "They'll . . . kill Conn as they have killed me! Do you hear me? . . . Away!"

Connor began to sob and clutch Burke's arm. "No, Da! I cannot leave you! Daniel came this far with me, Da! He said I should tell you!"

At the mention of Daniel, Old Burke sank back with relief and nodded once. "Daniel will care for you. Glad I am that Daniel's come. I have the proof of what they've done." He turned his face toward the maid. "Here, Molly. Take the key from under the mattress." The serving woman did as he bid. "There. Now lift the plank as I showed you before. In the small casket. The papers. Their letters. Marlowe. Stone. It's all there, what they have done to me. Hide them well till Connor can . . ." He faltered. "Get the boy to Daniel tonight." Another fit of coughing seized the old man, and when it ended he collapsed into a deep sleep without another word.

Connor clung to his father and cried, "I won't go! I can't leave him now! I won't go!"

Molly stroked the child's hair and tried to calm him. "Come now, Connor lad. It is your father's wish. The Burke's command. You must go." She glanced fearfully over her shoulder as if expecting Marlowe to crash through the locked door at any moment.

"I'll never see Da anymore!" the boy said, sobbing.

"Come now, Connor! Don't make me sorry I sent for you!" She lifted him up. "Kiss your da good-night, lad. We must be away before Marlowe finds you here. I'd no thought there could be danger to yourself. For the sake of your da. . . ."

Connor nodded and brushed back his tears. Molly boosted him nearer to Burke's face.

As the boy touched the broad forehead, then brushed his lips across his father's cheek in final farewell, the latch of the bedroom entry rattled. This sound was followed by the heavy pounding of a fist against the door.

"Who's in there?" shouted Marlowe. "Open up at once!"

Molly's face ashen, she groped beneath the floorboard for the hidden documents. Paralyzed with fear of his uncle, Connor gaped wide-eyed as the bolt strained against Marlowe's furious attempt to enter.

"Blessed be!" Molly gasped as her fingers closed around the brass-bound box. She crammed it under her arm, grabbed Connor's elbow, and dragged him toward their escape. Marlowe laid off pounding and ran to the stairs.

Terror gripped Connor as the shouts of Marlowe boomed through the house. Connor's legs would not move. Molly grabbed him up and threw him over her shoulder like a sack of meal. She clambered down the spiral stairway and, not daring to stop for her cloak, sprinted for the kitchen door and the obscurity of the dark night.

She was panting and exhausted by the time they neared the front gate. "You'll have to make it on your own, child. Come to your senses! Four miles to go to Daniel and Ballynockanor!"

Hearing her urgent voice the old gatekeeper tottered out of the gatehouse and held up his lantern. "You're late with my supper, Molly," he croaked. "And it's young Master Connor with you."

Lamps were being lit until all the house was illuminated, as though in flames.

"What are you doin' with the young master, Molly?" queried Liam.

Molly retrieved the potato from Connor's pocket. She fumbled with it for a moment, then tossed it to the sentry. "Here's your prattie. Eat up. Marlowe's on the prowl, old man. Don't let him see you. Don't tell him who brought you the prattie for supper, or I shall be discharged as well."

The old porter nodded and took a bite. "If that's the way it is . . ." He blew out the lantern and retreated into the darkness of his shelter as Molly gave Connor a fierce hug and then a quick shake. "You can run, lad. I've seen you do it. To Daniel then and don't look back!"

The baying of hounds in the kennels, excited without knowing why, combined with shouts of men at the house. The pursuit was coming! The boy started toward the gate, faltered, looking over his shoulder toward the window and the last glimpse of his father.

"Go! Across the fields with you," Molly hissed from the shadows of the fuchsia vine–covered walls. "They don't know you've been here. Only go!"

Connor bolted through the opening and lunged into a culvert beside the drive. He heard a voice shouting, "Shall I call out the lads, Master Marlowe?" It was the whining tone of John Stone.

"No!" Marlowe bellowed gruffly. "Not before we know what's stirring. But someone was in with Burke. Come on!"

Creeping along the culvert toward the shelter of the bawnditch wall that enclosed the south pasture, Connor heard pounding on the door of the gatekeeper's cottage. "Open up there, Liam!" Connor heard Marlowe demand. "We saw your light, man! We know you're awake."

The door creaked open. "What is it, then, sirs?" Liam inquired in a perplexed and sleepy tone.

"No time for your foolishness, old man!" Steward John Stone retorted. A sharp smack as of a fist striking a cheekbone and a groan reached Connor. Stone continued, "Who was here with you just now? Quick man, or it'll be the worse for you!"

When Liam did not respond soon enough to suit the steward, there was another distinct crack. Connor edged closer to the stone embankment. The boy wanted to run, but dared not move in the darkness for fear of dislodging a rock and giving away his whereabouts.

Liam's voice was thin and panting when Connor heard it again. "I don't know why you abuse me this way," Liam said. "I've done naught. It was only the young master was here."

"Connor? Here?" Marlowe exploded. "Hurry, man! Who was with him?"

"No one, sirs," Liam insisted. "He was dropped off by the coach an hour . . . some hours . . . since. Did you not see him up to the Great House?"

His uncle swore a terrible oath as Connor stretched upright in the darkness and gripped the topmost stones of the wall. "He was in the room with his father, and there'll be the devil to pay if we don't get him back."

"Shall I fetch the horses, sir?" Stone inquired.

"No use. If he's fled he'll go across the fields, and we cannot jump the walls in the dark. We'll bring the hounds!"

The hounds! The terrible wolfhounds that could haul down a running deer and tear the throat out of a bull! Connor trembled as a shiver ran along his spine. At the next words the hair on the back of his neck prickled: "And fetch the guns too!"

"Aye!" Stone agreed.

"But sir," Liam protested. "You'll not be runnin' the boy to earth to harm him, surely. The young master? I'll not let you hurt the lad."

There came the rustle of grappling in the darkness, then Stone's voice demanded, "Let go, old man!" Connor heard the noise a shillelagh makes whistling through the air and then a wet crunch like an egg dropped on flagstones. A short shriek, abruptly cut off, lifted Connor over the wall, his legs churning before he ever hit the soft mud on the other side. He heard footsteps running toward the kennels and his uncle's voice bellowing, "And send for Constable Carroll too!"

Where was he to go? What had Molly said? To Daniel, that was it! To Daniel at the priest's house in Ballynockanor. But which way was Ballynockanor in the cloud-shrouded night? Up the river and up the hills! That was it! He must find the river and follow it to the village.

Behind the lad hounds bayed and the pinpricks of lanterns bobbed through the gate of the manor. Away he plunged, slipping on the rain-slick grass and tripping over tussocks. Tumbling down the lip of a depression, Connor rolled into something that moved and bleated, frightening him. The boy was into the flock of sheep before he even saw them, bunched together against the cold and damp.

Pulling himself upright, Connor pushed between the oily heavy-fleeced bodies. It was like swimming in mud as the flock parted and then coalesced around him. The whole mass moved toward the far wall of the field.

"There's something amiss with the sheep," John Stone's voice called out. "Shall I loose the dogs?"

Marlowe's piercing cry of "No!" came too late. Their claws scrambling at the wall, the hounds broke from Stone's grasp and hurled themselves across the pasture just as Connor reached the far end.

It was down the slope to the river now and no time to lose. Connor's legs could not move fast enough to keep up with the downward plunge. A rock rolled under his foot, flipping him over into a headfirst slide amid the rubble of the incline. Thornbushes scraped bloody furrows in his cheeks as the boy spilled into a heap of gorse. He lay there, dazed and gasping, willing his legs to lift him again, knowing the hounds were only moments behind.

Savage barks and growls were succeeded by a terrified explosion of bleats. The scattered pounding of many hooves and high-pitched squeals of panic cascaded over the rim above the boy. The hounds caught the agitated excitement of the men and the wild feel of the night. The slavering animals tore into the flock of sheep, driven by the killing lust of their kind.

"You stupid fool!" Marlowe shouted. "They're slaughtering the sheep!"

Up and running again, Connor lunged forward, away from the smell of hot blood carried on the breeze. When he reached the bank of the river, he turned northwest to follow its course up into the hills. How long before the men dragged the hounds away from the herd and set them on his track again? And how in the darkness would he find the right turning that would bring him to the village and safety?

Connor racked his brain for the answer, trying to recall times he had gone for walks here with his father. Was it three canyons or four? In the blackness everything seemed so unfamiliar and so far.

A night bird flew up in his face. The startled boy stumbled through the ice at the verge of the stream, chilling him still further and adding to his suffering.

Far off on the wind behind him he heard his uncle calling, "Connor, lad! It's your uncle Marlowe. Don't be frightened, boy! Stop this foolishness and come into the house." Connor hesitated mid-stride. "Connor!" Marlowe hailed loudly. "Your father is asking for you, boy! Come back at once! He needs you!"

Da? Needs me? Connor thought. *What if it's true? What if this madness isn't real?* Then suddenly he remembered the guns . . . the sound of Old Liam's skull shattering under the blow of an ash stick . . . the cries of the sheep savaged by the hounds. He shook himself free to dash on again.

He had crossed three drumlins, the stony ridges that seam the Galway countryside, when he hit a gully lined with beech trees. A sense of recognition washing over him, Connor sighed with relief. This was the right place, the branch that would lead upward toward the chapel and safety.

It was a steep climb away from the river, and there was no discernible path. The skeleton fingers of trees interred in winter's tomb plucked at his flimsy wool jacket. Just as the boy broke free of the copse the clinging mist changed to the first icy flakes of snow, landing on Connor's face and dotting the back of his neck.

He fell again, pitching headlong over a pile of stones. When Connor collected himself he found that it was no chance heap but a marker cairn. From this point on the slope there were two recognizable trails leading upward. The mound of fist-size rocks stood beside the left-hand fork; but why? Was it a guiding sign or a warning? Connor did not recall the division of the path. What if he was lost after all?

The whine of dogs held to short leashes made up the boy's mind for him. The swirl of the snow-burdened air muffled the sounds from below, and who could say how close the pursuit had come? Onto the left-hand track he sprinted.

Another half mile upward and the snow was heavier than before. Connor was soaked, aching with cold and the climb and the falls, and now the torment of thirst was added to his misery. He licked the drips that ran down his face. He should have come to the village by now, or at least to the high road that connected Ballynockanor to Castletown. He had taken the wrong path after all, but to retrace his steps into the darkness toward the fearful hounds was unthink-able.

Another line of thickly planted trees confronted him, and the path he followed abruptly vanished. There was nothing to do but push through, and this Connor did, scraping between branches tipped in frosty dagger-points.

Ducking low, Connor crawled the last dozen feet over a high berm of earth to tumble into a small meadow. The boy ran across the ice-hardened turf, confronted a solid wall of interlaced trees that gave no hint of a passage, then followed the curving barrier, looking for an escape.

Frantic now, Connor could not even relocate the spot he had pushed through to reach the center of the ring. He had trespassed in a fairy rath . . . a charmed grove that some said might hold you prisoner forever for violating the solitude.

Connor wanted to sit down and cry. He wanted someone to lead him, better still to carry him. Gulping back the added terror in-spired by the place, the boy tried to recall what his da had taught him about such haunted rings. *Ancient they are,* his father had said, *and yet made by mortal men. Round hilltop forts . . . built of earthen walls . . . and trees have grown up in the turned soil. Re-spect them, lad, but do not fear them.*

This recollection calmed the boy, but still gave him no clue as to the exit. Breathing a prayer, he pushed aside some branches at ran-dom and dropped to his knees. The darkness under the trees was complete, and Connor groped forward one handhold at a time, fearful of having an eye put out by an unseen bough.

He felt as if he had been crawling through the ring forever when he heard a low growl. It came from everywhere and nowhere. Con-nor halted to listen, his teeth chattering. Which direction were the hounds, and how far away? Should he hurry forward, or lie com-pletely still?

The snarl came again, this time definitely behind him, and close, much too close. Connor struggled forward. The spear-point of a branch caught in the collar of his shirt, holding him fast. When he hurled himself against the restraint, it stabbed him painfully in the neck. When he tried to roll free, the limb snapped with the crack of a pistol shot!

And then the hound was on him, howling its triumph to the leaden skies. A heavy furred body landed on Connor's back, pinning him to the ground. Hot breath reeking of gore flooded into the boy's ears and neck and tore a ragged scream from his raw gullet.

The dog pawed at his back, jaws snatching at his clothing as Connor covered his throat with his hands and yelled for help. The beast tucked its bloody muzzle under the boy's side, rolling him over easily, and plunged its nose down to . . . lick Connor's face.

"What? What?" Connor struggled with disbelief and release. "Finn, is it you?" The dog whined and wriggled in mutual recognition.

Off in the night another voice called the dog's name. John Stone, somewhere lower on the slope, was also seeking the animal and climbing toward the rath.

"Show me," Connor urged. "Finn, show me how to get away from here."

The hound obediently pushed through the grove, allowing his young master to cling to his back. The dog wove and crawled, but in the span of two minutes was free of the maze. Connor wanted to keep the creature by him, but every time Stone called, Finn looked around toward the river and whined. Afraid that the hound would give him away, Connor ordered, "Whist now, dog. Get by with you! Go home!"

Finn slunk away a trio of paces, then turned as if to inquire if Connor would insist. When the boy repeated his command, the dog trotted off into the darkness.

Free of the fairy ring, Connor could once more sense the uphill slope that must sooner or later lead onward to either village or road. He pressed forward again, hoping that his pursuers would be misled by the dog or become tangled in the labyrinth of trees themselves.

Above the peak of Ben Beg a sudden gust of wind parted the clouds and let a single shaft of moonlight pierce the gloom. The moment of illumination revealed to Connor another heap of stones and a trickle of water falling into a basin hewn from a single boulder. "Saint Brigit's well," the lad breathed, crossing himself at the sight of the holy spring. An instant later he had drunk his fill, blessing Mary of the Gaels for the use of her well. More than refreshed, Connor now knew exactly where he was. He had taken the wrong track indeed and passed the chapel, but at least he knew where it lay.

When Connor reached the stone cross on top of the hill, there before him was the road and the last cottage of Ballynockanor. Its frosted windows, blazing with the orange light of a turf fire, beckoned the boy toward warmth and rest. Fiddle music danced free of the walls and thatch to add to the invitation. The dairyman's house, Connor knew, was full of laughter and children. He desperately wanted to go in and yet knew he could not. There was no safety for him apart from Daniel, and he might bring danger on the Donovans too.

Past other lighted homes he ran, ignoring the welcome of lanterns, candles, and the aroma of food until he came at last to the graveyard beside the church of St. John the Evangelist. No time now to think of the dead of Ballynockanor and their hurling matches with the deceased of Allintober; likely it was too cold a night for even the dead to walk abroad.

Behind the church was the one-room stone bungalow of Father O'Bannon, where Daniel had said to seek him. Connor was already pounding on the planks of the barred door before he noticed that no light escaped around the cracks of the entry; no glow came from the lone window. "Daniel!" he cried. "Daniel! It's me, Connor Burke! Help!"

Connor's numb fingers felt no pain as his impassioned rapping tore the skin from the knuckles. Someone must answer; they must!

Just as the boy's cries turned to wheezing sobs, there came the sound of the bar being lifted and incredibly the door opened. Connor fell forward into Daniel's arms.

"Young Burke," the big man exclaimed, lighting a candle. "And nearly frozen through too. What's afoot then?"

While Daniel's broad hands tenderly bandaged the boy's fingers and swabbed dirt and dried blood from his cheeks, Connor gasped out his tale in halting fragments. "And I think Stone killed Old Liam the porter!"

Long before Connor had finished the account of fleeing for his life, Daniel's face was set and grim. "We must get you clear from here," he vowed. "You'll not be safe this side of the Shannon, I think. We'll away before daybreak, but eat a bite now and sleep while I think what's best to do."

But it was not to be.

No sooner had Connor taken a single bite of boxty bread than the sound of hooves came pounding toward the churchyard. Daniel hurriedly blew out the light and peered through the window.

"Marlowe," he said tersely, "and some other. He must have guessed where you were headin' and gone back for his horse while Stone kept after you. And I would fare no better at his hands than you. Lively now! Out the back with my cloak around your shoulders." Back up the slope toward Ballynockanor they went. Daniel whispered his plans as they trudged over the snow. "And I know a grade that we can use to reach the Cornamona. We'll try to cross the river and then make our way through the hills of Ben Levy. If we can reach Clonbur in time, there's a coach will carry us clear of pursuit." The snow had stopped and the sky lightened in the west as the moon struggled to break free. "Hurry, lad," Daniel urged. "We'll make for fair targets against the snow if we don't bustle."

The last field of Ballynockanor perched above the river. The top of the wall that marked the descent was shrouded in snow, but Daniel seemed to know the place he sought. "Blood Field," he muttered, and then recognizing the dark import of the words added, "It's but where they bleed the cattle, that's all." Clambering over the embankment, Daniel stood on the narrow lip above the plunge into the canyon and reached back to help Connor across.

Wind tore apart the veil of clouds, and moonlight shown on the boy, transfixing the child atop the wall. From the direction of Ballynockanor came an exultant roar from the lips of Uncle Marlowe. "There he is, Carroll! After him."

"There's someone helpin' him!" Constable Carroll shouted back.

"Then shoot, man, shoot!"

Connor leaped toward Daniel's embrace, and as he did so, something hit him a hammer blow to one shoulder. The boy cried out, twisting and falling toward darkness. He barely heard the crack of the gun and Daniel's anguished cry before Connor felt himself snatched up and carried.

Sliding, skidding toward the river, more shots followed their descent. "I've got you, boy!" Daniel encouraged. "We'll cross the river on the ice . . . we can . . . we must!"

Connor felt rather than saw the bottom of the hill. The precipitous slither was replaced with a few steps of level ground. Then the expanse of the Cornamona was just ahead. Daniel did not hesitate at all, but rushed onto the ice.

Through a haze of pain, his stomach spinning, Connor heard another crack of a gunshot. Then it seemed the air was filled with gunshots, snapping all around them. No, it was the ice giving way!

Two more lunging steps forward, then Daniel gave a cry of despair as the crust broke beneath him. Man and boy were plunged into the icy river's flow. Connor caught a last glimpse of moonlight before the surging waters closed over his head.

PART I

I will go with my father a-ploughing
To the green field by the sea,
And the rooks and the crows and the seagulls
Will come flocking after me.
I will sing to the patient horses
With the lark in the white of the air,
And my father will sing the plough-song
That blesses the cleaving share.

—Joseph Campbell "I Will Go with My Father A-Ploughing"

∽ 1 ∾

The sun was a round silver ball hovering in the mists just above the Maumturk Mountains. Approaching dusk brought the distant sounds of moving water and the skirl of wind to the stillness of the valley floor.

It was four o'clock on the afternoon of December 24, 1841, in the village of Ballynockanor, county of Galway, province of Connaught, Ireland.

There might have been a song of promise on the breeze that Holy Eve, but none in Ballynockanor could decipher the words.

True, a sense of expectation had simmered for weeks at the hearths of all twenty village homes. It was after mass on the first day of Advent that the old woman, Mad Molly Fahey, had smacked her gums and rolled her eyes and told Father O'Bannon (as well as every farmer, farmer's wife, and child) that a great miracle was coming to visit the poor of Ballynockanor.

On the stone step outside the church she laughed, "Joseph and Mary! Before Christmas morn we'll see wonder and mercy come here to Ballynockanor!"

Tom Donovan, widowed with five children, inquired, "And if we might be askin'? What will this wonder be, Widow Fahey?"

Mad Molly scratched her grizzled hair beneath her dark wool shawl and cackled, "Glory be! The matter was right here before me.

'Tis . . . 'tis . . . the babe! 'Tis Joseph and all the tears of Mary. 'Tis butter and soda bread and salt on our porridge!" Then the old woman paused and screwed up her face. She cocked an eye, shining like a cloudy blue marble, at patient Father O'Bannon and whispered, "Loaves and fishes, Your Honor. Who could know they would run short of potatoes? Loaves and fishes! A secret miracle, Father, but a miracle it will be, never doubt."

It was a fine thought indeed because everyone in Ballynockanor was poor and sorely in need of a miracle, even a secret one.

From that moment on and for each day of Advent, everyone in the townland buttered their bread with expectation, salted their porridge with anticipation, and smoothed their ragged dreams with the oil of hope. Father O'Bannon knew Molly Fahey was mad; she had been so since the day old and young Masters Burke had perished in the same hour. Still, he could not help praying for the visitation of some angelic host to dance along the slate gable of the parish church. One thought led to another and he contemplated corresponding with the Holy Father in Rome. What if coveys of pilgrims should flock to worship in Ballynockanor? Might they not ask for blessing and offer their tithes to build a shrine? And might there not be enough left over to repair the leaky roof of the crumbling church of St. John the Evangelist?

Whatever else might follow, Father O'Bannon noticed instantly that the pews were packed each morning for mass. Something wondrous was indeed taking place in Ballynockanor.

The exact composition of the coming miracle was also speculated upon within the warm, dim confines of O'Flaherty's Pub.

"And you know, Tom Donovan, as sure as you're born, Mad Molly Fahey has been fey these fifteen years past." Paddy O'Flaherty, owner of the tavern, tapped his gray temple to emphasize the point.

Tom Donovan raised his glass and offered this toast, slurred though it may have been: "Then here's to Mad Molly's madness. Our children get out of bed each morn and smile at the thought that this day may be the day the secret miracle will come to redeem poor Ballynockanor and all of Ireland from the English! But until then, here's long life to the landlord. As bad as Old Marlowe is, better he than his son!"

Fourteen farmers drank with Tom Donovan. They clapped their calloused hands together and hooted their approval. "To Mad Molly! And long life to Old Marlowe."

More ale was drawn from the kegs by Paddy O'Flaherty. So progressed a litany of toasts to freedom and miracles and holy treason against the fine young queen Victoria across the Irish Sea in London. It was a spirited assembly, full of many pints of good cheer.

From the warmth of such gatherings, the farmers staggered into the night and searched the starry skies of Connaught for some sign that all landlords might vanish before Christmas morn.

No such star appeared to guide them.

Closer to home and in the daylight, women leaned upon their half-doors and dreamed golden visions of pounds and shillings dropping from heaven like scattered crumbs to the chickens.

One day during Advent, Mad Molly Fahey got free from her room and thus became lost in the village of her birth. A dozen children who had considered her a witch before now took her gnarled hands and walked past the broken walls of the deserted schoolhouse. Mad Molly smiled in toothless bliss because of the companionship and forgot that she could not remember where she was.

"Good friends," she said, sighing. "Never lost with good friends at my side."

The youngsters begged her to share the mystery of the Ballynockanor miracle.

"We'll not tell a soul," pleaded six-year-old Mary Elizabeth Donovan.

"It's there!" Molly Fahey replied with a wild light in her eyes that made her audience squeal and hop and cling to one another although it was not after dark. "The miracle? Joseph and Mary! I see it everywhere! In the grass. In the river! In the grave. In your porridge and my potato! Father, Son, and . . . bless me . . . I have a hole in my shoe!" Mad Molly held up her foot and it was bare. "Mary Elizabeth, will you take me to my home?"

The children led the old woman to the cottage of her daughter and son-in-law. They locked her up in a pleasant room with bars on the window and fed her. Mad Molly was content and sang all night long.

For the youngsters porridge and potatoes took on an aura of fascination, but stirabout and spuds produced no revelation. In pastures and on hillsides the rye grass whispered no hints. The normally babbling waters of the river Cornamona were frozen solid and still. Even the monolithic boulders marking ancient Celtic graves did not offer a clue.

Eleven-year-old Martin Donovan sat on the stone wall that enclosed Blood Field and gazed down the slope of the hill. Far below, and on the opposite side of the river, a stranger and a gray donkey hesitated on the bank of the ice-covered Cornamona. Even from a distance Martin could see that the ice, though deceptively solid near the traveler, was dangerously thin just beyond a small sandbar that rose from the center of the stream.

Behind Martin, Mary Elizabeth stroked the nose of one of the half dozen dairy cows and called, "You don't think he means to cross there, brother?"

The boy squinted and leaned forward slightly as the stranger below stepped warily from the shore and led the donkey onto the ice. "Aye," Martin replied. "That he does. At the very spot where they say young Master Burke vanished."

Mary Elizabeth nodded gravely. "Mad Molly says the fairies stole him." With that pronouncement, Mary scrambled up her own height in jumbled granite rocks to sit beside Martin on the wall. She did not want to miss the sight of the alien breaking through the crust and disappearing into the current. All six Irish Moiled milk cows perked their ears and sauntered down to flank the Donovan children. Three sweet roan faces peered over with interest at the right elbow of Martin and three tan faces to the left of Mary Elizabeth. Unbeknownst to the wayfarer were both his peril and his audience.

"That's a pretty little donkey. Will the donkey drown too, Martin?"

Martin considered the precarious footing of the beast on the river. Hooves, which were surefooted and true on the most dubious paths of the cliffs, slipped and faltered on the slick surface. Knowing the danger, the creature shook his long ears and held back as his master pulled him forward toward death.

"A pity," Martin replied. "To die so, on Christmas Eve."

"Maybe not." The girl's blue eyes brightened. "Maybe not at all. Not if it's the Holy Family, come to Ballynockanor."

Mary Elizabeth, black curls blowing in the breeze, leaped from the wall and skipped down the hill.

"Where are you goin'?" Martin called.

She waved away his question and began to run.

Martin tugged his ear and adjusted his round wool cap down tight over his dull brown hair. Hesitating a moment, he glanced at the twisted right foot, which kept him from skipping and running. He slipped off his perch, steadied himself against the fence, and called to Mary Elizabeth to come back. She ignored him. It was her way when she set her mind to disobey. The cows lowed resentfully as Martin limped down the boulder-strewn cliff face to retrieve his sister and tell the fool on the brink to turn back. Six bovine faces gazed reproachfully over the stone wall like brown birds perching there.

The fool and his donkey reached the sandbar at midstream at the exact instant the ice behind them cracked with a sound like a whip and caved in. Water lapping their heels, man and beast struggled forward to the bar.

Mary Elizabeth stepped gingerly onto the frozen mud at the river's edge.

Cupping her hands against the howl of wind through the canyon she piped to the stranger, "Are you Saint Joseph?"

Lunging for a clump of gorse to save himself from tumbling,

Martin muttered, "No matter his name. He is a dead man if he comes farther."

The traveler, a tall, fair young man wearing worn-out riding boots and a heavy wool sailor's coat pulled up around his neck, cocked his head as though he could not hear the words of the girl. "What was that, child?"

Mary Elizabeth called louder, "I see the donkey, but what have you done with the Virgin Mary? You've missed the road, you see. Had you come the proper way you would have all the candles of Ballynockanor to guide you." She stretched out her left foot and tested her weight on the river's surface.

Martin quickened his pace and stumbled. His sister meant to walk out across fifty feet of thin ice and onto the sandbar. "No! Mary Elizabeth!"

The stranger shouted, "Stay back, child!"

But Mary Elizabeth, who at the age of six was fully of will what she would be if she lived to be twenty-six, ignored the two frantic males and moved forward onto the river. First one, two, then three steps. Balancing and skating awkwardly with the rushing current clearly visible beneath her feet, she crept toward the sandbar where the fool waved her back and the donkey trembled and snorted.

Martin's heart drummed in his ears. Surely the ice would break apart. Certainly Mary Elizabeth would fall through it, be trapped beneath it, to drown and be swept away to Lough Corrib where she would not be found till spring! He reached the icy verge of the stream, but at his first step farther the crust groaned beneath his weight. To advance would endanger Mary Elizabeth even more.

What would Father say? He who had lost a wife and child to the terrible fire?

What would sister Kate say? She, whose neck and arm were scarred, and who at twenty-three would surely never marry again or have babies, who doted upon little Mary Elizabeth as though the willful sprat were her own child?

Kevin, who was eighteen and strong and whole, and worked in

the stables of Landlord Marlowe, would blame Martin. Brigit, who was sixteen and vain and loved the drama of tragedy, would hate him openly and fiercely as her role demanded she do!

Halfway across the frosted sheet as thin as a pane of glass, Mary Elizabeth slipped and fell on her backside. She laughed, spun around, groped forward on her hands and knees, and attempted to stand again.

"Stay where you are, child!" warned the newcomer. "There is already a crack between you and here."

Mary Elizabeth said in a clear voice, "But I cannot drown, sir. Mad Molly told me so. I will never drown, you see. The caul was over my face when I was born and so I cannot drown."

Martin knew that Mary Elizabeth believed the old lore. It made her careless near the river. Though Martin half believed it himself, he was always frightened when Mary Elizabeth dabbled by the water's edge and teased the rapids that smashed against the boulders in the gorge above the village.

The girl peered at the liquid that rushed past a mere fraction of an inch beneath her hands. "It's very fast, isn't it?" she said to the stranger, who crouched as though he would leap in after her when the ice gave way.

"You must go back, child. You must. See here." He pointed to the paper-thin surface two yards between them.

"But I cannot drown," she said, smiling sweetly.

"But you can freeze and die. And so you will if you do not turn back to the shore."

This was a new thought for Mary Elizabeth. Death was a very cold thing indeed. The water was cold and so was the day.

"Are you comin' to Ballynockanor, Saint Joseph?" she queried as she positioned herself to crawl back toward Martin.

The man was panting, fighting to keep his voice calm to instruct Mary Elizabeth. "Spread your weight evenly, girl. Hands and knees. Yes. That's it now."

She was persistent. "Are you comin' to supper, Joseph? It is Holy Eve. But you cannot bring Mary this way, not now."

"Tonight. Yes. Yes. When the river freezes solid I will cross."

"You are the miracle then. Mad Molly said you would come." She slid forward as Martin stood silent with terror, his hands reaching across the gulf to her.

"That's it!" the traveler encouraged. "Mind that spot there. Do you see it, girl? Very thin! Go around. Go around!"

Behind her the ice suddenly snapped and gave way. Cold water washed over the lip of the break and soaked her red plaid skirt. "It is very cold!" she called to Martin.

"Father will beat you with a stick if you live!" Martin shouted.

This threat caused Mary Elizabeth to hesitate and consider. She glanced back. "You must come to our house tonight and meet Father. The dairyman's house at the end of the lane." Then to Martin she said, "I will just wait here unless you promise not to tell."

Martin felt like he would faint from fear. Blood drained from his cheeks. He covered his face with his hands and replied sweetly, like he was coaxing a wild animal to take a piece of bread. "Come along then, Mary Elizabeth. I won't tell, but come along or we shall be beat for dallyin' when the cows need milkin'."

At this the girl's face clouded. She jerked her head in solemn agreement with this sound judgment. She moved more quickly toward Martin. The river exploded through its concealment at the toes of her shoes, and she scrambled forward to escape.

"It's givin' way!" shouted the stranger. "Hurry, girl! Faster!"

All around her the surface fractured, leaving her on a single sheet, three feet from the safety of thicker ice near the shore. On both sides of her, the Cornamona thrust out watery claws to grab the child.

Martin jumped onto the meager hide that covered the growling river. It broke instantly beneath his weight. He sank into the freezing stream, painfully soaking his thin legs to mid calf. Lunging for Mary Elizabeth, he grasped her wrists, pulling her into his arms and tumbling backward into water, ice, and mud.

⌁

The cottage of widower Tom Donovan was, like himself, small, plain, and sturdy. His daughters, Kate, Brigit, and little Mary Elizabeth, assured the house maintained a feminine air. His sons, Kevin and Martin, tended the barn and the fields and the livestock.

The building was long and narrow. Tradition demanded that the dwelling of a true Irishman not be more than one room deep or there would be misfortune to the family who lived there. There had been tragedy enough for the Donovan family and so the breaking of tradition was never considered.

Inside and out the stonework was rendered with three coats of lime plaster. According to the command of eldest daughter Kate, who managed the household, the whitewash was renewed yearly— too often, according to the neighbors. The walls shimmered clean and bright in the sunlight beside white nightshirts and nightdresses dancing on the clothesline.

The yellow of a newly thatched roof above the Donovan cottage sloped down snugly over four rooms. Two sash windows of twelve square panes of glass, trimmed in hand-crocheted lace, flanked the green door. Inside, above the entry, hung many St. Brigit's crosses, twisted from bog rushes.

The half-door let in the fresh air and light while keeping out the hens that clucked and waited for the fistful of bread crumbs Kate tossed morning and night onto the cobbles of the yard.

A long table with eight straight-backed chairs dominated the center of the stone floor. Opposite the windows was a dresser stacked with jugs and blue-flowered plates. An assortment of teacups hung from hooks beneath the shelves. Within two drawers of the wide base was the cutlery. The bottom shelves held the pots for cooking.

Behind the fireplace was a tiny kitchen. Meals were prepared and tea brewed in heavy black kettles that dangled from an iron crane over a blazing peat fire. In an alcove in the masonry to the right of the mantel perched a fiddle, dusty with disuse.

There were two bedchambers; one, a large dormitory, contained three beds for the girls. A smaller cubicle adjoined the kitchen and held three beds for the dairyman and his two sons.

The house and barns and the pens for the small herd of milk cows were a half mile beyond the parish chapel of St. John the Evangelist along the main road that wound through the village of Ballynockanor.

This evening every cottage was swept and cleaned in anticipation of the Nativity. Laundered shirts, blouses, trousers, and skirts were pressed and laid out in readiness on the cots. Socks were darned and worn-out boots brushed and made to stand in soldierly rows beside the door.

A single tall unlit candle was placed in the windowsill among the sprigs of holly. With the sounding of the Angelus bell at sunset the youngest girl child of the family would light the candle to illuminate the road for the Holy Family as they passed by on their way to Bethlehem. It was right that the honor belonged to the youngest in the family, for would she not be the one to live the longest and thereby keep the custom alive for many years?

So it was that Mary Elizabeth Donovan, the littlest Mary, had looked forward eagerly to the lighting of the candle. She had worn out the ears of Kate with speaking of it. She had practiced the joyful ritual a hundred times, placing an unlit twig to the wick and imagining the flame.

For this reason, as the sun sank lower over the mountains there was concern in the Donovan cottage.

Kate lifted the loaf of soda bread from the coals of the hearth and glanced briefly at the darkening sky. Where was little Mary Elizabeth? And Martin?

Had not Mary Elizabeth rattled on all the morning about her duty to help Mary and Joseph find their way to the manger? And all afternoon had not the child passed the hours chalking stick figures of angels and donkeys and the Holy Couple on a slate? And was there any end to the chatter about Mad Molly and the coming miracle?

Kate, who did not entirely believe in miracles, merely smiled and inwardly fumed that the priest had not put an end to speculation about the ravings of poor Molly Fahey. It was better not to hope than to have hope crushed by disappointment.

As the Angelus approached Kate worked quietly in the kitchen. She did not express her concern to Brigit, who brushed her hair and stared out the window at the empty lane and the lowering sun.

Brigit broke the silence. "Isn't it a half hour till Angelus? Where are they? Sure and she'll need a bath."

"The kettle is on," Kate remarked as though she were untroubled by the absence of the children. "No doubt they've met Molly on the road and she's fillin' their heads with nonsense."

"And Da is doubtless at the pub havin' a wee drop to drown his sorrows." Brigit tossed her fiery red hair back from her face and turned away from the window in disgust. "Late on such a holy evening. We'll go to mass without them."

"We'll do no such thing." Kate placed another turf on the coals and glanced at her pretty sister dressed in crimson. Brigit, she knew, had no real care for the holiness of the evening. Brigit simply did not want to miss the gathering at the parish church. Being the most attractive girl in all the village and perhaps in the surrounding countryside, Brigit cherished the coming in and the going out when the eyes of every young man in Ballynockanor followed her with admiration.

"I shall go alone if I must."

Kate swung the kettle over the fire. "They'll be along."

Brigit sighed and limped across the floor in imitation of Martin. "He is the slowest thing! Why didn't Kevin fetch the cows today of all days?"

From his room Kevin bellowed, "Did I not have important matters to tend to in Castletown? Why did you not go fetch them home yourself, Brigit Donovan?"

Brigit retorted, "Aye, important matters? Was it the driver's daughter in Castletown you're meanin'? And did she tell you how Protestants spend their Christmas Eve?"

Kevin's reply was vehement. "And you have not cast a glance or two at the landlord's devil of a son?"

Kate's eyes sparked. "Sha! Both of you! Lower your voices and mind your tongues. If Da was to hear such things even in jest! Or good Father O'Bannon . . . he'll read your names out at the mass!''

Brigit shrugged and raised her chin in defiance. "The priest? Are we expectin' him then? And Da? Sure and he'll be drunk again tonight. As he has been every night since . . .''

"Enough." Kate rose from the hearth.

"Why do you defend him, Kate? Da will not look at you unless his vision is blurred with the drink. Your body bears the memory of our sorrow. . . . Every tongue clucks as you go by. Poor young widow Kate. Aye, she's doomed to care for her drunkard father forever now.''

Kate put her left hand to the scars that engraved forever the path of the flames that had flayed her throat.

Each day as Kate looked at her reflection and at the warped fingers of her right hand, the stark reminder of tragedy overwhelmed her.

Her face had not been touched by the fire. She wore high collars above her somber, dark blue dresses to cover the worst of it. Warm brown eyes, high cheekbones, thick plaited auburn hair—all proclaimed the beauty of the widow Kate Donovan Garrity. But only at a distance.

Each time she carted the milk to Castletown, she felt the furtive looks of the townspeople. When she stopped to talk, she turned slightly to the right and tucked her chin so the shiny mark that bronzed her throat was in shadow. The crippled right arm was concealed beneath her shawl. In church, she crossed herself with her left hand.

Kate was glad each evening when the bright sun went down, and candlelight softened the sharpness of her scars. Over time the curiosity and revulsion of others had destroyed her gratitude for life. Shame filled the vacuum. Why had she lived and not the others? Not Sean?

There were long and lonely nights when Kate dreamed of being loved. Sleep made her arms strong and whole again. In dreams Sean kissed her throat and whispered that her body was soft and smooth.

Desire sang sweet songs as she slept. Truth mocked her when she awakened.

Brigit was right about their father. Tom Donovan, when sober, could not look at Kate without pain. He was seldom sober these days.

And there was no music played in the House of Donovan.

As for other men in the village of Ballynockanor? The memory of that night five years before was horrible and sharp. It cut away the possibility of love, leaving only pity for the once-beautiful and once-whole young widow.

Now the room was silent except for the soft hiss of the fire.

Kevin, tall and lean, his clean white shirt unbuttoned, filled the doorway. He brushed back the lock of brown hair that fell across his high forehead and glared coldly at Brigit.

"What are you starin' at?" Brigit challenged.

Kevin's deep brown eyes narrowed. "Can it be that you are cut from the same cloth as Kate? For all your satin looks, you are coarse and cruel and vain. Were it not for Kate and her Sean . . ."

Brigit opened her mouth to speak. Kate stepped in front of her and held up her disfigured right hand. The sight made Brigit blink and step back.

"Enough," Kate whispered wearily. "It was a long time ago."

At that instant the door crashed open. Martin tumbled in with Mary Elizabeth behind him.

"It's about time!" Brigit whirled around and stormed out of the room. "We'll be late to mass."

Kevin rolled his eyes and returned to finish dressing.

"Where's Da?" Mary Elizabeth shouted. "Where?"

Martin cleared his throat. "Still at the pub is he?"

Kate, grateful for the interruption, viewed Martin and the youngest Donovan with alarm. "Mary Elizabeth, you've been at the river again. Look at you!"

Dripping and caked with mud, the two children began to chatter at once.

Mary Elizabeth hopped across the flagstones as she spilled the news. "We saw Joseph, sister Kate!"

Kate cocked an eyebrow at her filthy siblings. "Joseph who?"

"Himself! The saint! Joseph! You know!"

Kate grinned and resisted the urge to embrace Mary Elizabeth. "Father O'Bannon will be pleased to hear it."

Martin removed his boots and stretched out his hands to the fire. "Could I stop her? My leg you see. Down she ran to the river's edge. . . ."

"Virgin Mary wasn't with him," Mary Elizabeth interrupted. "But Joseph has a donkey, a gray one it is, and they talked to us from the sandbar in the river!"

Martin added, "A fool and a strange man he was. He did not say where he was from. Truth to tell, I was busy fetchin' Mary Elizabeth back and so forgot to ask. Best cook a few more spuds. He'll be cold from the river."

Mary Elizabeth stared into the stew pot. "Joseph says he'll come to supper! I don't know what he did with Mary."

"Sha!" Kate scolded. "There is no time for your foolishness, Mary Elizabeth. Nor you, Martin. It's surprised I am to find you so laggardly tonight of all nights. Mary Elizabeth, have you forgotten that it was your duty to light the candle?"

Mary Elizabeth whirled around to see if someone had usurped her place, then sighed with relief at the sight of the still flameless wick. "I have not forgotten," she replied sharply. "Did I not have to tell Joseph which house was ours? I'll do it right now." The child stooped toward the broom to pluck a straw.

Kate's sound left hand shot forward to grasp Mary Elizabeth by the ear. "You shall not! Not until you are cleaned and made presentable."

"Why not let her alone?" Brigit teased. "Is it not true that the Holy Family ends up in a stable? What better sign could they wish than Mary Elizabeth covered in mud?"

Kate rounded on her. "That'll be enough out of you! To make mock so of this night! For shame. You will help Mary Elizabeth wash and get into her clean things and brush her hair."

Brigit thought about refusing, but the imperious look in Kate's eyes quelled the notion of rebellion. Martin had already prudently withdrawn to change.

The sun had dropped below the rim of the mountains and the air was noticeably cooler when Mary Elizabeth reemerged. Her face was clean and shone red where Brigit had scrubbed with too much enthusiasm. The soft, melodic chiming of the Angelus bell floated up from the church. "It's time, isn't it, sister?" Mary Elizabeth urged. "May I light it now, please?"

Kate nodded, smiling. It was difficult for her to ever stay cross with her youngest sister for long. "Go on, then," she agreed. "Perhaps Da will hear the bell and be home soon as well."

Brigit snorted, but said nothing.

With a broom straw that Mary Elizabeth ignited at the hearth fire, the girl reverently approached the creamy yellow tallow candle on the window ledge. She turned toward Kate with a question in her eyes.

"Go on," Kate said softly. "You know what to say."

Taking a deep breath, Mary Elizabeth touched the flame to the wick and solemnly intoned, "Behold the virgin shall be . . ." The child screwed up her face with the effort of recalling the words.

Kate prompted her. "With child . . ."

Continuing, Mary Elizabeth resumed, "With child and bear . . ."

"A Son," Kate whispered.

Mary Elizabeth, not to be upstaged, broke in, "And shall name Him Emmanuel!" The child beamed proudly, then stood tiptoe at the windowsill to peer out as light from the candle flickered and pooled on the cobbles. Suddenly she cried, "There he is, oh, there he is! Sister, see! I told you Joseph would come!"

Mary Elizabeth gestured so eagerly through the window that all the Donovans present rushed forward to look, each to a square of glass. Their breath fogged the panes in an instant, but not before they caught a glimpse of a man leading a donkey, and on the donkey a human burden.

"You see," Mary Elizabeth proclaimed triumphantly, "he has come, and he's brought Mary with him!"

The glass squealed under his sleeve as Martin rubbed a clear patch. "It is the same man," he declared, making Kate look down at him in sudden regard.

Through the topmost pane Kevin squinted at the approaching travelers and declared, "Joseph and the donkey it may be, but that's not Mary I'm thinkin', slung over the beast like two sacks of meal. It's . . ."

"Da," Brigit announced scornfully. "Drunk as I said!"

∽

So it was that the family Donovan caught their first impression of the stranger. And first impressions, it is said, are seldom far from truth.

"Saint Joseph!" cried Mary Elizabeth again and again.

Martin remarked, "Perhaps he *is* the miracle."

Clearing his throat, Kevin declared, "A patriot on the run, I'd say."

Kate raised her chin in regal disagreement. She watched with suspicion as the stranger hefted Tom Donovan from the donkey, wrapping a strong arm about the little man's waist to help him unsteadily toward the house. "On the run, aye. But a patriot? An outlaw, rather. A highwayman. A rapparee of the first order. Look at his tall boots. He's too poor a fellow to be wearin' such boots."

Brigit, smiling coyly through the pane of glass, said, "But he is very handsome, isn't he?"

At that assessment Kevin's eyes narrowed. Kate shook her head in disgust. Martin looked amused.

Her normally placid brow furrowing with concern, Mary Elizabeth reprimanded Brigit, "Joseph is married to the Blessed Virgin! You'll not call him handsome to his face and be shamin' us all, will you?"

The latch lifted and a blade of wind slipped between the green-painted plank door and the frame, throwing the portal wide open with a crash. From behind the staggering pair, a gale risen with the sunset howled into the room. The candle flickered and threatened to die. The peat fire crackled and sparks swirled upward.

Da, leaning heavily against the stranger, raised his head and peered at his children through one red eye. "Kate, daughter . . . I've brought the stranger home for supper. . . ."

Doffing his cap, smiling nervously, and attempting a slight bow while maneuvering Tom Donovan, the wayfarer greeted the wide-eyed welcoming committee. "God bless all in this house."

Kate tilted her face slightly to the right and glared at him with misgiving. She opened her mouth as if to speak.

Stepping deftly between Joseph and Kate, Mary Elizabeth curt-sied and said, "Enter, friend, and welcome." She helped the fellow guide Da to a stool near the hearth. Then she said to Kate in the warning tone of a child who has taken the book of manners to heart, "I invited Saint Joseph to table, Kate. Now see, the kind fellow, he's brought Da home. Not very late a'tall. Da may be almost sober by mass. And it was very cold on the sandbar." The child curtsied again. "A cuppa tay and supper, Saint Joseph?"

The stranger laughed. "You may call me Joseph, but I am no saint. I am Joseph Connor, and I could use a bit of thawin'."

"Then welcome to the House of Donovan." Kevin clasped hands with Joseph and made introductions all around.

Joseph extended his hand to Kate. Eyes lowered, she did not reciprocate. His smile faltered. Piercing blue eyes lingered a bare instant on the scar beneath Kate's chin.

Flushed with shame, Kate hid her hand behind her back. He had seen it, she knew. And like all the others, he could not hide the thoughts that swept through his mind. Kate made for the kitchen, her words trailing off. "I'll not neglect feedin' a beggar on such a holy night. Sure, and we'll all be beggin' at Saint Peter's door one day, and I do not want him turnin' me away."

2

The Protestant Church of St. Stephen, Castletown, stood on a low knoll at one end of the market village. As befitted one of the props of the community, its square steeple was visible for miles around and its presence dominated the Castletown landscape. It had been planned that way by Old Marlowe since the church neatly balanced the refurbished bulk of Marlowe Hall, which rose on the opposite end of town.

Marlowe's carriage clattered through the paved streets of the village, the noise of its approach warning pedestrians to jump out of the way. There was no actual need for haste. The Marlowes, father and son, were not late for the Christmas Eve service. Even if they had been, Vicar Hodge would never have considered beginning the proceedings without them.

Of the two thousand residents of Castletown and the townlands around the region, about one-tenth were Protestant Church of Ireland. And of these two hundred souls, nearly all were filing into the comfortably warmed and well-lit interior of St. Stephen's on this Christmas Eve. No Constable Carroll inspected Protestant faces for suspected rebels. No British soldiers stood guard in Castletown against the Irish terrorists called Ribbonmen.

As the black carriage with its gleaming brass lamps drew up at the side entrance of the church, many in the crowd of worshipers nodded respectfully toward the coach.

The sounds coming from inside the conveyance were anything but merry. Even before the uniformed footman had hurriedly unfolded the step and opened the door, the other churchgoers heard, "Blast you as a profligate wretch, William! I will not . . . I say I *will not* advance you another penny for your gambling debts and your fancy women!"

The stout upper half of Old Marlowe's body shook with rage even as his spindly lower limbs were cautiously stepping down to earth. *A lumpy prattie on broom straws* was the way many of the locals viewed Old Marlowe. They might have added, *a graying potato at that.* Old Marlowe's hair and complexion were both off, like a loaf of speckled oat bread gone to mold.

The slim, erect figure that followed his father out of the carriage was a distinct contrast to the elder Marlowe. Young Marlowe, "Viscount William" as the English styled him, was darkly handsome in a way his father had never been. Broad of shoulders, narrow of hips, his athletic legs encased in fashionably tight tan trousers, William Marlowe was widely regarded as the most eligible bachelor in Dublin society. Many of the onlookers questioned what he could be doing back in the rustic setting of Castletown, even at Christmas.

"Lower your voice, Father," William suggested, bowing in the direction of a pair of young ladies dressed in their Christmas finery. "Must keep up a show of unity, eh?"

Old Marlowe snorted, but nevertheless complied. His tone was still peevish when he continued, "And what sort of show are you making in Dublin? Not another cent, I say. You live too high, too high, William! And that solicitor's letter, extorting money from me! A bad business, that."

William gave a careless toss of his chin. "You need not have paid, Father," he argued. "You know how they are. A hundred different men might be the father of that slut's child. Besides, did I not return here as you requested?"

"Well," agreed Old Marlowe grudgingly, his tone softening, "that you did, and it'll be for your benefit, you'll see."

Leaning heavily on a silver-headed cane, Old Marlowe led the way into the family's private box elevated at the side aisle of the church. Vicar Hodge bobbed his head toward the Marlowes with such visible delight and admiration that his stole slipped off his shoulders and fell to the floor. As he bent to retrieve it, his spectacles likewise fell. In fumbling after stole and glasses, he lost his hold on his prayer book.

Neither of the Marlowes paid any attention, nor did they allow the booming of the organ and the opening notes of a hymn to interrupt their discussion. "In what way will I benefit?" William inquired.

Joy to the world, the choir sang. *Let earth receive her king.*

"I want you to learn the basis of our family income at firsthand," Old Marlowe suggested. "I want you to accompany John Stone in his rent-collecting activities. It will encourage him to be thorough and will teach you something about the value of money when you see how hard it is for us to collect what's owed us."

Let every heart prepare Him room . . .

Now it was William's turn to look peevish. "Stone? That farcical toady?" William's gaze swept over the congregation until he spotted Steward Stone and his wife. Both had been eagerly awaiting the moment when the gaze of their masters would light on them, and both of them beamed when it did. "Would you make a tradesman of me, Father?" William concluded with disgust.

"Not at all," corrected Old Marlowe. "Besides, since you are so fond of spending money, perhaps you can improve our income. I am certain we are not receiving all that could be squeezed out of this land. As of today it's your duty to see that we do."

And heaven, and heaven, and nature sing!

B y the time the ladle scraped against the bottom of the stew pot, it was clear to Kate that Joseph Connor was a man who kept his personal business to himself. He related the news of the world he had traveled. Great matters of politics and commerce that had little bearing on life in Ballynockanor were passed along as casually as the bowl of potatoes.

" 'Tis said that Britain and America may go to war again . . . something to do with a boundary way off in the Oregon territory."

He seemed to know the events of every province and county in Ireland.

"Rebel Ribbonmen hanged an informer in county Wexford. The English are up in arms about it and vowin' justice and revenge. Our own Daniel O'Connell says we can gain freedom for Ireland without violence."

But as for his own personal history, Joseph Connor remained an enigma. Kate noted that his accent was the soft brogue of a Dubliner. Palms were not calloused as the hands of a farmer would be. Nor was his complexion toughened by sun or wind.

Kevin, who devoured every scrap of information offered by the stranger, remarked, "It's plain you know the world, Joseph. Aye. As well as any Irish farmer knows his own fields."

"Politics is idle talk in the coffeehouses of France. I studied at the Irish university in Paris as my father did before me."

The mention of France sparked Da's interest. Many an Irish patriot escaped to France after the failed rebellion of 1798 and another wave in 1803. "An exile then, your father?"

"Aye. Left Dublin in '03."

Da, who was well on his way to sober by the end of the meal, pounded his palm against the table in sound approval. "So. I remember that bloody night in '03 when Emmet's men stormed through Dublin to try for the castle." Da nodded. "Emmet was a good man, in spite of the fact he was a Protestant and a lunatic."

The corners of Joseph's mouth turned up. "I grew to manhood with the tales of those days ringin' in my ears. What was it Emmet said before they hanged him? 'Let no man write my epitaph until my country is free.' Aye, well, as for myself, I have no story but this: I've been travelin' alone since my return and learnin' what I could from the land itself."

A half dozen more questions burst from the mouths of those at the table.

Da wiped his whiskered chin with the back of his hand and proclaimed to his children, "That's enough now! Leave the poor man to his supper. It's clear he does not wish to give us the story of his own life, but only the glory of his father's deeds." With a nod and a wink at Joseph he declared, "A wise man, you are. A stranger is always more interestin' in Ballynockanor if his past is left to imagination and invention."

Speaking around a mouthful of bread, Joseph replied earnestly, " 'Tis not my intention to remain a mystery, Tom Donovan. I've truly led an uneventful life."

At this, Kevin arched his eyebrows as though he alone knew the truth about this patriot.

Kate's face took on a distinctly cynical expression as she observed the brigand.

As for Brigit? She sighed. "No wife? No family? It must be lonely for you." It was clear from her soulful look that she had already created a role for Joseph of rejected lover giving up on life, friends, and family, and taking to the road like a common tinker. Kate could plainly see that the cogs and wheels of Brigit's brain were already spinning out the plan of how she might relieve the sorrow of Joseph.

Mary Elizabeth whispered to Joseph in a conspiratorial tone, pronouncing every word distinctly, "Don't tell them anythin', Joseph, for they would not believe you. They never believe me."

At this Martin added respectfully, "But can you tell us why you've come to Ballynockanor, sir?"

Joseph seemed relieved to come to the point. "Sure, and I can. When we speak of the present I am quite capable of answerin'. And as for the future? I am full of grand plans."

Everyone at the table leaned forward so as not to miss one morsel of information that might be later repeated to the people of Ballynockanor.

"Well then, here it is . . . ," he began.

But his explanation was cut off by the thump of a fist upon the door and a gruff Irish voice. "Open up! In the name of the Queen! Open up in there."

Da sighed and shook his head. "It's Constable Carroll. There's been trouble over the border. There's been talk he'd be makin' rounds tonight. Lookin' for . . ." The old man's eyes flashed a look of comprehension at Joseph.

Kate rose as the pounding increased. She said to Joseph, "It's the Holy Eve. The night that friends and family come from afar to be together. You're one of us. Do you hear me?"

His eyes fixed on the flame of the candle, Joseph nodded once. Mary Elizabeth scooted close against him, picked up his arm and slung it around her small shoulders. "Cousin Joseph," the child said, and smiled.

"Kate!" Da hissed. "You know what to do."

The hammering came again on the planks, jolting the woven reed crosses that hung above the entry.

Rising and smoothing her skirts, Kate looked around the room once and said loudly, "Brigit, Cousin Joseph's glass is empty. Pour him more buttermilk if you please, while I see who calls." Then she unbarred the door.

A burly form, with shoulders that spanned the width of the entrance, filled the space. The man was muffled in a dark blue cloak that nevertheless did not conceal the uniform of the village constable.

"Sure, and it's Constable Carroll," Kate crooned.

Kevin remarked wryly, "Come to carol on Christmas Eve, have you?"

Embarrassed by the remark and yet compelled by duty, the officer replied gruffly, "There's been trouble in Cong. Ribbonmen burned the house and barns of an informer and . . ." At the mention of the word *informer,* the constable shuffled uneasily. Constable Carroll was, after all, the chief informer and traitor in all the townlands.

Kate queried, "And was the traitor hanged as well? We heard the Ribbonmen are hangin' informers regularly in the North."

Angrily Carroll replied, "It's Irish rebels who are to be hanged." He jerked his thumb over his shoulder at a half dozen mounted British soldiers in the yard. "And there are the fellows who'll do the hangin'. They've followed a trail toward Ballynockanor it seems and since I know every man and child . . ."

Kate stepped aside to show that she had nothing to hide, then looked around the officer at the soldiers, their muskets unslung and held across the saddlebows. "Saints above!" Kate said with astonishment. "Will you all be comin' in then? We turn no one away this night, but the stew is nearly gone already. Mary Elizabeth," she called over her shoulder. "Put more potatoes into the pot."

"Potatoes?" scowled the constable, his gaze lighting on Joseph Connor. "Stand aside. We're not here for supper, Kate." He pushed his way into the room.

"But the night is bitter cold," Kate suggested. "Would your men not like to come to the fire?" She gestured toward the yard where the breath of man and horse alike made frosty plumes in the night air.

"Never mind about that. Who is this fellow?"

Kate shrugged and closed the door gently behind Constable Carroll.

"You," Carroll demanded roughly, pointing his finger at Joseph. "What's your name, and where do you come from?"

Mary Elizabeth piped up again, "This is our cousin, Joseph."

"That's right," Martin agreed. "Joseph Connor, from Dublin."

The captain's eyes narrowed in suspicion. "What is your business here, Mister Connor?"

Jumping to his feet, Kevin snarled, "He's here for Christmas, and what right have you to come here and interrogate us?" Tom Donovan laid a restraining hand on his son's arm.

"Constable," Kate said sweetly. As she spoke she took her right arm from behind her back and turned so that the firelight shone directly on her. "Why would you look to us for your fugitive? As you can see, we are at supper before going to mass. Hardly a desperate character amongst us all, would you not agree?" Kate gestured around the room with a broad, sweeping motion of her ruined fist.

"You . . ." The constable stammered, cursed under his breath, then stopped, frankly staring. Then he looked away uneasily; but wherever he turned, Kate was in plain view in front of him. "It's a hangin' offense, and they think there was some rebels comin' to Ballynockanor. We're askin' through the village for . . ."

The query paused again as Kate used the three remaining fingers of her crippled hand to hook a mug of buttermilk and offer it to the constable. Kevin, still bristling, raised his chin and said, "You're wastin' your time and ours and on such a night."

The constable studied the low timbers that supported the roof. "Mister Connor," he said, "you never told me what business would bring a man from Dublin all the way to Ballynockanor."

"Not just from Dublin," Kate replied. "He has no wish to make much of himself, but he has a fine education. He intends to be a teacher. . . ."

Joseph interrupted. "Not a teacher only, but first a priest, cousin Kate." Then to the constable he added, "I return to seminary in the fall. Whitefriar Street. But first I've come to study the church history of Galway with your own Father O'Bannon."

"Is this so, Tom?" the officer inquired, trying to look past Kate's scars directly at Da.

"You know where to find Father O'Bannon," Da affirmed. "Although you have not been to church among your own kind since you took an oath to serve the English."

Carroll's eyes sparked. "If you're lyin', Tom Donovan, and this chap ain't who he says and what he says, it'll mean eviction! And I'll personally see that not a stone of your house remains standin'!" The officer spun on his heel and yanked open the door to stomp out. He was already shouting orders to the soldiers as he slammed it shut behind him.

⌒⌒

Constable Carroll stood in the shadows beyond the torch that flickered above the gate of the Catholic Church of St. John the Evangelist. There was no sign of the English soldiers, although Kate did not doubt that they were within earshot of the constable.

It was a certainty that every family in Ballynockanor had been scrutinized and interrogated by the official. The brooding presence of Constable Carroll at the entrance of the chapel assured that Father O'Bannon had already been questioned as to the validity of Joseph Connor's story.

The thoughts of every parishioner now turned from the Christmas vigil and the hope of a miracle to the threat of soldiers outside the churchyard. It had happened ten thousand times within the living memory of Ireland that a son or a brother or a father was falsely arrested, tried, and transported or hanged for some offense he did not commit.

Kate passed beneath the portal, fully expecting that Joseph Connor would be proved a liar and detained on the spot as a rebel and traitor against the Crown of England. But it did not happen.

When Carroll let them enter, Brigit looked at Joseph with astonishment and whispered to Kate, "Sure and they've asked Father O'Bannon about him! Joseph Connor was tellin' the truth!"

Kate did not reply, but felt inexplicably ashamed of herself for doubting the stranger's story.

It was the sight of the newcomer that drew the thoughts of the congregation away from Constable Carroll. Every eye asked, *Who is this fellow? Where did he come from, and why is he here in Ballynockanor on this night of all nights?*

Martin and Mary Elizabeth, believing they were walking beside the Promise, beamed proudly, as though they had caught the largest trout in the history of Connemara fishing.

Mad Molly, guarded by her daughter and son-in-law and positioned by the left rear column for a hasty exit, spotted Joseph. In spite of her daughter's efforts to keep her still, the old woman began to hum "Morrison's Jig." She nodded sagely and blessed herself three times while muttering loudly, "Father, Son, and bless me, it's Joseph and Father, Son, and he's a fine-lookin' man for the father of the child. Father, Son, and it's in the grave. In your porridge and in my potato!"

Strangers had this effect on Molly, but tonight the parish of Ballynockanor was looking for an Irish rebel on the run or an angel. They gaped long and hard at Joseph Connor. Which was he?

If he was the predicted miracle, he looked disappointingly mortal and ordinary and oblivious to the hopes of the village. If he was the criminal wanted by the soldiers, the population would come to his hanging, pray for his soul, and be glad that he was not their kin.

Like everyone else at the Vigil of Christmas, Joseph repeated the gradual,

> *This day you shall know that the Lord will come and save us:*
> *and in the morning you shall see His glory.*

Perhaps a bolt of lightning would come down and strike Constable Carroll and the soldiers. The officials would be cinders and that would be something to talk about for years to come!

Molly shouted joyfully and turned in circles at the next words:

> *Tomorrow shall the wickedness of the earth be abolished: and*
> *the Savior of the world shall reign over us. Alleluia.*

No thunder boomed, but Molly added loudly, "Auld Marlowe! Dark devil! The fairies stole 'im! Ye did not search beneath the ice!"

At a stern look from Father O'Bannon, Molly's daughter blanched and took the old woman out.

Joseph leaned forward and cast an inquisitive glance at Kate. He mouthed the question, "Mad Molly?"

Kate nodded. Brigit looked disgusted. Da blew his nose loudly. Martin and Mary Elizabeth cast sideways squints at one another. Kevin was seized by a fit of silent, painful, ill-concealed laughter that shook the pew and finally ended in a spasm of coughing just before Holy Communion.

So it was that all of Ballynockanor met Joseph. And so it was that Joseph met Ballynockanor.

Five minutes after the benediction, however, the curiosity and hopes of the villagers dissolved entirely when Joseph stuck out his hand to Father O'Bannon and said, "Your Honor, I am Joseph Connor. . . ." He pulled an envelope from his pocket.

Father O'Bannon smiled broadly, showing that he had only four teeth in the front of his mouth. "Aye! Bless you, boy! I was not expectin' you here so soon! Mid-January, his letter said! The queen's soldiers were in hopes you were their man, but I told them the straight of it."

"I wanted to start the work sooner than planned, if you'll take me."

Kate stood pressed in the crowd of friends and neighbors and cousins, all of whom were whispering about the newcomer.

Brigit gave a haughty sniff. "So you didn't believe him, Kate? Well, look at that, will you? Sure, and he's close with His Honor. And you would have made him out to be a Ribbonman or worse."

Kate blushed. "The mackerel is out of the English nets. I've nothing to apologize for. It is natural to suspect . . ."

It was indeed natural to suspect a stranger in Galway. No one came to Connaught by choice. The hands of disgusted Ballynockanorians waved in dismissal. Joseph Connor was but a poverty-stricken student whose arrival was expected by the priest all along.

The glow upon the cheeks of Mary Elizabeth and Martin faded at the revelation of fact.

Where was the miracle? The hour struck midnight. Christ was born in the manger. The midnight mass was said. Constable Carroll and his soldiers went back to warm themselves at the barracks in

Castletown. There was not so much as a hint of heavenly lightning bolts to strike down the oppressors. Ballynockanor was still desolate and without hope of freedom.

Joseph Connor, the fool who crossed the icy river, was no one. Not a miracle. Not a saint. Not a patriot. Not a thief on the run. He was not even an eligible bachelor.

"It's disappointin', I tell you. Does the world need another priest?" Brigit asked.

Mad Molly would not be dissuaded. She charged Joseph and Father O'Bannon as they left the chapel arm in arm. Falling to her knees she raised her clasped hands to plead with the stranger, "I've done all I could do! The fairies stole him! Then the uncle Marlowe threw us out of the manor, you see! Oh my sweet boy! It's in the grave! It's in your potato and in my . . ." Mad Molly babbled on and was weeping still as the kind Joseph Connor helped her to stand. Her daughter led her home and locked her in the commodious bedchamber with bars on the windows.

Christmas morn came to Ballynockanor, and no chorus of angels danced upon the gables of the chapel of St. John the Evangelist.

In the morning brightness, shadows stretched long across the ground. Joseph Connor walked with Father O'Bannon among the tombstones of the churchyard. The old priest's head was bent. His hands were clasped behind his back. The hem of his cassock was trimmed with mud.

The young man, tousled blond hair shining in the sunlight, recited the names carved upon the monuments. He commented in amazement that among them were folks he had always imagined would live forever.

"And where," he queried, "is the memorial to young Joseph Connor Burke who some say died beneath the ice on the river Cornamona?"

The priest scratched his cheek thoughtfully. "The congregation voted to set a pillar beside the river where you drowned. But when your uncle Marlowe took over the estate, back rents came due and taxes were raised. So the collection was never taken up. Later on, when Daniel's letter came and I knew the truth of your escape, I discouraged the talk of spendin' money on such a thing. I told them that God had carved a tablet recordin' your brief life and that He holds the name of Connor Burke dearly in heaven."

"And no one must know my real name until the matters here are settled, and I am on my way back to seminary."

"Indeed, Connor. I'll not speak of it. But why did y'come back now? Stone is just as flint-hearted, and your uncle Marlowe just as graspin'."

Joseph grimaced as he replied. "It is about me," he said slowly. "Bein' sent now was not entirely of my own will. Father Elias at Whitefriars saw it first: my grief, my anger, my resentment of old wrongs. Daniel, who has been like a father to me, recognized it too. I cannot go on toward my callin' until I have laid the past to rest, one way or the other . . . and my past, though these fifteen years gone, is here. What of Molly Fahey? She recognized me, sure."

"She has been mad since the night your father died and you vanished. She wanders through these graves and chats with her long-dead neighbors about you. 'Father and Son,' she cries, 'Father and Son. . . .' Poor woman. Harmless enough. There's no one left in Ballynockanor who'll believe her if she says you are who you are. She cannot hurt you with what she knows. But neither can she help you, Connor."

Satisfied, Joseph Connor Burke quietly asked Father O'Bannon, "And where did they bury my father?"

The priest paused on the gravel path and raised his hand toward the white marble crypt with the name Burke engraved on it. "He's laid beside your mother in the family tomb. But when the will was read, your uncle claimed there was not money enough left to carve his name upon the stone. Imagine, boy! A man like The Burke without so much as a name to remember him."

"I remember him well. And I have come home to write his epitaph."

∽

After that first morning Joseph kept to himself. For seven days he ate only bread and water. Seeking solace in the musty quiet of the crumbling chapel he did not speak to the priest of his father or his uncle Marlowe again.

Kneeling before the cross of the suffering Christ, Joseph thought only of his own suffering and that of the people of Ballynockanor. He tried to pray, but his words were hollow echoes lost among the dark and ancient oak beams. Leaving his studies at seminary he had returned to Ballynockanor in hope of finding peace. Instead the old sorrows and rage seeped into his soul. He remembered only what had been taken from him and grieved anew for the loss.

On the evening of the seventh day Father O'Bannon touched his shoulder as he knelt at the altar.

"Connor, boy?"

Joseph did not take his eyes from the spike that pierced the feet of Christ. He murmured the thought that had passed through his mind a thousand times, "It's written that by His wounds we're healed. Sure, and why's my soul still lame, then?"

"You've come back home on your knees to find the answer. If you can't walk He'll carry you."

The last ray of sunlight withdrew from the chapel. Flames of red votive candles illuminated the altar. "How can I serve the God of peace when my heart wants only vengeance?"

"You'll not find the Lord you seek in your father's tomb. Nor is He there still dyin' on the cross. He vanquished our darkness. He's risen, Connor boy, and walks among the people of Ballynockanor. Your answer's with them."

PART II

This contest of ours is not on our side a rivalry of vengeance but one of endurance—it is not they who can inflict most but they who can suffer most will conquer.

—Terence MacSwiney from a speech in Cork

3

Joseph Connor Burke, leaving behind the *Burke*, which was the most essential part of his name, set out from the house of the priest in daylight. Raising his face to the sun he started off across the hills that swelled above Ballynockanor and led to Castletown and the place that had once been his home.

Joseph Connor feared he had forgotten The Way after so many years gone by. But The Way remembered his footsteps and urged him on. Once familiar paths appeared magically from beneath the new grass. At every turning some old landmark leaped into the sunlight to remind him.

He stopped to gaze down for a moment as a cloud passed before the sun and brushed the valley with shadow and light. Though he had grown older and changed, the land of Connaught had always been old and timeless. Here was a place unaltered by his absence. Below him were the fields and fences, the barns and cottages, the cattle and the grazing sheep: all the same as when he was a boy. Had Ballynockanor been waiting for his return?

But things were not the same. The people were not the same. Headstones in the churchyard gave mute testimony to that fact.

Joseph sat on a broad slab of granite that had soaked up the sun's warmth. Smoke rose from the chimney of the Donovan cottage. A woman was hanging laundry on the line. Was it Kate Donovan there, shaking out the nightshirts and pinning them up and staring at the sky in hopes it would not rain? Kate Donovan all grown up. Unlike the land, she was changed indeed. What tragedy had altered her forever? Joseph made a mental note to ask Father O'Bannon why she never smiled. And what happened to the hand that once played the violin so sweetly?

Now the old melody caressed his mind.

He spoke the words aloud in the Gaelic,

> *Is méanar do lucht an dobróin . . . Blessed are the gentle;*
> *they shall inherit the land.*

Katie Donovan at eight years. Small and bright she was. Her hair was red like a sorrel filly. She knew her lessons better than anyone else in the catechism class. Her hand was raised in proverbial correctness until Father O'Bannon would not call on her anymore. Little Katie Donovan had played an angel and performed on her fiddle in the Christmas pageant. Joseph Connor Burke, although he was destined to be the master of the townlands one day, was but a lowly shepherd. She hissed his lines to him on stage when he forgot, and he hated her for knowing everything. Later, when his father took ill and Connor stood waiting for the coach that would carry him to boarding school, Katie Donovan pressed a purple flower in his hand and told him she would not forget him. And he had loved her for that. From the distance of a lonely Dublin dormitory, Connor had loved her.

As if sensing his thoughts, Kate paused and gazed up into the hills. But she did not see him. Martin's dog scampered around her skirts and she scolded him, gathered up the empty wicker basket, and returned to the house.

"Don't go in, Kate," he whispered. "I've been here all along watching you!"

As she closed the door behind her, Joseph drew his breath in sharply. The dull ache of loneliness filled him with the understanding that everything had changed in Ballynockanor!

He remembered her as an angel with music in her hands. She probably had not thought of him at all in years.

In memorial to him and his father, no doubt the villagers had gathered by the river, at the very place where he had vanished from their lives. In loyalty they had spoken of what kind of boy he had been and what a shame it was he would not grow to be a man.

The Burke lands passed into the hands of a stranger who never loved the farmers or cared for their burdens. The old Burke house sat empty. It stared out, waiting for the new master to build it back to glory again by the sweat and burdens of the gentle farmers who loved the land they would never inherit.

How long did they mourn for him? How long did they grieve for The Burke who had loved them all?

Joseph was sure they had come and bowed their heads out of respect for father and son. And then they had returned to their simple lives, to the work and the cattle and the fields.

That much of Ballynockanor was unaltered by time.

Joseph gazed up at the passing cloud and wondered if the voice of God was silent and waiting to speak from within the shrouded mists. When would the promises be fulfilled?

Is méaner dóibh seo. . . . Blessed are those who mourn; they shall be consoled. Blessed are those who hunger and thirst after righteousness, for the righteousness of God shall be theirs.

Joseph Connor Burke mourned for what was lost to him, and he was not consoled. Hunger and thirst for righteousness had drawn him to the peaceful table of seminary. But the righteousness of God remained beyond his reach. Joseph's appetite for justice had taken its place.

Why did The Voice remain silent when injustice ruled openly along the banks of the Cornamona?

"If You're there, Lord, only speak to my heart and I'll obey," he whispered. "Tell me how to lay the past to rest, and I'll leave here forever!"

Wind whistled over the hill, but the voice of the Lord was not in the wind. The cloud scudded across the sky like a ship in full sail, but the voice of the Lord did not answer from the cloud.

∽

Joseph returned to Father O'Bannon with Kate on his mind. Over a cup of tea and a thin slice of toast the first history lesson of Ballynockanor began. "I remember what she was. Her fiddle and her songs."

The priest stirred a dollop of Donovan cream in his cup. "There's been no song in the Donovan cottage for these five years since the fire." Testing the brew he furrowed his brow. "Kate married Sean Garrity. Right here in St. John's it was."

"I well remember wee small Sean."

"He grew. Six feet four inches and fifteen stone. A good man, Sean. A bull. A dove. A gentle lamb without the quick wit of Kate. But the match was made in heaven."

"And how did it end?"

Father O'Bannon found a memory hidden in the cobwebs of the corner between beam and roofline. "New thatch was needed on Tom Donovan's cottage. All the family was sleepin' under the roof of Kate and Sean, save for Tom and Kevin, who were at the barn for calving, Lord have mercy." He crossed himself and was silent a long moment. "They were all asleep. A candle fell against the curtain, and all the house was aflame. Sean saved Brigit. Kate carried Mary Elizabeth to safety. Kate's mother, an infant boy, and Sean all perished when the roof fell in on them."

"And Kate?"

"Heroic. Sure, and she swam through the flames after them and pulled Martin free. His leg was burned. She went back, but there was no savin' the others." He sighed and frowned at the smoldering embers on the hearth. "For three long years she wore widow's weeds. At last I told her God would not have one so young wear the black of mournin' forever. Aye. But she swears she'll never love nor marry nor play her fiddle again." He cocked an eye at Joseph. " 'Tis my opinion she wishes she'd died as well. Sure, and she nearly had her wish, so great the sorrow. Kate waits for her own death and will welcome it. And Tom Donovan, poor fellow. False guilt is comrade to the drink, and the pair of them have had him by the throat from that day to this."

$\backsim$

Father O'Bannon arranged for Mad Molly to meet with Joseph before vespers. She was most calm and reasonable inside the tiny musty structure of St. John the Evangelist. "Almost in her right mind," the priest explained.

Molly and Joseph sat together in the soft glow of the votive candles that flickered at the feet of Jesus. Each light was the reminder of a prayer. Some shone for mercy, some for repentance, others for love or a field of potatoes or a new cow. One burned for the answer to an unanswerable question.

"Do you know me, Molly?" Joseph cradled the face of the old woman in his hands.

"Oooh," she breathed, nodding her grizzled head and arching her eyebrows. "Aye. Ye're the changeling, ye are. Stole little Connor they did and put ye back in his place. But I mean ye no harm. No harm! I'll not say a word to the uncle that ye're about."

"It's me," he urged, glancing up at Christ as he had done in his childhood. This quiet and holy sanctuary was the only place where Joseph Connor Burke was certain of his own identity. Beneath the quiet gaze of his Savior he knew he was known and loved. Always in the back of his mind had been the memory of Ballynockanor and Jesus gazing down at his child's heart in the chapel and whispering that one day he must come home. As years passed there had been days he thought the village, the church, and his father had been only a dream. But now fragments of the past came back to him.

"Sure, Molly. It's myself, Connor Burke. All grown up, I am, and come home to claim what's mine!"

"Ye'll claim what's His." She grinned up at the rafters of the chapel, then motioned to Christ crucified and still suffering for the souls of Ballynockanor. "Ye'll serve Him, will ye, boy?" A glimmer of reason entered her eyes.

"I've given the Lord my life, Molly, for I'd have no life a'tall if His hand had not saved me from the river that night."

"He saw everything, Connor. Aye."

"That He did. And you did as well, Molly." He searched her face and found recognition. "But I did not. So you must tell me."

Sanity vanished all too quickly. The old woman grimaced and scratched her head with both hands. "Hmmm. See all? That I did. But I cannot remember." The hands slipped down to cover her face, and she moaned. "Horrrrible! Poor man. Poor Connor. Poor Liam! His brains spilled and I stepped over . . ." Her face screwed up as though she were trying to move the heavy weight of time and memory.

"You must tell me," he pleaded. "I was . . . wee Connor was so very young, and it was such a long time ago. If you don't tell me I can't set it right."

She nodded in vigorous agreement. "It's in yer porridge and in my potato. It's in the grave, Connor! He took it with him, don't you see! Took the truth of it and there's an end to it and I'll not speak of it lest the uncle murder the child in Dublin too! And ye, as well, Joseph Connor. The uncle'll see you dead if he knows ye've come to unlock the casket and bring forth the dead to accuse him! No matter ye're intent on becomin' the priest. He'll murder ye again as he did the first time. Cold and wet were ye. A drowned kitten in a sack." She went to her knees, raised her clasped hands to the cross, and cried out, "Oh Lord, Lord! Breath of life! Christ have mercy on the child! Mercy on wee Connor! For there is none can save us but Ye, Jesu!"

With this final outcry Mad Molly's shoulders sagged. She crouched still and silent on the stones like a marionette dropped by the puppeteer.

Joseph sank down beside her. For a time he prayed for Molly and himself and Kate and the poor people who slaved on the lands that once were of the family Burke. What had become of them all? Placing his hand gently on Molly's head he entreated, "Christ have mercy indeed! Say the word, Lord, and we shall be healed. . . . Will You not unlock the door and take the bars from her windows?"

Mad Molly sat up slowly and cackled, "I saw it plainly! Joseph and all the tears of Mary! The babe! A miracle!" She closed her eyes, still wild, and chortled to herself.

Joseph put his arm around her frail shoulders as though she were who she had been years before when she fed him in the kitchen of the manor house.

"Molly Fahey, well do I remember your kindness to me. I'd make you whole again for your own sake, dear woman . . . and not just because I need your memory back again." He raised his eyes to the dark oak rafters of the ancient church. "But you saw it all, sure. And I am certain you hold the key!"

She moaned and sighed, "Aye. It's in your potato. . . ."

Brigit let Martin and Mary Elizabeth climb from the milk cart at the gate of the hated National School in Castletown. After a break for Christmas and the New Year, in mid-January came the time for student servitude to resume.

The matron, Mrs. Rush, stern and implacable, waited beside the high-arched doorway and glared as the two moved too slowly toward the building. Martin glanced nervously down at his awkward limp, then back at Brigit. His expression pleaded with her for an instant. Brigit inclined her head impatiently.

It was difficult to pass under Mrs. Rush's piercing stare. Martin felt himself scrutinized and judged, from his combed hair to his recently brushed shoes. Patting Mary Elizabeth consolingly on the shoulder, Martin pushed her firmly toward the girls grouped on the far side of the cobbled courtyard. With a final look back toward the gate to see if some reprieve was possible, Martin joined the cluster of lower-form boys.

Looking very much like a prison, Castletown's National School was a grim-faced building. Two stories of brick high, its sturdy facade was meant to suggest that education was a serious business intended to produce sober-minded citizens. The flat exterior was only relieved by two large windows, and these were set into the second floor. This was entirely appropriate, the English planners felt, since students should not have such distractions as glimpses of the outside world. Views were reserved for the superintendent's office and, grudgingly, for the other office into which ten instructors were crammed. Light for classrooms came from narrow slits placed high in the side walls so as to cause no diversion of the learning process.

Over the two front windows were pediments of white stone, meant by the designer to advance a connection between the National School and classic Greek and Roman thought.

Martin looked at the windows and shuddered, as he did most every day of school. Though he had never told anyone, the white stone triangles resembled the heavy eyelids of a watchful, crouching beast. This likeness was increased by the matching triangular pediment over the double door; it appeared to Martin to be a pointed beak ready to snap shut on the unwary.

Just under the prow of the gable was a clock. As Martin raised his eyes toward it, the minute hand closed the gap that separated it from vertical and ten o'clock struck. In contrast to the joyous ringing of the chapel bell, the schoolhouse chime made a dull, thudding sound.

As the last ponderous stroke rolled away, the heavy oak doors were flung wide and Steward John Stone, as acting superintendent, emerged to conduct the morning roll call. His stock was knotted high up his throat, forcing him to keep his jaw elevated. The effect would have been regal if Stone had possessed a chin to raise. In the absence of such a facial feature, the superintendent merely looked like one on whom the hangman had practiced and failed, leaving a permanently elongated neck.

Stone cleared his throat and, beginning at the eldest of the enrolled students, forcefully called each surname and Christian name. The correct answer, indeed, the only acceptable response, was "Present, sir." When a pronounced name met with silence, Stone repeated it once, then again, each time louder than before, as if he could summon an absent student by the power of his will.

Daring for an instant to break the rule that required perfect stillness in the ranks, Martin turned his head fractionally to the left to dart a glance at a foursome of students being sternly watched over by Mrs. Rush. Even though he knew what was coming, Martin cringed at the thought and silently breathed a prayer of thanks for the mothering provided by sister Kate.

Roll call finished at last, Superintendent Stone announced, "Two hundred five enrolled, sixty-three present." This was a typical turn-out for the school, many children being kept at home to help with farming. But not Tom Donovan's children, not often. Da insisted his younger offspring learn everything they could, even though every school day was a misery. "Missus Rush," the superintendent continued, "bring me your charges."

Prisoners he might have said, Martin thought. The four children who trooped forward to stand in front of the assembly had their heads bowed in shame and despair.

"Margaret O'Toole," Mrs. Rush announced crisply, holding her hand above the head of each offender in turn as if offering a blessing. "Dirty hair and ears. Billy Mulrooney," she said, sniffing and elevating her nose, "dirty about the person. Both to be sent home."

From the moment the unerring eye and nose of the matron had detected the transgressions, it was a foregone conclusion that the two unwashed children would be sent home. The cruel refinement practiced by these school authorities was to hold the convicted up to ridicule before sending them away. The two children left the grounds silently, but not before Martin caught the look of loathing and hatred on Billy Mulrooney's eight-year-old face.

What came next was almost as bad. "Finn Carolan and Seamus Kilpatrick," Mrs. Rush intoned, hands suspended over the pair of barefoot boys to impart an anointing of humiliation. "No shoes." The truth of this assertion was obvious, but the two had to endure the gaze of the schoolyard while their respective teachers were required to leave the ranks. From the school storeroom, each instructor returned with a pair of cheap, used shoes with paper-thin soles, which Finn and Seamus were forced to borrow and wear for the day. The shame bestowed on the students was thus shared in part by their instructors. Finn and Seamus would have no easy day even after this part of the ordeal was over.

"Master Carolan has undoubtedly been careless and lost or spoiled his shoes," Superintendent John Stone proclaimed to the gathering, "but Master Kilpatrick, this is the third time for you. If your father would reduce his daily dozen glasses of whiskey by just one dram, he could afford to buy you shoes of your own."

Kilpatrick colored beet red and choked on the retort he wanted to make. Martin knew that the Kilpatricks were a family of nine, living on three acres of the rockiest land in Galway. That Seamus had clothes to wear, let alone shoes, was something of a wonder. The head of the Kilpatrick clan, Old Seamus, had taken the pledge of Father Mathew's national temperance movement to lay aside alcohol forever, but Superintendent John Stone would never have believed it; in his mind, all male Irishmen above the age of fourteen were drunks.

Superintendent Stone clapped his hands together. "Very well. To class now, all of you."

Another day of National School in Castletown had begun.

The men were in the fields; the children were in school. Brigit, after dropping Martin and Mary Elizabeth at school, had taken a kettle to the smith for mending. Kate was alone with a pregnant heifer named Nancy whose belly was wide and round and tight to bursting with the calf she carried. The soft brown eyes of the docile creature stared absently over the gate of the calving pen as Kate mucked the stalls and spread fresh straw over the floor. This was to be the first calf sired by the prize bull of Tuam. Da had great hopes for introducing new blood into the Donovan dairy herd.

The first contraction seized the heifer at half past seven in the morning. There was little for Kate to do but watch and wait. She had witnessed the miracle a hundred times, and it was always as wondrous as if it were the first.

Kate did not dread it or fear being left alone with the little moilie at such an hour. Da always said the milk cows preferred Kate to any other in the family when calving was upon them. Da would be pleased to find a new baby when he and Kevin returned at dusk.

Kate stroked the nose of the creature and sang softly to soothe her, "There, there, Nancy girl. There now. It'll be over in no time a'tall."

But it was not over when it should have been. The morning passed and the fierceness of the contractions increased. Agony transformed trust to terror. Pain seized the little cow and brought her to her knees and to her side.

Kate threw off her blouse, stripping to her camisole. Lying down behind the straining cow, she eased her arm into the birth canal and touched the head of the calf.

"It's all wrong," she whispered. "Lord Jesus, where are his legs?" She reached beneath the chin of the unborn creature, groping along the neck, searching for a small hoof to grasp. The forelegs would have to be maneuvered forward, straight beneath the head and neck so the baby could be pulled to freedom.

The uterus seized up, gripping Kate's arm until the pain of the heifer was shared by Kate. Fingers turned numb. Spasms of fire shot into her shoulder. Her reach was not long enough.

Bracing her feet against the wall, she grimaced and eased into the heifer again. Face plastered against the hip bone, she groped for a handhold but found none.

It would take the long arm of Kevin to capture and hold the calf's leg. It would take the strong backs of two men to pull the creature from its mother's womb.

Kevin and Da would not be back for hours. If she ran to fetch them in the far field, both heifer and calf would be dead by the time they returned.

Another contraction crushed Kate's arm. She groaned as the calf moved slightly and the right knee inched forward. "A little more, Nancy girl. Just a bit. There now."

The cow bellowed, thrashing her hind leg, the hoof painfully striking Kate's thigh. Another wave of rippling muscle clamped down from fingertips to shoulder, bringing tears to Kate's eyes.

She cried, "Lord have mercy! Don't let me lose her, then. Christ have mercy! Don't let her die and the calf with her. Da is countin' on . . ."

A man's voice spoke her name. "Kate. Have you lost somethin', girl?"

It was Joseph Connor, gazing down at her from outside the pen. Never mind his stupid remark. Never mind that she was stripped to her underdress, and the scars on her arm and neck were plainly visible. It was Joseph Connor with his long limbs and five thick fingers to hold a spindly leg. Joseph with a strong back to pull!

"The calf . . . it's turned all wrong, y' see," Kate panted, pulling her blood-soaked arm from the heifer. "My reach is not . . . I'm not strong enough. We'll lose them both unless . . ."

In an instant the amusement was gone from his eyes. Throwing his coat to the side and removing his shirt he lay down behind the animal. "And what am I fishin' for?" His arm vanished to the shoulder into the birth canal.

Kate coached him. "And can you feel the nose? Aye. That's it. . . . Move down the neck of him now and see if you can . . . the knee. There's a good fellow. Just below the knee. Pull the first leg forward until the foot is . . . and then again . . ."

Twenty minutes later, with spasms wringing wrists and hands and spindly calf legs, two small hoofs emerged. Kate grasped them and sweating, helped Joseph pull with the next contraction.

The great weight of the baby heaved out of the mother as free as a fish in the current. Kate and Joseph fell back, the calf across their legs.

The mother turned to look with amazement at this thing that had broken out of the prison of her womb. The calf raised his head and breathed. The cow licked his wet hair and Kate's scarred right arm with it. Kate laughed, unconscious of her deformity, joyful in the new life. "A bull calf!" she cried. "Da will be glad of it! We'll call him Abraham! The father of many nations!"

"He doesn't look like much now."

Joseph helped the calf gather his legs beneath him, and Kate lifted him to stand. The legs wobbled. As Joseph reached out to steady him, his hands grasped Kate's hands.

Their eyes met, gentle and searching. His gaze, almost hungry, locked upon her face. No man had looked at her in such a way since Sean. Did Joseph not see the scars? For an instant she thought he would kiss her. The warmth of expectation filled her. Then panic set in.

Straightening, she turned away and wrapped herself in her shawl. ". . . and me dressed in nothin' but my skirt and shift." Her comment shattered the sweet moment between them. She stammered, "It's work well done, Joseph Connor . . . even if you're a priest and not a farmer . . . and I'm thankin' you for it."

"I'll need washin'," he replied flatly, retrieving his coat and shirt and leaving the pen and the barn.

Kate cleaned herself in a bucket of water and dressed without leaving the stall. Stroking the bull calf with fresh straw, she guided the tiny creature to his mother's teats. Kate remained in the barn until she was certain all was well.

She half expected Joseph to come back, to sit on the rail and take pleasure in his handiwork, but he did not. Was he waiting outside for her?

When Kevin and Da arrived home they remarked that they had met Joseph Connor on the lane. He abruptly told them the calf had been born. That was all. Nothing extraordinary.

The original purpose of Joseph's visit to the Donovan dairy remained unexplained. And why Joseph Connor had left Kate alone in the barn and gone away without a word of farewell was an even greater mystery.

Joseph Connor Burke made his home in the empty cow shed at the back of the chapel. Made of stone, it was warm enough. Pigeons nesting in the crevasses purred to him as he rested in the straw. A small peat fire burned in the center of the dirt floor. Smoke escaped through the broken slate roof.

The night passed slowly. Trying to sleep, he could not take his mind away from Kate and the day. Life had showed them its joy. The cow had cleaned her own blood from the new calf and had forgiven him for the pain his new life caused her. There was a portrait of Christ's love in that, Joseph thought.

He longed to talk with Kate about it. She, whose small and perfect hand had flagged all the answers in catechism class, had probably always understood why the Lamb of God was born in a stable.

Together they watched the miracle of love vanquish the memory of pain and yet he did not speak of what he knew. He saw in Kate's eyes that she waited to be loved in such a way. Why hadn't he told her? When he touched her hand he longed to take her into his arms and whisper, "Though we have been apart, we have been together."

Kate was, in his head, what she had always been: a gold coin shining on the riverbed. Bright and perfect, but unattainable. Another man's coin, another man's wish.

Joseph wrestled with his thoughts for hours. His calling to the priesthood, far from being clarified, seemed more obscure. The cloud of confusion over his future was thicker than ever.

4

It was January thirty-first, the Eve of St. Brigit's Feast. It was a time Kate keenly felt that she was without a proper place, and drifting.

For years in the house of her parents, Kate, as the oldest daughter, enacted the role of the saint. Married, she relinquished the task to her sister.

She was again the eldest unmarried daughter in the Donovan cottage. But tonight, as she had for four Februaries past, Kate refused to accept the task.

Brigit, red cloak replaced with a white shawl, prepared to personify her namesake.

Gathered inside the cottage were all the Donovans except Kevin, who was laboring late at Marlowe Park with a mare in foal.

To the family assembly was added Joseph Connor, who had come to collect the tithe of butter for Father O'Bannon but had been invited to stay to share the meal. Three times during supper as Da and Martin bantered about the repairing of the stone wall surrounding Blood Field, Kate felt Joseph's curious gaze upon her. She dared not raise her eyes from the plate. Her appetite left her as the stirring of unwanted longing for his quiet company filled her. She was grateful when the performance of St. Brigit's play finally began.

Kate watched Mary Elizabeth shiver with delighted anticipation. At the slightest sound from the yard the little girl shushed the others, as she had done three times before. "It's really her," she insisted.

Outside on the step Brigit's voice, deeper than normal, demanded dramatically, "Go upon your knees, all you within. Go on your knees and let Saint Brigit enter!"

"Greetings!" Mary Elizabeth shouted. "What are y'waitin' for?" she asked the others. "Invite her in, before she goes away!"

Hurrying forward, Mary Elizabeth threw open the door, bowing low to her sister in a sweeping gesture of welcome. Brigit's arms were full of rushes, cut from the bog a week earlier and dried for the purpose.

Mary Elizabeth begged, "Will someone not show me again how to make the cross?"

Joseph helped the child weave the rushes into the form of a cross, as St. Brigit had done fourteen hundred years earlier to teach a dying pagan about Jesus.

Mary Elizabeth clapped her hands. "Did y'know, Joseph," the little girl queried in her turn, "that there is a giant stone cross upon the hill where Brigit preached the gospel to a thousand pagans? And they were all baptized at the ancient well, not far from this very house?"

"Yes," Joseph acknowledged. "I did know of that."

Kate saw the man momentarily get a distracted look in his eye, as though he had suddenly fallen into a pool of memory.

The woven crosses were finished.

From the pocket of his coat Joseph produced a small glass bottle, stoppered with a cork. From its appearance it once held ink, but now the contents were clear. "Father O'Bannon sent water from Saint Brigit's well for the blessin'," he said. He laid his rush-symbol on the table by him and extended the bottle toward Brigit.

"Since Mother died," Kate said, "we've borrowed an old custom. We each light a candle to remember the Lord will guide us the next twelvemonth. Here, Da," she said, "you begin."

Each in the home, except Brigit who was still portraying the saint, lit a wick. The flames were ignited first by the oldest, in order down to the youngest, as was fitting, since tradition held that the first candle to go out reflected the first to die. When all had touched a broom straw to a candle, there was one remaining. "This is for Kev. Seein' as he's not here," Brigit explained, "I'll light it for him."

When the ring of six candles glowed on the sideboard, Brigit gathered the crosses together and sprinkled the water on them in memory of the first great baptism in Connemara. Tomorrow, on St. Brigit's feast day, they would be hung over the cottage entry, to join all those from other years.

When Brigit was done with the play, she looked very pleased with herself. She set the now empty bottle down on the sideboard with a flourish. It was only a gentle tap, but it made all the flames dance. The bump knocked over Kevin's candle, which sputtered and died in a trickle of thin blue smoke.

"It's Kevin's candle gone out," Mary Elizabeth cried with dismay. "Will he be the first dyin' among us?"

Joseph relit it and replaced it to burn with the others. "Old Molly's been fillin' your head with fairy tales again. There. It burns as bright as ever."

The Feast of St. Brigit was an important annual milestone in the lives of the people of Connemara. It was the day when folks let winter slide to the back of their minds, confidently expecting spring. Though February's winds blew damp and chill, new grass and new lambs meant new hope.

Except where the National School was concerned.

As if to taunt Martin, Mary Elizabeth climbed the rock wall that bordered the road home to Ballynockanor.

"Come on, Martin. Let's have a footrace. Me on the wall, and you on the road."

He envied the ease with which she skipped along the stone fence. He hated her for being so cheerful after another difficult day of

Superintendent Stone, Mrs. Rush, and Martin's own instructor, dottering Professor Larson.

Cocking an eye at his sister, it came to him how easily he could reach up and knock her off her perch.

"What do you say then, Martin?" she chirped. "A footrace from here to the chapel?"

He growled at her. "Have you no . . . no sense of the injustice of this day? Can you think of gallopin' along when the bricks of the National School still stand one upon the other? Where is your sense of propriety, girl?"

At his reprimand, which Martin was certain she did not entirely understand, her glee melted to glumness. Eyebrows knit together and lower lip protruding, she raised her finger in the air. "A fine idea," she concluded. "We'll ask the Ribbonmen of county Mayo to come and burn it down."

Martin's eyes narrowed. "We don't know any Ribbonmen a'tall. And if we did, do you think they'd come this far to burn the school?"

She leaped from the embankment and walked backwards as she gave the matter further thought. "They branded the *T* upon Protestant tithe cattle in Cong, didn't they? And no one would buy them because they were stolen from the Catholic farmers by the magistrate."

"Well? What of it?"

"Are tithe cattle more important than Irish brains, I ask you? A happy English child I am not!" Mary Elizabeth exclaimed. "They'll steal our wits, I say, and that is worth the burnin' down of the school."

It was a delicious idea. Martin savored the image. Mrs. Rush shrieking from the upper floor as the flames reached higher! At last the truth about her would come clear as she grabbed her broomstick and flew away to escape into the night!

"It wouldn't work a'tall," Martin replied. "There are no Ribbonmen in these parts to do the deed."

Mary Elizabeth gazed pensively skyward. "Then we'll form a

committee. Everyone hates the school. Even the Protestant children. We'll set a torch to it ourselves."

Martin snorted. "You? A girl can't be a Ribbonman!"

"I'll dress in your clothes and . . ."

"Sure, and then Constable Carroll would arrest me twice and transport me to America like they did to Da's great-uncle Cormac . . . or worse!"

"Then you would send for me, and I would grow up free and marry an American Royal and be very, very rich."

"There's no Royals in America!" Martin scoffed. "They threw over the king and Crown because of a tax on tea."

"Just tea?"

"They were Irish. What do you expect? Everyone there was an Irish convict. Transported to the colonies as rebels against England, they were. There were some Scots among them too. Father O'Bannon says the English made a terrible mistake. Aye. They should've known no man of Irish blood would stand for havin' his tea taxed."

It did not matter to Martin that his facts were garbled in the retelling; rebellion and victory over tyranny in the American colonies inspired Martin and Mary Elizabeth to form their own plan of attack against the English National School in Castletown.

Lanterns in the stables of the manor house burned long into the night. Joseph knew that Kevin Donovan was tending the master's favorite brood mare within the barn. Old Marlowe had remained at his country house to await the arrival of a new foal.

Joseph lurked beside the fountain in the garden just outside the terrace of what had once been his own home. Inside, shadowed figures moved across the windows. In the room that had once belonged to Joseph Connor Burke was young William Marlowe. Joseph held no resentment against his vain and selfish cousin. William shared no complicity in his father's sin, although his father's evil and arrogance splashed his life as well.

Uncle Marlowe, keeper of the keys in the days when The Burke had fallen upon ill health and misfortune, was the only focus of Joseph's visit tonight.

Joseph studied the bank of windows and the narrow second-story terrace of the master's suite. The lamp still burned. Pale smoke rose from the chimney. He knew the way up into the quarters. As a child he had climbed the tall rose trellis, then clambered over the balustrade and into The Burke's study a hundred times. His father had never minded the intrusion. Old Marlowe would feel differently.

Wrapping his cloak closer around him, Joseph settled back for a time. He carried the message he had waited a lifetime to deliver. In his boot was the hunting knife he had received from his father the last Christmas before the House of Burke had fallen to Marlowe. The hilt was made of elk horn capped with silver engraved with the family crest.

The lamp was extinguished at last. Other candles winked out within a quarter of an hour. Joseph delayed another forty-five minutes before he moved quickly from the shadows and effortlessly climbed the lattice to the terrace. Sliding the blade of his knife between door and frame he lifted the latch and entered the bedchamber, then softly reclosed the door.

Thick brocade curtains concealed Joseph as he listened to the deep, even breathing of his uncle. The fire crackled. Old Marlowe slept on, blissfully unaware that the dead had returned to haunt him.

The room smelled of the old man's breath and the wood smoke from the fire.

In the glow from the hearth Joseph could make out familiar furniture, though new silks and satins replaced the threadbare fabrics of his father's day. The portrait of Joseph Connor's mother still hung above the mantle. It was some tribute to the fact that Old Marlowe had loved his half sister deeply. Perhaps too deeply, Daniel had once told Joseph.

Joseph saw his own reflection in the steadiness of her eyes. His features were much like her own, and her gaze seemed to follow him as he crossed the thick oriental carpet to stand beside the bed.

The bed curtains were drawn. Joseph parted them slightly with the knife blade. How easy it would be to slit the old man's throat and listen as his last breath gurgled in blood. How right it would be for Old Marlowe to die on the same spot where he had slowly poisoned The Burke to death, where little Joseph Connor Burke had said farewell to his da for the last time.

Joseph's fingers flexed around the hilt of the knife as he contemplated the pleasure of such a revenge. But would the act not make Joseph into the image of his uncle? The sin of the old man's murder would be extracted from the hides of the people of Ballynockanor. The authorities would demand a hanging for the offense and never mind if the guilty man was hung. Joseph knew someone innocent would pay for the crime. As long as an Irish Catholic died it would matter little who had actually carried out the deed. By killing his uncle, Joseph would be guilty of taking two lives.

This certainty restrained him. There was the judgment of Christ for men like Marlowe. It would be much more terrible and just than a blade drawn across the throat. And a man like Old Marlowe, who lived with guilt, also lived with fear. Fear of discovery. Fear of death.

Joseph paused a moment before removing the scroll from his shirt. On the parchment he had carefully copied the words Thomas à Kempis had written in his work *Imitation of Christ:*

> *Every action of yours, every thought, should be those of one who expects to die before the day is out. Death would have no great terrors for you if you had a quiet conscience. . . . Then why not keep clear of sin instead of running away from death? If you aren't fit to face death today, it's very unlikely you will be tomorrow.*

Joseph signed the document simply and truthfully, *Your Servant in Christ, Thomas à Kempis.*

He added a postscript, *The dead walk among you.*

Joseph cut away the embroidered initials of Marlowe on the pillowcase and stuffed it into his pocket.

Opening the scroll, he pinned it to the headboard with his knife. What would Marlowe say when he awakened to the crest of Burke and a razor-sharp blade shining above his head?

Joseph saluted his mother's portrait and slipped out of the room the way he had come. Leaving the doors wide he let the wind wake Old Marlowe from his pleasant dreams to frightening reality.

Agitation among the poor farmers in the west country was growing. The animosity of secret organizations was concentrated against the landowners. By an act of the English Parliament they now not only collected their own exorbitant rents, but were also responsible for paying all the mandatory tithes to support the Protestant Church of Ireland. Naturally, in order to do this, they merely raised the rent still further. Connemara had yet to feel the full impact of the change.

Landlord Marlowe mounted the step of his carriage, grunting with the effort. Once balanced on his broomstick legs, he pivoted to lecture the circle of men gathered in front of him.

Though there were only three others present, they did not constitute a single rank beside the door of the coach. Nearest the rig was his son, chin raised, arrogant as always. One pace behind was John Stone, fingers plucking at his waistcoat buttons, a look of fawning solemnity on his narrow features.

At the rear of the group, several feet away, stood Constable Carroll, his chin stubbled and greasy. Even though the throat latch of his uniform was undone to accommodate his ample neck, folds of flesh still lapped over the band of his collar.

"Now pay attention to me," Old Marlowe demanded. His voice quavered, and he stopped to clear his throat. "Outrages over the border in Mayo are one thing, but here! Intolerable! I could have been murdered in my sleep! A whole gang of cutthroats in my private chambers!"

Stone glanced over his shoulder at Carroll. Nothing had been stolen except a scrap of cloth, but the bit of night-haunting had certainly put the wind up their master.

Old Marlowe noticed the look and sought to regain his composure. He knew better than to show fear to his hirelings.

"And those cattle in Cong!" Marlowe continued. Two spots of color, each the size of a tuppence, appeared on the landlord's gray cheeks. "Outrageous! And why has this happened?" Old Marlowe did not really want an answer to this query, and the three onlookers knew it. They simply waited for him to proceed. "I'll tell you why! It is because the authorities did not maintain discipline! Here, we will control our people. Carroll, I want a guard patrolling my grounds. Stone, you must not allow the wretches to have any say in the tithe matter. If they cannot pay in coin, then you select from their herds, not them. Show William here how to get what we are entitled to from the best, not from their leavings!" Marlowe paused and looked at Constable Carroll. "Use Carroll there as a sample of the animals we want. Look at him, William," he urged. "Fat as a butcher."

William Marlowe did as instructed, but he lifted his fingers to his nose at the same time.

"You see there?" his father resumed. "Fat cattle, stout hogs, well-fed sheep. Animals that will travel well and still command the best market price."

Constable Carroll looked pleased with himself despite the comparisons being made. "We'll do right by you, sir," he pledged.

"See that you do," Marlowe said coldly. "What have you found out about that newcomer . . . Joseph Connor? Are you certain he's not a Ribbonman?"

"Bless you, sir," Carroll returned, "he's not got the makings of a rebel. He's a scholar and wants to be a priest." The way Carroll sneered when he emphasized the occupations made it clear that both *priest* and *scholar* were synonymous with *weakling*.

"A scholar, eh?" Old Marlowe mused, remembering the threat

left behind in his bed chamber. He shook his head while his audience waited patiently. Connor was a newcomer. Only local people would remember The Burke. "You make certain that he is what you think," Marlowe admonished finally. "If he shows any sign of political activity, he is to be expelled from the district at once. Control, William," he addressed again to his son. "Firm from the beginning. Never show weakness, or you will have to work twice as hard to reestablish control. Isn't that right, Stone? Carroll?"

Both men nodded obsequiously.

"Now I must return to Dublin, but I shall escort Archbishop Whately back with me."

Stone and Carroll nodded respectfully. The expected visit of the Protestant cleric lent a certain plausibility to Old Marlowe's abrupt departure.

"Don't worry about a thing, Father," William asserted. "You may be going back to Dublin, but there is still a Marlowe in charge here."

∽

It was nearing twilight when the church of St. John the Evangelist came into Martin's view. His leg ached and he was cold. A ribbon of smoke rose from the chimney of the rectory. It was still another mile beyond to home and a warm supper.

"Thar she blows!" Mary Elizabeth called in imitation of a sailor she had once heard on the wharf at Galway City.

The object of her exclamation was Mad Molly Fahey, who stood wildly gesturing among the leaning gravestones in the churchyard.

"She's loose again," Martin muttered, hoping that Father O'Bannon would not spot him and request that he return the old woman to her home. "How does she get loose?"

Mary Elizabeth's eyes grew wide. "Mad Molly always says they cannot keep the wild bird caged. . . ."

"Sure, sure. She's wild enough."

". . . nor keep truth bound nor the river from runnin' free."

This was repeated reverently by Mary Elizabeth as though it made sense of Molly's escapes.

Martin ignored her. "Now look at her. Dancin' among the graves. And who's she talkin' to, I wonder?"

Mad Molly raised her scrawny arms skyward and turned in circles before the large square crypt that contained the bodies of almost all the Burke family. All but the young master, Connor Burke, who had drowned or been stolen by fairies or whatever.

Martin heard Mad Molly cackle.

Mary Elizabeth made an India-rubber face and shuddered. "She's playin'."

"With who?"

"With *what*, you mean. Cross yourself."

Martin did so. "Well, then?"

Hands on hips Mary Elizabeth whispered, "Mad Molly's the goalkeeper for the Ballynockanor spirits. She told me they'd soon be havin' a hurlin' contest with the dead Protestants from Castletown."

Martin shrugged. "That explains it," he remarked dryly. Then he shivered as he glimpsed a shadow move across the side of the crypt. "Wha . . ."

Mary Elizabeth saw it too and stopped dead, as it were, in the road. Her face fluctuated between horror and fascination, finally dissolving into disappointment as Joseph Connor came clearly into view.

"Look." Mary Elizabeth sighed. "It's only himself. Saint Joseph."

"He's not . . ." There was no use trying to convince Mary Elizabeth. She was the last in Ballynockanor still to cling to Mad Molly's prophecy. "Poor fellow. She's cornered him. Like a cat with a sparrow. He'll learn," Martin said, then added, "Well then, and he can take her home to her cage, can't he? Walk on, Mary Elizabeth. Pretend you don't see them."

This might have been possible except for the sound of iron-shod horses and carriage wheels bumping and rattling toward Ballynockanor.

A shriek arose from the graveyard as Mad Molly ran for the road. " 'Tis himself! The very devil himself in his coach and four!" She trilled an unearthly wail. " 'Twas murder! He drank the porter dry, then smashed the cup! Old Liam! Liam! Me friend, what have they done t'ye!"

The coach rumbled nearer, sending Martin and Mary Elizabeth scrambling up to safety on the wall. Mad Molly reached the edge of the road and flung handfuls of dust toward the approaching team. Behind her, in the shadow of the gate, Joseph Connor hung back and glared darkly at the curtained vehicle.

Molly shouted louder, "A curse upon ye, Old Marlowe and Young! Ye and your brood of vipers! Aye! Death follows close behind ye! It's in your porridge and in your bread! The secret's in the grave! In the grave, I say!" She spat upon the enameled green door of the carriage as it passed. "Oh, Connor Burke, poor wee Connor caught in the fairy rath . . . and the dog! Ye shall see the truth, ye devil! A little child shall lead them!"

The coach vanished in the dust of Ballynockanor, seemingly unaware of the curses that had been hurled at the occupant. And it was over. Molly sank to her knees. Joseph stepped from the gate and lifted the old woman up, enfolding her in his arms as she wept against him.

Martin and Mary Elizabeth climbed down from the stones and walked slowly toward them.

"Shall we take her, sir?" Mary Elizabeth asked.

Joseph shook his head in the negative and waved them on toward home.

The gales of March carried seabirds far inland over Connemara, white specks wheeling high above the hills. So, too, the breezes of tangled recollections swept Molly Fahey from her pleasant cage toward dimly remembered scenes.

Mad Molly capered among the tangle of overgrown vines at the side of the gatekeeper's cottage on the Marlowe estate. "It's in my potato," she sang. "It's in your porridge."

Joseph Connor called from inside the derelict stone cabin, "But what is, Molly? And where?"

He did not expect an answer, of course. Joseph harbored the notion that somewhere in the tortured workings of Molly Fahey's addled wits there still lurked an element of truth: the key to the mystery of Joseph Connor Burke's lost inheritance.

Earlier that day Joseph had encountered Molly in the churchyard of St. John the Evangelist. As usual she was speaking to the tombs of the departed as if they were all gathered at a céilé; a storytelling fest. "Oooh," she murmured to the headstone of long-dead Will Lynch, "from the fury of the O'Flaherty's may God and all the saints preserve us!" Molly pointed a twig of a finger at a nearby tomb on which the name O'Flaherty could still be dimly seen. Joseph grinned at that: Molly was quoting a bit of ancient lore that pitted the two named families against each other. "But," she remarked to the graves of both O'Flahertys and Lynches, "there is no fury as will be seen at the comin' of The Burke."

Joseph stopped short in his tracks at that. The advent referred to so calmly by Mad Molly would require Joseph's father to return from the dead. Then a sudden thought struck him: inheritance or no, the right to be called The Burke was now his own.

"What did you say?" he inquired.

It was as if Molly had been waiting for him in the churchyard, expecting his arrival as by appointment. "It's time," she urged. "The egg is cracked."

This was a new bit of nonsense, but even so, Joseph allowed the muttering madwoman to lead him over the bog. The abandoned cottage beside the Marlowe gate was their destination.

But inside there was nothing to be found. The accumulated debris of fifteen years' neglect and nothing more. If the Marlowes were not so peculiar they would have allowed a village family to clean and occupy the lodge, but such was not their way. Old Marlowe wanted no villagers living so near to his manor.

Joseph idly kicked at a bit of turf ash beside the hearth. When something scraped under his boot, he bent to examine it and found only a horseshoe nail.

Approaching hoofbeats mingled with shrieks and curses. Around a jumbled heap of broken roof slates, Joseph saw John Stone alight from a horse and move angrily toward Molly. His riding crop was raised over his head. "Devils and vipers," Molly howled. "To set the dogs upon the child! Oooh!"

Joseph heard the whistle of the riding crop, but even before it slashed into Molly's upper arm he was running. Gone was any thought of concealment, of being fearful his true identity would be discovered. In that one moment he not only wanted to wrest the whip from Stone's hand, he wanted to break the arm and the face as well.

Driver Stone was raving almost as wildly as Molly as he drew back his fist for another blow. "I'll not have you around here," he screamed. "Keep away, or I'll set the dogs on ye!"

Cowering at Stone's feet, Molly raised her hand to ward off the next strike, but it never fell. Joseph Connor intercepted Stone's wrist in mid swing. He twisted the limb so violently that the driver was flung backward to the ground. Stone's top hat bounced and rolled across the gravel.

Towering over the goggle-eyed man, Joseph stood with clenched fists and eyes that blazed with fury. "Enough!" he demanded, flinging the captured riding crop away into a thicket of thorns. "You'll not beat a crazy woman who never did you harm."

If Stone expected to employ his usual bully-and-bluster, the notion faded in the second he looked into Joseph's eyes and read there murderous hatred. The driver swallowed and shook his head carefully from side to side as if being flung to the ground had loosened something inside it.

"Come on, Molly," Joseph said, assisting the old woman to her feet.

Passing by the reclining form of John Stone, Molly made the sign against the evil eye, but when she reached the clump of vines she carefully leaned over and spat on his hat.

⌒〜

Joseph Connor was quietly seated in a dim corner of O'Flaherty's Pub. He was eating a plate of lamb stew that was long on potatoes and short on lamb, but very filling and only tuppence a serving.

A crew of young men crowded noisily through the doorway. Among them Joseph recognized Kevin Donovan. They gathered around the countertop, bawling for pints like so many calves penned away from their mothers.

There was much clinking of glasses, and then Kevin spotted Joseph. "There he is now, Tim," he said, nudging a tall, muscular fellow next to him and pointing. Kevin dragged his friend over to meet Joseph. "Mulrooney here is a Protestant, but a fine upright sort for all that he is a heretic. Mister Connor is a patriot even if he is a scholar."

"Do you ever let people speak for themselves, Kevin?" Joseph teased. "Or shall we just hear all about us from you and save our energy for eatin'?"

"But say," Kevin continued, not in the least embarrassed, "let me buy you a pint. Kate told us what really happened, with the birthin' and all. The Donovans are still in your debt."

Joseph reflected that he had returned to Ballynockanor too late. There was a time when having at least one of the Donovans beholden to him would have been a fine thing indeed. "No, thank you kindly," he said, indicating a glass of ginger beer at his elbow. "I have taken Father Mathew's pledge, and I've given up the liquor."

"Conversation then," said Kevin, squeezing beside Joseph on the narrow bench and inviting Mulrooney to sit across from them. "Y'would not be unwillin' to talk a drop of treason?"

Joseph allowed that talking politics was agreeable to him.

"Will we be gettin' our own government back?" Kevin inquired.

"That we will if Daniel O'Connell has his way," Joseph agreed. O'Connell, a member of Parliament and lord mayor of Dublin, was the leading Irishman in British politics. Called "the Emancipator"

because of his successful fight to give Catholics the right to vote and
hold office, O'Connell had lately turned his attentions to repealing
the enforced marriage of the Irish and British Parliaments. " 'Twill
not be an easy thing, what with the Tories back in power and Peel
the prime minister. The Irish in Westminster Hall are too few to
carry the laws we should be votin' on among ourselves," he said.

"It can't happen too soon," Tim Mulrooney growled in agreement.

Joseph looked at the young man with interest. "Do you say so?"
he asked, "and you a Protestant?"

Shrugging, Mulrooney drained half a glass of dark brown ale at a
swallow and wiped the foam from his lips with his sleeve. "It is not
a matter of religion," he said, "though there's some would like for
us to be at each other over a few candles more or less. No, it is this:
the English want us to stop bein' Irish altogether, and they force it
down our throats. Why, even my little brother come home from
their school spoutin' how every other nation was more civilized
than us!"

"That's it exactly!" Kevin agreed loudly. "We must convince
them to leave us be. You may be content to wear a temperance
ribbon," Kevin said, flicking the lapel of Joseph's coat, "but others
of us find another sort of ribbon to be more appealin'."

"Whist, man!" Tim urged. "Are y'daft?"

"Lower your voice," Joseph likewise suggested. The discussion
of ribbons was a thinly veiled reference to the Ribbonmen, the
secret anti-English societies who had been making clandestine raids
on landlords and their agents. "Lower it," he repeated. "You cannot know where an informer is lurkin'."

"Ah," Kevin said, arching his eyebrows. "You speak like one on
the watch himself. But know this: a few well-placed torches and we
will soon convince the English to leave us alone."

"Convince them that we are as uncivilized as they say," Joseph
retorted. "Lawlessness bears out that we are not fit to govern ourselves. The English soldiers swat petty outlaws like flies. Besides,
Daniel . . ." He stopped himself suddenly, but too late. He saw by
the gleam in Kevin's eye that his use of a familiar reference to the

Emancipator had confirmed Kevin's suspicions. "Lord Mayor O'Connell," Joseph continued, "does not hold with violence in any form. He says the temple of liberty cannot be built on blood-soaked ground."

"And what else will persuade the English?" Mulrooney inquired.

"If thousands of us feel the same way, Catholic and Protestant all standin' together . . . about our Irishness, I mean . . . they will get our message much clearer than from burnin' hayricks or brandin' cattle."

∽

Across the border in Mayo the Ribbonmen rode in defiance to the pleas of Daniel O'Connell for peace. By mid-March clandestine acts of violence in Mayo had put the English authorities in Connaught on alert. As yet the pot had not boiled over in Castletown, but there was a general consensus that one small incident would lead to revolt.

Joseph's advice about standing together as peaceful Irishmen had made him suspect among the young men who ran with Kevin Donovan. Strangely, Joseph was not troubled about losing their good opinion of himself. The only opinion that had come to matter to him was that of Kate.

Night after night Joseph lay down on his bed of straw and asked God about her.

He recited the words of the ancient hymn,

Athairatá I d'chónaí . . .
Father dwelling in light on high
When you look down on Magdalen,
The flames of love you wake in her
And make soft a heart once frozen.

The power of his desire for her alarmed him. He had not expected it. Was it love he felt for her or merely pity that moved him to want to touch her? Was it something in his past that bound him to her, some forgotten promise he had made in childhood to love her always? Or was it only his fear of living in service to God and dying unremembered?

> *A Chriost, is tusa ár n-aonghrá fíor . . .*
> *O Christ my true and only love,*
> *Rid me of my failings.*
> *Fill you my heart with living grace,*
> *Give back my heavenly reward.*

Like a man lost in the forest after nightfall, Joseph lay still in the darkness. Hoping for some reply to guide him home, he held his breath and listened.

God's voice was not in the darkness. There was no answer, only the troubling awareness that Kate was yet another complication, perhaps temptation, which could draw him from his goal.

But what if it was love he felt for her? Could he not wean himself away from desire? There had been other women who had stirred him. Yet seeking the righteousness of Christ he had turned his back on them easily. After all they were strangers to him, as he was a stranger to them.

But Kate? The sight of her was a familiar landmark, his home-land. She had been part of the life and years in which he had lived his only happiness. Like a wanderer raking solace from the feel of native soil beneath his feet, Joseph looked into the eyes of Kate and knew well the paths that wound to her heart. They were the same paths as his.

∽ 5 ∽

March the twenty-first was market day in Castletown, and it dawned fair and warm.

The Donovan stall was set among long aisles of tables in the exact center of town, between the courthouse on one side and the brooding hulk of the National School on the other.

Da had a meeting at Joe Watty's tavern to arrange the sale of a pair of yearlings. Kevin's presence was required there for him to observe the bargaining. Kate remained at home with Mary Elizabeth, who was down with the sniffles. This left Brigit and Martin to mind the table where butter and other goods were sold to the townspeople.

For a couple of hours Brigit was actually helpful. She would engage the shoppers in lively conversation and, in the talking, convince them that the deep yellow Donovan butter really was richer than that of their competitors. Martin marveled at the way she could get a penny more per pound and at the same time persuade the buyers to take twice as much as they had intended.

Things went smoothly until the clock chimed ten and Constable Carroll, accompanied by a dozen soldiers, sauntered through the square.

Along with dairy goods, the Donovans bartered household items of their own manufacture. Kevin and Martin gathered rushes and bound them to bog oak limbs for sale as brooms. All three Donovan men stitched shoes from cowhide, and several pair of these were displayed. Finally, Brigit had knitted three pair of knee-length wool stockings, and these were draped over a corner of the table.

When two young men of the townlands, Tim Mulrooney and Chris O'Neill, wandered into view, Martin had a sudden premonition that the quiet morning was about to be disturbed. Twenty-year-old Tim and nineteen-year-old Chris both had eyes for Brigit.

Brigit was animatedly discussing the merits of her stockings with the leathery-faced Mrs. Casey. "The toe loop is lined with linen, so it is. It lasts longer and does not chafe so."

Mrs. Casey, whose feet were innocent of any stockings, nodded sagely. Wool stockings were worn for warmth and against the chapping effects of wintry air on exposed shins. Martin doubted if Mrs. Casey's toes still had the ability to notice whether they were being chafed or not.

Smoothly, Brigit continued, "And do y'see the extra roll I've stitched into the tops? It keeps the stockin' from saggin', so." With that, Brigit deftly flicked her mid-calf-length skirt to knee height to show how well her stockings stayed up.

Just as glibly, Brigit straightened her skirt again, never missing a beat of her discussion or diverting her attention from her customer. She never gave any sign that she had noticed anything out of the ordinary.

But others had noticed, Martin thought. The boy saw Chris O'Neill make a remark to Tim Mulrooney and receive a shove in return. Both men were leering openly at Brigit from across the path, next to the fishmonger's stall.

For the sake of family honor he had to say something, Martin thought. Da would. Kevin would. But what was the right thing? He had just opened his mouth to challenge Tim and Chris when Constable Carroll rounded the corner.

"Tim Mulrooney," the constable called.

Leers evaporated, replaced by sullen resentment on the faces of Brigit's admirers. Conversation and bartering along the aisle fell away as two soldiers appeared at the opposite end of the row to block any escape. A wave of silence swept over the crowd. Heads pivoted to stare at the encounter.

Mulrooney turned his back on the policeman.

"Come now, Mulrooney," Carroll crooned. "Is that any way to greet an old friend? Are you still haulin' fertilizer, boy? If so, we'll be needin' some for the cabbages behind the prison."

Chris O'Neill scowled defiantly at the soldiers and made a pretense of patting his pockets for a pipe.

The constable, his eyes hard, strolled to the two young men. "Look at me when I'm speakin' to you, Mulrooney."

"What do you want with him?" a woman's angry voice shouted.

Martin recognized Mrs. Mulrooney as she broke through the crowd.

Carroll cocked his head to one side. "Ah. It's your mother, Mulrooney. Think she'll save you from the noose this time?"

"Stay away from this, Mother," Mulrooney warned her. "They've got nothin' on me."

At this the constable's smile broadened. "Have we not? You were among those who burned a house in Cong on the night of December twenty-third last. You were seen about after curfew."

Mrs. Casey had just handed over sixpence for a pair of the stockings. Brigit shoved it back into her hand and stepped from behind the counter. "Tim Mulrooney was with me, y'great lout! All night!"

"Brigit!" Martin hissed, and he put out his hand to hold her back. It was too late. She shoved the officer away from Tim and linked her arm with his.

Chris and Tim exchanged a smile. Mrs. Mulrooney blanched and cast a hard look at Brigit, then at the constable. Could he argue with this?

"Aye," Mulrooney agreed. "I was with Brigit Donovan."

Carroll glanced over his shoulder at the waiting soldiers. "With

her, were you? Well then, we'll be arrestin' Brigit Donovan too. For
we have it on good authority that you're a rebel. Word of an eyewit-
ness, you might say. That's right. One of your own, Mulrooney.
Says you threw the torch onto the thatch. . . . And so, Brigit Donovan. You're one of them too, are you?"

She clung tighter to Mulrooney's arm. "He was with me, I tell
you. We were together in my father's barn the whole night long."

Now the cruel smile on Carroll's thick lips vanished. He towered
over Brigit. "Stick to this tale, girl, and shall I tell you what will
become of your father's barn? And his house? You'll all be turned
out and not even the chimney will be left upright."

At this threat her defiance wavered, but still she clung to Mulrooney.

Mulrooney, the color drained from his face, pried her fingers from his arm. "Well done, Brigit, but he's made up his mind
to arrest me, no matter what. No use your family goin' down as
well."

The young man's mother began to wail. Brigit remained rooted
by him. An angry murmur rippled through the marketplace.

"You'll not take him," Brigit spat.

Constable Carroll snapped his fingers, summoning the guards
like dogs. "Arrest Mulrooney, and the girl as well."

There was stunned silence as the soldiers came forward. Martin
thought to run and call Da at the pub, but his legs would not move.

"Quite extraordinary," interrupted a cultured English voice
from behind them. "To think that I grew up here. I tell you,
Stone," said William Marlowe, "a man has to travel before he can
appreciate the fine things he has left behind."

"Quite right," agreed John Stone at Marlowe's elbow. "It's just
as you say."

The officer quickly doffed his cap and tugged at his forelock.
"G'day to Your Lordship. We're makin' the arrest, you see. This
Mulrooney chap and Brigit Donovan as well."

"Do you know, Stone," Marlowe continued, as though he had
not heard the petty official. He walked around Brigit, looking her

over as he would a brood mare. "I have heard a Dublin artist say that every peasant girl in Connaught could model for a sculpture. But I never believed it . . . till now." He tipped his hat to Brigit. "You've grown since last I saw you."

Martin was amazed to see Brigit flush. "Good day to Your Lordship," Brigit said, lowering her eyes with a brief curtsy.

"And what's all this about?" Marlowe challenged Carroll, who ducked his head.

"Your Lordship can see we've apprehended the rapparee who burned the house of the informant in Cong. We have a witness, but the girl here says he was with her all night and so we'll arrest them both and . . ."

Marlowe raised his hand to stop him. "You doubt the lady's word, Constable? And she with her honor at stake?"

"But . . . but . . . Your Lordship . . . ," Carroll stammered.

The expression on William Marlowe's face hardened as he glared at Constable Carroll. "Let them go, I say. And let these people get on with the business at hand. I'll see you at your office."

Brigit exhaled with relief and covered her face with her hands. "Get home, Tim," she whispered.

The young man, not waiting for Marlowe to change his mind, bowed stiffly and backed away to vanish in the press. The faces of the villagers turned quickly away from the young lord and the retreating policeman. A low hum mixed of terror and anger and relief buzzed about the square again.

Marlowe smiled down at Brigit. "Now, Brigit Donovan, what have you got to sell?"

She returned to her place beside Martin. "There is nothin' from Ballynockanor worthy of Your Lordship's attention."

"Not all the products of Ballynockanor are poor or unworthy." Marlowe took her hand and lifted it briefly to his lips. "You are a brave girl." Then, "Come on now, Stone," he said with a last sweeping look at Brigit. "Constable Carroll will be expecting us." He gave a brief bow, during which his eyes never left Brigit's, and then he was gone.

∾

Joe Watty's tavern was just off Main Street on a narrow lane beside a stone watering trough and black iron hand pump. The original structure stood before Castletown ever existed to be built up around it. Despite the fact that the building now boasted a slate roof, its low ceiling and the beams of bog oak darkened by two centuries of peat fires proclaimed its honorable age. Joe Watty, present owner of name and pub, was reputedly the sixth man to possess both. In earlier days the pub brewed and purveyed poteen, but now Watty dealt in strictly legal, bonded goods (except when dire necessity demanded otherwise, of course).

When Martin entered the slightly askew black door, his nostrils were assaulted by a mixture of smells: turf smoke, tobacco smoke, the yeasty, fresh bread smell of the black beer called "porter," the spicy tang of sausages grilling, and a faint reminder that cabbage had been on the menu the night before. Now that Martin was away from Brigit, he discovered he was hungry.

Sound, too, stormed Martin's senses in prodigious quantity. The front room of the pub was filled with the midday crowd of men with pints in their fists. In a corner Fiddler O'Rourke scraped through "Rose Coneely." Martin darted through the mob, dodging elbows and the punctuating hands of many impassioned speakers. The boy's plunge across the packed room brought him into a collision with the stout proprietor. Watty juggled two pewter pitchers of porter, yet still managed to cuff Martin good-naturedly on the back of the head.

Martin found his father and Kevin alone in the small room next back, where business was conducted. Da's glass of Guinness was half empty, and from the expansiveness of his gestures, Martin guessed that it was not the first. The two older Donovan males were seated in a dark alcove. On the wall above them hung a cracked china platter that read "Remember the men of '98."

"Do y'see what I mean, then, Kevin?" Da was inquiring of his elder son. "Y'must make the buyer feel that he has bested you in some way. That way he'll be the more eager to have another go.

Was it not my plan to sell both calves to O'Brien all along? But little did I want him to think that! Didn't I tell him that I promised first pick to his neighbor Kinney? And me knowin' all the time what great rivals they are? Now a sound trade would be to let him talk me in t'dealin' with him first. More: let him pay top price for one or t'other, though them calves is as like as two peas." Da held up two gnarled fingers pressed tightly together, but hardly paused for Kevin's nod of agreement before continuing. "But a great man of commerce, a great man, I say, goes beyond that! He . . ." Da caught sight of Martin and that stopped the recitation. "Martin!" Da exclaimed. "Why are y'not at the stall? Is ought wrong, then?"

"No, no, Da." Martin hastily shook his head. "Tim Mulrooney had a spot of trouble with Constable Carroll, but the young land-lord put a stop to it. Then Kate returned early and gave me leave to come and find you." The less said about Brigit's encounter with Young Marlowe, the better. And as for what Brigit had said about spending the night with that Protestant lunk, Mulrooney. . . . For once Martin actually preferred to think that his father's fuddled brain would not take it all in. "Kate said I might get a bite to eat."

"And so you shall!" Da agreed, pushing over a plate of drisheen and potato cakes. "And never too young you are to be learnin' the ways of business either. Now where was I? Ah, no matter, I'll just begin again."

Kevin rolled his eyes and jumped into the conversation. "Da," he said impatiently, "now you hear that young Master Marlowe may not be as bad as you have always said. Will y'not give me an answer to my question? Martin is big enough to take over for me with the milkin'. Is it not right for me to earn a bit more of the ready? And didn't the driver Stone send word that rents was to be raised next Gale Day, and them so high already? What with Glen FitzGibbon run off to sea, will the big house not be needin' me as a full-time stablehand?"

"Black slavery it is!" Da declared, sloshing Guinness on the floor with a jerk of his arm. "Would y'put yourself into the grip of the devil, then?"

Kevin eyed Martin from under lowered brows, warning the boy

to say nothing about Kevin's friendship with flaxen-haired Jane Stone, the driver's daughter. Martin sighed and jerked his head downward toward the platter. Stuffing a bite of black pudding into his mouth was signal enough to his older brother that he would do nothing to raise Da's suspicions. Still, Martin hated all the burdens that the secrets of his older siblings put on him.

Satisfied that Martin would not disclose any awkward revelations, Kevin argued, "You know I have a way with beasts, Da, if . . ." He paused significantly. "If, that is, they'll even take me on for exercisin' the bloodstock."

Da's shaggy eyebrows lunged together like two curly horned rams fighting. "And why would they not take you, and you a deft hand with all manner of creatures?"

Ducking his head with embarrassment Kevin said, "I hear tell that Chris O'Neill is seekin' the position himself, and him known about town for dealin' with cattle."

"Cattle!" Da exploded. "Manure is what he deals with, him and all that Castletown O'Neill clan! Since when does shovelin' up after moilies prepare a man for carin' for horses? What makes you think he should get the preferment over you?"

"There's been talk," Kevin said, his eyes still on the tabletop. "You know that Tim Mulrooney's mother takes baked goods to the big house. What with Tim and Chris such great friends and all, she likely will put in a good word for him."

"Then what are y'sittin' about here for?" Da demanded, grasping Kevin by his shoulder and jerking him upright. "March straight to Driver Stone and tell him your thoughts. Tell him you have been carin' for a great many beasts since you were a sprat and he could not do better by his master's animals than to employ you full-time. And mind y'make him think that you are doin' him a favor! Go on w'you! Chris O'Neill, indeed!"

On his way toward the door, Kevin found a moment to slip his younger brother a wink. It occurred to Martin that Kevin had indeed learned a great deal from their father's instruction in the ways of commerce.

The tall tin containers of milk had been sitting in the April sun for days. Not just outside, but beside the southern wall of the dairy, so as to concentrate as much warmth as possible. Brigit, driving the donkey cart toward Castletown, had no doubt that the contents were past sour and well on the way to clabbered.

The thought made her smile.

She was transporting the milk tithe to the home of the Protestant Vicar Hodge.

Ever since the days of the English queen Elizabeth, the Roman Catholic Irish had been forced to support the Protestant Church of Ireland. One-tenth of all the produce scratched with difficulty from the rugged hillsides of Galway was payable to the Protestants.

Of course, out of every hundredweight of potatoes, it was likely that ten pounds were mealy or mushy. Wool at shearing time always contained some fleece that was so full of cockleburs as to be almost uncardable. Fisherfolk on Lough Corrib had no difficulty producing a brace of eels or suckerfish from their catch.

All in all, it was a very Irish response to an English law.

Brigit was whistling "Willie the Wisp" as she drove along. For half a mile she warbled the cheerful tune, and then a tall bay horse bearing the unmistakable form of William Marlowe trotted into view.

With a glint of devilry in her eye, Brigit switched tunes abruptly. In loud ringing tones she raised "The Cotter's Life":

> *My mansion is a clay-built cot. My whole domain a*
> *garden plot.*

Marlowe, recognizing the girl, spurred his horse so as to come up to her more quickly. He tipped his hat, but Brigit nodded coolly, then turned her face toward the rock wall that bordered the lane and continued,

> *For these, each annual first of May full thirty shillings I must pay.*

Wheeling his horse to follow in the wake of the cart, Marlowe trotted alongside. "Good day to you, Brigit Donovan," he said politely. "Don't you know any love songs?"

"And if I do, do you think I would carry on in front of the likes of you?" And she resumed the ditty about the poor farmer:

> *Ye who in stately homes reside, abodes of luxury and pride.*

William Marlowe looked grieved. "The likes of me?" he repeated, making a show of fanning himself with his top hat. "How have we come to be foes, you and I?" Brigit did not respond, but she did stop singing. "I can see you in a stately home," the young lord commented. "Dressed in satin and lace. I tell you, Brigit, you are the prettiest milkmaid that ever was."

A retort about the necessity of hauling milk to pay a mandatory tithe to a foreign religion sprang to her lips. But Brigit choked off the angry response at the look of frank admiration on William Marlowe's face. "I shouldn't even be talkin' to you," she said simply.

Looking up and back down the road, Marlowe replied, "It seems safe enough at the moment. No one will see you consorting with the enemy." This phrase was uttered with such good humor and such a winning smile that Brigit allowed the young master to walk his bay alongside the cart until the steeple of St. Stephen's appeared on the horizon.

⌒

Yet another market day came to Castletown. Clooney's flute and O'Rourke's fiddle sailed into the sixth chorus of "The Wild Rapparee." They were joined in the rollicking anthem by Patrick O'Brien, the blind piper. The crowd in Watty's Tavern were all in good voice, and none more so than Tom Donovan, his throat lubricated by three pints of the best.

When the song ended Da led the cheers by shouting, "Good man!" and "Well done," until Kevin jogged his elbow.

"Da," he hissed. "Look there!" Kevin indicated the low doorway at which Constable Carroll entered.

The tune of "Bold Jack Donohue" died on the line "to wear a convict's chain." O'Brien's pipes lurched to a stop, squalling.

"God bless all here!" Constable Carroll called heartily.

There was no response. Everyone knew that Carroll was a professional traitor, a landlord's man, a tithe proctor for the Church of Ireland and, by simple nature, a bully.

O'Brien squeezed his elbow against the bag of the pipes and the drones made a rude noise.

The policeman glared at the musicians' corner ferociously, wasting a scowl on the sightless piper. Quiet mirth rippled around the room.

His attempt at good humor exhausted, Carroll switched to compulsion. "Outside, all of you," he ordered.

"Here, now, what's this?" Joe Watty demanded. "This is no illegal meetin' to be busted up by you. Go on with ye."

Looking angry and frustrated at the same time did not raise the constable's stock in the pub. In an exasperated tone he said, "Steward Stone and young Master Marlowe have a message to deliver. And they cannot be deliverin' it in a black den of iniquity such as this, can they?"

"Fastest done is soonest mended," Tom Donovan offered. "Come on then, lads. Quicker back to our cups, y'see."

Grumbling, the men in Watty's trooped outside. They could have balked, but wrangling with the authorities would not save them from bad news.

Stone stood on a mounting block beside the public well and watering trough. "You should all hear this at once," he said without preamble, "since it concerns you all. Our Parliament has decreed . . ."

"The English Parliament," someone corrected from the middle of the mob. "No Irish Parliament since '01."

As if there had been no interruption, Stone continued, "Tithes you all owe to the Church of Ireland are to be collected by the landlords. Some of you have been wrongfully withholding these tithes. That practice will stop at once. Each of you will be notified of what is owing." A rumble of discontent ran through the crowd. "You have more than a fortnight's notice," Stone announced, as if offering a great boon. "To be paid in cash or kind, along with your regular Gale Day rents on the first of May."

"And if we don't?" another voice shouted from the throng.

"Then your goods will be confiscated to the full value of the arrears."

Seated on the milk cart at the end of the block and also listening to Stone's harangue were Kate and Brigit. William Marlowe's wandering attention lit on the pair of women. Brigit's hair glistened in the sunlight, and Marlowe stared at her boldly.

She studied him just as frankly, nor did she look away when their eyes met.

Marlowe nudged Stone, who was continuing to describe the dire consequences of failing to heed his warning. "That's enough," William said. Then, loudly, he observed, "We are all neighbors here, and neighbors need no harsh words between them before they do what is right."

Kate's wicker basket was only half full with salt, tea, and soda. There were a dozen items yet to purchase, and each required at least a quarter hour of pleasant chat with the seller. Mrs. O'Shaunessy, who had a town-square stall filled with brown clay jars of sweet clover honey, had kept her for nearly three-quarters of an hour with gossip about the true reason William Marlowe had returned to his father's estate.

". . . I hear she was a clergyman's daughter. Young Marlowe

was a bull in the Dublin heifer pen, you know. Aye. And he says that the little calf isn't his a'tall. Think of it!"

"For shame." Kate shook her head at the disgrace of it. She had, of course, heard some variations of the story from each vendor. Yet, for the sake of the bargaining, she was obliged to listen as though this were the first telling. "Now about this honey, Missus O'Shaunessy. Tuppence a jar is a bit steep. . . ."

Bored by the endless talk, Mary Elizabeth tugged at Kate's skirt and said pertly, "There's himself you're speakin' of. William the bull. Is he lookin' for another heifer, Kate?"

Mrs. O'Shaunessy's broad ruddy face lit up as she followed Mary Elizabeth's gaze toward the Donovan stall. "Aye. So it is. Handsome devil, ain't he?"

A rush of resentment filled Kate as she spotted William Marlowe, sauntering away from Brigit and the Donovan booth. He leaned his head close to John Stone and muttered something, then leered over his shoulder. Brigit tossed an interested look back to him.

Kate slammed the honey pot onto the wood plank. "He's a bold one," she growled.

A broad hand rubbed across her mouth could not hide Mrs. O'Shaunessy's smile. "Mind my words, Kate. He'll be makin' little Marlowe bastards all over Connemara. Tell your father to get that girl married or send her to a convent."

Kate opened her mouth to reply, but caught herself. To respond to the implication that Brigit was his next target would open the family to a round of vicious gossip. " 'Twould be wiser, I'm thinkin', to turn this Marlowe bull into a steer, Missus O'Shaunessy," Kate said, smiling.

Roaring with laughter, Mrs. O'Shaunessy slapped an ample thigh, making her plaid ground-length shawl flap around her. "Well done, Kate Donovan Garrity! Tragic circumstance has not robbed you of your fine wit." She laughed again and wiped tears from her cheeks with the back of her hand. "We'll see if we cannot find a committee to undertake just such a thing!" More howls. "He'll be singin' soprano!"

Kate had won the round. Wit always prevailed in the court of public opinion. Now the story would be retold with Kate's retort as the focus rather than Brigit's encounter with the young master. She collected two honey pots. "Tuppence for the pair, then?"

"Could I turn you down, my dear?" Mrs. O'Shaunessy took the coin, and Kate, still smiling in spite of the fact she was seething inside, placed the honey in her basket and turned to find herself face-to-face with William Marlowe and John Stone.

Master and steward tipped their hats. Lecherous grins faded as Kate raised her burned hand as if to greet someone across the square.

Pushing past them, she grabbed Mary Elizabeth's arm too tightly as she made for Brigit and Martin. The child yelped her protest, so Kate let her go again lest anyone know she was angry.

As Kate dodged around a draft horse hauling a cart loaded with oak casks of salt beef, Brigit and Martin spotted her approach at the same instant. Brigit looked at once guilty and defiant, Martin both guilty and angry.

Mary Elizabeth chirped, "Did you sell him anythin'?"

"Him who?" Brigit brushed her skirts absently.

Martin snorted in derision. "You know very well who." Each of his words was punctuated by the clop of an iron-shod hoof.

Kate's eyes narrowed in spite of her attempt to keep the pretense of coolness. She whispered hoarsely, "You'll have the whole wide county talkin', Brigit."

"Me very words," Martin agreed.

"You're to keep your big gob shut about this, Martin," Kate warned. "Do you hear me? I'll not have Da knowin' the young monster made bold with your sister."

Batting her eyelashes, Brigit murmured, "Me very words." The distant trill of a tin whistle competed with the cries of starlings on the rooftops.

Mary Elizabeth remarked, "Every boy makes bold with her."

Kate shushed her. "And that'll be all from your mouth." She passed Martin the basket. "Now you get along to the pub with Da and Kevin. I want a word with Brigit alone."

"Me very thoughts." Martin lifted his cap in disgusted farewell and muttered himself away from this female domain.

Then Kate snapped at Mary Elizabeth, "Now go on with you."

"Where?" The child perched on a crate and gazed up expectantly. Something was about to explode, and she did not want to miss it.

"To play. But not beside the river, mind."

To Kate's frustration, Mary Elizabeth did not budge. "I'm tired. I want to sit down."

At last Kate boiled over. "Then first fetch me a stick, and when I have used it, you will not wish to sit down for a day or so."

At this Mary Elizabeth spotted one of her friends and, with a hearty wave, scampered off across the cobblestones to play.

Kate closed her eyes and breathed in deeply. When she opened them again, Brigit was grinning at her. Maybe sneering?

"Well?" Brigit queried flippantly, casually straightening her tangle of red hair.

"If we were home . . . ," Kate said through clenched teeth as she pretended to smile and straighten the wares on display.

"We're not." Brigit gestured at the wide crowd in the market. She pointed from Marsh, the rug seller, to Drummond, the spice merchant. "And I am safe."

Kate clasped her arm and pulled her back toward the cart out of full view of the square. "Did you think the whole town did not notice His-High-and-Mighty himself lustin' after you?"

"What's that to me, then? Can I help it if I am not . . ." Her voice faltered.

"Scarred as I am?" Kate finished the cruel thought.

"As you wish. Can I help it if men enjoy lookin' at me?"

"I'll speak to Father O'Bannon about this."

"So will everyone in the parish. Is it my fault if William Marlowe . . ."

"Stay clear of him, Brigit. You know what he is. It will break Da's heart. You know there is nothin' good can come out of a man like himself."

"No, I do not. Nor do you, Kate. And I'll be thankin' you to stay out of my affairs. I'm a woman grown. You were married when you were a year younger than myself."

"Married to a man of our own sort. An Irishman. A good man."

"And since the fire took him and Mother and the others, you laid aside your fiddle and the music died in your soul too."

"I cannot play."

"You can. But you will not. Where is the music now? You and Da. You mourn in silence, and he consoles himself in the drink."

"This is not about Da or me."

"Is it about me, then? Because I have not stopped enjoyin' life like you and Da?"

"You bring shame upon us all. We are a proud family and you . . ."

"For all the good pride does any of us," Brigit retorted. "Ah, we may be poor, but we are proud, we Donovan Irish. Too proud to sing again five years after the sorrow."

"Too proud to make fools of ourselves with the English."

"There's little enough to eat, but we have our pride. Is that it, Kate? I think it is not pride that makes you so grim, but the truth that no man will ever look at you with love and smile again. There is no hope left alive in you." Brigit glared at Kate and the pretense of civility evaporated. "I have bigger plans than livin' on pride and memories and inheritin' the drudgery of my mother and my mother's mother before me. I have somethin' the Englishmen want and their own Englishwomen cannot give it them. I have looks, Kate. Not like you. It isn't Irish butter or Irish bread or Irish potatoes these Englishmen are hungry for. I am young and beautiful, which makes me what is most desired by the English, don't you see? And I can barter this. . . ." She swept a hand over her body. "For somethin' better."

Kate wanted to slap her, to shake her and tell her to come to her senses. But all the marketplace would see it and know the sisters were at one another again. Pride told Kate it wouldn't do to carry on so in a public place. Pride was the leash of self-control that held Kate back by the scruff of her neck.

Eyes lowered, Kate replied in a barely audible voice, "Go home,

Brigit. Go now before I forget myself and thrash you here and now for the shameless hussy you are."

Brigit showed her fist. "If ever you lay a hand on me, it'll be the last thing you ever do."

Raising solemn brown eyes, Kate continued in an even tone that left no doubt of her intent, "Go home, or I'll tell Da you've made bold with Young Marlowe and he with you. Da'll marry you off to the first Irish tinker who drives his wagon through Ballynockanor. Or maybe to a veteran of the rebellion of '98? Someone ancient and grizzled who lost his teeth to the butt of an English musket, like old Brian Lynch. He's been nosin' about. Askin' after you. 'Is that Brigit Donovan married yet, lads? Aye! There's a girl could make a man feel young again. . . .'" Kate smiled pleasantly as Brigit's defiance was replaced by fear. "And think of it, Brigit darlin', old Brian's got three good acres and a dozen sheep."

Brigit blanched for an instant at Kate's threat. If Brigit's encounters with William Marlowe were repeated and enlarged upon, Tom Donovan would indeed marry her off to the first son of Ireland who would have her. After a moment, Brigit composed herself, tossed her hair, pulled up the hood of her scarlet cape, and strolled away into the market crowds as though nothing whatsoever were wrong.

⟿ 6 ⟾

Kate held tight to the spoke of the cart wheel and stared after Brigit's red cloak as she rounded the corner of the school building. The happy strains of "Trip to Sligo" sang out from blind O'Brien's pipes and drifted above the hum of the market. Bursts of laughter punctuated the rhythm of the melody. The brightness of the tune was like the glare of too much sunlight against the gloom of Kate's heart. Painful in its illumination of her sorrow, she longed to hide herself from the joy of others.

Her fury served only to separate her farther from Brigit. Nothing was solved, nothing gained. The chasm between the sisters simply widened. One day, Kate knew, there would be no crossing over.

Loneliness gripped her in spite of the pleasant bustle of friends and neighbors around her. Could anyone read the emptiness behind her eyes? She looked heavenward and breathed a weary prayer for help. Would life never be easy again? Brigit was right, wasn't she? The music of Kate's soul had died within her. That was the true reason she would never pick up the bow or sing again. Bitterness was the very explanation of why there was no happiness or harmony within the walls of the Donovan home. So much had vanished with Mother and Sean and the little one who had not been saved.

Kate glanced at her hand. *She had reached through the flames, but too late. Too late, and everything was lost.*

Feeling as though she might weep, she tucked her fist beneath her navy blue shawl and forced a smile onto her face. Mary Elizabeth was weaving through the press, dragging Joseph along behind her.

He grinned as though he was embarrassed to see Kate waiting behind the crock of butter. Had he hoped to find Brigit there instead?

"Look who I found!" Mary Elizabeth was exultant. "Himself! Joseph!"

Kate noted that the scuffed riding boots, ragged jacket, and drooping hat were unchanged since her first sight of him. He was the very picture of the impoverished student. Joseph carried a wicker basket over his arm. "Shoppin' are you, Joseph?" Kate asked.

"I've come to fetch a pig for Father O'Bannon from Joe Watty. Payment for his daughter's wedding."

Kate scooped out a measure of butter onto butcher paper, wrapped it, then laid a small round of cheese beside it. "Aye. And Kevin owes him for . . . somethin' or other. Kevin said His Honor himself would be by to pick up butter and cheese today, but I'm guessin' you'll tote it for him?"

Joseph placed the basket on the table and tipped his hat. "God bless you, Kate. Are you well, then?" He tilted his head slightly, peering curiously into her face.

"God bless you, Joseph. That I am. Well, I mean. And yourself?" Lowering her eyes from his penetrating gaze, Kate gave a curtsy.

"Well enough, God be thanked. But Father O'Bannon is not. The damp he says has got into his bones."

Kate deposited the goods into the basket. "A pig is too much to manage when the lumbago is upon a man."

Mary Elizabeth piped, "Did you give Brigit a thrashin'?"

With a stern look, Kate silenced her. "That I did not."

Mary Elizabeth peered over the table. "We saw her pass by. She was very gloomy. Where is she, then?"

"She went home." Kate flashed a nervous grin at Joseph.

"You sent her home, did you?" Mary Elizabeth would not be stilled. "I'm sorry I missed it."

"You missed nothin' a'tall," Kate defended as Joseph gave Mary Elizabeth an encouraging pat.

The little girl would not be silenced now. "I followed William Marlowe and Mister Stone. They was still talkin' about her. I knew you'd be in a fury over it, and it's always so fine to watch when you and Brigit . . ."

Kate clamped her hand over the child's mouth and gave an uneasy chuckle. "Brigit is high-spirited, that's all. Young Master admired her. It was nothin'."

With a nod, Joseph replied, "There's been talk about him. I heard about it from Clooney. And what you said. Makin' the bull a steer. A grand sentiment, that, and widely approved of, I can tell you. He's also made bold with Clooney's daughter . . . Watty's girl as well, and her bein' just married. Which brings me back to why I came to Castletown for Father O'Bannon's pig."

"We've come full circle, then." Kate laughed, genuinely relieved that Brigit was not the only girl in the marketplace who had received the attentions of William Marlowe. "I thought it best Brigit be out of his line of sight."

"True. True. Very wise, Kate," Joseph agreed solemnly. His deep blue eyes locked on hers, making the color rise to her cheeks.

Words hung back in her throat. She chided herself for noticing how handsome he was. More than handsome, he had a kind face. She blurted, "How are the studies comin' along?"

"My friend was right about Father O'Bannon. He knows his battle sites, both new and ancient."

"And every saint in Ireland and holy well . . ." Her voice trailed off as she spotted William Marlowe's top hat bobbing through the crowds.

He followed her glance. "There may be a few more battle sites in Galway if this fellow is not more circumspect." He grinned broadly. Kate noted his teeth were white and perfect. "In London such boldness with a lady would be cause for a duel."

Kate dismissed the thought. "London is not wee Ballynockanor. In London the Protestant gentry keep duelin' pistols. They are free and welcome to shoot one another. In Ireland we Catholics cannot have even a fowlin' piece, as you well know. Perhaps a duel with pitchforks?" She laughed at the absurdity of the image: Marlowe and some offended Irish father or brother squaring off in some barnyard to do battle for honor's sake with farm tools as weapons.

Joseph winked at Mary Elizabeth, who was listening wide-eyed to the exchange. He showed her his fists. "This is one way an Irishman can fight." Tapping his temple he added, "But quick wits, good humor, and fiddle music will win the day every time." Again the penetrating gaze into Kate's eyes. A question. "How can anyone fight when there is music in the air? The toes begin to tap and soon . . ." He raised his hands in triumph as the fiddle of Mike O'Rourke joined O'Brien's pipes. Two old women danced the jig before their stalls. Children linked arms and began to sing as they skipped across the cobbles. Joseph picked up Mary Elizabeth and twirled her around.

In spite of herself, Kate's foot was tapping. "It's fine. Aye. It is fine, isn't it?"

Joseph placed Mary Elizabeth onto the table, and she danced amid the crocks and cheeses.

He said cheerfully, "Now, Mary Elizabeth, here's a bit of history! Who do you suppose is the finest fiddler in all the west country?"

"O'Rourke!" shouted Mary Elizabeth.

Joseph shook his head. "You'll never get into seminary with such an answer. Not O'Rourke! It is not a man a'tall! Father O'Bannon says your sister Kate is the finest fiddle player in all the west country."

Kate tucked her hand beneath the shawl again, remembering herself as she always did in the end.

"Sister Kate?" Mary Elizabeth cried in disbelief as the tune scrolled away. "There's an old fiddle in our cottage, but she does not play it. No one does!"

Joseph turned full onto Kate and spoke softly. "I was wonderin' why you do not play?"

Shame overwhelmed her. "If the good father has taught you the history of every family in Ballynockanor, then sure, you know the answer."

"Aye. I heard the history, Kate. But not the answer."

She stepped back as though he had laid into her with a blow. "Have you come to duel with me, Joseph Connor?"

"I was curious. That is your bow arm. You can surely hold a bow. I saw you use your injury as a weapon against the constable Carroll. You hide behind your scars very well. But I also saw how you labored with birthin' the calf. It is not so severe that you cannot still play your fiddle."

"You are not a priest yet. And you will never be my confessor. There are some questions good manners leave unasked."

He shrugged. "There are other things I need to learn for my vocation besides history. Matters of the heart. But I see I have trespassed."

"Indeed, sir."

"You are quite beautiful, you see."

"You mock me."

"Not a'tall, Kate. Music, they say, is the reflection of a soul, the true prayer of the heart singin' to the Almighty."

"If that is true, then you have answered your own question as to why I play no more." Now the music began again, sad and soulful, the tune of "Lord Inchiquin."

"Are you so bereft of hope then, Kate?"

She would not reply to this. Coolly she returned his basket to him. "Greet His Honor, Father O'Bannon, for me. I know he enjoys Donovan butter and Donovan cheese."

Joseph nodded and opened his mouth to speak. There was apology in his expression, but the probing curiosity remained in his eyes. "One day I would like it if you would play for me."

Kate stopped him. She would hear no more, tolerate his prying no longer. "You are pleasant, but you cut too deep for those of us in Ballynockanor. If you think we take to meddlin', then you are so green, sir, that if you went into a field the cows would eat you. Keep to your history lessons, and you will be better liked hereabouts."

With her rebuke he bowed slightly at the waist and tipped his hat. "I am vanquished, ma'am," he said. Patting Mary Elizabeth on the head, he backed up a step, then left them.

❦

Joseph Connor was still musing about fiddle music and Kate Donovan Garrity and being so green that cows might eat him as he passed down Castletown's main street. He reflected that she was right; he was well intentioned, but clumsy. Joseph chastised himself for doing harm when he meant only good. His own father and Daniel afterward had both said the same thing: the good Lord gave us two ears and one mouth so we would listen twice as much as we speak. But how could one listen if the other party would not oblige by talking? And how could she be encouraged to converse if he did not first speak to draw her out? It was a tangle.

The tangle was not one bit unraveled when Joseph, looking up at the sign of a teapot hanging over the street, collided with someone coming out of the shop: Vicar Hodge. A half-pound sack of black tea went one direction and the cleric's spectacles the other.

It had been fifteen years since Joseph had last seen Castletown's plump little Protestant parson, but there was no doubt as to his identity. "I beg your pardon," Hodge said, puffing.

"No, my fault," Joseph corrected. He stooped to retrieve the aromatic bundle of peppery leaves while Hodge located and replaced his eyeglasses. Their combined actions brought them nose to nose, two feet above the ground, like the wary encounter of a pair of dogs.

Watery hazel eyes stared into clear blue ones.

"Dear me," Hodge sputtered. "Don't I know you?"

"Not likely, Your Worship," Joseph said. "I am not from around here."

"Wait a moment," the vicar argued. "Just let me think. I'm not as good with faces as I used to be . . . not that my memory was ever very good, you understand. . . . Are you certain you have never been in Castletown before?"

Joseph was already retreating, his back to the vicar. He had seen a spark of recognition on the parson's face, something that after fifteen years' absence he did not expect and something that absolutely could not be permitted to develop. Over his shoulder he called, "Sorry, Your Worship." It worried Joseph that when he turned the next corner and glanced back, the portly clergyman was still rooted in place, deep in thought.

∽

The market stalls were dismantled, produce packed and carted away home with much singing. Kate remained late in Castletown to clean the house and fix the supper of the blind widow MacDonagh. This Kate did half in penance for her anger and half because she did not want to go home to face Brigit again.

The flagstones were swept, the fuel stacked beside the hearth, and the old woman fed. Sightless, Widow MacDonagh always spoke without pretense to Kate. Having no vision to remind her, the widow forgot about "poor Kate's scars."

Conversation ranged from the eight new chicks peeping in the yard (the widow counted the number by the sound) to Kate's mother (God rest her soul) and what she did to silly Maggie Berry at the mayor's funeral twenty-five years before.

Kate left the place laughing. The pleasure of the deed and the good company entirely vanquished her anger toward Brigit and the impertinence of Joseph Connor.

The curfew bell echoed across the empty square of Castletown. How had it come to be so late? Mindful of the penalty for being caught in the street after nightfall, Kate considered returning to the widow's house. The recollection of early morning chores at home drew her on. Once out of Castletown she would avoid the road and cross the hills by way of a path seldom patrolled by soldiers.

Far away a dog barked. Moonlight illuminated the slate rooftops of the townhouses and shone on the cobbles like a lantern. Kate pulled the hood of her cloak up and ducked down a crooked back alley. The narrow passage separated a pub from the brick wall of a deserted coaching inn. Plunged into darkness, Kate brushed her fingertips across the rough face of the bricks to steady herself against the uneven surface of the cobbles.

She stumbled and paused. In that moment she imagined she heard the tread of a footstep behind her. Regaining her balance she continued, suddenly afraid. Glancing over her shoulder, she consoled herself that she could see a slit of moonlight beyond the entrance of the alley. No one was pursuing, she told herself. And why should anyone care if she had been delayed after market day and had only just started for Ballynockanor?

The glimmer of false hopes vanished as a shadow crossed in front of the entrance. The thin frame of a man blocked the light.

An amused voice called past her, "The rabbit's in the snare!"

A terrifying reply bellowed just in front of her, "Leave her to me, then!" A harsh laugh followed.

Kate gasped and plastered herself against the wall. She recognized the voices. Constable Carroll and John Stone had stalked her as though she were game in the forest to be captured, gutted, and spitted!

Her heart pounding, she turned to run back, praying she could slam against the weakling John Stone, knock him to the ground, and escape.

Two steps, a sharp cry, and the thick, cruel grip of Constable Carroll grasped her hair and pulled her back!

His meaty hand clamped over her mouth, muffling her scream and cutting off her breath. She struggled for air, battling to free herself as the dancing sparkles of near-unconsciousness played before her eyes.

He laughed again as his free hand groped her breast.

"This one's mine," Carroll panted.

John Stone chortled with pleasure. "That'll teach the little slut what it means when a woman is out after curfew in Castletown."

Kate knew the driver was gone, leaving Carroll alone to take his pleasure.

The hand lifted a brief instant. Kate gulped air into her starving lungs. No chance to scream. He slapped her hard, then slammed her head against the wall. Senses dimmed in a dreamlike nightmare as her body went slack. He shoved her face down onto the pavement.

Sitting on her back, pinning her battered cheek against the rough-edged cobbles, he muttered cheerfully, "Sure, and I been watchin' you. Did you think I wasn't? It ain't like you don't know what's comin'." She struggled to free herself. Carroll enjoyed the battle.

"They'll hang you. . . . ," she managed.

His tone gathered more pleasure the harder she fought. "Who? Your Ribbonmen friends? If they lay a hand on me, they'll be hanged. And if you speak a word of it, you'll be transported for breakin' curfew. For conspiracy. You know what convicts in New South Wales do with their women? There aren't enough to go round and so they share." He slid his fingers along her calf. "Well now, don't tell me you don't miss havin' a man."

She kicked against the crushing weight and tried to reply. He plunged his knuckles into her side, knocking words into a groan of agony.

"First I'll kindle a fire in you, girl." He leaned close, his hot, boozy breath on the back of her neck. "You'll not be half-bad in the dark. . . ."

Kate cried out as he locked his massive forearm around her middle and tore her cloak from her.

There followed the whistle of a blackthorn stick and a resounding crack against the skull of Constable Carroll. He slumped forward. His full weight pressing her down, he lay motionless atop her as she sobbed.

Then the urgent voice of Joseph Connor whispered as Carroll was rolled to the side. "John Stone's guardin' outside in the square. Can you walk, Kate?"

Free from Carroll's bulk, she struggled to stand. There was no time. Only moments remained before John Stone would sense something had gone wrong.

Joseph threw Kate over his shoulder and carried her the back way out of the alley as John Stone called in to Carroll, "Have y'had her then?"

Joseph paused a moment, then replied harshly, mimicking the constable's voice, "Leave me to it!"

Kate slipped in and out of a dim consciousness. A narrow, winding track led over the mountain. Mercifully, clouds covered the moon and sheltered their flight from any curious eyes that might glance up toward the hillside. She did not know how long or how far they traveled.

She awoke to the sound of rushing water and the cool touch of a damp cloth against her lips. Pushing the hand away she asked hoarsely, "Did they follow?"

The reply was light. "No. We're safe."

She sat up, and the river stretched out before her. Light danced on the current. Joseph, his eyes full of worry, searched her face.

She asked, "How was it you came?"

"I was waitin' outside the widow's. To see you home. To beg your forgiveness for my boldness. I saw the two of them trap you, and when Stone stepped out of the alley I ran around the back way."

"You came in time."

"He split your lip."

"You split his skull."

"My aim was off a bit in the dark."

"Did you kill him?"

"I tried. But that pleasure will belong to some other man another day . . . or to his wife."

Kate raised her fingers to her swollen eye and bruised cheekbone. "Kevin will kill him and Stone. Or Da will! If ever they find out what Carroll tried to do! Sure, and then there'll be Donovans on the gallows for certain!" She clutched Joseph's sleeve. "Promise me you'll not speak of it! I'll say I've fallen on the slope or tripped on a rock or . . . somethin'! I can pass the night at Father O'Bannon's and in the mornin' you take word to Da I'm not badly hurt. Promise me, Joseph Connor!"

He wrapped his arms around her and pulled her gently against him. His cheek was damp. Did he weep for her? "They'll never hear of it from me," he promised, stroking her hair. "Dear Kate. Sweet Katie," he murmured as though he were comforting a small child.

K ate awakened in the cottage of Father O'Bannon. The priest, who had given up his bed to her, nodded in a chair beside the fire. Joseph had gone on to the Donovan cottage last night lest the family worry about her.

It was just past daybreak when Kate heard the hooves of a dozen horses galloping toward the church.

So the soldiers had come calling upon the residents of Ballynock- anor. She shuddered with revulsion as the clear picture of last night's events came back to her. Had Carroll and John Stone put out a warrant for her arrest?

Father O'Bannon's head jerked up. He glanced at Kate with con- cern. "Are you all right, daughter?"

She ached all over. "I am."

He peered out the glassless window. "The driver, John Stone, rides with them, but there's no sign of that brute Carroll." He nodded gravely. "If they've come to take you, I promise they'll not lay a hand on you while I'm livin'. Are you up to facin' John Stone, daughter?"

"Aye," she replied in a troubled tone.

"Trust me."

Not waiting for their command, Father O'Bannon burst angrily out the door. "Have y'come t'mornin' mass, gentlemen?" he called.

Stone's voice replied above the snorting horses, "Last night as Constable Carroll was making pursuit of a curfew breaker he was attacked from behind by a band of Ribbonmen loose in Castletown."

Father O'Bannon replied brightly, "Is he dead then? He was a Catholic . . . but that was before he made his pact with the devil. You'll not be buryin' him here."

Stone cursed the priest soundly. "He's alive enough and will have his revenge."

"Alive is he?" Father O'Bannon allowed great disappointment to radiate from the question. "I suppose you'll be wantin' to arrest the perpetrators?"

"Aye," spat the driver.

"Well then, come in, Mister Stone. No, no. Just Superintendent Stone alone, if you please. Come in. I'll fix a cuppa, and we'll discuss the matter."

Stone dismounted and followed Father O'Bannon into the cottage. The priest slammed the door behind him and pulled the curtain back to reveal Kate lying battered on the cot.

Stone blanched at the sight of her and stammered, "You . . . you! Who was your accomplice, woman? You'll confess or be hanged!"

The priest smiled up into the crimson face. "Accomplice is it? That was my question exactly. Who was the accomplice of Constable Carroll when he tried to rape a decent Irish woman who was on a mission of mercy last night in Castletown?"

"I don't know what you're talking about," Stone blustered.

Father O'Bannon nodded and narrowed his eyes. "Y'see here, Mister Steward. There is a devil loose indeed in Castletown. Two devils. Both are married men who conspired to violate a certain respectable young widow woman of Ballynockanor. She was beat insensible. Aye. Her face tells all. And the marks of the vile fellow's fingers are plainly on her neck. I am certain the wives of two rapists would be interested in hearin' the facts."

"Our wives would never . . ." Stone caught himself.

"Your wives would never believe it? Sure, and rape is a nasty business, Driver Stone. And the woman was only defendin' her virtue when Constable Carroll slipped upon the cobbles and hit his head. But surely he'd had a drop too much to drink. His wife . . . and perhaps the wife of the other fellow . . . would understand and forgive. Gentle trustin' women, the wives of these two animals are. They don't know what goes on after curfew, surely."

Stone drew back. His eyes hardened as the image of his cool, stern wife materialized before him. He glared at Kate and then at the priest. "There was no woman involved in Constable Carroll's incident. It was a gang of . . . conspirators . . . knocked him . . ." His voice trailed away.

"Ah. I see, I see. Well, never mind the wrath of your wife then." Father O'Bannon hefted the fire poker, paused a moment as though he considered swinging it, then turned and jabbed at the peat fire. His reply was low and threatening. "If word of what you've done gets out there'll be ten thousand decent Irishmen, Catholic and Protestant alike, who'll be waitin' in the shadows every time you take a stroll."

"Is that a threat?" Stone said menacingly.

" 'Tis a fact. The law may hang them all for your murder, but ye'll already be boilin' in perdition and not able to enjoy a moment of their executions." Replacing the iron Father O'Bannon added, "Ride on now, Driver Stone. Chase your Ribbonmen shadows, but not in my parish. Not in Ballynockanor. Sure, if I was yourself I wouldn't dare come round for a while lest some observant Christian notice that the marks on Kate's face match the fist of that swine of a constable. And you and himself bein' so close."

A tremor of fear passed over Stone's face. He lowered his eyes, clenched and unclenched his fists. Opening his mouth as if to respond, he turned on his heel and charged furiously out the door.

"There's nothing here," he instructed the troops, and they rode away as Father O'Bannon put the kettle on the crane and swung it over the flames.

Once again Kate fought back tears of relief. "Well done," she whispered.

The priest pointed skyward and winked. "Do not worry about what to say or how to say it . . . for it will not be you that speaketh but the Spirit of your Father speakin' through you." He sat beside her bed and patted her hand. "Truth is the Lord's most powerful weapon, Kate. Like the sun, its brightness'll burn out the eyes of any man who's so arrogant he thinks his stare can keep it from risin' in the east. There never were two more dark and arrogant than Constable Carroll and Driver John Stone. Hypocrites! They have played the bluff with man and Christ and truth too long. They pursue shadows because they are terrified of what the light will reveal. Truth is our best defense. A sword it is!"

She squeezed his fingers. "Sure, but I'll not be tellin' Da or Kevin about what they did."

"Wise. Very wise. The virtue of silence is often praised in Scripture when the speakin' might injure those we love." He smiled, hesitated, and then asked, "Have you anythin' else you wish to talk to me about?"

"I . . . I don't . . . know what you mean."

"Ah. Well, girl, you were callin' for Joseph last night in your sleep."

Kate closed her eyes in shame and covered her face with her hands. "Did I?"

"Aye." He patted her hand again.

"I did not mean . . ."

"You love him, do you?"

Tears spilled down her cheeks. "I think of him. I don't want to, but I do. I know he means to be a father, and I don't want to stand in his way."

"A father. Hmmm. Aye." Father O'Bannon ran his tongue over his lips in thought. Was that a smile? "Well, and that's good of you now not to prevent himself from becomin' a father. Aye. But there's much yet to be settled in the affairs of Joseph Connor. He was born to be the shepherd of a great many poor folk who need him desperately. I'm certain of that. But Kate . . . what if Joseph Connor cares for yourself more than his callin' to duty?"

The thought of it terrified her. "I mustn't. . . . I'll not be a stumblin' block to a man so good, so pure of heart and kind and . . ."

"Love, a stumblin' block? Quote me a chapter and verse before you say that, woman, for I've never found such a sentiment in the Scriptures."

"I'll not speak with him again privately," she vowed.

"Sure, and you call for him when you're sleepin'."

She stared at the priest. "Did you not just warn me away from him? Say he has great things ahead of him?"

"Warn you? That I did not. And have you not considered his heart might also be callin' for yourself?"

She put her hands over her ears. "I'll not hear of it. I've made up my mind. Love again! It's too much and . . . I'll put him out of my mind now."

Father O'Bannon sighed and rose from the chair. He leaned against the window frame and gazed out. "Lord, and the sunlight is so bright this mornin'. Bright enough it hurts the eyes."

∽

Two days after Kate's narrow escape, Joseph Connor sat wrapped in thought on the stone rail of Castletown's Charity Bridge over the Cornamona. The sun was warm on the back of his neck, but despite its rays, his hands were icy and his pondering grim.

An early morning inquiry informed him that John Stone and William Marlowe were already abroad in the town. They called on the injured constable Carroll at the barracks over the river; they would have to recross the bridge.

Joseph tossed pebbles into the swiftly tumbling stream. When two figures drew near, he glanced up. One was tall and angular: John Stone, and no mistake. The steward was describing with great animation how dastardly the attack of the Ribbonmen had been and how Stone himself had doubtless barely escaped injury or death.

It was clear to Joseph that no part of the actual events of that night were being communicated to the young landlord.

William Marlowe was the first of the approaching pair to look at the man on the bridge. A quick glance took in Joseph's worn clothing, and then the aristocratic nose went up in the air and turned away.

Not so with John Stone. Joseph willed the man to look him in the face, silently dared him to match gaze for gaze. The steward's contemptuous look swept over Joseph's features once, then darted back to Joseph's eyes. Joseph watched Stone's countenance widen in surprise: not with anything like recognition, but in astonishment at the flinty hatred he encountered. He remembered the fierceness with which Joseph had defended Molly Fahey. And what with the young master speaking so fair to the townspeople . . . better not mention it.

Stone looked off up the river, back at Joseph's face, down at the gravel of the road, again at the adamant cobalt orbs and stuck there. His feet likewise refused to carry him farther, and Joseph saw the man's throat work as if he had taken a mouthful of raw fear that could not be swallowed. He could not escape Joseph's eyes.

Marlowe went on several paces beyond Joseph before noticing his fawning lackey was no longer at his side. "Stone!" he said impatiently. "Did you hear me? We'll have no troubles here, even if we have to send to Dublin for troops."

For the first time since Young Marlowe's return to Castletown, Stone was not paying attention. "You," he said tersely to Joseph. "What're you doing there?"

"Sunnin' myself," Joseph replied. "Is there any reason I should not? Is it not a free country?"

"What's your business here?" Stone inquired nervously, flinching from Joseph's stare as if he had been struck.

"What are you yammering about?" Marlowe demanded.

"This fellow is . . . he might be the one . . . I mean, one of them who . . ."

Joseph shifted his attention briefly to the young landlord to see the reaction to this statement. He read only derision and sarcasm in Marlowe's expression.

"Get a grip on yourself, Stone! Here in broad daylight not half a mile from the barracks and even less to the courthouse?" Marlowe's tone was full of contempt. "See here, man," he said civilly to Joseph. "We've had rough work done last night by some rebels. Will you tell us your business?"

"Aye," Joseph agreed. At the sound of his voice, Stone made the mistake of looking up again and Joseph's stare transfixed the steward like a rabbit caught in a garden by lanternlight. "I am a student come here to learn of Connemara before returnin' to my seminary exams. Father O'Bannon will vouch for me; I've already met with Constable Carroll, and Driver Stone here for that matter."

"There, now, Stone, you see?" Marlowe said with finality. "This is the man of whom my father already had word before his departure for Dublin. Your pardon, sir," he concluded, preparing to leave.

Like a dog summoned to heel, Stone twitched and moved to follow his master.

"Galway has rich traditions for my study," Joseph remarked into their tracks. "Take the story of the High King, Rory O'Conner of Connaught. He drove out the invaders, but first he hunted down their hirelings, base-born wretches who carried out abductions. . . ."

∽ 7 ∽

Just past the middle of April, the oat crop was knee-high and pale green against the darker verdure of turflands. Rain, which had been bucketing for a week, eased off a bit, and the sun smiled on Connemara. It was a rare, fine day.

It was Flynn's tooth that caused Kevin to be exercising the black hunter. For three days the face of the Marlowe stablemaster had been more wrinkled and his conversation more curt than usual before he admitted he had a toothache. When even his home-brewed willow-bark tea failed to take the edge off the pain, he finally consented to go into Castletown and have it drawn.

"Now mind," he said sternly to Kevin. "Nought fancy. Ride him out easy. Let him limber up and stretch out. Young master says he shies at water, so take him across the pool jump a time or two. Then cool him out good and walk him home. D'ya hear me now, Kevin? You may have the gift of speakin' with the beasts, but you're still a shoneen when it comes to jumpers."

Kevin was agreeable. His increased duties as chief stablehand were still largely confined to leading the colts in circles and the feeding and the mucking out. Occasionally he was allowed to saddle and exercise the mares, but never as fine an animal as the black. "I'll take good care of him," he shouted.

Flynn nodded and walked off, holding his swollen jaw.

Beyond the formal garden of Marlowe Park was a large area of bog. Though many lumps of peat could have been cut and stacked there, it was reserved for the use of the Marlowe bloodstock. The turf was soft underfoot for the tender legs of the foals and running in the heavy sod built up their strength and their wind. Kevin completed his other chores in double-quick time and hurried to saddle the hunter.

The muscles of the black rippled under his glossy coat, and his mane tossed in the northwest wind. He strained into the bit, and Kevin had to fight him to keep him down to a trot on the first two circuits.

As soon as the animal was loosened up, Kevin trotted him to where a brimful water hazard stood near the rock wall. The rail barrier was only three feet high, but the takeoff leap came from in front of a ten-foot-wide pool.

At the first attempt, the black shied, dancing sideways around the puddle. Kevin reined him in and dismounted. Then with his mouth to the ear of the horse, he whispered, "Are y'too dainty to be gettin' your feet wet?" Walking the animal back and forth through the water he said, " 'Tis nothin' to be frightened of. A thumpin' great power like yourself will clear it altogether." Sure enough, on the second attempt the black made a perfectly timed leap and vaulted pool and rails with ease.

It was not until he had dismounted again to praise the animal, rubbing its face and neck, that Kevin noticed his audience. Slim and flaxen-haired, Jane Stone sat atop a sidesaddled mare, smiling at him from across the stone wall. "Don't let me interrupt," she said, laughing. "I'm glad to see you have speech, even if it is only for horses."

"I have a voice when I have somethin' to say," Kevin protested.

"I don't believe it," Jane returned. "Do you find it easier to speak to animals than to people?"

"Some animals and some people," Kevin admitted, scratching the star on the black's forehead.

"Me?" Jane asked, shaking her blonde curls.

"Nay," Kevin protested. "You have a fine, quiet way about you.

But it is not proper for the stablehand to be conversin' with a grand lady like yourself." His words were carried on a smile. They had known each other since childhood and bantered like this for years. Indeed, they chattered away whenever they were alone together, which had been much more often of late.

Jane laughed again. She had a clear, genuine laugh, like the tone of a silver bell. It was neither harsh nor mocking. "Don't belittle yourself so," she said. "My father is a steward, nothing more." Then to direct the conversation away from social status, she asked, "What magic spell do you whisper to horses to make them mind you?"

"No magic!" Kevin argued. "I just explain what is wanted, and they, when spoken to civilly like good Christians, oblige me."

When Kevin had taken the black over the water obstacle a dozen more times without difficulty, he judged that the practice was done for the day. Still on the path across the fence from the marsh, Jane said abruptly, "I'll race you back."

Before Kevin could even protest, Jane clapped her left heel into the mare's side and spurted into motion. There was nothing to do but follow, it seemed, and Kevin set the hunter into pursuit. Not wanting to overheat the black when he was supposed to be cooling down, Kevin contented himself with keeping the faster creature to a steady pace in the spongy turf, planning to let the girl win.

All that changed when a hare darted across the track directly under the mare's hooves. The bay horse bucked and plunged, and Jane lost her grip on the reins. The leather straps flipped over the mare's head, and her animal bolted, galloping.

It was a sudden nightmare come to life. If the mare stepped on the trailing reins it could pull itself head over heels, crushing Jane or throwing her into the stone wall. Encumbered by the sidesaddle, Jane could not even lean forward far enough to grasp the bridle. It was all she could do to get a double handful of mane and hang on.

In three strides, Kevin knew that he would never catch up to the runaway mare if the black had to fight the bog. Kevin tucked his heels into the hunter's flanks, and they flew over the barrier to take up the pursuit on the harder surface of the road.

For a half mile they pounded along before Kevin drew up along-side. Jane's face was white and strained, but she was not screaming or crying. The mare shied away from Kevin's first attempt to grab a cheekpiece, but he nudged the black still closer and lunged for the strap and grabbed on. Stretched far out between the two animals, Kevin was still able to turn them both in a wide circle until the panicked mare was reined to a halt.

Vaulting out of the saddle, Kevin ran to Jane's side. "Are y'hurt, Jane?" he asked. "Are y'injured?"

"No," she said, "but I think I . . . I'm going to . . . ," and she fell sideways off the horse into Kevin's outstretched arms.

Later, when she had revived, they walked and Kevin led the two horses the rest of the way back to the stables. Once there, Kevin massaged the legs of both creatures with witch hazel since they were swollen and hot. He spent an hour more than usual on the rubbing down, and Jane stayed in the barn with him the whole time.

The event known forever after in Ballynockanor as the Children's Rebellion came just two days after Kevin saved Jane Stone.

It was a fine, soft day. The drops that fell were too light to be called rain and too heavy for mist. In spite of the softness of the morning, it was to prove to be a very hard day.

The cobblestones in the National School courtyard were slick and shining. Martin's cap was plastered down to his head. The weather caused no change in the usual lineup and roll call, except that Superintendent Stone and Matron Rush stayed under the portico.

"Be on your very best behavior today," Stone warned. "We are going to have a special visitor this afternoon. Archbishop Whately, who has come from Dublin as the guest of Lord Marlowe and his son, will be observing some of the classrooms, and then we will have a reception for him in the assembly."

Everyone knew that the real purpose of the archbishop's visit to the area was not to view schoolrooms, but rather to tour the holdings of the Connaught landlords and make a personal assessment of the tithes due to the Church of Ireland. Old Marlowe and his son had made a particularly strong point that there would be no uprising among the tenant farmers of the Castletown area as there had been in Mayo. Old Lord Marlowe had a ruthless pride in his ability to control the people who worked his lands. To defy him meant eviction. To fail to pay the additional taxes would mean eviction. Rebellion would lead to transportation halfway around the world to the penal colonies of New South Wales.

In his classroom, Martin looked at the vacant desk ahead of him in the row and frowned. It had been a week and more since his friend Robert McBride had last come to class. He had, it seemed, made good his threat to stay away. The McBride family, unable to pay the additional money, had already been served their eviction notice. Robert's absence made school feel even more lonely and pointless, and made the morning hours drag on forever. Professor Larson was unusually curt and short-tempered.

Just before the noon meal break was the hour for the archbishop to observe the studies. As the classroom door opened Professor Larson shrank back into the corner of the room, almost as if he expected some disaster to follow.

"It is the education obtained in National School, Your Honor," Superintendent Stone remarked to the archbishop. "There is no other explanation as to the cheerful compliance of these creatures to the laws of parliament."

Two men accompanied Superintendent Stone. They wore the dark clothes and clerical collars of Church of Ireland prelates. Martin recognized one of the two: he was the Reverend Mr. Hodge, the vicar of Castletown.

"Attention, boys," Stone demanded. At this command, all the students rose to their feet and stood stiffly beside their desks. "Today our school has the singular honor of receiving His Excellency, Archbishop Whately of Dublin, as well as our own vicar hodge. As you know, Archbishop Whately is the author of our Political Economy curriculum, and I know how impressed you must be to meet such a highly educated and famous man in person." Stone's words dripped with the oil of compliment and the honey of flattery.

Martin exchanged a look with Billy Riley. Whately was as broad as he was tall, with a gold watch chain so stretched across his girth that it seemed to be the only thing keeping his stomach from exploding. Of course the students recognized the name of the author of the hated study called "Political Economy."

"Professor Larson," Stone continued, "don't let us interrupt your lesson, which I believe should be in political economy." Here was the reason for Professor Larson's surly nervousness; he had known he was going to be observed at the most critical time of day.

Larson nodded mutely and looked wide-eyed. It seemed to Martin that their instructor was as apprehensive as the students, if not more so. "Master Riley," Larson said, finding his voice at last. "You will remain standing. The rest of you, be seated and open Archbishop Whately's excellent text to page seventy-three. Master Riley, begin reading the section entitled 'On Value and Labor.' "

Billy Riley found the place, licked his lips to wet them, and traced the first line with his index finger. "To have value, something must have three qualities. The object must be scarce, it must be desirable, and it must be transferable."

"Stop there, Master Riley," Larson instructed. "Master Donovan, stand up and give us an example of something that has value."

Thank goodness for an easy question. Martin rose to his feet again and fixed his gaze pointedly on the archbishop's belly. "A gold watch chain," he said simply. "It is rare, men want to have it, and it can be passed from one man to another."

The schoolmaster grew pale at this reply. Then the archbishop's fat lips curved in a smile. "Well spoken, lad."

Larson breathed a sigh of relief. "Continue, Riley."

Billy Riley resumed reading. "It is false, however, to think that labor can make a worthless object valuable or increase an object's worth. Things are either valuable or they are not. Thus we see that labor has no value of its own."

Afterward Martin could never explain what made him raise his hand, made him speak up when he could have stayed silent.

"Please, sir," he inquired of the Protestant archbishop, "does land have value?"

The subject of the value of land had been scrupulously avoided in the archbishop's written discussion. Land was to be owned by the hereditary English landlords or by the Crown; it was rare and desirable, but seldom transferred, nor did the English want their Irish tenants to think about land ownership.

The archbishop coughed into his hand and replied with irritation, "Yes, certainly. Land is very valuable."

"Then," Martin continued, "if a farmer clears a field of rocks and builds a wall around it, has he not made the field more valuable by his labor?"

Dead silence in the room. "That is an impertinent remark," the archbishop observed.

Advancing like a stalking bird menacing a frog in a pond, Stone bent over Martin and hissed, "I shall report you to the priest and to your father as a detriment to this school!" Then loudly he continued, "Professor Larson, are you going to deal with this unpleasantness, or shall I?"

Shaking himself out of his dumbfounded stillness, Larson ordered Martin to the corner to stand upon the black stool. "One hundred times," Larson demanded. "Begin reciting now."

Stone swept the visitors out of the classroom, but Martin knew they could hear him reciting the school's favorite punishment phrase, "A child of the dust must not be proud. A child of the dust must not be proud. . . ."

And so this one small incident was the beginning of what came to be known as the Children's Rebellion of Ballynockanor. Martin Donovan's defiance and punishment over the archbishop's economic theories led to further uprisings throughout the fine soft day of the churchman's visit to the school. When the final tally was taken, there were thirty-nine expulsions. The count included wee small Mary Elizabeth Donovan, who when asked to recite a poem in praise of English learning, instead sang a loud chorus of "The Wild Rapparee," then danced a jig upon the black stool.

∽

A regular council of war was held in the Donovan cottage that same night.

Mary Elizabeth burst in joyfully, declaring she would never, ever return to that hateful school again. Kate, who was scooping oats into a simmering kettle, let the little girl sing a verse of "Bold Jack Donohue" and dance about the room. It was some time still before Kate could draw from the girl the circumstances of what actually happened.

" 'Out! Out!' cried Matron Rush, and she swooned away and lay droolin' on the step in a heap! We cheered! Thirty-nine of us! There'll be hardly anyone left in the school!" the child cried gleefully. Clasping her small hands beneath her chin she put on a pious face. "A miracle! Saints and holy martyrs we shall be called!"

Mindful of his responsibility to the moilies, Martin was some time behind his younger sister. By the time he got home, Kevin and Brigit were also present, and Kate pieced together the day's events.

"Sure, and we'll burn the school to the ground," Kevin declared. "It and that John Stone and that old witch, Rush, and the heretic Dublin clergyman!"

"Sha!" Kate scolded. "We'll have no talk of burnin' and killin'. Would you be after callin' down more bad luck on this house, Kevin Donovan?"

"Kate's right," Brigit agreed. " 'Tis the Donovan temper has caused enough trouble already. If Mary Elizabeth and Martin had said the lessons like proper students, there'd be nothin' to fight about."

"Spoken like a true believer in the landlord's son," Kevin replied.

Brigit threw a cup at him that shattered on the wall beside the hearth. A shard bearing the words *Souvenir of Belfast* rattled and spun to a halt on the floor.

Kate rounded on her. Waving the wooden dipper under Brigit's nose, Kate said sternly, "And I suppose you'd have meekly recited what a happy English child you are? I say I am proud of Mary Elizabeth, and of Martin. I will hear no criticism of either."

Kevin called loudly again for the destruction not only of the school and its superintendent, but of all the English. He vowed to raise an army from O'Flaherty's tavern that very night, and out of the house he stormed.

Brigit, skipping back out of Kate's reach, muttered darkly that the Donovans would soon have the reputation of rapparees: men living wild in the hills and without civilization.

Sighing heavily, Kate gathered both Martin and Mary Elizabeth to her. "My little rebels." She hugged them both, but her words were addressed to Brigit: "Don't you see?" she asked. "It's their way to turn us Irish each against the other. They want us to think that our da and all our forefathers were savages and drunken failures. If they drive us to anger and bloodshed born of poteen," she said pointedly, staring at the door through which Kevin had raged, "then they have proved their point." Then locking eyes with Brigit, she continued, "But if they succeed in makin' us ashamed of who we are and who we come from, then we are adrift in the world! Mark my words, Brigit Donovan, no matter what they make you recite, they will never let you be English. If you said it ten thousand times, you'd be no more to them than a trained ape, mouthin' words to be laughed at and scorned."

Brigit burst into angry tears and likewise fled from the cottage. In her hasty exit, she collided with Joseph and her father, who were just entering. Without so much as an apology, she ran past them both into the evening air.

The arrival of the two men gave Kate a new target for her wrath. "And what will you say now, Da?" she demanded. "Will you still insist that your youngest children endure humiliation every day? Is it worth the torment to their young souls just to receive an English education?"

Tom Donovan, as well he might, looked baffled at the sudden assault.

Joseph caught on at once. " 'Tis not right to shame children for bein' proud of their parents and their country," he asserted. "But it's equally true they cannot hold their own in the world without proper learnin'."

"And just what are you goin' to do about it?" Kate snapped, giving a savage stir to the porridge and banging the ladle more forcefully against the kettle than was necessary. "You who can go on your way at any time?"

"That is just what I have been speakin' to your father and to the good priest about," Joseph responded. "I cannot be a burden to the community, and I must earn my bread. I have little skill with my hands, but my learnin' may be of some use. With Father O'Bannon's help, we'll start a school for the thirty-nine small martyrs of Ballynockanor."

For once, even Kate was speechless.

∽

The soft day had become a soft evening before the final act of the day of the Children's Rebellion was played out. Profuse apologies from Marlowes senior and junior accompanied Archbishop Whately to his coach. Despite a lavish dinner laid on for his enjoyment at Marlowe Park, Whately abruptly decided that his wounded dignity needed to leave immediately.

Just past the village of Farnaght on the way to Maam Cross, the road used a series of switchbacks to scale the hill called Glenlusk. It was on the third of these S-shaped curves that the horses strained against the combined weight of the archbishop and his carriage, and progress slowed to a walk. The coachman was leaning forward as if he could aid the struggling animals when four men appeared from the verge of the highway. Two were on each side of the archbishop's team and two more flanked the coachman. Their faces were blackened with burnt cork and their shapes made formless by grain-sack tunics belted on with bands of woven straw. Reins were seized and the rig wheeled out of sight of the road behind the hill. As the coachman was menaced with a blackthorn stick, the archbishop was invited to alight. Actually, Whately was told that his choice was to step down or be dragged out.

The churchman emerged, preceded by his gold watch and chain, which he thrust toward the nearest phantom and blubbered, "Here! Take this, but spare my life!"

"Tush, man," the leader of the Ribbonmen intoned. "Put back your watch and save your tears. Have we not come to improve the quality of your education? Can you recite, 'A child of the dust must not be proud?' "

The prelate agreed that he could. Then do so, he was told.

"A child . . ."

"Hold, hold," the captain insisted. "You are not in proper form. Where is the black stool?" The other Ribbonmen spread their hands in dismay. Apparently the required black stool could not be located. "We'll have to make an accommodation then. Take off your boots and stand upon one leg."

Ponderously hoisting one pale fat foot aloft, in his black coat and trousers the archbishop looked like a performing bear.

"A child . . ."

"Hold, hold," the leader of the rebels interrupted again. "This is still not quite right. Take off your trousers."

Soon the archbishop, naked from the waist down, was again on one leg and rehearsing "A child of the dust must not be proud."

"It is a fine thing that we did not take your watch and chain," the Ribbonmen's leader commented dryly. "You would be quite indecent otherwise."

One hundred recitations later (fifty on each leg) the hoarse archbishop was allowed to stop and sit beside the road. "Now it is but two miles into town," suggested the rebel chief. "But we, however, have much farther to go. So we'll be borrowin' your coach. I'm sure your Lordship does not mind walkin'?" Whately shook his head wearily. "That's fine, then, fine. Just let us get the boots from your driver, and we'll be on our way. Oh," the Ribbonman added, "you may keep your watch."

8

The immediate result of the theft of Archbishop Whately's pantaloons was much harsher than any of the participants in the Children's Rebellion could have imagined. What began with the stamping of Mary Elizabeth's foot led to the arrest of Tim Mulrooney one day later. Within two more days he was tried, and, on the basis of the testimony of paid informers, condemned and sentenced. When less than a week had passed, he was aboard a convict ship leaving Bantry Bay astern and bound for the prison colony of New South Wales.

Nor was that the end of the consequences.

The penal laws established by the Puritan tyrant, Oliver Cromwell, had been abolished; an Irishman could no longer be arrested for practicing his religion nor a Catholic priest hunted down like a wild animal. But the relaxing of the strictures on freedom of conscience did not mean a loosening of English law. Since 1800 a whole series of coercion statutes had been introduced. Each measure was designed to suppress rebellion, and each was harsher than the preceding. Wherever these rules were enforced, it was a jailable offense to be out after curfew, deportation for wearing a disguise.

And perhaps worst of all, any family convicted of aiding a criminal was subject to eviction.

Such was the case with the Mulrooneys.

As soon as word of Tim's conviction spread beyond the walls of the Castletown courthouse, friends and neighbors gathered at the Mulrooney cottage. Joseph, Kevin, Martin, Da, and others loaded stools, a table, a dresser, and a precious mirror onto two carts.

The womenfolk gathered shawls, feather pillows, and cook pots.

Mary Elizabeth corralled a laying hen and tucked it under her arm.

Billy Mulrooney went around and around the home, looking for his cat, which was scared and hiding from all the commotion. Clancy, the black-and-white feline, had still not been located when a gang of men led by Constable Carroll and accompanied by John Stone tramped up the road from town. On their backs they carried axes, crowbars, and coils of rope.

"Clear off with you now!" Carroll demanded harshly. He read a court order making it clear that what was about to take place had the full force of law and the approval of the English Parliament.

Kate dropped an armload of threadbare blankets and rushed toward the doorway, only to be barred from entering by John Stone. "You may not go back in," he said, sneering. "It's too late." She clenched and unclenched her good fist as she backed away. Seething with frustration and anger, there was nothing to be done.

Interfering with the carrying out of an eviction order made the trespasser and family also subject to forced displacement.

The gang of men who accompanied Stone and Carroll were not soldiers or policemen. Convicts themselves from Galway City, the "destructives" had been offered one chance to save themselves from transportation to Australia: aid the law in turning out others.

Mrs. Mulrooney ducked under Carroll's arm and back inside the cottage to emerge a moment later with a baby cradle tucked under her arm. When the constable roughly pushed the woman out of the way, Kevin started forward. An ash branch was clutched in his hand.

Kate saw Joseph catch Kevin's collar and drag him backward. "Tim Mulrooney had the good sense to keep silent and spare his comrades a sea voyage," Joseph hissed. "Even if you would throw his good deed away, think about what you would bring on your own family, and keep still!"

Two of the destructives chopped holes in the thatching and tied a cable to each end of the beam that supported the roof. A third sawed partway through the middle of the bog oak timber. While two more attacked the masonry around the girder mountings, the rest hauled away at the ropes. "Heave-ho, lads!" Carroll shouted, as if he were a sea captain ordering the hoisting of a sail. "On three again. One! Two! . . ."

Mrs. Mulrooney dropped the cradle and sank to her knees, sobbing. Kate and Brigit, surrounded by the Mulrooney children, flanked her. They all hugged one another in a mass of heaving shoulders and dirt-streaked faces.

Billy Mulrooney circled the scene, calling, "Clancy! Clancy!" The boy would have rushed back inside to search for the cat, but Joseph collected him. He called Martin over to help.

It was only the work of minutes for the great beam to crack under the strain of the crowbars, the axes, and the sideways pressure of the ropes. "Look out, lads!" Carroll called cheerfully. "She's going!" Only minutes were required to ruin a home that had sheltered generations of Mulrooneys.

The two men still on the roof jumped clear just as the oak timber burst in the middle. With a roar, the roof caved into the interior of the cottage, and one end wall and one side wall collapsed as well.

John Stone nodded his approval, then turned to Mrs. Mulrooney. "You may have the thatch and wood," he said. "But don't carry away any bits of stone . . . they all belong to Lord Marlowe."

The house wreckers and the officers marched off toward the promise of a hot meal and a pint of stout, leaving a heap of rubble and a haze of dust that attacked Kate's throat and eyes. Mrs. Mulrooney's crying changed to a high-pitched wail, keening for the loss of a loved one.

"Clancy!" Billy Mulrooney called over the bawling of his mother, sisters, and neighbors. "Clancy!"

Martin rushed forward, and Kevin joined his little brother in digging frantically into the rubble. In the mound of plaster, thatch, and rock, it was impossible to see anything, certainly not a tiny kitten.

Joseph stepped forward. In a loud voice he commanded, "Everyone keep still!" A few sniffles and sobs resisted the order, and then silence fell. Thatch straw, still sliding downward, made a hissing sound. A rock, balanced on one of the remaining walls, fell clattering into the mass of debris. And then . . .

There was a weak meow from the far end of the ruined cabin. All the men and boys rushed forward, tossing aside chunks of rock. Kate saw Joseph tear his fingers on a bit of splintered beam. Next she watched him dive into the shards, disappearing up to the waist in straw and plaster.

He emerged a moment later, clutching a very dusty, very frightened black-and-white kitten.

❀

The day after the tossing of the Mulrooney cottage, Martin watched as Mary Elizabeth handed over a penny to Mrs. Mulrooney. "To help you go to America," the little girl said. She hoisted a scollop of thatch to her shoulder, though the straw parcel was half as big as herself.

"Let me help you with that," Martin offered.

"No," Mary Elizabeth said firmly. "I have paid for this bundle, and I'll tote it to the school me own self."

A line of villagers from Ballynockanor waited their turn to hand Mrs. Mulrooney a penny or tuppence or a sixpence. Each murmured something similar to what Mary Elizabeth had said: "For the crossin' . . . to speed you to America . . . toward the passage money."

If Ballynockanor was to have a schoolhouse again, then the building would have to be repaired and reroofed. If the Mulrooneys could no longer live in Ireland, then they would go to America, and the thatch and lumber allowed them by John Stone would make up their fares.

Martin thought how life, even when it was not fair or just, could be made to balance somehow.

Two Kilpatricks, Old and Young Seamus both, tipped their caps. "Give her the pennies," Old Seamus urged his son. " 'Tis a fine rafter," he said to Mrs. Mulrooney as he patted the bog oak timber. "Just the right length to patch the hole above the southwest corner of the schoolhouse."

Da rested his hand on Martin's shoulder, and the boy snuggled back against the comforting weight of his father's gnarled grip. "It'll be a good thing indeed to see the school reborn," Da said. He and Kevin carried a stack of wood for which they had paid a whole shilling.

"Aye," Mrs. Mulrooney agreed. "It's like a part of us will be built into the place, to remain after we're gone."

⚬∽

Joseph looked around the swept floor and scrubbed walls of the schoolhouse. It had been like this in his father's day, he remembered. Uncle Marlowe had decided that educating the children of the land was a needless extravagance that gave them airs above their station.

In less than a week, missing bits of mortar were rechinked and the roof, thanks to the Mulrooneys, was sound and thatched again. The building, about the size of two cottages, would serve well for the rebellious children of Ballynockanor. Best of all, it stood on land belonging to the church of St. John the Evangelist and could not be molested by Marlowe or his henchmen.

Tonight, however, the bare floor was pressed into service for a different purpose: to "wake" the Mulrooneys on the eve of their departure to America. Leaving Ireland for either America or heaven had the same result: no one in the old country expected to ever again on earth see the face of the departed. A funeral celebration was called for, and one was arranged.

As Clooney and O'Rourke struck up a tune, Father O'Bannon helped himself to a finger of tobacco from the bowl on the trestle table in the center of the floor and joined Joseph. "Fine night to hold a feast of departure," the priest said in the Gaelic. He regarded Joseph with such a quizzical look that the younger man recognized a challenge behind the remark.

Grinning at the wordplay, Joseph responded, "Ah, Father, you'll not be catchin' me that easy. It may be so called over the border in Mayo, but here we say 'a farewell supper.' "

Father O'Bannon beamed with satisfaction. "You'll not have any trouble with your examinations," he vowed. "You are a quick one."

While the fiddle and the pipe soared, Clooney left off playing his flute to take up the words of "Castle Garden":

> *Farewell my old acquaintance,*
> *My friends both one and all.*
> *My lot is in America*
> *To either rise or fall.*

The singing would go on until after midnight, together with the storytelling and the swapping of advice about the new world. Joseph saw Kate come in the door between Brigit and Kevin. "Excuse me, Father," he said to O'Bannon. "There's someone I've been meanin' to speak with."

The priest noted the direction taken by Joseph's eyes and nodded the young man away. With a rueful shake of his head, he muttered, "Quick you may be, but still far from settled in your own mind, I'm thinkin'."

Kate saw Joseph approaching and, reaching into a deep pocket, pulled out a book. She held the volume in front of her like a shield to keep Joseph from coming too close. "For the school," she said over the top of his greeting. Thrusting the book into his hands, she announced, "It was my mother's. *Castle Rackrent* by Maria Edgeworth. Perhaps you'll read aloud from it."

"I will, and I'll treasure it," he replied.

She appeared that she might bolt, so Joseph put out his hand to stop her. They had scarcely spoken since the night Constable Carroll had assaulted her. That must be the cause of her distress, he reasoned. Perhaps the sight of him reminded her of what almost happened. He felt guilty and ashamed somehow that at his first glimpse of her, his recollection of that night had been of sitting beside the river cradling her in his arms. The memory of that sensation flooded back strongly, and he shook his head against the vision.

As if facing up to the demons, she looked him in the eye and said, "I thank you again for what you did . . . and what you are doin'."

Joseph shrugged, certain she did not want to speak of it further. "I've not seen you about," he said.

"And haven't you been busy preparin' for the school? The whole village will be watchin', y'know. You must really be a teacher, Joseph Connor," she challenged. "And a good one."

Joseph agreed he had been absorbed in study. "And yourself?" he asked gently. "How have you fared?"

"Well enough," she said. "There is always a great deal to be done about the place, and Mary Elizabeth is so underfoot. School will be good for us both."

Shouts of "Good man" concluded Clooney's performance, and he was encouraged to sing another: a love song this time.

Two hearts drew together into a fond embrace. The stream it murmured words of care in a moonlit secret place.

Kate sprang away from Joseph abruptly. "I must help Brigit with the oat cakes," she said, leaving him with half-formed words on his lips.

Joseph swallowed hard. He was not certain what was the more difficult thing to bear: being near her, or being rebuffed.

∽

It was two nights before Gale Day, when the semiannual rent payments came due. It was also the time when the Connemara landlords would collect tithes for the Protestant Church of Ireland as well as their own fees.

Father O'Bannon invited Joseph to sit down in the single room that was his living room, bedroom, kitchen, and dining room. At the moment, however, the chamber was functioning as the priest's office. He waved a letter under Joseph's eyes.

"I have received," he began, "a note from Archbishop MacHale, dated . . ." The priest squinted at the cramped print. ". . . dated the twenty-seventh of April, just two days past, which he has added to a letter from Daniel O'Connell. In it the two men agree that it is time to move forward toward repeal, but stressin' again that no violence will be countenanced. The two men want to know what the sentiment is hereabouts; is there support for disunion and can disorder be prevented?"

Joseph nodded his understanding. The Catholic archbishop MacHale across Lough Corrib in Tuam was a powerful voice for Irish self-rule and equally as opposed to bloodshed as O'Connell. "What is it they want you to do?"

Father O'Bannon grinned slyly. "It's not so much what they want of me as of you, I'm thinkin'. I am forbid to address political meetin's, except to preach amity and calm. I am instructed to find another in the district who can lead, who commands respect and admiration. Daniel O'Connell suggests you."

∞

Joseph saw by the tenseness in Kevin's jaw and the flush on his face that expectation was running high. Joseph had called this nocturnal meeting in the schoolhouse, but had left the inviting of others to Kevin.

Gathered around the plank table still heaped with books and slates were the eager young men of Ballynockanor and Castletown. To a dozen from the village and the market city were added a half dozen more from Alintober and other outlying areas. It was clear the eve of Gale Day carried significant meaning.

All wore expressions of excitement mixed with determination—firebrands, every one. Joseph thought to himself how well Kevin had done; these were exactly the ones whom Joseph had to convince.

Kevin did not wait for Joseph to speak first, but took the initiative himself. "So it's time, is it? We have done with waitin' and are ready?" Kevin's words were seconded by grim nods around the table. "We have come as you ordered," he said to Joseph.

"Requested," Joseph corrected, "and I thank you. I recognize that because of the curfew you will have to stay the night so as not to be violatin' the law." The scowls on the faces of the men told Joseph how much they scorned the English law. "I have a message for you from Daniel O'Connell," Joseph continued. Kevin's face lit up even brighter. Joseph recognized the glow of self-importance connected with being summoned by the Great Liberator. "Actually, it is a message penned jointly by Mister O'Connell and Archbishop MacHale of Tuam."

This information made the gathering all the more significant. MacHale was the spiritual leader of Catholic Galway. He and O'Connell had suffered political differences in the past. If they were now sending joint communiqués, then the time for rebellion must truly have come. "God bless the archbishop, and God bless the Liberator!" proclaimed Brian O'Malley. "Aye!" and "Amen!" rattled the straw of the thatching. Palms thumping agreement on the table bounced a copy of *Homer* onto the floor.

Anxious to regain his role as second-in-command, Kevin inquired, "And may we be hearin' this message?"

"Indeed," Joseph agreed. "Here it is: 'The time has come to work for the repeal of the union between Ireland and England and to restore an Irish government of Irishmen.' "

"Aye!" and "Good man!" echoed even louder than before until Joseph had to caution the group to quiet down.

"What do Their Honors want first?" Chris O'Neill asked. "Do we burn the courthouse or the manor?"

Joseph said nothing in reply to this. In fact he studied each face in turn, trying to read what truly lay behind the ferocious looks. His silent scrutiny went on so long that the men grew uncomfortable, shuffling their booted feet and rustling a heap of arithmetic papers.

"Mister O'Connell and the archbishop know what an uphill struggle it will be to gain our freedom," Joseph said at last. "Requirin' much dedication and much money. The important task they have entrusted to you is the collection and safekeepin' of the Repeal Rent."

"The what?" Kevin exploded. "Gatherin' pennies from old women like we was beggars?" Growls of unhappiness came from the others.

Patiently, as if speaking to a particularly unruly and backward group of schoolchildren, Joseph explained what was wanted. He told them how O'Connell and Archbishop MacHale were planning mass meetings for that very year. He spelled out that there would be gatherings of thousands of people to show the English how much sentiment there was for repeal. He stressed the need for funds for offices and publications.

"What about Ribbonmen?" Kevin suggested. "How long will we let the lads of Mayo do our fightin' for us? How long will we go on bein' sheep?"

"O'Connell and the archbishop are set firm against violence and illegal acts," Joseph said sternly. "No secret bands of hooligans, no waylayin' carriages, no burnin' of hayricks, no maimin' of cattle."

"When the Protestants have soldiers and guns and the law on their side?" Kevin challenged. "Tim Mulrooney . . ."

"Tim Mulrooney *is* a Protestant," Joseph challenged. "And this is not a matter of Catholics and Protestants. But I was waitin' for you to mention Tim. D'ye see where it got him? Australia and his family's cottage tossed. Do y'want to bring that upon Ballynockanor and your own families?"

"I'll hear no more of this," Kevin announced, jumping to his feet. "Tim Mulrooney was a good man, better'n the rest of us up to now. You are a traitor, Joseph Connor, and a weaklin'. I want no more to do w'ye." With that Kevin stalked out of the school. Most of the others left as well.

In the weeks that followed, three Connemara cows and twenty-five Connemara sheep gathered for tithe payment were secretly branded with a *T*. To any merchants who sought to purchase these animals at auction it was whispered that the letter not only invoked the hated Tithe, but stood as well for the even more abhorrent word *Traitor*. Eventually Stone and Carroll drove the beasts to Galway City and sold the lot to a merchant ship bound for England. They brought only a fraction of their worth.

Just outside Ballynockanor, a hayrick set aside for tithe mysteriously caught fire and burned the same night that Carroll and Stone were away.

9

It was obvious from the way William Marlowe leaned back against the rock wall and watched Brigit's approach that he had been waiting for her to come along. He held the reins to his bay horse as the animal cropped the grassy verge. "Good day to you, Brigit Donovan," he said with a tip of his top hat. "A beautiful May morn."

"I'm not speakin' with you," she said curtly. She was carrying a teakettle that had been to the smith for the repair of its handle. She shook the vessel at him. "After what happened to the Mulrooneys, I can't think why you'd expect me to."

"I had nothing to do with that!" Marlowe said forcefully. "That was the work of the magistrate and the constable, not me."

"But you did naught to prevent it, either, did you?"

The girl passed by without stopping, forcing Marlowe to drag the horse away from his feed. "I don't want us to be enemies," he said with feeling. "You are the most beautiful girl I have ever seen . . . and you deserve better than milking cows in a mud-hole village. You should be dressed in satin and lace and live in a fine house."

Despite her aloofness, Brigit turned her head and her attention toward the young landlord. "Meanin' what?" she asked.

"Come away with me. I'll take you to Dublin . . . even France, if you like. You'll have money to spend on any whim and servants to wait on you."

Stopping dead in her tracks, Brigit inquired, "Marry with me . . . you, a lordship?"

To her distress, Marlowe laughed in her face. "Marry you? Are you mad? But I am offering you a chance to get away from this bog."

Brigit swung the teapot toward his head, making Marlowe jump back. "What do y'take me for?"

Leering, Marlowe replied, "You already told me that in the market when you spoke up for that poor peasant, Tim Mulrooney. I'm sure you and I could come to an . . . understanding."

"Just you listen," the girl said, shaking the kettle in Marlowe's face. "I said what I said to save Tim from the constable, little good though it did! Now be off with you before this kettle and your skull come to an understandin'."

The second-floor withdrawing room at Marlowe Park was furnished in shades of pale yellow and amber. It was altogether too cheerful a location for the kind of wickedness being plotted there, but neither of the conspirators noted the irony.

"I can't believe she refused me today!" William Marlowe exclaimed with exasperation. He pounded his fist on a light oak side-table, spilling a tumbler of brandy. "Who is she to reject me? The nerve of the slut, Stone. Practically offering herself to me in the street and then spurning me. I tell you, it is not to be borne!"

John Stone mopped up the liquor and made sympathetic noises. "She's too far beneath you to trouble yourself over, sir."

Marlowe's tirade continued as if he had not heard. "I will have her, I say. You and I can . . . can . . . hang it, man, she's only a peasant girl. We can abduct her."

His obsequious expression slipping, Stone's face showed alarm. "Rape . . . is . . . such an ugly word," he said at last. "Sentiment among these wretched tenants is running high already. You might even be endangering your life."

A wave of Marlowe's fist suggested both his petulance and his disbelief. "Constable Carroll will keep the bog-trotters in line," he argued. "Do you think the poor wretches would sacrifice their hovels for one girl more or less?"

"Constable Carroll cannot protect you every dark night," Stone warned. "Besides," he added, "Carroll is not trustworthy. He might sell you out for the right price. But there is another way."

"What?"

"Marry the girl."

William Marlowe rocked back on his heels as if Stone had struck him in the face. "Are you mad? Be shackled to one like her? Give her a share in the estate?"

Stone hurriedly protested that he had been misunderstood. "What if she *thought* she was married . . . long enough to go with you willingly? When she protests later it will just be her word against yours."

The peevish cast to Marlowe's face was replaced with one of cunning. He refilled the crystal beaker with brandy. As an afterthought, he poured one for Stone. "Yes," he murmured. "I see. At the hunting lodge, away from prying eyes. Now, who can I get to play priest?" A small sip of brandy and Marlowe's expression lit up. "Roger Peel!" he exclaimed. "Perfect! My Dublin whoring companion. He looks emaciated and scholarly . . . just perfect for a priest! And I have so much scandal to hold over his head, he dare not refuse me. Now listen, Stone," Marlowe continued, just as if the entire plot had been his own idea, "here's what we'll do. . . ."

∽

Brigit Donovan was waiting for Joseph outside the schoolroom at the end of the day.

Wisps of red curls framed her face beneath the hood of her cloak. Beautiful and wild, she was, like a storm reaching the headland from the sea. Unbidden the words of the old tune came to his mind:

I have never seen Maid Quiet,
Nodding in her russet hood,
For the winds that awakened the stars
Are blowing through my blood.

There had been talk about secret meetings between her and William Marlowe. Joseph felt certain the whispers contained some element of truth. A man like William could not pass such a work of art and not want to possess it.

Joseph waited inside the school. Brigit hung back beside the mile marker as Martin and Mary Elizabeth approached her.

"I've come to have a word with your schoolmaster," she informed them. "Now get along to the pasture with you. The cows are waitin'."

Mary Elizabeth questioned her. "And what will you be talkin' to him about?"

"None of your affair," Brigit retorted.

Martin's eyes narrowed. "We'll not be goin' till you say."

Disgusted and certain there was no getting rid of her siblings, Brigit sighed and pulled out a folded and well-thumbed copy of *London Illustrated News.* "I've a question. A matter of politics and the English."

Joseph smiled at her quick wit. The comment touched on the day's lesson. Tedious stuff at best, the workings of the Whigs and Tories and the English Parliament was a topic certain to send Martin and Mary Elizabeth happily to fetch the cattle.

The younger Donovans hurried on. Joseph bent his head under the lintel and emerged blinking into the bright sunlight as though he were unaware of Brigit.

She cleared her throat. "Pardon, sir." She was ill at ease and clenched the *News* in her hands.

Joseph nodded. "A fine day, Miss Donovan."

She looked up into the cloudless sky as though she had not noticed. "That it is." Then, "The primroses are in bloom."

"A fine day," he said again, slinging his satchel of books over his shoulder. "Your brother and sister are doin' well with their lessons. They're a pair of wits, those two."

"Aye." His reference irritated her. She glanced over her shoulder furtively. "But that's not why I've come. . . ."

He waited patiently. "I see."

Stepping forward two strides, she halted with her bare feet hidden in the clover like a timid doe beside the road. A dozen paces separated them. She stretched the folded copy of the London paper toward him.

"The Galway mail coach driver brought it for me. He does sometimes."

"A fine publication." Joseph came near enough to take it from her. On the cover was a woodcut of a gondola floating through the canals of Venice. Seldom did the *London Illustrated News* dwell on London politics. So why had Brigit come?

She blurted, "My brother and the others say you're a traitor."

He laughed. "Do they now?"

"But I told Kev you're a man of peace. Harmony and reason, said I. That is Joseph Connor. Sure, Kevin, said I, no doubt Joseph Connor has a friend or two among the English, and he bears no malice without thinkin' the matter through."

"That would be my choice."

She smiled with relief and moved closer, pointing at the picture. "And you've seen the world as well. France. Venice. Places where it never rains."

At this remark he scratched his chin to hide his smile. "The rain is often warm in the South of France. I've never been to Venice."

"No matter. When you're a priest you'll make pilgrimage to Rome, no doubt."

"Aye. Perhaps I will. And then to America I hope."

Delight filled her. "A man of the world, who knows much beyond our little Ballynockanor."

"All the best in the world is here in Ballynockanor, Brigit Donovan. That much I'll tell you before you set your heart on travelin' far. If . . . if that is what you came to discuss."

Her exultant expression faded. A cloud passed over the sun.

"Aye. The very matter. I . . . I wanted to know if ever in your travels you met . . . a good Englishman or a truehearted landlord."

"Many."

Again, relief flooded her features. "Sure, and I knew not all were bad as Kevin says."

"Many Irish landlords are for repeal of Irish union with England." He considered the strangeness of the topic briefly, and then the true nature of her questioning came full on him. William Marlowe was the veiled subject of her interest. He added quickly, "But some nearby are calloused and dark-hearted men." He shot a glance toward Castletown so she would not mistake his meaning. "They have no care for Ireland or her people. Nor for England. Scavengers in silk waistcoats and top hats they are. It is themselves they love and none other."

She took the paper from his hand and studied the image solemnly. "The rain is warm in the South of France you say?"

"Aye. Brigit . . ." He wanted to cut through the charade and tell her what he knew about William Marlowe. But what good would it do? She had been warned by others no doubt. He briefly considered speaking to Kate on the matter; but no, Kate was troubled enough without causing her more grief over what was certainly just a flight of fancy.

Brigit's deep blue eyes were almost pleading as she searched his face. "Men can change. Love can change a man, they say: can change everythin' he ever thought he was or wanted to be."

Joseph could not argue with that. His longing for Kate had turned his world upside down. The dull ache of knowing she would never have him pushed Joseph back to old dreams again. "Careful, Brigit. You walk a dangerous path, girl."

There was no need to say more. She thanked him, and turned toward home.

Once more Joseph wondered if he should do more than warn Brigit: inform Father O'Bannon perhaps? But what solid evidence did he have of anything wrong? Then Joseph recalled how much

Father O'Bannon hated unfounded gossip. He decided to let the matter drop.

Joseph sang the phrase softly as he watched her go,

I have never seen Maid Quiet,
Nodding alone and apart,
For the words that called up the lightning
Are calling through my heart.

The late May sun was well past its peak and Brigit had still not seen William Marlowe.

Earlier that day she had gone to keep the market stall in such high spirits that she did not wrangle with Kate and forgot to chide Martin. Her younger brother looked at her suspiciously when she allowed him to go play with some friends, but the boy did not openly question her unusual display of good humor. He agreed to return later to help transport the unsold goods and then scampered quickly away.

Throughout the trade in milk and cheese Brigit loaded and prepared to fire her brightest smile every time a male shadow hove into view. Although this drew a flock of young men to the table, the landlord's son never appeared.

After several hours the smile of Brigit Donovan faded. Dust from the market day traffic dulled the gleam of her carefully brushed hair. Errant globs of butter added unwanted shiny streaks to her best red cape. Market day was ending without William coming by to see her.

Like every girl in Ballynockanor Brigit knew the old Irish proverb about women who give in too easily to a man. "Why buy the cow when the milk is free?" Mrs. Clooney said regularly to any young female within earshot.

As the daughter of a dairyman, Brigit knew the worth of a fine milk-producing bovine. She would not give herself away and yet . . .

Mrs. Clooney stopped to chat. "A fine day, Brigit. Two pennies for a pound of butter?"

Brigit muttered moodily, "I'll not be givin' it away, Missus Clooney. Every cow has its price. I told him I'll not be givin' it away."

Puzzled, the florid-faced woman blinked at Brigit. "Who would ask you to give it away free?"

"William Marlowe."

"Ah. Himself. Monster Marlowe. And why would he be wantin' your butter and cheeses, girl? He's got all he wants and when he wants it and from whoever he wants to give it to him!" The matron raised her finger in warning and declared, "If the likes of himself is sniffin' about your stall, you can be certain he's not interested in buyin' your milk, dear! Remember what me sainted mother used to say! 'Why buy the cow if the milk is free, darlin'!' Aye! He's playin' the same game of sally rod with my pretty girl, Maeve. I've told Maeve to sell him nothin' a'tall! Not so much as a cabbage! Nor even speak to the man! Aye! He's as randy as a bull among the heifers, that one! And he's been payin' for his pleasure in Dublin with cold hard cash. But he'll not find the girls of Ballynockanor so willin'!"

At this the voice of Mad Molly piped up from behind. "He's a saint and a gentleman, the young master is! Aye! A saint and the son of a saint, God rest him!"

Mrs. Clooney rolled her eyes heavenward. "No, Molly dear. It's the Marlowes we're speakin' of. Old and young, them two are the devil's own."

Mad Molly plugged her finger into the butter, stuck it in her mouth, and winked at Brigit. "I always said Kate was the pretty one." At that she cackled, spun on her heel, and wove her way back through the market square.

Mrs. Clooney tapped her temple. "Poor old darlin'. Lives in another world, she does. Still thinks the Burkes are up at the old house and that the taxes never will come due. Well now . . . sure, and don't let your lovely face get you into trouble! You attract young men like a honey tree to bees. I said the same to me own sweet Maeve. Don't let him turn your head with flattery or promises. Mark me words, darlin'. If your own dear mother were livin', God rest her, she'd say the same. Don't sell that William Marlowe so much as a wheel of cheese when he's wantin' somethin' else from everythin' in skirts! Now then? Two pennies for a pound?" Then noting the brimming eyes and downturned mouth of Brigit, she asked, "Are y'unwell, darlin'?"

"Nothin' a'tall, Missus Clooney. It's just spring is all. It troubles my eyes."

"Boiled houseleek!" cried the woman. "The very thing for sore eyes."

Another fifteen minutes passed in conversation about the medicinal merits of houseleeks, nettles, and gardener's bane. By the time Mrs. Clooney took her butter and gathered her eleven children from the four corners of the market, Brigit was pale with irritation. The information about William's boldness with Maeve Clooney and the young master's absence from the Donovan stall shook Brigit's confidence. Free milk notwithstanding, had she set her price for love too high? Had she lost control over his affections? What if he found her tiresome and cast his eye elsewhere?

When Martin was still a block away, Brigit angrily called to him to hurry over. Where had he been dawdling for so long? The boy shrugged a good-bye to his chums; this at least was the Brigit he expected. "And pack it all up yourself," she demanded. "I've got a fiercesome headache and need a cup of tea."

Wounded in pride and at the same time afraid her pride had pushed William Marlowe away forever, Bright rounded the corner between Flanagan's Coaching Inn and the courthouse. From the concealment of a stack of timbers and slap bricks, a hand shot out to grab the girl's elbow and pull her aside.

Her rush of fear was not relieved when she saw the face of her accoster: John Stone. The driver's words were instantly pleasant and consoling. "I'm sorry for this conduct, miss," he said, bobbing his head. "But the young master was certain you wanted secrecy, and this was the first chance I've had all day to speak with you in private."

"Secrecy about what?" Brigit demanded, her eyes narrowing. "Secrecy or dread, is it? Too afraid to tell me himself that he wants no more to do with me?" She shook her head, angrily flinging cascades of hair.

"No, no!" Stone protested. "You misunderstand completely. He has agreed to everything you ask."

"Everything I have asked. . . ." Then she gasped. "Do y'mean he has agreed to marry with me?"

Stone nodded solemnly.

"A proper weddin', with a priest?"

"Just as you said," Stone responded. "Master Marlowe wants you to know, and I am his emissary, that he cherishes and honors you. Can you get away tonight?"

"Tonight?" Again a gasp of disbelief. Brigit's hand flew to her throat in a gesture of astonishment that for once in her life was real. "How? Where?"

"Master Marlowe recognizes that the difference in your stations . . . while of no concern to him . . . may be awkward for both of you for a time. He suggests that you marry in secret: tonight, if you are willing. He has arranged with a priest to perform the ceremony in private and keep it in confidence until you and he conclude the time has come for all to know. You will continue living in your father's house, saying nothing, until then. Are you agreeable?"

There was obvious wisdom in taking the course of secrecy. Da stormed and Kate raged at the merest mention of Kevin's interest in Jane Stone. And what height would the outrage in the Donovan cottage reach over she and the Protestant son of the English landlord?

"Of course," she said, recovering her composure. "Tell William . . ." She addressed Stone as though he were already her servant. "Tell Master Marlowe that I accept. What's to be done then?"

"Can you stay behind in Castletown after the close of the market?" Stone inquired. "If you can arrange to be away from home . . . all night," the driver added delicately, "Master Marlowe will see to everything else."

Flushed with excitement, Brigit tossed her curls in a flurry of agreement before she rushed away back to the booth. She was smiling again as Mrs. Clooney waved farewell. It was only minutes before Martin would leave, and she would be joining her husband-to-be.

∾

It was late afternoon when Joseph took up the ax and walked to the apple tree that had bloomed each spring for thirty years behind the house of the priest.

"A gift from your father, it was," explained Father O'Bannon. "Like an old friend it presented me with barrels of fine apples each autumn. And now it's died. I've not the will nor the strength to chop it down, Joseph Connor."

And so the task fell to Joseph. He leaned on the ax handle like a walking stick and stood apart from the tree for a time. Gnarled branches, without leaf or bloom, were in stark contrast against the bright green hills of the Connaught spring. The renewed world was shining through the blackened branches.

He remembered the words of Christ:

> *Every tree that bringeth not forth good fruit is hewn down and cast into the fire.*

Soon enough the grass would fade and the blossoms of the primrose would fall. The face of Brigit Donovan came to mind. She, like all of creation, was yearning for a world where the rain was ever warm and the sun shone every day, where true love coaxed apples from a corrupt tree.

Joseph understood such longing. Had he not returned to Ballynockanor to resurrect the ancient pride and power of the Burkes? His fathers had sent their roots deep into the soil of Connaught and drawn their strength from the labor of the common people. The fortunes of Burke had been won by men who had little to warm them but contentment and the love of their families. They were the silent men of Ballynockanor, day-blind stars, waiting patiently with their light till the sun would set for the last time on earth and Christ would return to redeem them.

Blessed are the poor in spirit, for theirs is the kingdom of heaven.

Unlike Brigit, Joseph was certain there was no peace or grace to be found in an earthly place where every living thing was doomed to go back to the dust. Her beauty would fade. The love of William Marlowe would be a blighted tree for her, without leaf or shade or nourishment. She had placed her hope in a man destined for the ax and the fire.

Joseph asked himself if he had also placed his hope in revenge against his uncle when the matter of the Burke estates was as dead as the apple tree. And then there was Kate. . . .

"Be still," he whispered to himself. "Be still. The way is clear."

He shouldered the ax and ducked beneath the brittle branches of the tree.

"Joseph!" Father O'Bannon called to him. "I say! Joseph!" The cleric bustled around the corner of his cottage. Kate Donovan, her face clouded with concern, followed close behind.

Joseph leaned the tool against the trunk and strode to meet them. "God save you both."

Kate returned the greeting without a smile. "And God save you and also my sister Brigit."

Father O'Bannon explained. "Kate has come out of concern for Brigit. It seems Brigit, very agitated and cheerful, sent a word with Martin and Mary Elizabeth that she was goin' back to spend a day or two with a friend. . . ."

Kate interrupted. "Martin said Brigit had come to have a word with yourself yesterday afternoon. Somethin' about English politics?"

"Aye. That she did."

"Brigit hasn't a brain in her head about anythin' English except for one. Did she mention William Marlowe, then?"

Joseph hesitated a moment. "No, she did not." The young man struggled with his conscience, not wanting to lie and yet unwilling to betray a confidence. Besides, Brigit had not actually mentioned Marlowe by name.

"You've heard the talk about my sister and young Marlowe?"

Joseph and Father O'Bannon exchanged looks. Joseph replied, "Aye. But there is always talk in Ballynockanor about William Marlowe and someone." Should he say more?

While Joseph still mused, Kate exhaled in exasperation. "If she's gone off to meet the rogue and you're not tellin' all, Joseph Connor, may her disaster be upon your soul!"

Father O'Bannon put a hand on Kate's arm. "A strong curse to put the sin of another on the guiltless."

"If he knows more, then he is as guilty as she," Kate defended.

"Kate Donovan Garrity!" Father O'Bannon scolded. "There'll be no more of this. Joseph Connor has done nothin' wrong. You've taken the gossip about your sister too seriously. Aye. That you have. And do you not think Brigit's confessor would know if any wrong has been done here?"

Shamed by the reprimand, Kate lowered her eyes. "Pardon, Father. I just . . . Brigit is foolish, but also, in her way, an innocent. Since Mother died I have tried to guide her. But . . ."

The priest scowled. "It's yourself needs guidance. I'll see you at confession tomorrow. Now leave off persecutin' poor Joseph and leave him to his task."

Without looking at Joseph she nodded and said quietly, "I am sorry to have troubled you. I beg your pardon."

"It is most freely given." Joseph tipped his hat and remained rooted as he watched her leave. He was relieved to begin swinging the ax. By the time the tree was felled, the physical exertion had pushed the moral dilemma to the back of his mind.

On the outskirts of Castletown was a tumbledown shebeen, the remains of a crossroads pub. The deserted one-room shanty still possessed its turf roof, overgrown with weeds. The walls were shrouded in the strangling vines called gardener's bane, and house-leeks grew from what little remained of the mortar between the stones. The one sign that anyone had ever dwelt there and cared about the home was the holly tree beside the eastern wall.

Brigit stood hidden from view by the drooping eaves of the ruin and the holly branches on which dark old leaves and lighter new ones were mingled. She had dispatched Martin homeward with a tale of needing to visit her friend Rose Kennedy, who lived on the far side of the district. The distance was reason enough for her to spend the night away from home with no one the wiser. She slipped out of town using the cover of the stone walls and arrived at the appointed rendezvous.

Along a cart track behind the shack rumbled a carriage. Though the weather was pleasant, the top was up and the side curtains drawn. John Stone wheeled the pacer into the yard beside the tree and hissed, "Get in, girl, get in!"

As soon as Brigit had her foot on the step, Stone abruptly whipped up the rig. The lurch forward tumbled the young woman awkwardly into the rear seat. "Where are we going?" she asked.

"Marlowe Hunting Lodge," was the reply. "Now keep back out of sight. We have to pass the tenant cottages, and it would not do to let your secret out this early, would it?"

This was more like an abduction than a wedding procession. Unspoken doubts were evident in Brigit's demeanor. Her hands were trembling as she pulled her cloak tightly around her. Why had William sent his steward for her? Why had he not come himself?

As though he sensed the quarry was about to bolt, Stone called back to her cheerfully, "Here you are, driven in a carriage like a proper lady past the homes of those who will someday be your tenants."

"I'll not put on airs to them," she replied, seeming somewhat relieved.

Marlowe Lodge was a structure built by the Burkes for hunting on their lands south and east of Castletown. A peninsula, four miles long and very narrow, jutted out from the shoreline into Lough

Corrib. Like an accusing finger, it admonished an island named Inishdoorus, to which it was connected by a short causeway.

Across a seven-arched stone bridge was the islet. There was little there except a two-story Gothic-style building topped by a brass weather vane in the form of a hunting dog. The carriage shed, which was the ground floor, was in darkness, but yellow light spilled out of the upper-story windows and cascaded down over a brush-choked yard.

Drawing back the leather side curtain, Brigit peered out. "And where's the chapel?" she demanded.

Stone snorted. "You are not married yet to be so overbearing," he scolded. "Isn't it enough that the young master has agreed to a priest from your own religion?"

It was the dream of every girl in Ballynockanor to be wed in the chapel of St. John the Evangelist with Father O'Bannon officiating. "I've not been to confession. Will the priest . . ."

Stone interrupted. "You've nothing to confess yet," he said, leering at her. "Now in the morning . . ."

The ridicule silenced her.

The coach passed directly under the center doorway of the lower floor and into a pitch-dark space that smelled of musty hay and the dampness of the lake. Brigit displayed uneasiness again, and then a door at the top of a flight of stairs opened to reveal William Marlowe. He swayed slightly, as though he had been drinking.

"Darling, Brigit!" he called to her, and suddenly Brigit flushed with excitement. She rushed up the steps before he could say another word and flung herself into his arms.

William crushed her to him, and she matched the fervor of his kiss as though no one nor nothing else existed in the world.

It was a respectful cough from John Stone that caused Brigit to recollect finally that others were present. She pulled back slightly, then put her hands on William's chest, forcing Marlowe to release her. There was a flash of annoyance in his narrowed eyes, quickly replaced by a smile.

"Come in, my beautiful Brigit," he urged. "Father Ross is waiting."

In the center of the dark wood-paneled room was a thin man of medium height. His cassock was too long in the sleeves, and the stiff collar apparently chafed his neck, but the priest smiled a greeting and called Brigit, "My child."

"Father," Brigit responded. "It worries me that the banns have not been read . . . is it not sinnin' to wed without it?"

The priest was goggle-eyed behind round-rimmed spectacles, and Brigit's question seemed to fluster him.

William Marlowe broke in smoothly, "The very thing I asked about, darling. And Father Ross assured me that since we will both swear we are not breaking a vow made to another, there is no reason why we cannot marry at once." Marlowe paused and looked deeply into Brigit's eyes. He squared his shoulders before asking, "That is . . . you have never given your heart to another, have you?"

"No, never!" Brigit replied emphatically. "You are my one true love, and will be so forever."

"Then hurry, Father," Marlowe said with urgency. "Marry us at once."

Brigit crossed herself and pulled a fold of her shawl up to cover her head in proper reverence. Behind her John Stone coughed again, a trickle of noise that briefly sounded like a snicker.

Father Ross fumbled with the mass book, having to pull his spectacles down on his nose in order to locate the proper page. "May the God of Israel join you together," he read, "and may He be with you." The priest ran a slim finger around the inside of his clerical collar before continuing.

"And will no one else be here?" Brigit interjected. "The witnesses?"

Marlowe's face flashed impatience. "If you interrupt, my sweet, the ceremony will never conclude. We two are here, the good father is here, and Mister Stone is here as witness . . . why do we need any others? Go on, Father," he ordered.

"Your wife shall be like a bountiful vine. . . ."

As soon as the vows were concluded, Marlowe jerked his thumb over his shoulder toward the stairs. "Now thanks and good-night, gentlemen. I hope you enjoyed the play." He pressed a gold coin into the palm of the priest, then dismissed him and Stone. Whispering to Brigit, he added, "As for the rest, I shall teach you your lines. We need no audience for act three."

The two men hurried out of the room, and Marlowe slammed the stairwell door shut behind them. Lifting Brigit into his arms, he carried her toward the only other door and kicked it open. The massive canopy bed was made up with fresh linens. A bottle of brandy and two glasses topped a bedside table. "Come," he said, kissing her hard as he laid her on the bed and fumbled with the buttons of her blouse. "Show me how bountiful you are."

PART III

For one armed man cannot resist a multitude, nor one army conquer countless legions; but not all the armies of all the Empires on earth can crush the spirit of one true man. And that one man will prevail.

—Terence MacSwiney from "Principles of Freedom"

∽ 10 ∽

High summer came again to Ballynockanor. The fleecy clouds flew like banners from the farthest peaks. Morning mists drew back from the valleys like fingers combing the lush, thick grass. The leaves on the gnarled branches of the blackthorns made even those venerable ancients look spritely. The copse of poplar trees glittered green in the hollow. The stand of ash along the water's edge shaded the banks with bright leaves.

The sun warmed Kate's face as she made her way toward St. Brigit's ancient cross, which topped the hill above the village and the pastures and the distant ribbon of the river.

Today, the time of the summer solstice, marked the seventh anniversary of her wedding. For five years since Sean's death, Kate, carrying a loaf of bread, made solitary pilgrimage on this date to the old stone cross.

The valley opened below her. Green fields sloped down to the banks of the stream. Houses, men, and grazing livestock grew small, and for a moment Kate willed herself to forget their names and their worries.

Along the slants and crooks of the path she imagined that Ballynockanor was some nameless place and today was some timeless day, filled with people who had lived before and before and before.

The cross, the fields and stones, held memories she could not know. They were witnesses to salvation, joy, and also to broken dreams and promises. Christ would return to Ballynockanor one day, and this cross and these stones would cry aloud what they knew. Then every knee would bow before Him.

Kate found comfort in that. All the lives this land had nurtured remained here still. Now, in their dying, they nurtured the land.

She thought of Sean, her mother, and the baby; their souls singing praises; their bodies beautifully transformed to earth and flowers and the green grass. The life that once had flowed inside them now coursed through the branches of the poplar trees by the river's edge and fed the buds of the blackthorn where the lark sang.

One day, Kate knew, she would be what they had become. Since she was childless, there would be no one left to bring flowers to her grave . . . and yet she would become flowers.

Her name, Kate Donovan Garrity, would be forgotten in one generation. But her soul, named anew by Christ, would live on and on, forever. With Sean. With Mother. With the baby. She would know all those others who bloomed centuries before her own brief hour in Ballynockanor and those who would follow.

Kate neared the tall granite cross, knelt before it, and blessed herself.

She lifted her eyes toward heaven. White clouds drifted across blue skies like sailing ships. She was free here. There was no one near to stare at her scars or to whisper, "Poor Kate."

She laughed and said aloud, "God bless all here!"

The cross replied, "Thank you, Kate."

She gasped and tried to stand, but stumbled and fell.

In an instant Joseph Connor leaped out from behind the cross and grasped her arm. "Did I startle you then?" There was amusement in his eyes as he pulled her upright.

Suddenly angry and embarrassed, she pushed him away. "And what do you mean spyin' on my private prayers?"

"Pardon." He tipped his hat. "But I came here before daybreak. . . ."

"And skulkin' there behind the holy cross . . ."

"I was dozin' peacefully until you came." He sat on the base of the monument. "In other words, I was here first."

Fuming, Kate turned away from him. "Then since you've been here so long, Joseph Connor, can you not go away and leave me to myself?"

He did not reply, and when she glanced over her shoulder he was smiling and staring at her with his chin in his hand.

"Well?" she asked.

"It's a long climb from Ballynockanor. Do you come here often?"

"And why should I answer?"

"Why should you not?" His voice was gentle, as though her anger hurt him somehow.

"Why are you here?"

"Father O'Bannon bid me come. You well know Saint Brigit preached salvation to the heathen on this very spot. To come here and remember that day is to partake in the glory of the moment. The cross was put here one thousand years ago. It is weathered now, but what it must have been like to see it new and fresh from the sculptor's chisel. . . ."

She broke in. "Father O'Bannon? He bid you come here this very mornin'?"

"He did, indeed."

"But sure, he knows this is my day. . . ." Her voice trailed away. This had the smell of a plot in it, but she could not think why the old priest would arrange such an encounter.

"Your day?"

"If you must know. Once a year I come here. I was wed on this very day seven years ago. I came here to pray on that mornin'. My mother was with me. We talked about Saint Brigit freein' her mother through kindness. When I come to this place I feel close to Mother and . . . to the others."

The twinkle was instantly replaced by remorse. "Ah. Well then. I have mistakenly partaken of your most private moment. My apologies." He looked up at the towering symbol and tipped his hat again. "God bless all here."

He turned to go, and on impulse Kate blurted, "Have you eaten breakfast then, Joseph?"

He paused in his stride. "I have not."

"I bring bread to share with the birds each year. Would you stay and eat with us?"

He nodded and retraced his steps to her side. Taking her hand he said, "I am glad you came here, Kate. Friend."

The color climbed to her throat. "I . . . it was good to . . . we're all glad you've come to Ballynockanor."

"Yes."

"Martin and Mary Elizabeth are enjoyin' your teachin'. They come home full of stories. Black Francis and . . . will you be stayin' here in Ballynockanor a while longer?"

"For a time, until I leave again for Dublin. Examinations."

Their eyes locked for an instant. What was his unspoken question as he searched her face? She looked away quickly lest he see her hopeless dreams and make her confess what she felt for him.

He stepped back and jerked his thumb toward a large boulder on the slope. "I'll wait there until you have done with your prayers."

It was hungry July, the month when last year's potatoes had all been eaten and the new crop was still too small to dig. The summer sky was pregnant with thunder; the dark clouds massing over Ben Beg gravid with storm. The very air was heavy: hot and oppressive, as though waiting to be delivered of some burden. Carrying Kevin's meal in his rucksack, Martin passed unnoticed beneath the arch of the stable. Beyond, on the far side of the cobbled yard, Old Flynn, William Marlowe, and John Stone stood in a small knot. It was clear to Martin that the trio discussed serious matters. Whether the subject was the foaling of a mare, the pedigree of hounds, or the attack of the Ribbonmen against the Crown's tax collector to the north in County Mayo, Martin could not decipher. The faces of the three men were set and grim as Stone spoke and then each of the others in turn. Martin studied them a moment, deciding that the subject of mares due to foal was most likely to be the topic at hand. Al-though the murder of tax collectors in Mayo was certain to make Stone sleep poorly at night, neither the young master nor Old Flynn would give the matter a second thought. After the first flurry of antitithe activity, Connemara was quiet again. No. There was nothing on the plate these days but the thoroughbred mares.

As for poor Kevin, the foaling was entirely his life. The Marlowe estate provided Kevin no bed to sleep upon, yet they demanded he spend his nights at the stables. No bread was offered to him by his employer, yet he was commanded to grain the horses regularly. For all the required extra work at foaling time, Stone maintained that he would receive no increase in wages. The trade of labor for Donovan rent was an even exchange according to the driver. True to both his title and his surname, Driver John Stone drove all who worked close by him into the ground.

Martin could not find the reason why Kevin continued to stay. Had he hopes of taking the place of Old Flynn when the stable-master died? If that was the ambition of Kevin then he would most likely be an old man himself before that happened. The Flynn family had the reputation of living for a century and working till they dropped dead.

Martin watched the three furtively. How could he deliver Kevin's meal without being seen as he crossed into the sunlight and through the half-closed doors of the barn? On the wall near him the boy spotted a ladder leading up to the hayloft. When Flynn gestured away from the barn up over the high walls toward some pasture or other, Martin scrambled up the ladder and tumbled into the sweet soft hay of the loft.

The sound of more urgently uttered words drifted to him along with the aroma of horses. Had Stone and Flynn and the young master seen him and followed him into the stable? Martin lay still, afraid to breathe. If he was caught around the place, Stone had warned, Kevin would be discharged and all the rents would come due at once. Stone would do it too.

"There is no other way for it!" This was Kevin's own voice speaking sternly from below. Who was he talking to? A mare? Or had Stone hired another stablehand? Martin would not stir until he was certain Kevin was alone.

It was after a long moment of silence that the second voice rang clearly into the rafters. "My dearest," cried Jane Stone, "you know what sort of man my father is. If you love me you will take me away from here forever." She seemed on the edge of tears.

"But take you where, my love?"

"America."

"But I have no money."

"Please, Kevin! I do! A small inheritance left me in my grandfather's will for a dowry when I marry. I can lay hands on it easily."

Martin felt the blood drain from his face. Kevin marry the driver's underage daughter? Kevin Donovan steal away with John Stone's eldest girl and with her money too? Kevin Donovan, the son of a poor Catholic tenant farmer, elope with the Protestant daughter of the meanest man in all of Galway? It was against the law and all reason too. Kevin would be caught and hanged for sure!

Martin crept forward to peer over the rim of the loft. A shower of straw fell from the edge, but the two lovers did not notice. Fine black mares nickered and snorted, bobbing their heads over the half-doors to watch. Jane stood on her tiptoes and stroked the cheek of Kevin tenderly. Kevin gazed down into her eyes with such longing. The fool! No good could come of this!

Martin gasped aloud as Kevin pulled the Protestant into his arms and kissed her. And the dark-hearted father just outside! Just across the courtyard!

Groping through the rucksack, Martin retrieved a still-warm potato; a fine big one it was too. He took aim and pitched it hard at the passionate couple. It sailed just past Kevin's ear, but the pair gave it little notice.

"Did you hear something?" Kevin mumbled. He hushed abruptly when the girl pulled his face to hers and kissed him harder than the first time.

Martin dared not shout lest Stone and the others hear his voice and come charging to the barn.

The girl whispered, "Take me here, and then take me to America. I am your own true love, Kevin." She tugged him toward the fresh straw of a stall, and they lay down together.

And then it was too late for anything. Martin did not see John Stone, Old Flynn, and the young master enter, but suddenly there they were, gaping down in rage at Kevin and the girl.

John Stone roared something unintelligible and horrible, and Jane began to scream.

The driver kicked Kevin hard in the ribs and then in the face. He put a hobnailed boot on Kevin's neck, then drew back his other foot to smash it into Kevin's belly.

"I want to marry her!" Kevin cried through the blood that spurted from his mouth. "Sir! Sir! Please!"

The appeals were punctuated by Stone's blows as William Marlowe cheered the driver on. "Kill him, Stone!" shouted Marlowe. "You've got the right, man! Kill the bloody little peasant!"

Old Flynn backed away toward the courtyard. The old man's toothless mouth puckered in silent consternation as the scene unfolded.

"Father, no! It is my fault!" Jane threw herself around her father's knees. "I love him, Father! We're to marry!"

"I'll kill you first for the whore you are!" Stone snarled. He booted her hard, slamming her slim body into the planks of the stall. Her head snapped backward against a partition, making the horses rear and plunge. She was silent after that, too dazed to move or protest.

Stone made as if he would stomp her again. Only then did Kevin lunge upright. "Me, you may abuse," he gasped, "but you'll not lay a hand on her!" Cursing Stone for a coward and a brute, Kevin grabbed Stone's heel and hurled the driver back hard onto the floor.

The young Donovan, his face running with blood from scalp to chin, stood above the prone driver with fists clenched. His voice shook with rage. "Stand up and fight me if you be a man! You've beat Jane for the last time, John Stone!"

Stone rose slowly. The driver's hands were spread wide in the face of the fury before him. Inwardly, Martin cheered. The driver was surrendering! Then the boy saw Stone move his gaze away from Kevin's face toward something over Kevin's shoulder.

Out of the shadows behind the two combatants emerged William Marlowe. In his hands he held a turf spade drawn back like a cudgel. He swung it toward the back of Kevin's head at the same instant Martin screamed a warning.

Martin's cry came too late for Kevin to dodge out of the way, but he turned enough so that the flat side of the shovel hit him rather than the blade. The force of the blow propelled him forward to crash into a post and fall face-first into the straw.

Martin was sobbing, certain Kevin had been killed. "He's still breathing," Stone reported. "Shall I finish him off?"

"NO!" Martin shouted. The boy began hurling potatoes. One struck the spade, and another splattered at Stone's feet. Startled by the unexpected presence of a witness, the three men stared up.

"Leave him be, fool!" Marlowe growled in a low voice to Stone. "In front of the boy?" Then to Old Flynn, "Out to the road with Kevin Donovan." Eyes cold and unfeeling, William Marlowe called up to Martin. "Boy! Get down and clear off. And if I ever catch you or any other Donovan lurking about here, I'll horsewhip every inch of hide off your body!"

Martin climbed down slowly from the loft as Marlowe and Stone swung Kevin's limp body onto a manure cart. Kevin groaned and tried to raise his arm. William slapped it down.

Martin, seething with hatred for the arrogant squire of Marlowe Hall, spat on the ground beside Marlowe's boot.

Stone cuffed him hard, knocking him to the ground.

Old Flynn spoke, "Sar, he's just a child."

Stone replied, "He's an arrogant half-wit and a crippled good-for-nothing."

Martin, still glaring at William Marlowe, struggled to stand. "Brigit told me you are a good man."

Marlowe's mouth twitched into a half-smile. "Did you ask her what I was good at?"

Stone laughed.

Martin looked from one cruel face to the other, at the downcast eyes of Old Flynn, and then squarely back at Marlowe. "I know Brigit thinks well of you, maybe loves you. But how can you do this to Kevin, her brother?"

John Stone laughed aloud. "He may be the first she loved, but he will not be the last, boy. In Dublin there are many fine houses where she can get employment."

With a downward slicing movement of his hand, William Marlowe said angrily, "Mind your tongue, Stone. She has nothing to do with this."

Martin bit his lip in shame and rage. He glanced at the bloody blade of the turf spade and imagined bashing the brains of Stone and Young Marlowe.

The squire read his thoughts. "Don't try it, boy," Marlowe remarked.

"When I am a man!" Martin cried and turned away, lest the driver and the young master see he was near tears.

As Stone had done a dozen times at school, he clouted Martin as a warning for silence. "When you are a man, Martin Donovan, you will still be a cripple and an unschooled half-wit and the son of a drunkard. Now get on with you and your brother."

William Marlowe ordered Old Flynn, "Stablemaster Flynn, tomorrow I leave for Dublin, and I shall make a full report of this day to my father. If you value your position here and that of your family on their land, you will not speak a word about this in the pub or elsewhere. Now take your countrymen outside the gate and dump this . . . in the road as a warning to all here that presumption by inferiors will not be tolerated."

∽

You saw what they did to him, Mister Flynn!" Martin cried as the old man helped to lower Kevin to the side of the road.

"I saw nothin' but your brother with the driver's daughter," Flynn snapped. "And I will say no more but that Kevin Donovan is a fool. I'll bear witness to nothin' but that, boy. Now go fetch someone to help you take your brother home."

With that, Old Flynn wheeled the cart around and rattled back up the avenue toward the manor stables.

It was plain to Martin that Kevin was in a bad way. He lay on his back, unmoving. There was no color at all in his complexion, and dark, newly congealed blood stained his clothing and his face.

Martin knelt beside him and took his hand. "Kevin? Can you hear me? Oh, Kev!" The lane into Castletown was deserted, and no one was in sight. The whole world seemed abandoned as the approaching storm glowered from the west and evening neared. Kevin should be indoors, Martin thought desperately. From the look of the black clouds, there would be a downpour soon. Kevin's cheek was clammy, his body limp. He needed Kate's care. But how was Martin to get him home? How could he fetch assistance? He clung to Kevin, certain that if he ran down the highway to Watty's pub, Kevin would die. It was as though the will of Martin alone kept Kevin's soul from letting go and floating away. "Stay with me, Kevin! Oh please don't leave!"

He glanced at the crumbling stone of the gatekeeper's cottage. It was shelter, sure, but the place exuded a sense of evil deeds and an evil night and untimely death. Martin would not take Kevin inside such a place, not for a pot of hot tea nor steaming bread nor a dish of stew to warm him!

Raising his face to the sweltering heavens, Martin heard the first growl of thunder, felt the first plump drop of warm rain upon his cheek. The wind howled out of the mountains then, bending the trees toward the ground.

"Help me!" Martin cried.

Lightning flashed, splitting the sky over the peak of Knocknagussy. Thunder shook the ground as it rolled over Martin and Kevin's prone body. "Oh, God!" the child cried. "Didn't You see what they did?" The peal of the thunderclap bounced from the heights of Ben Levy and echoed down the valley of the Cornamona.

Martin tore off his coat and held it above Kevin as the torrent reached them. Rain hid his weeping, and Martin sobbed openly. "Kevin! Don't die on me now! Da would have only one son if you should die! Please, please, Kevin! Do not leave me!" A stream of salty tears coursed down the boy's cheeks, and rain drizzled from his hair.

A streak of jagged light ripped the clouds again, and thunder boomed as if to bring the mountains down. Somewhere over the Maumturks, another stroke of lightning forked, branching and splitting. There was a crash of thunder so near overhead that the ground quivered, and the puddle of rain and tears beside Kevin trembled with the impact. Kevin's eyes snapped open. He stared blankly upward into the heavens, and then his lids closed again.

Was he dead?

With a wail, Martin embraced him. He cried his brother's name again and again. He called for help and yet despaired that help would come, for his shouts were lost amid the fury of the storm. Looking wildly around, the boy saw only sheets of water sluicing down and the bleak, uncaring stones. He beat his fists on the ground, and even that, softened by the downpour, yielded no response.

Suddenly there was a firm hand on his shoulder. A calm voice said his name, spoke to him softly. The words, though gentle, cut through the roaring wind.

"Martin! Stand up, boy."

It was Joseph, with his donkey and a small cart loaded with canvas-covered turf.

Martin raised clasped hands and begged, "Help me! It's Kevin, you see! I think he's dead!"

Joseph dropped to his knees in the mud, laid a hand on Kevin's forehead, then checked the wounded man's pulse. "He's with us still, Martin." Squinting into the downpour, Joseph cast a black look toward the stone cottage as though witnessing again the death of Old Liam, the porter of the Burke house, some fifteen years before.

Martin, seeing the anger on Joseph's features, cried, "They did this to him! The two of them against one! They did this! The cowards. William Marlowe and John Stone together! I saw it all! They did this . . . beat him down and cracked his head with a turf spade and . . . and . . . now they've thrown him out to die here by the side of the road!''

Joseph nodded grimly as though he saw the full picture already. "Calm yourself, Martin. It is an old story with such as them. Kevin is a strong lad. Not like . . ." He left the thought unspoken. "He'll not die. Help me get the turf off the cart. We'll take your brother home, and you can tell me all you witnessed here.''

∾

Lightning struck thirteen times upon the treeless hills and fields surrounding Ballynockanor. Tom Donovan observed to his daughters that many a grazing moilie and lamb had met its end in such a storm.

Brigit remarked that a boy the size of Martin, head and shoulders taller than a cow, would make a fine target for the heavenly hurlers tossing down bolts of fire.

The fierceness of the storm subsided, God be thanked, but Martin still did not return by ten o'clock. Tom Donovan lit a torch and set out toward Castletown, half expecting and wholly dreading that he would find the dead body of his younger son laying by the road.

Kate paced from one window to the other, peering out into the darkness at each turning.

Brigit, who had of late spent many nights away from home, supposedly with friends, sat wearily on the creepie beside the smoky hearth. Mary Elizabeth slept soundly on a blanket at her feet. "Sure, and Martin's stone dead," Brigit announced as she gazed up at the reed cross above the door. "Mark my words. It came to me like . . ."

"Auditionin' to play Mad Molly's role as Ballynockanor doom-crier, are you then?" Kate snapped. "You'll not utter such things within Mary Elizabeth's hearin'. It will give her dreams."

"She's sleepin'." Brigit pouted at the rebuke.

"Soundly. And so is Martin, no doubt. He's stayed the night with Kevin in the stables. Or maybe taken shelter at Clooney's.

Sure, Missus Clooney with eleven of her own would not mind another mouth to feed or notice another boy in the bed."

Brigit conceded the likely probability. "If he's alive, then Da will kill the little sprat for makin' us sick with fear."

"It's Da I fear for," Kate said, glowering at Brigit. "Martin's not such a fool that he doesn't know when to come in out of the rain."

"Not like Da, then," Brigit mused and stretched like a cat beside the fire. "Da will be knockin' on every door, and they'll all think he's drunk again and has lost his way home." Rising from the four-legged stool Brigit poked idly at the embers of the single turf brick as rain renewed a fierce drumming against the panes. "It's supposed to be dry in summer. All my life I've been waiting for Ballynockanor to dry out. I'm tired of it bein' damp all year 'round. Someday I'll go off to the South of France, and there I'll never be sodden again. Someday you'll know I'm well and wed . . . and well . . . me and the husband, we'll steal away to the South of France where it doesn't always rain." She smiled.

"Be certain to write, Brigit darlin'. Till then you've cows to milk in the early light of an Irish morn."

Brigit dismissed Kate's comment with a wave and gathered Mary Elizabeth in her arms. "We're goin' to bed. Wake me when Da drags Martin through the door. I'm not wantin' to miss the slaughter."

Kate was grateful to be left alone with her worries. The wind died, and the house was silent except for the crackle of the fire. She sat upon the creepie and stared into the low flames. The loneliness of the silence pressed on her. How she envied Brigit her foolish dreams of love in faraway France!

In spite of her longing to love and be loved by a man, to bear a child, Kate had no dreams. She carried no hope beyond the four walls and the obscurity of a lifetime alone in Ballynockanor. She let her mind drift to Joseph. There was compassion in his eyes when he saw her isolation, her certainty of one day being buried and forgotten in some overgrown corner of the village churchyard.

Kate shook her head and whispered to the hissing peat fire,

"Sure, and Joseph'll make a fine priest. But for myself, Jesus, I wish I could call such a man my husband and not Father."

So there it was. Stark and unveiled, the truth of what she felt for Joseph Connor tumbled out of her mouth. The thought made her blush with shame. How could she love a man whose only goal in life was to serve God? How could even the barest hope remain alive in her that any man would ever love her in return? She glanced over her shoulder at the door to the bedroom and hoped Brigit had not overheard.

With a sigh, Kate went again to the window and peered out. A bright glow illuminated the trees beyond the hill climbed by the lane. Wind whipped the branches into frantically waving arms. Kate drew her breath in sharply as the certainty of disaster knotted her stomach. "Christ have mercy!" she cried and crossed herself.

Bobbing flames rose from behind the rim of the hill, followed by the shafts of torches, hands, arms, and heads of a mob. Two score men topped the rise and Kate clearly saw the canvas-covered cart pulled by Joseph Connor's mule as Joseph walked beside.

Who lay on it? Da or little Martin?

Kate tried to call for Brigit, but she could not speak. Groping for her cloak, she threw the door wide and ran into the night.

"Kate! Daughter!" It was the voice of Da! Was it Martin who lay dead beneath the tarp?

Then Martin darted from the group and shouted to her, "Kevin's hurt! He's dyin'! Oh Kate! Quick, make a bed beside the fire!"

Torches flickered in the yard where full thirty men of Bally-nockanor kept vigil.

Inside the Donovan cottage, Kevin lay unconscious on the long table in the center of the room. Beneath the blood and swollen blueness of his bruised face, there still was no color in his complexion. Mercifully, Mary Elizabeth remained asleep behind the closed door of the bedroom. Da and Martin were ashen. Brigit, in her nightshift, trembled and wept loudly. Martin cast a sideways glance of fury at his hysterical sister.

"Kevin! Oh, dear Kevin! He's dyin'!" Brigit sobbed, wringing her hands and falling to her knees between Da and Martin.

Joseph's eyes locked briefly on Kate's as they stripped the filthy, gore-soaked clothes from Kevin's limp body. The look seemed to validate the truth that Kevin was very near death. A three-inch laceration split flesh and muscle in a jagged line along his left side.

"From John Stone's ridin' boot," Martin volunteered bitterly. "He meant to stomp him to death."

"This will need stitchin'," Joseph said as he leaned close to examine the wound.

Brigit clenched her fists. "I'll kill who did this to poor Kevin!"

"And here," Kate blotted a flap of scalp and hair that oozed blood onto the pine planks.

"The blade of a turf spade from behind," Martin declared. "In the hands of William Marlowe."

At this revelation Brigit's keening broke off. Her eyes grew wide with disbelief. "You're lyin'! Not William!" she cried. "William could not . . . I will not believe it!"

Martin turned on her. "Have faith! Aye. All things treacherous are possible with William Marlowe, Brigit Donovan! This happened because Kev loves Jane Stone, and the girl loves him as well! Marlowe and John Stone together meant to beat him till he was dead. They near did it too!"

Da staggered back, groping for the stool. Brigit again screamed that Martin was a liar. Fingers clawlike, she lashed out at the boy. Joseph spun on his heel and grasped her wrist, twisting it hard until she cried with pain.

"Claws in, cat!" Joseph commanded. "What Martin says is true."

Brigit struggled against his grip and kicked out at him. "It can't be! Not William! He wouldn't! He loves me! Joseph! You said sometimes love could change a man!"

Kate stiffened and glared at Joseph. "You swore she never spoke to you about Marlowe!"

Joseph's brow furrowed. "It was not . . ."

Brigit sobbed, "Not William! A man can change you said! He loves me!"

Martin retorted, "William Marlowe love the likes of you?"

"It isn't true!" Brigit shook her head. "You're lyin'! You're lyin'! William loves me! He wed me!"

Da rose to his feet and staggered forward as if he would kill Brigit with his own hands. He reached for her, but Joseph stepped between them.

"Go on now, Tom," Joseph urged gently. "This will not do."

Da hesitated and stepped back. "Wed to William Marlowe? Then it is two children I lose this night," he muttered. "Christ have mercy! Better I lay in my own grave than live to see this!" Face filled with sorrow, the old man ran a trembling hand across his brow and turned away to face the wall and weep.

Brigit begged Kate, "Kate! Kate! You loved a man once! Are you dead as a stone inside? Look at me! Can you not look at me?"

Kate did not dare look up at Brigit or speak. The worst of everything she had imagined about Brigit was true. Instead she focused her rage on Joseph. "You could have helped me stop her!"

Joseph, trapped by the half-truth of Kate's accusation, pulled Brigit to her feet and held her there with her toes barely touching the floor.

"You're hurtin' me!" she whimpered.

In a barely audible voice Joseph said, "Brigit! For once in your life, think of your family! Your brother! Your da!"

"But William!" Her body shook with sobs.

"There is Kevin. He'll need washin'. Fetch the water, girl, and heat it."

She broke away, her face hard and cold as she grabbed her cloak. "I'll not stay where I am reviled! I have a husband who loves me! You'll see! We were leavin' this dreary little place soon anyway! I'll not stay here with the likes of you! Do you hear me?"

None but Martin watched as she threw back the door and charged out into the crowd of onlookers. Fighting her way through gentle, outstretched arms of friends who meant to comfort her,

Brigit ran back down the road to Castletown and vanished into the stormy night.

Kate heard the voice of Clooney call from the mob into the house, "Has Kev gone to be with Jesus, then? Is Brigit goin' to fetch Father O'Bannon?"

Through clenched teeth Kate replied, "Kevin'll not die from somethin' so slight as the blow from a Protestant turf spade, Mister Clooney!" She lowered her voice and laid her hand against Kevin's pallid cheek. "But we may all perish from the breakin' of our hearts this night."

Da ordered Martin, "Shut the door after her, lad, and wipe your feet." The old man lifted his fingers toward the dusty fiddle in salute to happier times.

Kevin opened one eye slightly and fixed a stare on Joseph. "Get him out of here. Out."

"You heard him," Kate spat.

Joseph nodded curtly, then averted his eyes from the sorrowing look of Martin. "I'll fetch Father O'Bannon," he muttered and backed out of the cottage.

The Donovan rage followed Joseph as he walked back to St. John's with Father O'Bannon. Could he have stopped Brigit? Would the girl have listened if Kate had gone after her? The cloud of unknowing was deep and dark.

"They blame me for everything."

Father O'Bannon nodded. "That they do. And I'm askin' you, Joseph Connor, did you know more than you told Kate?"

"Suspected."

"Then why did you not tell Kate what you knew? It might've prevented the girl from tragedy."

"She came to me in confidence."

"You're a priest and confessor, are you now?"

A pang of regret stabbed Joseph. "I am not. Nor likely to be."

"Sure, and you might've come to me with it."

Joseph stopped in the road and put his hand to his forehead. "I warned her."

The priest harrumphed. "And if a blind man was but one pace from a precipice, would you be sayin' for him to mind his step? You should've taken her hand and led her to safety and reason, man."

"I could've intervened."

"And why did you not?"

"I've . . . no answer for it."

"To let a soul rush to destruction and not do all you can to stop it is a grave sin. By your silence you're an accomplice."

"What can I do?" Joseph pleaded.

"Can you not see it yourself? Brigit gone. Kevin near dyin'. Tom Donovan off at the pub to drown his sorrows. That leaves poor Kate to mind the dairy and hold what family is left together. Give Kate your hands and your back and your strength. Kate'll need your help, even if she'd rather take help from a devil instead of yourself. You'll have to delay your return to seminary till next year, for I'll not recommend you to the priesthood."

Joseph was silent for a long time as he considered the consequence of his inaction. Another year of his life spent in the obscurity and turmoil of Ballynockanor. Another year living within the shadow and the threat of the men who had raped the land and the people of Connaught, who had stolen his identity and his life. At last he replied, "I'll manage the Donovan cattle and the milkin'. It's little enough. But Kate'll hate me all the same. A year may pass, but still I'll have no answer for her."

"God's voice will speak to your heart from the cloud by and by, Joseph Connor Burke. When tragedy comes . . . as it surely must now . . . none but the Holy Spirit can tell where your duty to the house of Donovan'll be."

∞ 11 ∞

Very bad fortune had indeed visited the house of Tom Donovan.
Father O'Bannon administered last rites to Kevin Donovan. Joseph Connor remained at the Donovan cottage to help with the dairy since Brigit had gone off to Dublin with William Marlowe and Kevin would certainly be in his grave very soon.

Mad Molly wandered by, peered into the window of the kitchen, cheerfully asked Kate for a cup of tea, and announced that she would be pleased indeed to come keen at Kevin's wake in sixty-two years. "I can wail and weep with the best of them," she said, "because I am fey and care not what any may think of me."

Kate thanked her and told her Kevin would not die if she and Jesus had any say in the matter.

Mad Molly then asked, "Then might I dance at your weddin', Kate darlin'?"

Kate agreed to the request and sent Martin and Mary Elizabeth to escort the woman home.

In Paddy O'Flaherty's pub, the absence and abstinence of Tom Donovan was noted by all.

Said Clooney, unslinging his flute, "Sure, and Tom Donovan is as sober as the pope. Sobriety robs him of his good humor. Me wife says he has not been so sober since the fire took his wife and the others, God rest them."

"Tom Donovan's taken the pledge," said Paddy O'Flaherty with a sad shake of his head. "You'll find him at mass every mornin' prayin' for poor Kev and foolish Brigit, who has disgraced her own and caused the murder of her brother in her defense."

The fact that Kevin's fight with Stone and Marlowe concerned his adoration of Jane Stone was not mentioned, if it was known. It seemed more noble to imagine that the battle had taken place as Kevin defended the honor of his sister.

The pub owner continued, "Tom Donovan told me himself he's sworn a solemn vow to give up the drink forever if Kev will live. Aye. Tom's wearin' the ribbon of abstinence and declared himself joined up with the movement of that teetotalin' priest, Father Mathew, who's preachin' against the evils of drink and turnin' every respectable pub in Ireland into a teahouse!" It was clear the great abstinence crusade that was sweeping the countryside concerned Paddy O'Flaherty. Tom Donovan was the first in the village to join, and he had been Paddy's best customer.

Said O'Rourke as he tuned his fiddle, "Tom'll be back to drink with us soon enough. The wife says Kevin Donovan'll not live out the week, sure, Mad Molly says she saw the face of death carved in the stones down by the river. She will not tell whose face she saw, but it must be Kevin Donovan. He'll be a dead man soon enough if his effigy is in the stones. Then when the boy is waked and buried, Tom'll be back to raise his glass with us and drink a toast to the demise of John Stone. Tom'll have blood in his eye, and he'll call upon us all to curse the man who killed his son and stole his pretty young daughter away to Dublin. And I for one shall join him!"

At this, a score of fists lifted pints in a toast that retribution would come upon John Stone and William Marlowe.

A moody reverie passed over the group. Clooney and O'Rourke struck up a sad song:

> *Oh, Brigit Donovan, ye were your father's dar-*
> *lin',*
> *Ye were his looking glass from night till mornin';*

He'd rather have ye home without one farthin',
Than see ye ill-wed with big house and garden.

∽

The squirt of milk into the pail made a steady *ting-ting-ting*. Joseph's forehead pressed against the cow's buff hide, and he spoke low, gentling words. Ever since the terrible night of Kevin's beating and Brigit's flight, none of the Donovan cattle had given as much milk as before. " 'Tis the tautness in air about here," Tom Donovan remarked. "Cows sense it. Makes the milk not let down, and it sours faster too."

For days as Joseph entered the barn he made an effort to stop his agitated thoughts. He set aside the clamor in his heart about Kate's animosity toward him, as best he was able, and talked kindly to the cows. At first nothing seemed to make any difference, and Joseph wondered if causing the cows to go dry was one more piece of misfortune that he was bringing down on the Donovans.

Then, just that very morning, he had recognized his worry about the milk as one more anxiety. Laughing at himself, he spoke to the moilie of how green and rich was the grass of summer and how pleasant it was under the shade of the trees on the inch. To his delight, that was the exact moment when the milk began to flow in its usual abundance, frothing into the bucket.

An orange tabby cat sat against the stone wall watching. Joseph deliberately missed the pail with the next two squirts, spraying the cat's face. The tabby did not even jump back; it was content to lick its whiskers as if merely accepting its proper portion.

Joseph chuckled. "Nought to spare the last few days, eh, puss? But I think it'll come right now."

From the doorway Mary Elizabeth's reproving voice scolded, " 'Tisn't right to laugh when Kev may die. 'Tis no time for fun."

Looking over his shoulder as he finished stripping the milk, Joseph said, "I'm sorry if I offended you, Mary Elizabeth." He reflected that the girl had been unusually solemn ever since that terrible night. She had gone to sleep with her world spinning in its usual orbit and awakened to an unconscious, seriously wounded brother and a vanished sister. The tension felt by the cows had also come from the heart of this small child.

Abruptly the little girl asked, "*Is* Kev gonna die? His candle went out, y'see." The fear in her words settled around her tiny shoulders like a dark cloud.

On the bright, sunlit summer afternoon, it took Joseph a moment to bring up the recollection of just what candle was meant. A night at a gathering in the Donovan home, when only Kevin was away, came to mind. "Ah," he said, comprehension spreading through him, "Saint Brigit's eve. The candle blew out, Mary Elizabeth. That's all."

The girl's face, already dark with worry, gathered into a frown. The explanation was not good enough. Mary Elizabeth was not content to be told to forget an old superstition. She was afraid that her brother would die and distressed because she could think of nothing she could do to aid him.

Rising from the milking stool, Joseph lifted the pail of milk and set it in the cooling trough out of reach of the cat. Then he gathered the little girl into an embrace and hoisted her to chest height. "Has Father O'Bannon given you this verse to learn: *Perfect love casts out fear?*"

"Aye," she said.

"Know this, then," Joseph said kindly. "Hate is not the opposite of love. Fear is. But God's love is like a warm cloak. We are tenderly folded in it . . . always, no matter what we see around us . . . so we can stop bein' afraid. Do you understand what I'm sayin'?"

Mary Elizabeth nodded.

"Run on, then. Whisper to Kev that you love and pray for him . . . he'll hear, even if he gives no sign."

∾

Kate lay on her bed in the darkness and listened to the murmuring of her father and Joseph as they smoked their pipes beside the hearth. What a terrible contradiction his daily nearness brought to her heart. Openly she swore her hate for him, and yet how grateful she was that Joseph had stayed. What comfort it was each morning to hear the milk pinging in his milk bucket and listen to his gentle voice croon to the moilies in the barn. In spite of her fury that he might have stopped Brigit from ruin by a word, there was a melody in his presence that she had not heard or felt since Sean.

Moonlight streamed in through the window and puddled on the foot of Mary Elizabeth's cot. The glow illuminated the smooth unmussed blanket on Brigit's bed. Kate wondered about her. Was she walking beneath the stars in the South of France with William Marlowe? Was she pretending she had not come from Ballynocka-nor? Was she daily forgetting those who loved her and who held up the mirror of truth for her to see her own heart? Ah, but Brigit had always been one to turn away from the soul's looking glass. Could Joseph have stopped her indeed? Could anyone?

"Well, she's gone from us then," Tom Donovan said, sighing. "As surely as though it was herself who died that terrible night. Brigit'll not be comin' back. I had hopes she'd marry Clooney's son, Barry. He's a fine boy and stands to inherit three acres and a cottage . . . I hoped . . . grandchildren to comfort me in me old age. Kate will never marry again or have a child to call her own. And then there's Kev. When I was his age I held Kevin in the crook of me arm. As my father cradled me. And in that moment I knew what love my da must've had for me. Our children teach us about our parents, do they not? I had hopes that Kevin would have sons. Then he'd know me well, and perhaps his judgment of me would soften some. By now I should have had a brace of Kate's little skogars climbing onto me knee. As for the youngest son, Martin, who can say? The fire may have made him a bachelor. Is there a girl in Ballynockanor who would wed a boy who can't dance? And little Mary Elizabeth? I'm sure to be gone by the time she's old enough to marry."

"You speak as if it is settled."

"Which?"

"That Brigit will never come home. Kevin will die. Kate never marry. No grandchildren. And all the rest of it."

"Almost certain."

"Whatever remains unsure leaves an empty space. Uncertainty makes room for faith to perch on the ledge and chirp hope into our ears."

"True. True," Da conceded. "Very wise indeed. You'll make a fine priest, Joseph Connor. You'll make a fine father." A long silence followed. The scent of tobacco smoke wafted in to Kate. Then Da spoke again. "Down at Paddy O'Flaherty's pub they're layin' odds on when Kevin'll die."

Joseph laughed. An odd response to such a bitter comment, Kate thought.

Lightly, Joseph replied, "I've taken the wager myself. Ten to one in Kevin's case the death knell will toll for him in fifty years or so. He's too angry to die. Mad Molly wagered on sixty-two years. She knows more than she tells, that one. It's been a week since William Marlowe mistook Kevin's brains for a turf bog. Kevin surprises every gossip in the county by livin'." Joseph's voice was tinged with humor.

"Sure, and if he lives or dies? Will I ever be able to forgive the daughter who married a man who'd kill her own brother?" Tom Donovan said bitterly. "Brigit is lost to me." Further silence. "Is she a Protestant, do you think? She did not say if it was priest or vicar who wed her to that fellow. I suppose she must be a Protestant, or the marriage would be outside the law."

Again there was silent consideration of this fact. Joseph did not reply at all, and at last Da yawned and said the pipe was finished and that he must be off to bed.

Kate listened to the rustle of Joseph making up his blanket beside the fire, taking off his boots and cords, washing his face, and kneeling on the hard floor. The whisper of his prayers, yielding the day and the night and tomorrow to God, stirred her. She wished she could kneel beside him, hear his words, and know what longings he shared only with heaven. "Amen."

She coughed once, wanting him to know she was still awake.

"Kate?" he questioned in a hushed voice. "Are y'not sleepin' then, girl?"

"That I am not," she replied, pulling the covers tight beneath her chin as his footstep neared the doorway. Light shone behind him, and his shadow hovered on the wall above her bed. She touched the outline of his hand where it rested on the white plaster and longed for him to come and sit beside her. The thought warmed her inside.

"Have your da and I kept you awake with our pipes?"

" 'Tis a comfort to hear him." Her voice trembled. Did he notice? "Da has not talked so much since Mother left. When I was a child, I used to drift off to sleep on the wings of their words."

"I can't sleep a'tall myself. If I throw my trousers on, could you use a cup of tea and a bit of a chat by the fire then?"

Unbidden, images of Sean came to her. How long had it been since she sat beside a strong man and shared the news of an ordinary day over a cup of tea? How long had it been since Sean had reached across and pulled her to the floor and kissed her as the peat fire crackled and the tea got cold? She dreamed about Sean's calloused hands touching the softness of her body. But tonight the memory of his face was replaced with the image of Joseph smiling down at her, his kind blue eyes hardening in a moment of desire.

The sudden hunger she felt startled her. The fierceness of her longing was frightening. How long had it been since she wanted any man to make love to her? It had been five years since Sean had been lost in the flames, and never did she think of anyone but him. Yet now! She longed for the passion of a man who knelt at night beside his bed and prayed as fervently as if he were already a priest. She loved the man she hated!

Kate jerked her fingers back from Joseph's shadow as though the cool white plaster was hot iron. Crossing herself she muttered, "God forgive me!"

"Kate?" he whispered louder. "Did you hear me?"

She swallowed hard, fighting to find her breath. "The mornin' will come early," she said flatly. "I'll be needin' my sleep. But I thank you for the thought."

The expectancy in the shadow relaxed. Shoulders sagged as he stepped back. Had she disappointed him?

"Sure, and it is gettin' late. Well then? In the mornin' . . . Kate, will you ever forgive me?"

She hesitated. To forgive him would mean yielding to love. "I cannot," she blurted. What she meant to say was that she must not.

He snuffed the candle out. She closed her eyes in the darkness and strained to hear his every move and sigh. She could not sleep until the even cadence of his breathing assured her he dreamed of cathedrals and cassocks and hymns and homilies. She was safe.

∽

To the amazement of all in Ballynockanor, Kevin Donovan did not die. Weeks passed, and he sat up in bed to hold the cup of broth himself. But it was remarked that he seldom spoke, not even to curse the men who had beat him and stolen his sister away.

When Joseph Connor came into the house to sup, Kevin turned his face to the wall. No matter that Joseph had found him and carted him home. No matter that Joseph did the milking and the mucking out and drove the herd to and from the pastures morning and evening. Kevin still thought him a traitor and an informer.

As for Kate, she hated Joseph in spite of his kindness to the family. If Father O'Bannon had not ordered her to accept his charity, she would not have let him set a foot on the land or lay a hand on the milk cows. She was heard to say to her father one morning, "Brigit would still be with us if it weren't for him."

The heart of Tom Donovan, however, was kindly to Joseph. Sobriety and the long workdays of summer had returned Tom to his former self, the self that had been before the fire.

Da labored long and hard and forsook the congenial gatherings of his neighbors at the pub. He went to church each morning to pray for Kevin and the children who remained to him. As for Brigit, he would not tolerate the mention of her name. She was, he said to Father O'Bannon, dead to the House of Donovan. Nor did any word of her come from Dublin.

The summer was passing. There were crops to be won and turf to be stacked against the coming winter chill. The grass was tall and dry enough for haying. All these things kept Tom Donovan busy, with Joseph Connor often at his side.

On August Quarter Day, when the Protestant tithe next came due, Driver John Stone and Constable Carroll passed by the Donovan house without stopping. Some said this boon was given because of Brigit and young William Marlowe. (It was more likely that after the attempted rape of Kate and the beating of Kevin, both men expected to be killed the moment they stepped onto Donovan land.)

Whatever the true reason for the favor, Tom Donovan would have none of it. Before daybreak Tom counted out the precious coins and walked with blackthorn stick in hand to the cottage of John Stone. He pounded on the doorpost with a fury to wake the dead and the Stones. John Stone, trembling at the appearance of Tom Donovan and without the constable to protect him, sent his wife to the door.

Tom hurled the pouch into the house. "Count it, you spawn! Every good man in Ballynockanor has paid the tithe with his blood and sweat. The House of Donovan'll take no charity from the devil!" Demanding a receipt for the coin, Tom cried loudly that everyone knew the driver was a thief and a liar who collected and kept more than was due.

Tom returned to the milking and said quietly to Joseph, "Know this: Kevin and Kate hate you, though Mary Elizabeth and Martin think you're a saint. Father O'Bannon says you'll not be returnin' to seminary because of all this. But I hold nothin' against you. The girl was bad seed, a wild thing of the forest, though I called her my darlin' colleen."

Tom's forgiveness streamed into Joseph like rich milk into the bucket. "I'm forever in your debt, Tom Donovan."

"You're a good man, Joseph Connor. Whatever debt you think you owe me and mine is canceled. Kevin'll be back to work in another month, and I told Father O'Bannon I'll not be keepin' you from your callin'." Tom peered over the back of a cow. "Unless, that is, you hear another voice callin' you to stay among us." He slapped the rump of the moilie. "This little heifer's got good hips for bearin' young. Aye. If she's like her mother was, she's willin' and eager as well. Well suited for all the joys of holy union, if you take my meanin'."

Upon this not-so-veiled reference to Kate, Joseph ducked his head and pulled the teats with such vigor that the sweet moilie lowed her resentment and stamped her hind foot.

"You said it yourself, Tom. She hates me."

"That's a woman for you. Many's the girl hates the man she loves." Tom harrumphed. "Take this little cow, for instance. She's left out to pasture too long, her udder so full of milk that she's in perfect agony with it. Likely to kick your head off, she is, unless she's in the stanchion. Ah, but the gratitude in her heart the minute a gentle hand is on the teats and the milkin' begins. What I'm sayin' is . . . you have my permission to change her mind if it can be changed. That is, unless you've a mind to go back to Dublin."

In this way, official permission was given by the father for Joseph Connor to at least consider the possibility of a different calling.

Clean nightshirts and crisp bed linen flapped on the clothesline that was strung from the limb of an oak to the nail on the tall post in the Donovan yard. In the window box Kate's flowers shone bright reds and yellows against the white limewash of the house. The lilac tree was laden with purple blossoms as heavy as clusters of grapes. The garden was in bloom. Myriad shades of green on hill and pasture sharpened or paled with every passing cloud.

Kate came out of the house with the laundry basket on her hip. She was barefoot, and her dress was red like the flowers.

At his first sight of her, Joseph stopped in his tracks within the cool darkness of the barn. She could not see him as he watched her. He longed to speak with her, but could not.

There was a rhythm to the movement of her work. Each article of clothing floated upward from the line, was pulled to her for a swift, crisp fold, and then plunged into the basket on the ground. Her body swayed, and a mischievous nightshirt molded itself to her shape. Matching voice to motion she sang softly in the Gaelic, *"A Athair atái . . ."*

Light glistened in her plaited hair.

Joseph sang with her,

> *Father dwelling in light on high*
> *When you look down on Magdalen,*
> *The flames of love you wake in her*
> *And make soft a heart once frozen.*

Kate paused and raised her face as though she had heard the echo of his voice. "Martin!" she called. "Come help me with the foldin'."

But Martin was long gone, sent to the far pasture by his father.

Joseph stepped into the light. "He's gone with your da, then. Can I help?"

The faint smile on her lips vanished. "I'll manage, thank you kindly."

"You were singin' in the Gaelic."

"And why shouldn't I, then?"

He strode quickly to her and, without waiting for permission, took the sheet from the line. "No reason a'tall. A lovely tune." He bowed slightly and hummed a bar. "I'm good for more than milkin'."

"Laundry's women's work."

"Too complicated, is it?" Without relinquishing his grasp, he extended two corners of the fabric to her. The clean scent of the linen mixed with the aroma of the lilacs.

"I'll finish myself, if you don't mind."

Joseph grinned. "Father O'Bannon would not be pleased that you deny me opportunity to do penance." The cloth stretched between them.

"I only wish you would do it elsewhere," she said wearily as she folded the sheet, bringing her ruined hand atop the sound one.

Her rebuke dimmed his smile. "Sure, and I understand how you feel." When they stepped toward one another, their fingers touched.

They stood close with the sheet between them. Now the scents of lilac and soap were forgotten by Joseph as the fragrance of the warm sun on Kate's hair washed over him. He searched her face for some sign of compassion. "Can you not forgive me, Kate? I meant no harm."

How he wanted to pull her to him, hold her and tell her he loved her, that he had always loved her. His breath quickened at her nearness. What would happen if he crushed her to his chest and pressed his mouth against her lips?

Kate's voice trembled as she replied, "Are you finishin' the foldin' then, or am I?"

He grasped her fingers, anxious for the moment to stay unbroken. "I'm askin' your forgiveness, Kate. Will you not let it go?"

Lowering her head, she whispered, "It isn't you. Not you! It's myself I can't forgive. If I had been a better sister to her . . ."

"You were mother and father and sister, dear Kate. How could you have been more? She wouldn't have it, that's all. She wouldn't!" He moved half a pace nearer. What if he tore the sheet aside and grabbed her shoulders?

Tears brimmed in Kate's eyes. Her anger returned. "You see everythin'. Everythin'! It's too much for a girl!" She wrested her ruined hand from him, released the cloth, and backed away. "I think you're gone, and when I turn 'round you're lookin' at me with pity in your eyes! It's more'n I can bear, that's all."

"Not pity, Kate! Never that! I want . . . I want you . . . to see me!"

She stumbled from him. "I won't hear it! Not another word, Joseph. There can never be more between us than . . . that bed-sheet!"

"I was hopin' there'd be less between us one day."

She gasped and, lunging forward, slapped him hard across the face. "Do you think all Donovan women are fools like Brigit?"

"I'd melt the ice that binds your heart if I could," he pleaded.

"There's no sun hot enough could warm me to the likes of you!"

Her rebuke was like a second blow. He nodded, slowly folded the bed linen, and placed it in the basket. "Sure, and I'll be goin' back to Dublin when Kevin is well enough and Father O'Bannon gives me permission."

∞

A single turf brick smoldered moodily on Father O'Bannon's hearth. On the sideboard that served him as table and desk a single candle likewise flickered, a sulky spiral of smoke trailing upward.

On a creepie between candle and fireplace sat Joseph, his head sunk in his hands. "And so I must return to Dublin, you see."

"No, I do *not* see," Father O'Bannon replied sternly. "You're givin' up and runnin' away, then?"

If Joseph was surprised at the rebuke in his friend's tone, it still did not make him lift his eyes. "It is the first day of September. I've been here nine months, and I've failed in all three things I came here to do," he explained. "I've failed Daniel. The young men will not listen to me, do not even trust me. Kevin Donovan says openly that I am an informer."

The priest nodded to himself. "Go on."

Shrugging, Joseph continued, "Mad Molly is no help. . . . I cannot break through the walls in the labyrinth of her mind. I will never regain my inheritance without proof, and I'll never find it if Molly holds the only clue."

"Never is a long time," Father O'Bannon murmured. There was a long pause, and it seemed that Joseph had finished speaking, but the priest was not about to let the young man off that easily. "And your third horrid failure," he prodded. "What of that?"

At last Joseph raised his face from his hands. Even so, he stared at the shimmering candle flame and did not look at his friend. "I am not fit for seminary. I have lost my vocation," he said at last. "I will never be a priest."

"Even so?"

Joseph shook his head. "I failed Brigit Donovan when she turned to me. I have brought shame and sorrow to the House of Donovan. And through it all, I have harbored hatred in my heart for the Marlowes."

"And yet none of this touches upon the whole problem, I'm thinkin'."

"And . . . I love Kate Donovan. I have tried to stop thinkin' about her, but I . . ."

To Joseph's amazement, Father O'Bannon broke into this painful confession with a question. "And which is the stronger in you? The hatred or the love?"

The words leaped from the young man's mouth without an instant's reflection. "If I could take Kate away from here with me, I would never give another thought to the Marlowes or my inheritance . . . but she will never have me."

Unseen by Joseph, the good father smiled gently. "Now hear me, Joseph Connor Burke," he said quietly. "Hatred is a sin akin to murder . . . but love is from God and given to men as a light in the darkness of this world. You must not equate one with the other. You have made a mistake, but it is not what you think. You came to Galway believin' your callin' to the priesthood was settled . . . but perhaps that was not why God brought you here at all. He . . ."

Whatever else Father O'Bannon was going to add was interrupted by a clatter of hooves and wheels and then a voice calling the priest's name. He rose to see to it and returned a moment later with a letter. With a whistle and a pop of the whip, the carriage drove off.

"The Galway mail coach with a letter for me," he said with alarm. "The reinsman, good Catholic that he is, brought it up the road from town. All the way from Dublin, he says, marked 'urgent.' Here boy," he continued, thrusting the folded pane of pale blue paper into Joseph's hands. "You can read it faster than I can locate my spectacles. Who is it from?"

Scanning to the bottom of the single sheet Joseph made out the name Jane Stone. " 'Tis from the driver's daughter," he answered.

"Go on, go on! Read it and tell me what it says!"

"She says she heard her father and Young Marlowe talkin'. Kevin must get away at once, or they will do somethin' to him. She says they did not think he would survive the beatin', and now she is afraid for his freedom or even his life."

"Whist, man!" Father O'Bannon spouted, grabbing Joseph by the elbow and pulling him to his feet. "If we have received the word, then so might Constable Carroll. No time to lose. Like your eyesight, your legs are younger than mine. Run to the Donovans and warn them!"

"There's more," Joseph said. "About Brigit."

"Later!" the priest ordered, shoving Joseph toward the doorway. "No time to lose."

Since Joseph was calling Kate's name from the time the Donovan cottage first came into sight, he was not surprised that the door opened even before his fist had pounded on the panels. Kate herself appeared, Mary Elizabeth beneath her arm. Tom Donovan and Martin came from the barn.

There was an instant, just the barest flash, when Joseph saw something on Kate's face like pleasure at the sight of him. This was quickly submerged, to be replaced by carefully practiced indifference. "What d'ya want, then?" she asked coldly.

"Where's Kevin?" Joseph said urgently, catching his breath. "Is he able to travel?"

From the men's end of the house Kevin called, "Well enough if there's need? Why should I?" When Kevin emerged from the shadows, Joseph could see that he was dressed, except for his boots. He still looked pale, but healthy.

Swiftly, Joseph explained about the letter. "You must go at once," he concluded.

Kevin was belligerent. "Jane is a true heart to warn me so," he said. "But unlike others I could name, I will be no coward and run away from a fight. We did nought wrong. I'll face Marlowe and Stone and any others they choose to send. Better still, I'll get an ax and take the battle to them first!" Kevin declared.

"Think, man!" Joseph warned. "Many a one has been arrested on a trumped-up charge and then come to a regrettable *accident* . . . a fatal one . . . without ever seein' sunlight again. Jane has cut herself off forever from her family by warnin' you. Would you have her sacrifice go for nothin'?"

"Shall I bring the ax from the barn, Kev?" Mary Elizabeth piped. "Will we need the spades too?"

"Hush," Kate said to her little sister, then, "Kev . . . y'must do as he says and go."

"What?" Kevin blustered.

"Remember what came upon the Mulrooneys," Kate implored. "Would y'have Mary Elizabeth and Martin turned out on the road? If you do anythin' other than leave, they will find a pretext for tossin' the cottage. Da, tell him so."

Martin said stoutly, "I'll help y'fight them, Kev."

Joseph noted in Kevin's eyes that Martin's remark swung the balance. Grudgingly Kevin said, "Kate's right, Martin. I must go. Da," he added, "do you say so as well?"

"Aye," Tom Donovan said slowly. "For now. Many a man of honor has taken to the hills at need. It is the wisest course. Gather your things."

"I'll take you to Dublin," Joseph offered. "I have friends there who . . ."

Kevin turned his back abruptly. "I thank you for bringin' the word," he said, "but I want nothin' more from the likes of you."

"But Brigit is in Dublin!" Joseph asserted, anxious to get to the second part of the message.

"I'll not have that . . . I'll not have her name mentioned in this house," Tom Donovan commanded.

"Da," Kate said anxiously, "take Martin and Mary Elizabeth and bring the knapsack and a blanket from the barn. Kev should away at once."

Understanding crossed Tom Donovan's face. "Come then," he said to the younger children. To Kate he remarked, "Be quick about it."

As soon as they were out of earshot, Kate hissed, "What about Brigit?"

"Jane says Marlowe did take her to France," Joseph reported, holding up the letter. Kevin snatched it from Joseph's fingers and stuffed it into the front of his shirt. Then he sat down to pull on his boots as Joseph continued, "They are back in Dublin now."

"Livin' as man and wife?" Kate asked dubiously.

"No," Joseph answered, shaking his head sadly. "Jane says he keeps her . . . as his mistress. He has already begun to tire of her, Jane says, and boasts about Dublin how he tricked her with a fake priest."

"You did this," Kate spat, seething with anger. "She is ruined, and it is your fault! One word from you, and I could have stopped it . . . saved her."

"Aye," Kevin agreed, looking fiercely into Joseph's eyes. "Marlowe deserves to die. I will meet him again, that much is certain."

Martin and Mary Elizabeth accompanied Joseph to the far end of Ballynockanor. It was the place where the Galway mail coach picked up passengers, but Joseph would be returning to Dublin the way he arrived: on foot, leading his donkey.

It was a spot to say good-bye; a boundary between those whose lives were wrapped up in Ballynockanor and the wider world beyond. It was a place of sorrow.

"But who will be our teacher?" Mary Elizabeth protested for the hundredth time. "We can't go back to school in Castletown, we just can't!"

"I'm sorry," Joseph apologized. "But I must go. God provided me as a teacher. He'll provide another. There are things I have to do far away from here."

"But you will be returnin' to be our teacher again, won't you?"

Joseph caught a look from Martin that said now was not the time for complete honesty. Martin knew that Joseph might never be coming back to Connemara. He also knew that with Kevin gone and Brigit gone and Kate so cross all the time, Mary Elizabeth's world had unraveled; his little sister was near to tears and snuffling into her sleeve.

Kneeling, Joseph took Mary Elizabeth by the elbows and drew her over to him. "Our lives are all in the palm of God's hand," he said. "And there is no better place to be. You are a fine student,

Mary Elizabeth, and any teacher will be proud to have you. Perhaps you will yourself be a teacher some day."

The little girl stopped sniffing and looked up. "Me?" she asked doubtfully. "Have all that book-learnin' in my head?" She made it sound as if she had been presented a bushel basket of potatoes and told to eat them all at one sitting.

Joseph nodded solemnly. "Aye, and your brother here is a scholar as well. You must both of you aid your next teacher, whoever it is. Do you promise?" Mary Elizabeth nodded. "Good," Joseph affirmed, giving her a hug. "Now it is a solemn vow between us." Joseph stood then as the coach swung into sight a half mile down the road. It was like a signal that the time of departure had come.

Martin stepped forward and thrust out his hand manfully. "I thank you for all you have done," he said. "I know sister Kate blames you for what happened with Brigit, but she does not mean the half of what she says."

There was an uncomfortable tightening in Joseph's throat. He had told himself that he would be glad to go, be relieved to get back to Dublin . . . but it was not so. What an unanswerable riddle: How could it be impossible to stay and yet so painful to depart? "Thank you, Martin. And there is somethin' I want you to do for me. I know you are takin' food to Kevin." Martin backed up a step and protested, and Joseph hurried to reassure him. "It's all right, lad. In fact, I'm glad of it. But here is what I need." The coach swirled past in a rush of late-summer dust and warm air. "If there comes any news, anything of importance about Kevin, don't be afraid to tell Father O'Bannon. He'll know how to get word to me."

12

Torrents of rain sluiced off the leads of the Dublin rooftops. Autumn wind swept in fitful gusts along the dark and deserted streets of College Green.

Ten days' walk from Ballynockanor had brought Joseph to the door of a stately old mansion known as Daly's Club House. Years before, the building had served as the exclusive retreat of members of the Irish Parliament. Since the dissolution of the national legislature, Daly's had fallen on hard times: it was now the gambling club and bordello of choice for many of the finest young gentry in Dublin.

Joseph knew William Marlowe would be among them.

The windows blazed with light. Above the drumming of rain, lively music and laughter emanated from the building. A doorman in red livery stood beneath the dripping eves.

Tying his donkey to the post, Joseph climbed the steps.

"Get on with you!" warned the porter, not moving from his shelter. "You'll not be tyin' up your bloody beast in front of Daly's!"

Joseph kept coming. "I've traveled long and far, man."

"I care not how long nor far you've traveled. Sure, and Daly's is not a public house. Be off with you!"

A steady stream of water ran from the brim of Joseph's hat. He grasped the lapel of the doorman's greatcoat and jerked the man into the rain. He growled, "I am Joseph Connor Burke, son and heir of The Burke of Connaught, nephew of Lord Marlowe of Castletown, first cousin of Viscount William Marlowe. My cousin frequents this establishment and is within tonight. I've traveled fifteen years to see this hour. Now tell my cousin I have come to discuss family matters."

Shaken by the menacing tone of Joseph's voice, the doorman nodded fearfully and opened the door to let Joseph pass into the warmth of the foyer. The entry was small and illuminated by the light from a coal fire that crackled on the hearth.

Joseph pulled off his gloves and stretched his aching hands to the blaze as the servant backed toward the paneled dining room beyond.

"Be quick about it," Joseph said menacingly and turned to stare into the flames.

Ten days of walking through the fierce cold from Ballynockanor had brought Joseph to a decision. He would reveal himself to the Marlowes, confront them with the truth that the son of The Burke was living and well. That would be enough to keep them looking over their shoulders for a while. And he would find Brigit Donovan. Joseph had not thought what would happen beyond that.

He felt, rather than heard, the approach of his cousin at his back.

There was amusement in William's whiskey-soaked voice. His words were thick. "Billy tells me a ghost has come to haunt me."

Not turning to face him, Joseph replied, "Not a ghost, William. Your cousin, Connor Burke. Do you not remember?"

William laughed. "He's long dead, and you're stinking up my club."

"Do you not remember the afternoon by the river, William? You slipped on the stone and fell in? Like to drown you were and called out to me to save you. Then I went in after and . . ."

William drew back in horror. "Who are you?"

"I sliced my right hand open on the rock. Molly Fahey stitched it up with horsehair from the black hunter whilst Liam played his flute in the kitchen. Remember, William?"

"Connor Burke was stolen away by a robber! He drowned in the river Christmas Eve! Fifteen years ago!"

Joseph tugged the brim of his hat lower over his eyes and turned to face his cousin. "Don't you know me, William? It was 'Morrison's Jig' Liam was playin' whilst the old woman darned my hand like a sock. You begged us not to tell your father how I came by the wound. And we swore we would not."

William's skin was ashen in the firelight. His mouth worked like a fish out of water. He croaked, "Who told you this?"

Stretching out his right hand toward the light of the fire, Joseph traced the scar across his palm. "Sure, and you remember then?"

"From the grave . . . no . . . take off your hat, man. You're all in shadow."

Joseph shook his head slowly from side to side as from his pocket he pulled a scrap of fabric embroidered with the letter *M*. Tossing it at William he said, "Return this to your father with my compliments. I am no shadow . . . tell him I am no dream. And as for you? You have stolen somethin' not your own."

"It was my father!" William cried. "I had nothing to do with the estate."

" 'Tisn't land I'm meanin'."

"What do you want from me?"

"Where is Brigit Donovan?"

"Brigit!" The girl's name exploded in derision from his lips. "Brigit Donovan, is it!" Fury replaced fear. William strode forward and grabbed the hat from Joseph's head. "You! Priest! Hedge schoolteacher!" Snatching up the iron fire poker, he raised it to strike. "Cousin Connor, are you? That old hag Molly told you of Connor Burke!" He took a swing at Joseph's head and missed. "Get out of here! Impostor! I'll have you arrested, convicted, and rotting in prison before daybreak."

William raised the iron to strike again. Joseph caught his wrist and pushed him back, pinning him to the wall. He threatened, "It's Brigit Donovan I've come for, Cousin. Now where is she? Where do you keep the girl?"

Beads of sweat formed on William's brow. His eyes were wild. "Want her, do you?" He gasped as Joseph gripped harder and the poker fell clattering to the floor.

"What have you done with her, Cousin?"

"You . . . want her?"

"That I do."

"Like every man in Dublin."

"Brigit Donovan, if you please."

"A whore. At The Flattery. Well liked by all, I hear." He managed a smile that dissolved into a grimace of pain as Joseph twisted the wrist back and brought William to his knees.

But Father! The hedge schoolteacher! It is Connor Burke indeed!" William was trembling as he paced the length of his father's bedroom and back.

Old Marlowe's nightcap was askew, and his face fixed in a permanent scowl at William's midnight disruption of his sleep. "You're drunk again! Dreaming of ghosts. Connor Burke fell through the ice of the Cornamona and died, saving me a lot of trouble!"

William, ashen in the dim firelight, shook his head slowly from side to side. "This is no ghost. He knew things about my childhood no one could know."

"Gossip gleaned from the madwoman."

"But think of his face. His eyes! Have you not seen them looking down at you from that portrait? Connor's mother! Think of his face! The features are the same as hers! And the pillowcase!"

The old man frowned and slumped back against his pillows. He pressed his hand against his forehead as the similarities between Joseph Connor and the beloved portrait tore away his skepticism. The possibility small Connor had not perished after all made him uneasy at first and then defensive. "And what does it matter who the rogue is? The estates of The Burke passed to me as they will pass to you. Nothing left behind by The Burke documented Connor's legitimacy. There were no documents recognizing the child as heir. We made certain of it."

"But why has he come forward now?"

"To frighten us. You. To intimidate you into giving him some portion when I am gone, perhaps. Or perhaps out of vengeance?"

"Vengeance for what?"

Old Marlowe was silent. He stared at the pendulum of the wall clock for a long time as William paced the room.

"Be still!" Old Marlowe spat. "Look at you! Coward! Connor Burke is a bastard in the eyes of the law! He cannot legally cause you a moment of unrest."

"He could kill me."

The words disgusted Old Marlowe. "You're worthless to everything but whoring and gambling!"

"He came to find the Donovan girl."

"Did he, now? Then pass her along to him. You've broken her in, I dare say."

"When he finds her . . . I cannot say what lengths he will go to if he takes it in his mind to avenge her."

"Fool! Coward! That's why you learned to use a pistol! Get back to Galway and be what I made you!"

The Flattery was a small, inexpensive bordello near Ha'penny Bridge over the Liffy River. Frequented by students from Trinity College, it had earned its name from the fawning praise with which the women of the house lifted the spirits of the visitors.

Brigit, with her wild and beautiful red hair, had been the most requested prostitute at The Flattery since her arrival.

"I've come t'take her home again," Joseph explained to the heavyset woman with a grotesquely painted face who ran the establishment.

"Beautiful, she was," sighed the madam to Joseph. "The lads'd come and keep that'n busy all night. But her heart weren't in her work. Nay. Not a'tall. In the mornin's, b'fore dawn, she'd leave the house, and I half expected she'd throw herself from Ha'penny Bridge. Then she'd come back 'round nine o'clock of a mornin' to sleep like the rest of 'em. Then one day last week she didn't come back."

"Where is she?"

"That kind don't leave a forwardin' address."

"But you must have some idea where she'd go."

"Her lover are ye, man?"

Joseph shook her head. "A friend of the family come to fetch her home if I can."

Satisfied with his explanation, she studied her nails and said in an instructive tone, "Well then. As you ain't attached, I'll tell you what I think straight out. Best if you never find her the condition she was in. Her belly was round like a little melon last I seen her, if you take my meanin'. Quite far along she were. Six months at least I'd say. Maybe more. And I'd have to put her and the brat out sooner or later. We'll have no babes here at The Flattery. Dampens the enthusiasm of the guests. Distracts my girls. Ruins their bosoms as well." At this she gave a broad wink and a nod. "Sure, and Brigit Donovan's at bottom of River Liffy most likely. Walkin' dead she was. Longin' to die. The gentleman wag what broke her inta this life broke her heart as well. She's done herself in and no doubt will pop up and float out to sea soon. Best for her and the child. Let it go, sir, if you have a heart. She'll not be wantin' to be found, even if she be alive."

The weeks that had passed since Jane Stone's warning letter had been a flurry of departures and arrivals in Connemara: Kevin catapulted out of Ballynockanor into the wild lands over the border in Mayo; Joseph Connor was driven back to Dublin by Kate's hostility and his own conscience; and finally William Marlowe was forced to return to Castletown as the official face against rebellion and lawlessness.

"The rapparees are terrorists, just like the rioting mob in the

Reign of Terror in France," Old Marlowe insisted as he sent William away from Dublin. "And you remember what happened to the landlords after the terrorists got control of the guillotine. We must lop off their heads before they take ours!"

Through it all, the one who made a regular pilgrimage in and out of Ballynockanor was Martin. Immediately after Kevin's flight, he became the go-between, supplier of both provision and news. In the mist-cloaked hours of predawn, he made his way to the stone cross atop the hill behind the village. There he found Kevin waiting for him.

"I've brought you a blanket," he said as Kevin materialized out of a clump of granite boulders. "Da says winter is comin' on, and you'll be needin' warm things."

Kevin acknowledged the gift and the basket of food. "Tell him we have a fine cave, I and six companions. Dry enough and proof against storms. Tell Da they are all patriots, driven off their lands, and not common thieves. What word of Brigit?" He tore off a hunk of soda bread and stuffed it in his mouth, all the time turning slowly and scanning the surroundings for pursuers.

Martin seemed reluctant to answer the question directly. "Young Marlowe and Driver Stone go about the country, collecting rack rent and tossin' cottages like the fiends they are."

"They and I will have a reckonin' one day," Kevin vowed.

Clenching twelve-year-old fists, Martin stiffened with a recollection. "I cannot stand the sight of the young master," he said, "since hearin' him laugh with Carroll about . . ." He stopped abruptly, suddenly conscious of a promise nearly broken.

"Laughin'?" Kevin probed. "At what?"

"Kate made me swear not to repeat it," Martin argued.

"You must," Kevin replied, "and she need not know you told."

Relieved to be able to unburden himself, Martin's words tumbled from his mouth like a mountain freshet after a thunderstorm. "He left her. Left her in a whorehouse! When he's drunk he brags of it. Says she owes her livin' to him!"

Kevin looked grim, his features as hard as the carving on the stone cross. "He has ruined her indeed," he said through clenched teeth. "I will no longer wait for a reckonin' . . . I will seek one out."

"Oh, Kev," Martin worried, "don't get killed. Da has burden enough without that!"

Not even listening, Kevin was already cinching the supplies into a makeshift backpack with the blanket. "Whatever I have need of," he said, "I'll leave word in the usual place. Don't be seen goin' away from here."

"I won't," Martin pledged. He continued to explain that he took a different route home every time, but when he turned to look, Kevin had already faded like a wraith back into the cover of the hills.

∽

After mass on Sunday morning, Father O'Bannon crooked his finger at Kate and took her to one side as the congregation passed beyond the churchyard wall surrounding St. John's.

"Come on, then," he said. "I'll have a wee word with ye, before y'hear it from someone else. The truth of the matter is known all over Dublin. Joseph's told William Marlowe, and there's an end to the secret."

Kate's heart dropped to her stomach. Was it some terrible news about Brigit? Her mouth was dry. "Hear what?" she asked, walking with him toward the Burke tomb.

Hands clasped behind his back, Father O'Bannon paused before the granite structure. He raised his eyes to the new carving on the stone.

"See here," he remarked.

Kate read aloud the crisp new letters.

In Memory of Joseph C. Burke
Lord of Connaught
A.D. *1842 by his loving son*
J. C. Burke

Father O'Bannon cleared his throat loudly. "Well?"

Kate replied cautiously, "The Burke has no son livin'. Little Connor drowned and . . ."

"You're wrong there, girl," the priest corrected. "The Burke's son came home to carve these words in the stone and . . . to carve other things on the hearts of some in Ballynockanor."

Kate looked over her shoulder at the departing parishioners. "But who?"

"Do you know what the J. C. on the stone stands for?"

"And why should I?"

"Well, then, I'll enlighten you. It stands for none other than the man you spurned. The man who loved you and who you loved but sent back to Dublin in shame! It's Joseph Connor Burke himself you've been cursin', girl!"

Kate clutched her stomach and tried to breathe. "But . . . he's . . . he said . . ."

"Joseph Connor. Son of The Burke himself. He said nothin' about his business, sure. He had his reasons for caution. The reasons were his uncle, Constable Carroll, and that lyin', cheatin' thief of a steward, John Stone! Joseph has no proof, and they would've killed him before they let him find proof." He pulled a letter out from the deep pocket of his cassock. "I'm sure he's written them all down for you, so read it yourself! As for me, I've never seen a more headstrong, foolish woman since Eve!"

He stalked off, leaving her alone in the churchyard to read Joseph's message:

Kate, my dearest,

By now you have heard the truth of who I am. It matters not at all to you, I am certain, that I have held sweet memories of our childhood together for all the long and bitter years of my exile. I dreamed often of sitting at your side as the waters of the Cornamona flowed gently past us. But I have not been free to speak openly of my identity or even to go where I pleased. I am in this respect no different from every true Irishman who is bound by the ice of injustice. We keep silent and often hide the truth for fear of vengeance. In Ballynockanor, as in all of

Ireland these days, only the river runs free. One day the warmth of God's love may melt the stubborn hearts of all true Christians, be they Catholic or Protestant, to stand and serve Him together as one nation. It is my dream.

Until then, perhaps you will have cause to forgive me my failings, and I may have an hour to tell you all. For now my past and future are of little consequence compared to Brigit. I shall do my utmost to find and restore your sister. Poor dear Brigit. I accept responsibility for her downfall and for her well-being. I assure you by my vow of penance that I will not rest until I restore her honor again. If it takes the sacrifice of my own life, it will be done. I ask only your prayers for now, and perhaps one day you will find it in your heart to forgive me.

Your faithful servant,
Joseph Connor Burke

∽

In the time of Tom Donovan's grandfather, of blessed memory, the family had acquired the lease to a field far to the west of all the others. It was called Queen Maeve's Field, after an ages-old tale that ascribed ownership of the pasture to Queen Maeve of Connaught in the days before the coming of St. Patrick. The southwest corner of the range came very near to the Marlowe manor house.

Long, streaky gray clouds chased one another across the sky. Dark, scrolling vapors piled up against Ben Beg like a coil of rope, turning afternoon sun into gloom. As Martin drove a trio of newly weaned calves into Maeve's Field, he spotted a figure moving furtively in the shelter of oak trees and boulders. He shaded his eyes against the westering sun and announced to Mary Elizabeth, "She's got loose again." The boy pointed to the black-cloaked form hopping from shadow to shadow like a skinny, oversized sable rabbit.

Mary Elizabeth did not even have to squint to know who was meant. "How does Mad Molly get out?" she wondered aloud. "Do y'suppose she's magic, Martin?"

"Nooo," the boy said slowly, drawing out the word. "But she's slippery, right enough. What is she about there, do y'think?"

Mary Elizabeth did not answer the question as her mind was going off another way. "She'll never find her way home," she observed, scrambling over the fence. "Not with dark comin' on."

Knowing it was useless to argue, Martin followed his sister across the wall and down the hill.

Before they ever got close, Martin could hear Molly's crooning chant. "It's there . . . ," she said to an oak. "Porridge and potatoes." The old woman stood on tiptoe and peered into the boll of an oak limb. "It's where it has always been."

"What is?" Mary Elizabeth inquired.

Mad Molly pirouetted on one bony foot. "I don't remember," she said cheerfully, not showing any surprise at the sudden appearance of the two children.

"Are you lost?" Mary Elizabeth asked.

Martin coughed into his fist. He thought the question was much the same as inquiring if the grass was green.

"No," Molly announced with emphasis, "but *it* is!"

"What is?"

Molly ran to a boulder that anchored a stone wall on the slope above Marlowe Park. "D'ya know Queen Maeve?" she said, rounding suddenly on the children. The way her cloak flapped in the air, Martin decided she looked more like a raven than a rabbit. He shuddered in spite of himself; a raven was a very ill-omened bird indeed.

"Joseph Connor taught us about her," Mary Elizabeth said. "She was a great warrior queen who fought against the Knights of the Red Hand. Oooh," Mary Elizabeth remembered suddenly. "I've said his name wrong. He's Joseph Connor Burke . . . the little Connor was not stolen by fairies after all."

At the mention of Joseph's name, Martin saw Molly stiffen. "Joseph and Mary," she said. "It's there." The old woman jumped onto the rock, stretched out her veined and knobby arm toward the Marlowe home and sang,

I found you there, all still and dead.
You had no prayers, your soul had fled.
Only a crooked crone who psalmed,
and I wiped your blood upon my palm.

"Queen Maeve!" she said abruptly. "Queen of the fairies. She took little Connor Burke to herself . . . but not for evil . . . no, not she! She took him to save him from the merrow who dashed out Liam's brains." Molly hopped down, her cloak floating around her. She thrust her pointed nose into Mary Elizabeth's face. The girl flinched, squeaked, and fell backward.

"Come on, Molly," Martin said manfully, trying not to let his sister see he was also shaken. "We'll be takin' y'home now."

Molly prattled on as if she had not heard. "The merrow took old Liam, but it did not get the treasure. No, no. It's in my potato, see?"

The afternoon had darkened to gloomy twilight, and the wind swirled overhead. A high thin cry rose and fell on the breeze, and Martin instantly regretted thinking it sounded like the wail of a banshee. "Home," he said firmly, but it was too late. Molly was running purposefully toward the ruins of the gatehouse beside the Marlowe's drive.

"Come back," Martin and Mary Elizabeth cried together, but Molly paid no heed.

"What's a merrow?" Mary Elizabeth asked. Her legs were churning, and still the children could not gain ground on the unbelievably spry old woman.

Shaking his head, Martin suggested, "Y'don't want t'hear." The boy knew that a merrow steals the souls of men and keeps them imprisoned under the ocean.

The children were panting and the first drops of rain were falling when Molly reached the vine-covered heap of rubble that was once an outbuilding of the gatehouse. "There," she said, pointing again. "See the blood from his poor old head."

One dark red flagstone, already moistened by the rain, did look like blood. It was right in front of the doorway leading into the ruin.

"It's in my potato," Molly said sadly, stooping to rub her fingers over the paving. She glanced at her fingertips with curiosity, as if surprised at the absence of gore.

Thinking the fit had spent itself, Martin said kindly, "Let's go now, before the Marlowes come and run us off."

At the mention of the name, Molly shrieked, bolted erect, and held her arms arched toward the clouds as if holding up a great weight. "Merrow . . . Marlowe . . . merrow . . . no, can't have it!"

When Martin put his hand on her elbow, she shook him off and ducked into the abandoned cottage. Leaving his sister gasping and hopping from one foot to the other, Martin plunged in after the old woman. "You've got to . . ."

Molly had stopped, her toes on the edge of the hearth. Dirt, pigeon dung, and the remains of a broken bench all obscured the outline of the fireplace, but Molly did not seem to mind. She hummed softly, nodding to herself as she used her bare foot to sweep aside the trash.

Unsure if the rushing sound was coming from the storm outside or only existed in his ears, Martin stood rooted in place. Molly bent over again and pried at some mortar with her nails. She tugged at a fragment of rock as if her life depended on winning a contest. When it slid out, she dropped the soot-covered stone and stuck her hand into the shallow crevice.

"It's gone," she mused with a disappointed sound, her fingers pattering around the cleft like mice in a cupboard. Martin stepped up behind the folded figure and put his hand on her shoulder. "My potato is gone," she lamented again. Then, yanking her hand out of the crevice, she exulted, "But here's the key to the treasure! I hid it in the potato, you see, and so they never found it!" and she flourished a rusty bit of iron in triumph.

By the time Martin, Mary Elizabeth, and Mad Molly reached Ballynockanor, the rain was bucketing. All three were soaked, but unlike the children, who covered their heads against the pelting downpour, the old woman lifted her face to the skies. She smiled and capered in the mud puddles. Martin had to scold and hurry her along, as if she were the child and he the parent.

"There's no more potato," she sang, "but it's in my porridge still."

Just outside the cottage of her daughter, Molly stopped abruptly and looked over her shoulder. Martin drew a deep, tired breath and sighed. If she was going to run off again, he thought, someone else would have to fetch her back.

Instead of fleeing, Molly bent lower and called the children to her. Spreading wide the shoulders of her cloak, she gestured for Martin to hold it over their heads like a tent. "Joseph and Mary," she muttered. "Little Connor Burke is gone with the fairies, but Mary is here, aren't you, Mary?"

Mary Elizabeth nodded, wide-eyed.

Molly nodded vigorously in return, twisting a long, straggly lock of hair around a gnarled root of a finger. With a sudden plunge into her pocket, she retrieved the heavy key and thrust it into Mary Elizabeth's hand. "Must keep this," she instructed. "Only, don't tell a soul . . . a soul," she repeated. Then her smile faded. "If you tell, the merrow will steal your soul. Promise!" she said fiercely, making the little girl squeal and Martin drop the hem of the cape.

"I promise," Mary Elizabeth vowed in a quavering voice.

Smiling again, winding the strands of hair into gray yarn, Molly nodded with satisfaction. When she again thrust her hand into the folds of her cloak, Martin could not see what she was about, which was just as well because this time she held a small knife with a blade curved like a fang.

Martin and Mary Elizabeth barely had time to gasp before Molly sliced off a length of leather tie from her cloak. This she passed deftly through the handle of the key held in Mary Elizabeth's trembling fingers and knotted it. Tossing the loop over the girl's head, she lifted the iron bar and dropped the cold metal inside Mary Elizabeth's collar.

Raising her chin, Mad Molly carefully inspected the barren roof of the cottage and the empty limbs of a nearby oak tree. "Don't let anyone know," she warned again. "Or the merrow will come for ye." Fearfully mimicking Molly's inspection of the darkness, Martin and Mary Elizabeth never saw the old woman melt away from them and disappear inside the cottage.

Night after night Mary Elizabeth awakened screaming from nightmares of the soul-seeking merrow coming for Mad Molly's iron key. She wet the bed again. Fear of a bony hand reaching out from beneath the cot kept her from getting up to use the chamber pot.

Martin knew the reason for his sister's terror, but the same promise for secrecy that Mary Elizabeth made to the old woman applied to him as well. He would not speak of the curse of the key except in attempting to console his small sister.

Kate changed Mary Elizabeth's nightdress and the bed linens, then rocked the child and sang sweetly to her until she was asleep again. Martin, barefoot in his nightshirt, watched from the doorway.

Kate asked him, "Martin? Do you know what could be troublin' her so?"

He shook his head, looked away, and then returned to his cot. A sense of evil weighed upon him in the gloom. The key to an unknown casket, long hid in a potato by an old woman long since gone mad, was now in their possession, wrapped in a kerchief and stuffed beneath his mattress.

Any creature would have to go through him to get the key. He wondered if the merrow had stolen Molly's soul as well as her sanity. Could such horror come upon him and little Mary Elizabeth as well? The thought of it made him shudder and pull the blankets over his head.

Come morning he washed and dressed and stuffed the key into the pocket of his jacket. There were circles beneath his eyes and poor Mary Elizabeth looked as if she had not slept in weeks. In the chill of pale sunlight they walked slowly toward the now vacant hedge school.

"What shall we do, Martin?" Mary Elizabeth asked.

His brow furrowed, Martin raised his face to the dim yellow sun as though the shine of it could melt away the fog in his brain. "Joseph said the way we Irish fight evil is with our wits."

And so it was that Martin searched the shelves of the schoolhouse for books about the legend of the merrow. What was this beast that lured men into his lair to steal their souls and lock them away in lobster pots?

"An ancient tale it is, of temptation and sin and eternal loss," Martin read. He then studied a gruesome story that made for much trembling and looking over shoulders.

> *The merrow is not a real creature but an allegory for all those worldly things that lure men away from the Christ and so they lose their souls. Moreover, those gifts entrusted to our care must be laid at the feet of Jesus and then they can never be stolen by darkness or used by the evil one.*

Martin felt the iron bar burning hot in his pocket. He replaced the volume, and they hurried from the school.

"So what do you think?" he whispered to Mary Elizabeth.

She shrugged. "I think . . . it's not going to rain."

He cuffed her. "No! Molly's merrow. It is allegorical."

Her face clouded. "Allegors live in rivers in Africa. They eat people."

"You weren't listenin'."

"I saw a picture of one at the National School . . . in the zoo book. Allegors eat natives who go to the river to wash their night-dresses." She acted out the part of the unsuspecting laundress at the river's edge and then the approach of the monster. "Sneak up and catch them in their long beaks and bite them with terrible long teeth and pull them under and . . . I'll not go so close to the river again. We must keep our promise to Molly about the key, Martin." She shuddered. "I don't fancy bein' served up to a pack of merrow allegors for supper."

Martin rolled his eyes. "There's no such creature."

"There is!"

"Sure, and you're hopeless." He put his hand on her shoulder as the steeple of the chapel loomed above the treetops. His eyes narrowed with determination. "Now I ask you, if you were listenin' a'tall to the lesson, what is it stops the merrow allegor from stealin' a soul?"

Mary Elizabeth stuck out her lower lip in an attempt to remember. She failed the test. "A spear."

He shoved her again.

For two days Martin considered the information he had gleaned from Joseph's book about the great thief of all men's souls. The Lord of Evil was not an allegory and only one thing made Satan tremble. That one thing was the cross of Christ, and those who hid beneath its protection were saved.

With the certainty of this truth set in his mind, Martin formed a plan of action. It would keep the mysterious key to the unknown chest safe from whatever merrow lurked in Ballynockanor to steal the souls of Irishmen.

Martin and Mary Elizabeth crouched behind the massive boulder across the lane from St. John the Evangelist. They were waiting for the last of the Thursday morning worshipers to leave the building. Mary Elizabeth whispered furtively, "And what if Father O'Bannon catches us?"

Martin shushed her. "You know he has his tea each morning after mass."

She nodded and blinked up at the shifting clouds. "I'd like a cuppa tea."

Martin nudged her hard for silence as the priest stepped out into the morning light after his parishioners and smiled and waved as they left. Content, the cleric stretched and rubbed his head as he made for the parsonage, then closed the bottom of the half-door.

"His tea," Martin remarked. "Sure, and I told you."

"He's left the top of the door wide. He'll see us when we cross the churchyard."

At this Martin frowned and put his mind to it. "And if he does we'll bid him good-day and come back another time. Boldly to it, Mary Elizabeth."

The two crossed the lane and entered the churchyard as though they had every right to do so. Of course they did have every right to enter the chapel, but the reason they did so was meant to remain a secret known only to Christ and His saints.

The dimness of the building was illuminated by the ever-present candles. One taper burned at the side of the ark where the bread of the Eucharist was kept, there beneath the feet of the crucified Christ.

Martin and Mary Elizabeth crossed themselves and moved hesitantly forward toward the altar.

"Is it not some sort of sin?" Mary Elizabeth queried and tugged at the tail of her brother's shirt. "They're lookin' at us, Martin." Her eyes glanced fearfully up at the sweet face of Mary and then at the agony of Jesus.

"Aye. And they're the only ones in Ballynockanor can keep a secret!" Martin cast a withering look her way and put his finger to his lips. A doubt flickered briefly in his brain. What if this unholy key brought some curse upon the chapel and the people of the parish? What was it Joseph's book said? "Gifts entrusted . . . laid at the feet of Jesus . . ."

Martin steeled himself. Pushing Mary Elizabeth into a pew, he tiptoed up the steps, knelt down, and took the key from his pocket. In Martin's hand was the awful burden that had been laid on him and Mary Elizabeth. There above them hung the Savior dying for the sins of the world, dying for the sins of Ballynockanor, banishing forever the merrow that hungered to steal their souls.

Martin studied the spikes that pierced the hands and feet. Blood spilled from the wounds to soak the small wooden shelf where the toes of the Savior touched.

Cocking his head to one side and inching forward on his knees, Martin could see there was a triangular gap between the sole of the foot and the shelf and the cross itself. Room enough to slide something behind! Space enough to hide the key to a casket beneath the feet of Jesus.

Martin bowed his head and crossed himself again. "Me and Mary Elizabeth . . . she's havin' dreams, you see, and I've been tryin' to sleep with the thing beneath my mattress. Whatever it means, it's too great for us to keep safe. And if Molly's merrow is real, then all our souls will be lost if the key is taken. The merrow fears only Your cross." He added in a fervent whisper, "Lord, hear our prayer."

And with that he stood and stepped forward. Conscious of trespassing on a holy place, his hand shook as he slipped the key behind and beneath the bloody feet.

"Can you see it?" he queried Mary Elizabeth as he backed away.

"Not a bit! We're saved," she said, sighing with relief. Crossing herself, the little girl blithely skipped back up the aisle and out into the daylight.

∽ 13 ∽

There were three bridges over the river Cornamona between its headwaters on the slopes of Lugnabrick and the delta through which it flowed before emptying into Lough Corrib. To be a triad of any object in Catholic Ireland almost guaranteed the use of the three divine virtues as names. The stone arch near Cromghlinn was styled Faith, while the last span, the one in Castletown, was called Charity.

In between these two was the trestle known as Hope. Ironically, Hope was planted where hope no longer existed. The gorge crossed by the middle bridge was squarely between the abandoned village of Duachta and a hillside made oppressive by a cluster of barrows: bronze-age tombs.

William Marlowe and John Stone were en route back to the Marlowe estate from the family holdings at the far end of the river valley. From the dozen small holders that made up Tonaglana, Driver Stone collected a hundred shillings in rent. He also warned the farmers that no more extension was possible for the amounts of their arrears; another hundred shillings was due within a fortnight or out they would go. Stone touched up the chestnut pacer with his buggy whip for the pull up a slight incline.

"You certainly have them trembling," Marlowe said, applauding. "But how can you make good on your threat? Don't they know that if they are turned out, then we will get no rent at all? Aren't they laughing behind our backs right now?"

"No, sir," Stone corrected respectfully. "You see, the well-to-do Protestant farmers, like Colonel Bilberry . . . and even some of the Catholic squireens, like O'Farrell . . . they are just itching to get their hands on more grazing land."

"And they will pay more than we are making now from those miserable wretches scratching the dirt for potatoes and oats?"

"Oh, aye," Stone agreed. "They will indeed. Makes them feel like grandees to lord it over the small-fry."

"Then why don't we turn them all out at once?" Marlowe exploded. "Collecting a shilling here and sixpence there is like extracting teeth! Pull down their village and be done, I say."

"Well, now, it isn't as easy as all that," Stone said patiently. "To empty a townland of its people, to make it 'perfectly untenanted' as I like to call it, takes a fine touch."

Stone was growing schoolmasterish and therefore tiresome to Young Marlowe. The driver gestured with his buggy whip toward the remains of Duachta. Grass grew over mounds that five years earlier had been cottages. The front and back walls of the abandoned church of St. Columba made jagged knifepoints against the evening sky where the roof and sides had fallen in. "It took your father and me three years of planning to empty Duachta," the rent collector said proudly. "See, if you move too quickly, you risk a rising and a general rebellion. But these rustic cottars are just like sheep; no, they *are* sheep: stupid and easily led and easily picked off one at a time. Do you know that after the first three boyos were turned out, we paid them a shilling apiece to come back and tear down the homes of their neighbors? And they took it! Pick on the weakest first. Then set them against each other in greed and suspicion, that's the play. How can they raise a rebellion if they aren't even sure who they can trust? Do you know . . ." Stone had to pause for breath. "Do you know, we even had one old woman apply to us for the shilling to pull down her own house!"

They continued their discussion of the finer points of preventing insurrection and accomplishing eviction as the evening shadows lengthened into full night. Stone guided the pacer into the turn back toward the river that led to Hope Bridge.

"What about Ballynockanor? Might it not be successfully cleared soon?" Marlowe suggested eagerly. "The people there are no better than brigands and cowardly at that. Might they not be turned out at once?" Iron-shod hooves clattered on the stones of the trestle, slipping. The Cornamona rushed beneath, making Stone's reply impossible to hear.

It was from the darkness under the far edge of the bridge that the first blackened face appeared. Visage smeared with burned cork, hands likewise disguised, the cloaked figure levered abruptly upright from the gloom like a scarecrow raised up on a pole. But this scarecrow was holding a pitchfork.

The horse reared in his turn, shied sideways, and jammed a wheel of the carriage into a post of the bridge rail. Stone slashed at the animal ferociously with his whip, cursing and swearing.

Marlowe, seeing that the way forward was blocked, jumped from the cart to run back the way they had come. When two more demonic forms advanced toward him, the young landlord leaped back aboard.

"What do you want?" Stone shouted as he got the horse under control. "Clear off at once!" His speech was as stern and arrogant as always, but the shudder in the tone belied the words.

The three figures closed around the rig. One laid hold of the bridle of the sweating, wild-eyed bay, and the other two flanked the carriage. "We have no money," Marlowe said. "What do you want from us?"

"Now that would not be strictly true," responded the man holding the pitchfork. "We know you drained Tonaglana, but it is not about that for which we beg your attention."

Emboldened by the politeness of the attackers, Marlowe put on a haughty manner. "Then you know who I am," he said. "Clear off at once. The wearing of disguises is forbidden by law. We could have you all arrested!"

"And who would you have the magistrate swear out the warrant against?" the leader inquired with a laugh. "No, there will be no arrests this night, nor killin' neither, unless you are even more foolish than you look." He accompanied this warning with a thrust of the pitchfork that left one of the flat iron tines an inch from Marlowe's chest.

"Don't kill me," Marlowe squeaked. "Here, take the money. It's in the bag by my feet. Only don't kill me!"

"Whish, man, have you not heard me?" demanded the leader again. "We'll take the coin since you're so generous to offer it, but it is not robbery for which we've stopped you."

"Then what is it?" squirmed Marlowe.

"You have wronged a young woman by the name of Brigit Donovan, and you must do right by her."

"I don't even know the name!" Marlowe protested.

"Nor anything about a sham marriage with some wretch posin' as priest!" cried the captain of the assailants. "The law looks harshly at sacrilege, even when practiced by a landlord. Now I ask you again . . . and think carefully before answerin', for your life hangs by a thread . . . will you acknowledge Brigit Donovan as your true wife?"

Marlowe writhed on the buggy seat. His face turned to all sides, seeking help from any source. Stone sat rigidly upright, without speaking, but his fingers crept spiderlike toward the pocket of his greatcoat.

"And if I will not?" Marlowe said, his voice quavering. "How can you call the law on me without revealing your own identities? You will be in much more difficulty than me, I promise you."

The face of the pitchfork-wielding phantom split into a hellish grin. White teeth gleaming in the skull-like mask of a face, the spokesman replied, "The law will have its due, but how if you stand before the eternal judge this very night? Are you ready to die, William Marlowe?"

Stone's hand plunged into his pocket and withdrew, flourishing a pistol. In that same second, the pitchfork was thrust forward. With a scream, Marlowe threw himself apart from Stone, believing that the thrust was meant for him. The prongs of the fork tore the flesh on both sides of the driver's arm, pinning his hand against the bullhide on the back of the carriage seat. The pistol spiraled into the air, exploding harmlessly as it struck the paving of the bridge before skittering over the edge and falling into the river.

Despite his scramble out of the buggy, Marlowe's flight was stopped by a pair of hands around his throat, and he was dragged, sobbing, up against the rear wheel of the rig.

With the sound an ax makes when withdrawn from a block of wood, the chief attacker withdrew the pitchfork blade, freeing Stone. The driver gritted his teeth, holding his bleeding wrist clenched in his other hand. A moment later Marlowe looked up to find the bloody tines presented at his eye level.

"The next thrust will be your throat," was the quiet promise. "Will you marry Brigit Donovan?"

"Curse you!" Marlowe shouted. "You cowards! You cutthroats! You come at me in ambush and in disguise and make demands. Have you no honor? You never would fight me man to man, in broad daylight."

The leader of the group drew himself up at that. He straightened, grounding the pitchfork on the stones with a spark that dazzled the eyes.

"Who are you to call me coward?" he demanded. "If you will not marry my sister, then I will fight you fair, however you choose."

"Your sister, eh?" Marlowe said lightly. "So, Kevin Donovan, you will meet me on a field of honor for the purity of your sister?" The young landlord said this lightly; fear kept sarcasm from his words.

"No, Kevin," one of the accomplices protested. "Marlowe has no honor. He will have the law on us, sure, and no help to your sister still."

The tines scraped across the paving once more, and Kevin placed a blade against the young landlord's Adam's apple. "No one takes the risk but me," he vowed. "It is my place and my right. But know this, William Marlowe, if you have reserved in your heart to cheat me of my right, you'll never rest easy again in Connaught. Another dark night and another bridge will be your end, and no more warnin' given. Do you swear?"

"I do swear," Marlowe agreed. "And the time, place, and weapons? How will I let you know?"

Kevin shrugged. "I would kill you with my bare hands, so the means is of no consequence to me. As to time and place, so long as it is private, between the two of us, I do not care. Chalk it on the wall of the old churchyard beneath the branches of the willow near the gate. The word will come to me."

"We'll not back you in this madness," one of Kevin's companions warned.

"It is well," Kevin concluded. "Until then, William Marlowe, I leave you whole and unmarked . . . see that you spread no other tale of this night than that you were robbed by bandits on the road." With that Kevin and his two comrades cut the reins of the harness and fled with the rent money into the cover of the skeletal remains of Duachta.

There was a swirling mist rising from the Cornamona, but despite this early morning shroud, Martin located Kevin exactly where he expected to. Below the stone cross was a path heading toward the rising sun and a rendezvous of death. The boy heard the snap made by a stepped-on twig and he set out following the sound.

The way taken by Kevin led along the river. Ahead in the darkness, a stone rattled against another. Martin stopped and thought. It could only mean that Kevin had climbed a bawnditch wall and struck out cross-country.

In another fifty paces, Martin found the spot. A fist-size rock had been dislodged, and the boy climbed over the barrier at the same location. He swung around on top of the stone fence to lower his legs on the other side. Something grabbed him around the waist and slung him to the ground.

"Y'little sneak!" Kevin snarled. "Who gave y'leave to be followin' me?"

Martin ignored his brother's anger. "You're goin' to fight Young Marlowe, aren't you, Kevin? I saw the place chalked on the wall. I won't interfere, I promise. Have I told Da, then, or Kate or Father O'Bannon? I have not. Let me come with you, Kevin."

"Go home," Kevin said abruptly, loosing his hold on Martin's cloak and letting the boy drop. "Go home and forget y'saw me. This is somethin' I must do alone. If I catch you followin' me again, I'll thrash you good."

At that Kevin whirled and ran off across the pasture. Martin knew that his brother figured to outrun him easily and lose himself in the mist. But the first light of dawn was already changing the hillside from black to gray, the haze was lifting, and Kevin was silhouetted against the pale, treeless slope. Martin picked himself up and stumbled after.

Marlowe property reached far to the north of Castletown, as far as the border of county Mayo, to the shores of Lough Mask. A meandering country lane ran through the bottomland between the square shoulders of Ben Levy and the frowning heights of Bothan. The downs were low and swampy, full of bogs and wickedness.

At the deepest point of the swale, about a mile beyond the village of Allintober, there was a lake. It was not a large body of water, like the great loughs Mask or Corrib. It was called Ballydoo and measured no more than a third of a mile in length and something less than that in breadth.

In its center, near the north end, was a crannog, one of the man-made islands said to be built by the Druids, but actually dating to a thousand years earlier. It was the presence on Marlowe land of this secluded heap of stones and earth, barely rising above the waterline, that had caused William Marlowe to suggest the place. When Kevin stepped from a wreath of rushes below the appointed spot, both William and John Stone were waiting beside a rowboat.

Martin kept above his brother on the hillside so as not to be seen or heard, but he could plainly make out the figures below. A trick of the breeze floating up the incline carried voices to him easily. Martin fretted about the rowboat. He could not follow if they meant to cross to the crannog. What could he do?

"What's this, then?" he heard Kevin demand of the two cloaked figures.

The whip-lean form of William Marlowe turned. "Donovan," he said with an amused sneer. "I have lost a wager. I bet Mister Stone that you would never show up, that we had seen the last of you."

"Think what you will," Kevin said curtly. "Your pistol will do my talkin' for me. Mister Stone should have more fear of collectin' than you of paying up."

"Will you get into the boat?" Marlowe said with a scoffing laugh, indicating where the dinghy stood ready to shove off.

"I will not!" Kevin retorted, mocking in his turn. "Peasant-born I may be, but you must not take me for a simpleton. Halfway out might you not kill me and drop me body over the side to be food for fishes?"

Even from his distance up the hill, Martin could see Stone and Marlowe exchange a look of consternation. Perhaps what Kevin surmised was exactly what they had been planning. But in this lonely place, what was to stop the two from carrying out such a scheme anyway?

Martin spotted a nearby boulder and onto this outcropping of granite he climbed, posting himself like a sentinel in full view of the men below. He was near enough to be a witness of what followed, but not so close that he could be easily caught. He waved his arms and set his cloak flapping until he was certain he had been noticed.

"If you and your friend persist in being so suspicious," Marlowe said in an irritable tone, "then the ground here beside the lake will have to serve. But I warn you, the footing is slippery. And what about your second?" Marlowe continued, waving a careless flutter of one hand toward Martin. "Do his manners not include coming any closer?"

"They do not," Kevin replied both firmly and loudly. "He is quite well enough placed where he stands." His words carried both warning and gratitude to his little brother.

After a peremptory gesture by his master, John Stone retrieved a flat wooden case from the thwart of the rowboat. When he opened it, a brace of pistols gleamed dully in the morning sun that broke through the gray skies atop Ben Levy. "You will watch me load both pistols," Stone said to Kevin, "and then you will have the choice of weapons."

Anxiety gnawed at Martin's stomach as he watched the preparations go forward. Martin had never seen a dueling pistol before, but from the muskets carried by the British soldiers, he knew how they worked. A flask was upended to pour a measure of gunpowder down the throat of each gun, then a lead ball, wrapped in a cloth patch, was rammed home atop the powder. More powder was then poured into the pan of the firing mechanism and a lid closed over it.

Loading process completed, Stone escorted Kevin to one end of a level pitch of about thirty feet in length. He then presented the box of weapons for Kevin's inspection.

Kevin picked up each pistol, hefted each one in turn, then said cheerfully, "It makes but little difference to me, since I have never fired one of these before anyway."

Shedding his ceremonial courtesy at last, Stone said, "You low-born scum! The best result you can wish is that he kills you cleanly. One way or the other, you are a dead man."

"My own da's father used to say that none of us will be gettin' out of this world alive," Kevin replied forcefully. "And the best thing a man can do is to make a good end. Could I but take the both of you with me, Driver Stone, I would consider my days well spent."

All Martin's attention had been on his brother, but when Stone returned to the other end of the pitch, the boy's eyes followed. He was surprised to see that William Marlowe betrayed some nervousness, fumbling the pistol when he drew it out of the case and stopping to wipe his palm on his pantleg. Martin recognized the symptoms of fear in the young master and for the first time in many days felt hope begin to rise.

John Stone planted himself near the center of the ground and nearer the water's edge, facing up the slope. In a strong voice he said, "My duty demands that I make this inquiry one last time: will no other solution satisfy you? Donovan?"

"Stop now, and I will still be arrested and transported to Australia, and my sister's life will still be stained," Kevin observed. "When

a mad dog needs killin', a man does not put the deed off on someone else. I will not draw back."

"Master Marlowe?"

William Marlowe looked pale even from Martin's vantage point,
but color rose into his cheeks at Kevin's words, and he shook his
head.

"Very well, then," Stone concluded. "Cock your weapons." In
the stillness that followed, the noise made by the two hammers
being drawn back sounded to Martin like a crash of drums. "I will
raise my handkerchief. When I drop it, you may fire. Do you understand?"

Curt nods of comprehension replied.

Martin hid his eyes behind his hands, and then because he could
not stand it, peeked through his fingers anyway. He saw the cloth
flutter briefly, then float earthward.

At the instant the handkerchief left Stone's grasp, William Marlowe fired. There was a snap and a roar from his pistol, then a jet of
flame and a cloud of bluish smoke shot from the muzzle. Martin saw
his brother stagger back, clutching his side, heard him groan, and
saw an exultant smile spread over Marlowe's face.

Martin also saw William Marlowe's look of triumph change to
one of horror as Kevin pulled himself up straight. With his left elbow
pressed tightly against his side, Kevin raised his right hand to dead
level, the pistol muzzle pointed squarely at the center of Marlowe's
waistcoat.

"Stop him, Stone!" Marlowe shouted, breaking from his spot and
throwing himself aside. John Stone rushed toward Kevin, then
dodged sideways when the young man waved the pistol toward him.

It was a strange jig Martin witnessed from the hillside: a circular
dance of death as Marlowe fled from Kevin's aim, Kevin circled,
trying to find a clear shot, and Stone alternately rushed forward and
drew back.

For all the movement, the capering lasted only a count of three or
four seconds. Stone threw himself on Kevin just as William Marlowe
lunged for the cover of some rocks. Stone fought Kevin for possession of the weapon, and in the struggle the pistol erupted. Flame

spouted beneath Stone's arm, and the driver fell backward, clutching at himself. Had Stone taken the bullet meant for Young Marlowe?

The scream that reached Martin's ears was not from the throat of John Stone. In knocking aside Kevin's arm, the driver had caused the pistol to discharge at the exact instant it was trained on William Marlowe's breastbone.

Like a tall, slender candle melting in a fervent heat, Young Marlowe telescoped downward. His knees already on the ground, his waist sank earthward, then his bloody waistcoat, and lastly his head lolled forward on his breast. At the end Young Marlowe's mouth worked soundlessly like the last flicker of a flame before it gutters out.

John Stone and Kevin both stood transfixed at the sight. It was Martin who first recovered his wits. "Run!" he shouted. "Run, Kevin! Get clear while you can! Go!"

"You've murdered him!" John Stone cried, bending over the crumpled form of William Marlowe.

Kevin stared stupidly at the body. "So I have," he agreed flatly. He hurled the pistol away from him. Martin watched it skip over the lake surface like a flat stone, then plunge beneath the water.

"You'll hang for this!" Stone menaced.

Kevin held his side with both hands, blood trickling between his fingers.

"Come on, Kev!" Martin urged again. "Are y'dyin' then? Can y'not run?"

Kevin gaped at the lifeless clay of William Marlowe, then forced his legs into a stumbling trot up the hill to meet his little brother.

"The ball grazed my short rib," he said, panting.

Even at Kevin's halting pace, it was only a matter of moments before the two Donovans were into the heath on the western edge of Lough Ballydoo and out of sight.

Martin expected Kevin to be arrested before the duel ever took place. Why had Marlowe and Stone not hidden a troop of soldiers in the bracken? Even so, it would not be long before Stone reached Castletown, and the hunt would be on. Then it would be horses and hounds and men with muskets on their trail.

Kevin stopped again, and Martin turned back to him. Pulling the length of his shirttail out of his trousers, Kevin said, "Help me with this."

Tearing a strip of cloth from the bottom of the shirt, Martin wound it tightly around Kevin's torso. "Just a scratch," Kevin said grimacing.

"You'll be wantin' Kate's needle and thread."

Kevin shook his head. "I'm a quilt already from her stitchin'. They'll transport you all and pull the house down. I'll not be goin' home ever again, Martin." Kevin glanced nervously over his shoulder.

"Over the border then? Mayo?" Martin suggested, meaning to the lair of the Ribbonmen.

Again Kevin indicated a negative. "Markin' cattle and burnin' hayricks is for transportin'," he said, "but murder means hangin', and I'll put no other man's neck in the noose for mine."

"It were no murder," Martin protested. When Kevin did not respond at all, Martin already knew the reason: in English courts and under English law, it would be murder and the rope, no matter what. "Where then?" he asked quietly.

"I've got a notion already," Kevin said. "I must keep clear of pursuit till I can fetch Jane and . . . maybe then to France or America. Ireland is death to me now."

The boy nodded, squared his shoulders, and helped Kevin to his feet. In spite of his wound, Kevin traveled at a faster pace than Martin.

The destination Kevin had in mind was south. "They'll expect me to try for the border to the north," he explained. "But it was Marlowe's own scheme gave me the other notion: the rowboat, I mean. We'll take to Lough Corrib and go by water."

Martin caught on at once. "The hounds will be no use to them!"

"True enough, nor horses neither. But we must first manage two miles of open country and cross the high road to get there."

Travel on the slopes of Ben Levy was easier than crossing the bog lands. It got easier still when they hit an overgrown but still recognizable path. Martin searched his memory for where it might lead.

"What is this track?" he asked, scanning both horizons for villages or any sign of human habitation. "It does not lead anywhere."

"Older than the villages, a thousand years and more, and part of the old pilgrim road to Croagh Patrick, before the highways were ever thought of. But look yonder," Kevin ordered, pushing Martin down behind a boulder.

Along the highway from Castletown cantered a troop of horsemen and the unmistakable form of John Stone. Sun glinted dully off gun barrels and the brass buttons of uniforms. As Martin watched, the unit split into two parties, one heading east to follow the highway. The other, led by Stone, wheeled northward toward the site of the duel.

Kevin breathed an audible sigh of relief. "They think to ride us down with the horses and have not taken time to bring the dogs," he said. "Once they are out of sight, we can cross the road and get on."

Martin nodded, watching the dwindling shapes of the pursuers. Kevin was already rising from concealment when Martin hissed at him to get down, get down! At the far reach of vision, one horseman detached himself from the party around John Stone and trotted back toward the crossroads.

It was Constable Carroll.

Kevin sank back with a groan. "They remembered to post a man between the two parties. And look who it is! We'll not get by unseen before dark, and by then the hill will be crawlin' with searchers."

The two brothers sat in dismal silence. It seemed that the escape was ending before it had properly begun. "Do y'see that line of willows in the bottom?" Kevin asked. "Crawl along it away east, as far as you can. When they have me, they'll not go on lookin' for you."

Martin nodded glumly. It was the only way. If Kevin had any chance remaining, it would be to run: something Martin's presence would only hinder. "God be with you, Kev," he said, preparing to obey.

To his surprise, Kevin was still studying the line of the willows and the placement of the lone guard. "Wait," he said, forestalling

Martin's questions, then, "it might work. You are a game lad, Martin. Listen to my thoughts." Swiftly Kevin explained his plan to his brother and just as quickly, Martin agreed.

Constable Carroll sat atop his bay so as to have a clear view in all directions, but his cap was pushed up on his forehead, and his musket was slung across his shoulder. Clearly he did not think that the quarry would be coming back into the teeth of pursuit.

Martin slithered on his belly to the edge of the highway about a hundred yards to the east of the guard. The rill he followed carried a trickle of water, and the front of Martin's shirt was soaked. Buttons, knees, and elbows caked with mud, the young Donovan had also smeared his face with black clay to keep it from shining in the brush.

What seemed like the length of a patriarch's life was really only a few minutes before Martin heard the signal: a soft imitation of the shriek of a hunting merlin.

Scrubbing the worst of the mud from his face and front, Martin stood upright in the ditch next to the highway. He stepped idly out onto the gravel with his back to the sentinel.

Even though in plain sight, it still took a few seconds for the sentry to spot the figure that had emerged from nowhere. "You there," he called. "You, boy! Stop!"

Martin continued walking as though he had not heard. The noise of hooves told him that the dozing horse had been spurred into motion. Now it was important that the watcher not come on too fast.

Turning abruptly around, Martin faced the constable. "Was you callin' me, sir?" he asked innocently.

"Yes, y'spawn," Constable Carroll retorted, slowing his mount again to a walk. "And don't pretend you didn't hear me the first time. Why was you lurkin' there beside the road?"

"Lurkin', sir?" Martin protested, spreading his arms. "I wasn't lurkin'."

"Is it you, then, y'gimp? Where is your brother?"

Martin stood completely still.

"What ails the daft beggar?" mused Carroll aloud. "Come here, I say!"

Remaining rooted in place, Martin saw exasperation spread over the constable's features. Once more the horse was urged into forward motion.

Three of the willow trees in the burn grew quite close to the road. The branches of the nearest and largest overhung the edge of the highway. Martin's position was twenty paces on the other side of the tree from the sentry.

"Are you addled, boy?" demanded Carroll as he rode beneath the willow.

A moment later, it was the brains of the constable that were addled as Kevin dropped feetfirst out of the tree to land on the policeman's head. The two men tumbled to the ground together, with Kevin uppermost and wrenching the musket away. The strap hung up under Carroll's chin. The stunned man struggled feebly. Kevin knocked the constable unconscious, and the weapon came free as the policeman sank down with a groan.

At the impact the horse shied violently, and Martin had an instant's apprehension that it would bolt back toward town. Instead it spun around twice, trotted off the road toward a clump of grass, and made no protest when Martin caught the trailing reins.

"The traitor is out cold," Kevin said, "not able to say which way we have taken." Quickly scanning the lane he added, "And time to drag him into the brush so no passerby will soon notice him."

Carroll was gagged and bound, tied with his back to the road. Kevin was aboard the bay and wearing the musket slung over his own broad shoulders. Martin stood beside the horse, expecting to be dismissed since Kevin had the means of rapid escape.

"Will you desert me now?" was the surprising question. Extending his arm, Kevin swung Martin up behind him. "You're a dab hand in a fight, young Donovan, and if you are willin', our road does not fork just yet."

Behind Dead Island was a small harbor, just large enough to shelter a few fishing boats when Lough Corrib rolled in the grip of violent storms. As soon as Kevin spotted the mast of a vessel in the anchorage he reined the gelding into a ravine, and the two brothers dismounted.

"This is as far as I go by land," Kevin said. "And this is where you and I must part as well." Before Martin could protest, he continued, "The word will be out to watch for two a'horseback. Even if the first ship will not take me, I'll go along the shore till I find one."

Martin nodded glumly. The wisdom of Kevin's words was plain.

The two brothers regarded each other without speaking. Kevin grasped Martin by the forearms. Both knew that this might be the last they would meet on earth. "God be w'ye, Kev," Martin said at last.

"And you," his brother returned. "I'm minded to go to America . . . one day you may join me there. A fiercesome pair of rapparees like us need great space for our exploits, do we not?"

Martin did not trust himself to reply and only hugged his brother around the waist.

"Go, then," Kevin said gently. "Leave the horse find his own way home. And remember me in your prayers." He turned Martin by the shoulders and nudged the boy toward the hills. Then Kevin jogged toward the harbor.

Behind some rocks near the water's edge, Kevin took the musket from around his shoulders and carefully concealed it. The low, black hull and rust-colored sails of the lone ship plainly revealed it to be a trading craft called a "hooker". Hookers properly belonged to Galway Bay and the seacoast trade, but occasionally one plied the reaches of Lough Corrib. The sight was a reminder that only twenty miles down the lake was Galway City and vessels that regularly set course for Dublin, France, and America.

A swarthy man paced the deck of the twenty-foot-long craft. He wore a tall-crowned leather hat and the short jacket and loose trousers common to sailors. As Kevin watched, the man hauled at a line, hoisting the dark mainsail. The mariner appeared to be alone on board, and he was obviously preparing to get under way.

Kevin stepped boldly from among the boulders and hailed the man on the deck. "Can y'take me downwater? I can work for m'passage."

The sailor seemed unruffled by Kevin's sudden appearance.

"Don't need you," he retorted. The northerly breeze puffed against the canvas, displaying the black-painted cross on the belly of the sail.

"I can pay," Kevin called urgently, seeing the ship gathering headway.

"With what?" the mariner challenged. "I saw you sneakin' about in the brush like a common thief."

Kevin plunged back into the rocks to wave the musket over his head. "Is not a fine weapon worth passage to Galway?"

Without a word the sailor dropped the mainsail, leaving the vessel floating just a few yards offshore. "If you do not mean to rob me," he said, "dump the powder from the pan and set the musket down on the sand there and back away."

Kevin did as ordered and the dark-complected figure splashed over the side and waded through knee-deep water to the shore. Once he had the firearm in his grasp, he invited, "Come on, then. Your passage is paid."

When both men were on the craft, the sailor hoisted the main again and put the tiller hard over to port, setting the hooker's prow toward the south.

"I was afraid you would take the gun and then leave me stranded," Kevin confessed. "I thank you kindly for your help."

Eyeing Kevin's bloodstained shirt the mariner asked, "Y'did not get such a scratch from a thornbush. Tell me plain: are you at odds with the law?"

Kevin hesitated a moment, unwilling to admit his predicament. "Who is askin'?"

"An Irishman and a Catholic." The sailor's gaze lifted to the cross on the canvas. "I did not think you traded a bushel of pratties for the musket," he said. "Have you a price on your head, then?"

Kevin shrugged. "Aye, or will soon enough, but I swear I am unjustly accused."

"As I am a good Christian and named for Saint Brendan the Navigator," the man declared, "I believe you. 'Tis fortunate you are to have come to me. There's many would turn you over to the authorities."

"Can you take me as far as Galway?" Kevin inquired.

Brendan stared up at the emblem on the sail and then squinted toward the horizon. "Near enough," he confirmed. "It will not be easy keepin' you from the clutches of the Protestants, but I know a few channels that should serve."

Waving Kevin to a seat on a coil of rope, Brendan produced a handful of smoked herrings and a morsel of dry bread. These he handed to Kevin with the words, "A man on the run must eat when opportunity presents." Kevin accepted gratefully and blessed the food to which words Brendan added a fervent "Amen."

The young man fell to eating while the sailor contented himself with a pipeful of tobacco. Brendan lounged in the stern of the vessel, one sinewy arm resting lightly on the tiller. "We'll run behind Inishthee and the Derry Rocks," he said, gesturing with a jerk of his square chin. "Then hug the western shore as far as Oughterard."

Kevin chewed another mouthful of the salty fish. "Have you a dipper so I might get a drink?" he asked.

"I'll do better than that," Brendan promised. "Here, take the helm." He uncorked a small wooden cask and poured a beaker of dark brown liquid.

Taking a swallow, Kevin blinked at the strength of the ale. "It has a bite."

"And so it should," Brendan agreed, returning to the tiller. "Fortified with brandy to keep your bones against the damp. Drain the cup, boy. Confusion to all Protestants, I say."

The sun was warm on Kevin's face. He watched the shoreline sliding past and relaxed for the first moment since the challenge of the duel had been issued. His shoulders drooped as the weight of worries slipped away.

Brendan kept up a soft crooning to himself, a litany of the islands they passed. Navigating by the memories of generations he sang: *"Inishthee, Oilean na Ghamhna, Rua-Oilean . . ."*

Soon Kevin was asleep.

When he awoke he felt uncomfortably cramped. He stretched to allow his arms to find a new position, but his movement was hampered in some way. "What?" he mumbled. Kevin's arms were bound to his sides. Another loop of rope secured his ankles as well. Blinking in the light, Kevin struggled to look around him.

"About time you were stirrin'," Brendan said from the stern of the boat. "And we almost into port."

"What is this?" Kevin demanded. "I thought we had a bargain."

Brendan laughed. "A sharp trader always looks to his own, boy. If it's any comfort to ye, the only item ever in question was how long I should luff about while waitin' your worth to climb upward."

"I'll tell about the musket," Kevin threatened.

"What musket?" Brendan replied blandly.

The hooker slipped toward the quay at Oughterard, and Brendan hailed a police constable. "I have caught a queer fish," he said grinning. "Tell your captain he may buy it off me."

"You are a traitor," Kevin said bitterly.

"Fine talk from a man who boasted of a price on his head," Brendan retorted. "Is it not our Christian duty to obey the law . . . whenever possible?"

14

For weeks of futile searching, Joseph had based himself at the home of his friend and benefactor, Daniel O'Connell. O'Connell was abroad when Joseph first arrived in Dublin, and the young man had been glad; he wanted to report at least one success to accompany the litany of his failures.

Later, after fruitless investigations of ever lower and more dismal brothels and hasty visits to the grim morgues where the unknown dead were taken, he had grown desperate for Daniel's return.

At last the big man arrived back at the five-story brick house at number fifty-eight Merrion Square. Joseph Connor Burke eagerly passed beyond the brass lion-head doorknocker to ask O'Connell for help. Joseph had put aside his student clothes, his worn boots and cloak. He was dressed in top hat and frock coat, as befitted The Burke, Lord of Connaught.

O'Connell clapped him heartily on the back and embraced him. Cheerfully he declared, "I hear you made quite a splash on your return to Dublin. Put the wind up Viscount Marlowe, eh? So much so he ran back to his da the same night the specter of Joseph Connor Burke reappeared!"

This was all too lighthearted for Joseph. He felt he owed it to O'Connell to explain all that had taken place in Ballynockanor. He described the treatment of the villagers by the Marlowes, Stone, and

Constable Carroll and the seduction and ruin of Brigit by William. Though he colored deeply with shame, Joseph did not gloss over his own failure to warn the Donovans.

"So Kevin lives as a rapparee, in fear of his life," he concluded sadly, "and it is all my fault. You see why I must locate Brigit and do what I can for her . . . if she lives."

O'Connell stood beside the oak mantel and stared at the painting of his wife, Mary, who had died some years earlier. When he turned to face Joseph, his great, bushy eyebrows were drawn together in a frown, but the words of reprimand he spoke were not as expected. "Connor," he said sternly, "there are two things I cannot abide in a man. One is if he takes too great a share of the credit when somethin' goes well . . . and the other is when he embraces as his own too large a portion of blame. Did you make Young Marlowe the scoundrel he is? No! Did you give the young girl flights of fancy or push her into the viscount's arms? No." He added abruptly, laying a fleshy finger beside his nose, "Now mind, I do not say you are blameless, but get a grip, man! Your useful life is not ended."

"No," Joseph agreed. "But I must not stop seekin' the Donovan girl until every last hope is exhausted. It is the very least I can do. It is why I come to you now."

"Then it is done," O'Connell confirmed, lifting his hand solemnly toward his wife's portrait as though taking an oath. "You already know Mary insisted we treat you as one of our own. All my resources are at your disposal. If Brigit Donovan still walks this earth, we will locate her. Is it enough?"

Joseph shuddered at the gruesome probability that Brigit was already dead, but nodded his acceptance. "And you are right that my useful life cannot be ended," he said. "My path has taken an unexpected turnin', but I find myself on old familiar ground at the last: squarely in your debt." O'Connell's protests went unheeded. "My course is set. I will not return to seminary. I can serve God and my people better at your side," Joseph said firmly. "Say what is required, and I will perform it. I am your man."

Sitting down in a red leather barrel-backed chair, Daniel expressed his satisfaction and then asked, "You say that the west is near to risin'?"

"Explosive," Joseph confirmed. "The young men, like Kevin Donovan, know there is no future for them without more land to raise crops and families. But the landlords are headed squarely in the opposite direction."

"And how many in Galway would support a peaceful assembly to hear our plan for disunion and a new Irish Parliament? Could you gather five thousand men, say?"

"Ten thousand!" Joseph asserted. "Only it must be yourself who addresses them."

"And who else would it be, then?"

The political discussion was interrupted by a discreet knock at the door of the study and O'Connell's white-haired manservant entered. "A message for you, sir," he said, extending a folded yellow sheet. Looking directly at Joseph, he added, "From Galway."

After a moment's silent reading, the bulk of Daniel O'Connell exploded upward out of his chair. "Young Marlowe is dead," he announced gruffly. "And bein' held for his murder is one Kevin Donovan."

∽

One week later Joseph sat on a park bench in Merrion Square with Daniel O'Connell. In Daniel's hands was a sack of stale bread and about his feet were a flock of pigeons. They bobbed and bowed and cooed as they scrabbled for each handful of crumbs.

"I have vowed not to give up searchin' for Brigit Donovan until I know her fate," Joseph said, sighing. "But what about *Kevin* Donovan's fate? Is there nothin' to be done to save him from the gallows? He is fiery, aye, but not treacherous. Whatever he is guilty of, it cannot be cold-blooded murder."

"Witnesses?" O'Connell inquired.

Nudging a pigeon with the toe of his boot, Joseph continued lamenting. "That's the worst of it. The Marlowe steward, John

Stone. It is reported that he saw it all. He is ruthless, that one, the kind of low scoundrel who would volunteer to be a hangman. Molly Fahey says a darker soul ne'er looked upon the sun without bein' burned to a cinder.''

O'Connell distributed another palm-load of largesse to the birds.

"Stone scruples at nothin',' Joseph continued. "At a rape he will help the attacker and not the girl . . . I know that to be absolute fact.''

"What do you mean?'' O'Connell inquired. Nothing in the demeanor of the broad-shouldered man changed; he still casually toyed with the pigeons. But his words were sharper, and his eyes locked on Joseph's.

Joseph recounted how his timely arrival had saved Kate from Constable Carroll and John Stone.

"And who has heard of this?'' O'Connell probed.

"Kate and the priest and the two men; no others as far as I know. Kate wanted to protect her family from reprisal, and the two villains were afraid of bein' murdered by Ribbonmen.''

O'Connell dusted the crumbs from his hands. Clapping Joseph on the knee, he said, "I will take the Donovan case.''

"You?'' Joseph sputtered. "But there is no money to pay, and it is too great a favor to ask in a losin' cause!''

Shifting on the bench, O'Connell startled the flock of birds into a rattle of wings before they crowded around again. "I agree that things are grim for young Donovan. A Catholic farmer cannot kill a Protestant noble and hope to escape. But I have said I'll take the case. Let's hear no more about it.''

Joseph shook his head sadly. " 'Tis your great heart that you would offer,'' he said. "But English justice, so-called, is swift in Connemara. You cannot leave Dublin before your term of office ends, and Kevin will be cold and dead by then.''

O'Connell was still smiling. "Y'have known me all these years, and yet y'do not credit me half enough. Is it not an honor to attend my farewell banquet as Lord Mayor?''

Joseph agreed that it was.

"And would not the Crown prosecutor for Galway and the Castletown magistrate give their very souls to be invited to Dublin on such an occasion?" O'Connell gestured toward the far side of Merrion Square. "Did y'know, lad, that the Iron Duke, Wellington himself, was born just around that corner? Aye, but when asked if that fact made him Irish, he retorted that bein' born in a stable did not make one a horse!" Flicking a single fragment of bread into the covey of birds with his thumbnail, O'Connell set off a frenzy. "It may be so, what he says," he concluded dryly with a wink, "but some men are pigeons who will chase the smallest of crumbs. When the Galway legal authorities are called away to Dublin, I think we can safely say that Kevin Donovan's trial will be continued until the December assizes. Plenty of time to prepare his case."

∞

At the close of October, 1842, Daniel O'Connell's term as lord mayor of Dublin would be ending. As he rode through the streets in his carriage of office on the fifteenth of that month, Joseph rode beside him.

As the conveyance traveled from Merrion Square to O'Connell's offices in Mansion House, he was loudly cheered on all sides. "Hail to the Liberator!" was the cry. "Hats off for the Emancipator!"

Joseph smiled as over and over his benefactor doffed his tricornered hat and waved it to the crowds. "Will you miss this?" Joseph asked. "They'd make you emperor for life if you would take it."

"And then murder me like Caesar when they found me too ambitious? The Tories already make that comparison." O'Connell fingered his ceremonial robes and laughed. "Truth, Connor? I cannot afford the honor. My poor estate is mortgaged to the hilt from all the obligatory banquetin'." At Joseph's look of alarm he hastily added, "No, don't fash yourself. This office takes too much of my attention, and I have more important matters to attend to than the municipal water supply! It is time for me to press the case for repeal.

Next year will be the most momentous since '01. Repeal, lad! Monster meetin's all over the countryside."

Mindful of his commitment, Joseph asked, "And how can I serve?"

The young man was startled when the reply came. "I am sendin' you back to Galway," O'Connell said. "If we can raise the west, all the rest will follow. Connaught is the key. Will you serve?"

It was the last thing Joseph would have wanted, but how could he refuse? "I will," he said.

"Good lad," the Liberator remarked as the carriage turned onto Dawson Street and arrived at the cobbled forecourt of Mansion House. "You should know two things: we will use Galway's rally as a test of our strategy." O'Connell paused to gaze speculatively at his protégé.

"And the other?"

" 'Tis a hornet's nest you're goin' into," he said. "To walk the brink between enthusiasm for repeal and violent uprisin'. Old Marlowe has gone mad. He vows to toss all of Ballynockanor and raze it to the ground."

While Joseph was still digesting this morsel of grim news, O'Neill Daunt, O'Connell's personal secretary, hurried down the steps toward the carriage. "I have an urgent message," he reported, "for Young Burke."

Jolted out of his reverie, Joseph prepared himself for the worst, certain that Brigit was dead.

O'Neill Daunt continued, "The young woman . . . or at least one of her description and giving the name Brigit Marlowe . . . has been found."

"Alive?" Joseph exclaimed.

Daunt nodded somberly. "But only just. She likely will not live out the week. She is very ill with congestion of the lungs."

"Where?" Joseph demanded, all other considerations forgotten.

"In a workhouse, near Killmainham Gaol."

"Daniel," Joseph said, "I must . . ."

"Take my carriage, lad," O'Connell offered. "Godspeed."

∾

Killmainham workhouse was adjacent to the implacable, leaden mass of Killmainham Gaol and was similar to it in feel. Both structures resembled bloated, bottom-dwelling creatures, into whose cavernous mouths helpless victims would be drawn, never to emerge. A gray, drizzling rain added to the sense of being at the bottom of a stagnant river.

It was due to the heraldic insignia on the lord mayor's coach that Joseph was given instant admittance to the overseer of the workhouse. When Joseph explained his mission, the sniveling governor, fearful he had done something wrong to draw such august attention, immediately led the young man to the infirmary. "She has had the best of care," Master Whippet proclaimed. "She came to us two weeks ago in dreadful condition. Even though she could not perform even the meanest task, I still ordered her to receive a bed and medical attention, just as if she were one of our regular wards." Whippet wrung his hands. "I didn't know she was somebody," he said apologetically.

The infirmary was a dark, airless space that smelled of vomit and urine. In the corner, against the back wall, in a cot next to a toothless old woman whose face and head were covered with scabs, lay Brigit.

"The doctor is due to come again tomorrow," Whippet said anxiously. "Every three days, you see. The best of care."

"Get out!" Joseph ordered abruptly. "Send two men with a stretcher at once."

"I don't know if your authority permits . . ." Whippet said, dithering.

"Now!" Joseph said coldly, "or Lord Mayor O'Connell will see that by tomorrow you are pickin' oakum and swillin' gruel like the rest of these poor wretches!"

Whippet scurried away.

"Brigit," Joseph said softly, lifting the girl's limp hand from the thin coverlet. "Brigit, it's Joseph Connor." There was no response. How pale she was . . . and gray, like the color of a gravestone. And how thin. Except for the bulge of her abdomen, the young woman seemed to have dwindled to half size. "I've come to take you home."

This provoked a response from the sunken, dark-rimmed eyes. Brigit's lashes fluttered, and she muttered, "No . . . no . . . can never go home again."

The pulse in her lathlike wrist was as faint as her words. "Listen," Joseph encouraged. "It's Joseph. I've come all this way for you, Brigit Donovan. You'll get well again, and you and the babe'll be safe and cared for with me. I swear it."

Though a fit of coughing seized her, racking her skeletal frame, Brigit's eyes opened and she murmured, "Joseph?"

"That's right," he agreed, stroking her cold fingers.

"Is it yourself, then?"

"It is. I'll take you home."

She moaned, "I've spent . . . myself . . . Christ has forsaken . . ."

"Hush now, girl." He stroked her hair as emotion constricted his throat. She mourned the loss of her soul. What could he say to comfort her? Throwing his head back, he gasped and prayed, *Lord, do You not see? Can You be silent even now?*

Brigit's ragged breath and the groans of the workhouse inmates were the only reply.

Joseph bowed his head in grief and kissed her fingertips.

The words of the old poem written to Mary Magdalen whispered in his brain:

> *O woman with the wild thing's heart,*
> *Old sin hath set a snare for thee:*
> *In forest ways forspent thou art*
> *But the hunter Christ shall pity thee.*

As though she had heard his thoughts, her eyes opened and fixed on his face. "Christ pity me," she managed.

"He does, sweet Brigit. He will."

"I've sold my . . . life." The eyes squeezed shut. A single tear escaped and coursed down her cheek.

Joseph wiped the tear away, suddenly aware he was weeping as well. Again, in a still, small voice he heard the ancient verse recited clearly:

> *O woman spendthrift of thyself,*
> *Spendthrift of all the love in thee,*
> *Sold unto sin for little pelf,*
> *The Captain Christ shall ransom thee.*

Vox de Nube! The Cloud of Unknowing parted for an instant and the Voice of God's Spirit spoke clearly to his heart. Joseph fell to his knees beside her, suddenly certain of what he must do. Kate's face came clear into his mind. For a moment he argued with The Voice, but the command remained unchanged.

Embracing Brigit gently, he said, "Brigit! By His dyin', Christ has already ransomed you! Only receive His forgiveness and your wounded soul will be healed!" She nodded and he kissed her cheek. "Do you accept the sacrifice of Jesus on the cross?"

"I do receive Him," she murmured. "Now I . . . can . . . die."

"Brigit! You must live and be my wife! And the child'll be my own dear child and bear the name of Burke. Do you hear me, girl?"

Her hand lifted slightly, then fell back as she slipped into unconsciousness.

"Hurry with that stretcher," he hissed over his shoulder to a pair of workhouse inmates just entering the room. "Bring blankets and take her to the carriage!"

ᖇᖰ

Doctor Mahony shook his broad face and wiped a palm over the white-fringed dome of his head. "It is congestion of the lungs," he said. "There is no doubt both airways are involved. And she is burning with fever. Apart from prayer, there is little to be done."

Mahony, Daniel O'Connell's personal physician, Joseph Connor Burke, and the Liberator himself were gathered in a corner of O'Connell's upstairs bedroom. The three men were speaking in low tones, even though Brigit, lying beneath the pale blue coverlet, gave no sign of consciousness. With tears streaming down his face, Joseph regarded the young woman. Brigit's glorious hair, all that remained of her youthful beauty, was fanned out around her head like a halo.

"And the child?" Joseph inquired brokenly. "How soon can it come and live?"

Mahony regarded Brigit for a moment before replying. "The baby is large and well formed." He stopped and all watched as Brigit's shoulders shuddered in her struggle for one more breath. Her form was so frail, so insubstantial, and pressed down into the bed so lightly, that apart from the swelling at her waist she appeared little more than a pencil sketch of a woman's face propped upon the pillow. The doctor shrugged. "The young lady is literally spending the last coin of her life's force on the child."

Daniel O'Connell, his booming voice lowered to a rumble, asked, "Will she waken?"

Again the doctor had no firm response. "She is young and was manifestly healthy before being terribly abused and starved. I have given orders to have strong broth and iron tonic spooned into her around the clock, as much as she can swallow . . . but . . ." His words faded into the unspoken horror of helplessness.

Squaring his shoulders, Joseph declared, "I want a priest standin' by," he said. "If she knows me . . . if she is alert for as much as five minutes . . . I'll marry her and give the child my name."

"Be careful, lad," O'Connell warned. "To make such a declaration in front of witnesses! If she were awake to hear it, you would be bound!"

"Such is exactly my intention. I am bound already."

The following day, Joseph posted a hasty letter to Tom Donovan, telling him that Brigit was found and that he intended to marry her when she was able. He briefly mentioned it was his intention to fill the Donovan household with many grandchildren very soon. Paying the driver extra, Joseph insisted the message be taken immediately to the Donovan cottage.

That duty performed, Joseph settled down to watch and wait for Brigit to come around.

∽

Vapor rose from the breath of the milk cow in the stanchion. Grateful for the warm hide of the little moilie, Kate finished the morning milking with Da.

Tom Donovan worked without speaking. He had been silent and sad for weeks since Kevin's arrest. He smiled not at all, even when his neighbors clapped him on the back and said that Kevin was a brave lad and had only done what was right.

Kate agreed that Kevin had done what true justice demanded. But what was true seldom defeated what was powerful. Old Marlowe was powerful, evil, filled with hate for every tenant farmer in the townlands. As Joseph had predicted, violence had brought destruction to the very gates of Ballynockanor.

Da, Martin, Mary Elizabeth, and Kate had only one comforting thought in all that had come upon them: Joseph Connor Burke, son of The Burke, was in Dublin searching for Brigit.

Perhaps he would bring her home again. Contrite, humbled by her folly and embraced by the love of her family, Brigit would truly be one of them again. Kate clung to this hope. Da had not spoken of accepting Brigit back, but Kate saw the grief in his eyes for her and knew he would not turn her away.

The blast of the horn from the Galway mail coach interrupted her reverie.

Da said, "Can that be soundin' for us?"

"Aye. Perhaps some word from Dublin, Da."

They left their buckets on the high shelf and went together into the coldness of the day.

The team slowed to a walk and stamped impatiently in the puddled yard as Da raised his hand to greet the driver.

"Peace to you, Tom Donovan," shouted the coachman as he dipped into the bag. "The word you've been waitin' for, no doubt!"

"Could you use a cuppa hot tay then, Jack?" Tom reached up to take the letter as though he were unconcerned with the contents.

Kate saw the lips of the coachman twitch as he licked his lips, stared at the sky, and then down at the sealed paper that bore the emblem of Daniel O'Connell, lord mayor of Dublin. Jack wanted nothing more than to sip the news contained within.

"A cuppa? It's the day for it. Aye. Don't mind if I do. But I'll have it here if you don't mind."

Da inclined his head to Kate. "Tay for poor frozen Jack, daughter," he instructed, holding the piece of mail to the light.

Kate, barely able to make her feet move away from the tidings, even for a moment, heard the paper tear as she entered the cottage. Had Brigit been found? She prepared the tea with her heart thumping in her ears. She heard the giggles of Mary Elizabeth and Martin outside as Da shared the information with them.

So it was good news! How they all needed good news! Brigit must have been found! Waiting for the tea to steep, Kate closed her eyes and squeezed back tears of joy and expectation. She blessed Joseph Connor Burke for the good man he was!

Da's voice drifted through the window. "Was ever a man so blessed by the Almighty? Glory to God! Martin! Mary Elizabeth! Run quick with the news to Father O'Bannon and to all the village as you pass by!"

The brew was weak, but Kate snatched it up and hurried outside.

Jack reached down from his perch and clasped Tom's hand. "Congratulations, Tom Donovan! Has ever a man had such a fine son-in-law as the son of The Burke himself! And your Brigit will be a happy bride indeed when she returns to your hearth!"

"Glory to God," Da cried, and then his eyes caught a glimpse of Kate's face as she stood frozen in the doorway, cups steaming in her hands. His smile faded briefly.

Kate knew her expression mirrored the blow of such a report. Mastering her emotions, she managed to speak: "It's good news then, Da?"

He was less exuberant in his reply. "Aye, Kate. That it is. Brigit is found. In ill health, he says, but he's taken her to O'Connell's house and . . ."

"Tell me all, for I can't help but rejoice that he's saved her."

"Himself . . . Joseph's a good man, that. He'll make a fine . . . husband for Brigit."

Kate forced a smile as she handed the drinks to the driver and to Da. "Bless him," she whispered. "I always thought a man so fine as Joseph would make a husband for Brigit!" She spoke the words, but her heart ached. She reprimanded her own regret. Had she not sent the man away? What did she expect?

"Aye." Da's unrestrained joy resurfaced with the redemption of Brigit's honor. "He'll have a handful with that girl! But he says here . . . 'I regret I could not wait to ask your permission in person, but I have a priest nearby, and I cannot wait to wed her. Have faith, dear Tom. You'll have a bushel of grandchildren around the Donovan house by and by!' "

Kate, knowing that tears would soon follow, thanked the coachman for coming so quickly and bringing such joyful news. Then she excused herself and returned to the milk bucket.

So she had lost him forever. It was only right, she thought. Had she given him any choice? Leaning her cheek against the warmth of the milk cow, she prayed for Brigit and for Joseph and let the flow of her weeping carry her far from the love she had held for Joseph.

∞

The basket of food Kate carried into the prison was thoroughly searched by the assistant warden. Dour, bull-necked, and smelling of whiskey, the official plunged his knife blade into the kidney pie, pierced every potato, and probed the butter with a dirty finger.

Licking gravy from his knife he intoned, "Well now, you're a good cook, but the question is, why waste such food on a man who's good as dead?"

Kate lowered her eyes for fear he would see her defiance and keep her from Kevin's cell. "Encourage me to feed him, sir, for wouldn't it displease the courts if my brother were to perish from eatin' too little thin porridge?"

The warden laughed and kept back the kidney pie. "Go on, then. I'll keep this portion on suspicion there may be a Ribbonman hid within who would burst out and attack the jailer."

"Sure, and that won't happen, sir. There are no Ribbonmen this side of the border."

"Only your brother, ma'am. And by feedin' him so well he may grow strong enough to seek escape. Hunger has its place here. A weak prisoner makes the bars that much stronger."

"Kevin has no mind to injure any man."

"Save the one he's murdered."

"Keep only half the pie, sir, and I'll bring you a whole one when next I visit."

The warden considered her request. She would not bring food again if this was confiscated entirely. Half a pie and a promise of more to come was worth the sacrifice. He scraped half the contents of the tin onto his own plate, then summoned two guards to accompany Kate into the gloom of the prison cell block.

Keys jingled as they entered a narrow brick corridor illuminated by a few candles in sconces. Dank and oppressive, the place smelled of latrine buckets. Six iron doors on each side of the corridor contained prisoners awaiting deportation for debt or homelessness or some petty offense.

At the sound of footsteps some captive began to sing,

> *To live at home*
> *And never to roam;*
> *To pass his days in sighin'.*

Voices from other cells joined in singing,

> *To wear sad looks,*
> *Read stupid books,*

And have no fear of dyin'.
O! Charley dear!
To me, 'tis clear,
You are not the man for Galway!

The song ended with a cheer from the men who were destined never to see their homeland again.

"They put a fine face on it, then," remarked a guard as they stopped before Kevin's door. "All but this one. Kevin Donovan'll not be singin' till he's swingin'."

Key plunged into the lock and turned. The tiny space contained no bedding except for dirty straw on the floor. There was a bucket for the latrine and a bucket for water. Kevin, filthy and bearded, red of eye and ashen in color, glared at the unfamiliar light like a mad-man.

Kate scarcely recognized him. Again she restrained the fury she felt at his treatment.

Controlling the emotion in her voice, she said his name quietly. "Kevin, darlin'."

He squinted against the light. "Is it yourself then, Kate?"

"Aye. With good food for you." She took the candle from the guards, thanked them as the iron barrier clanged shut behind her, then moved toward Kevin.

"I'm half blind from the dark," he croaked. "There's been no sun for days. Or is it weeks? I can't tell. What's the month?"

"November."

"I'll not live to see Christmas, Kate. They'll hang me sure, before then. Why'll they not allow Father O'Bannon in to visit me? Or Da? How is it you've come after so long?"

"Joseph Connor has a powerful friend in Dublin: Daniel O'Connell himself. He arranged it so one member of the family could come. Better me, a woman, than Da. They'd be some gentler, we thought, with me." She pulled the fractured pie from the basket. "I managed to get this in to you, Kev. Da couldn't have done it."

Kevin inhaled the aroma of the still warm dish. "Da would've et it himself or got arrested tryin' to save it." A smile wavered on his lips. He lowered his head and began to weep quietly. "I've done it all right, haven't I? What good is all of it?"

"Martin saw it all. It was an accident. He'll testify."

"No! He mustn't say a word about it. If he was there and saw it, then that makes him an accomplice. I'm for the gallows. And if Martin breathes a word of what he knows, you'll be tossed off the farm. They say every farmer in Ballynockanor'll be turned out because of me if I get off! Ah, Kate!"

She shook his arm and hissed, "Shaaa, Kevin! Be a man. Do you want them to see you broken?"

He wiped his cheeks with the back of his hand and pretended to be interested in the contents of the basket. "Good," he said, holding up a potato. "Good big pratties."

"Aye."

He caressed the spud as if it were a treasure. "Fine soil, our prattie patch. Always grew the biggest potatoes in the townlands. I've missed the harvest." He paused. "But I'll be early home for plantin'." A look of sorrow fixed in his eyes. "Will they let you bury me at Saint John's, do you think? Beside Mother?"

"No more of that," she chided, although the certainty of his condemnation and execution filled her mind as well. "But Kevin, I've brought enough good food for the week, you see. And somethin' else that'll strengthen your spirits."

He did not respond for a moment as if the vision of his grave hung before his eyes. "What then?"

"Brigit's found," Kate said cheerfully. "Joseph searched all of Dublin till he found her."

"She's alive then? She's well?" Suddenly he became animated. The old Kevin returned.

"Aye. She's alive." Kate did not tell him all. "And here's the most surprisin' news of all. You were right about Joseph not bein' who he said he was. He's none other than the lost son of The Burke. That's right. Connor Burke didn't die. He came home. And now he's found our poor sister and married her himself. Proper, before a real priest and with Daniel O'Connell himself as witness."

Kevin laughed and tossed the potato into the air, catching it with one hand and taking a big bite. "God be praised!" he cried. "William Marlowe in hell while Brigit is married to the true lord of Connaught, Connor Burke himself!"

Kate patted him on the shoulder. "There now. Better?"

"Will he bring her home then? I'd like to speak to the man. I maligned him fiercely, didn't I, Kate?"

"That you did."

He nodded vigorously, then his joy faded a moment. "But what of you? I always thought if he wasn't a priest, the two of you would . . ."

"Shaaa, Kev! I've not given it a thought. The family honor is restored. Brigit's saved. And never mind myself."

He looked her in the eye. "Then never mind what comes of Kevin Donovan. But Kate . . . if I could . . . I've been thinkin' of Jane. I'll be writin' my farewell to her. Now seems I've two letters to write: one to Joseph as well. Could you bring me ink and paper?"

The rattle of keys in the door interrupted them.

The guard barked, "Come along now, missy. Time's up."

"Aye." She promised Kevin she would bring the stationery. "All the village prays for you. Remember you're loved. Even here in the darkness you are not alone, Kev."

"God bless all. . . ."

With a rough shout from the jailors, the visit came to an end.

The vigil at Brigit's bedside passed slowly over many days and nights. Her hand was like a small bird in Joseph's fist. Through the long hours he rested his right palm on her abdomen and felt the baby move and kick. The life growing within her became his own. Inexplicably Joseph came to love the unborn baby as though he had conceived it and waited eagerly the nine months for its birth. Joseph prayed for Brigit's life. He whispered softly to the baby and told him plainly that if he were male he would be named for The Burke of Connaught.

Joy illuminated Joseph's soul. He would be a father, a husband. What had begun as a command to the duty of loving was transformed miraculously into love.

"You must live, Brigit," he whispered in a barely audible voice. "For the sake of the little one."

The priest, an old friend of Daniel's, sat at the foot of the bed. Doctor Mahony read by the fire.

The doctor spoke. "If she dies, we must be prepared to take the child from her womb within a matter of minutes or he will die with her. Can you bear it?"

Joseph's gaze met the priest's. "She'll live," he insisted hoarsely.

At that, Brigit's faint voice spoke. "Are you still here, Joseph?" She smiled and glanced down at his hand on her stomach.

Words caught in his throat. He nodded and forced himself to speak. "That I am."

"The baby . . . he's a lively one."

"He'll be needin' a father. Will you take me, Brigit?"

Radiant, peaceful, she touched his face. "I've had sweet dreams of Mother dressin' me like a virgin bride in white. I thank you for helpin' me find my way back. Mary Elizabeth said you were Saint Joseph." She wheezed and fought for breath. "I believe it myself now."

"Will you be my wife?" he pleaded.

"You must tell Kate I love her. . . ."

"You'll be tellin' her yourself."

"Aye. That I will one day. And the others. Da . . ."

"Will you marry with me now?"

She touched her belly. "Feel him kickin'? I will . . . marry you." She inclined her head slightly to the priest who came swiftly to the bedside and clasped the couple's hands in his.

"Witnesses?" asked the priest. "Who'll stand with you?"

"Fetch Daniel for me, will you, Doctor?" Joseph asked.

Brigit sighed. "My mother is watchin' from heaven. Be quick about it."

Daniel, rumpled in his evening clothes, joined them.

The ceremony began as the first light of dawn seeped through the tall windows of the bedchamber. Brigit's replies were barely audible until she repeated the phrase, "Till death do us part . . . dear Joseph . . . I am . . . so tired. Bless us now, Father. We are well and truly wed."

The priest obliged her with the final "Amen."

Brigit smiled up at Joseph. "Aye. For the sake of the child you've done this, and I'm grateful. I'm a respectable Irish wife, sure. . . . And I'll make you happy, dear Joseph. One day you'll love me too. I promise. Kiss me, husband."

Joseph bent low and kissed her pale lips. "My wife."

"He'll need a fine father . . . to watch after him," she said, breathing faintly.

"And mother . . ."

"I owe you everythin'."

" 'Twas Christ paid your debt."

"There's one debt left for me. For everyone."

"Don't speak of dyin', Brigit, when you have found life."

"I've prayed for his little soul. Asked God not to count my sin against him."

"One day he'll find his own path and carry his own load to the cross. As we all must."

"I thought God would take us both . . . baby to heaven, and myself? Myself never to hold him . . . in this life or the next. But Christ saved me from that sorrow."

"Heaven is yours and life here as well. Think of livin'." Joseph rubbed her hand, hopeful at the renewed color on her cheek.

"Aye. Joseph Connor. Life."

She drifted off to sleep. Joseph remained at her side, watching as the child shifted and moved within her. He bent to kiss the bulge that was soon to be his son or daughter.

"Sweet dreams," he whispered. "I will learn to love you, Brigit."

Daniel interrupted his reverie. Joseph followed him quietly into the study. Daniel's admiring gaze locked on his face. "The Burke would be proud of you."

"A boy child will have his name, and that of Brigit's father."

"Aye. I'll stand at your side at the christenin'. Now. To other matters. The chief prosecutor in charge of Kevin's trial is on his way back to Galway. I have used my connection with the lord lieutenant to have a new magistrate appointed, one not under the thumb of Old Marlowe. I told them both I'll be defendin' the lad myself. There is a mountain of false testimony from Constable Carroll and John Stone in the case.''

"They cover their crimes by accusin' another of wrongdoing." Joseph felt the anger rise in him again.

"They fool only themselves. God knows the truth and so do we all. Do they look into the eyes of their companions and know everyone sees they are liars and thieves? Ah, well. Perhaps not. But they've lied enough to stretch Kevin's neck and have all of Ballynockanor turned out of their homes."

"They use the courts to do injury when their own cruelty has been exposed. An odd method of revenge then, is it not?''

"I became a barrister for the defense," Daniel said, "because it came to me clearly: those who twist the law to steal and destroy'll receive some special punishment on the day when every knee shall bow before almighty God."

"May all they've done to others come back upon their own heads."

"So it is written by God's own hand. Perhaps it'll not be in our lifetime, but justice'll be done. Until that judgment we mortals must use wit and truth to fight those who hide behind the name of Christ though they are in league with the Old Deceiver."

"Till now the truth has won the cause little ground," Joseph said. "What do you have in mind?''

"This mornin' I'll leave you here with Brigit and hurry to defend Kevin or he's a dead man sure. Tell me all you remember about your uncle and that last night in your father's house. Voices and shadows and faces if you can. Surely goin' home brought old things newly to your memory. Then give me every detail about Constable Carroll and John Stone from the time you came back to Ballynockanor until the moment you left for Dublin. The key to unlock the prison door may be here." Daniel tapped his temple, gave a wink, and rang for strong tea and breakfast.

15

In her dream Kate walked beside Joseph along the banks of the Cornamona. She was whole and beautiful again, and there were no scars on her body or in her memory.

Sean stood watching on the hill above them beside St. Brigit's cross. He shouted down to her, "Go on then, Kate. Love him! Connor Burke always was my friend."

Kate stopped and turned to embrace Joseph, but as she did, the water of the river froze and on the opposite shore Brigit beckoned and called, "Joseph, I need you more than she does!" Her gleaming hair shone in the sunlight.

Joseph cupped Kate's face in his hands and kissed her gently. "Tell me to stay, Kate, and I'll never leave you."

Kate nodded, opened her mouth to tell him of her love, but said, "She's right, you know. Brigit needs you more than I do."

"Aye," Joseph agreed sadly and turned away. "I'll wed her then." Stepping onto the icy stream, he walked across without looking back and enfolded Brigit in his arms.

Kate was awakened by a fierce knocking on the cottage door. It was Father O'Bannon standing outside in the rain.

"Kate, girl! Wake up!"

"Comin'!" She wrapped her cloak around her shoulders and

hurried to open the door while the rest of the family moaned and stirred in the darkness.

"What is it?" Kate asked fearfully.

"My lumbago!" moaned Father O'Bannon. "It's bucketing and no mistake!" He shook the rain from his coat and stretched his hands toward the faintly glowing embers on the hearth.

"But why have you come?"

"A cuppa tay, girl, if you've a mind for my condition."

She obeyed as Da, buttoning his cords, wandered out and greeted the priest.

"And what brings you here before the chickens are awake, Your Honor?" Da remarked through a yawn.

"None but the Emancipator himself. Daniel O'Connell."

"Had a vision, have you?" Da smiled, took the cup from Kate, and sniffed.

"Not a vision. But glory be! Daniel O'Connell at three o'clock in the mornin' knockin' at my door. Listen then! He's come to Bally-nockanor himself to defend your own Kevin! Aye! And he's asked me to come here straightaway and fetch Kate for a chat."

"Daniel O'Connell," Da questioned. "To defend wee Kev? And to chat with Kate?"

The priest sipped his tea and grinned with his four teeth, making him look like a very old infant just teething.

"Aye. 'Tis Kate he wishes a word with first. Then Martin about the shootin'. Then he'll speak with Kev in his cell."

Daniel O'Connell's face was weary as he questioned Kate about the attempted rape by Carroll and John Stone. He made careful notations of the details on lined paper, then compared them with another scrap of paper signed by Joseph Connor Burke and witnessed by a Dublin magistrate.

"Identical to Connor's story in every respect," O'Connell said. "My question is, if you'll be up to speakin' out about it in the courtroom?"

"It shamed me. But if it can help save Kevin somehow . . ."

O'Connell shrugged his massive shoulders. "We must do all we can. I'll not lie to you: Kevin's is a terrible uphill struggle." Changing the subject, O'Connell remarked, "Most likely Connor . . . Joseph as you call him . . . won't be here. His wife will not be able to travel for some time."

Kate swallowed hard at the reference to Brigit as Joseph's wife. "Is she growin' stronger, then, Your Honor? I've said a novena for her, and prayed every day that all would be well."

"Then all will be well. She sent the message that she loves you and the family." The Emancipator patted her hand reassuringly.

Emotion rose in Kate's throat. She had forgiven Brigit. Had Brigit likewise forgiven Kate? "I'll be glad to have her home again. To embrace her."

"And Joseph sends fond greetin's as well. He wishes you to know he'll bring Brigit back as soon as she's able. She's stronger than she was at first. And . . . I'll add to this . . . she has the best of care. Mahony's a fine doctor."

Kate lowered her eyes. " 'Twould be a miracle to have us all safe and home in Ballynockanor again."

"And may I be here to see it. Joseph says you are the finest fiddle player in all of West Ireland. He asked me to ask you . . . if your brother goes free and Brigit comes home again . . . will you play me a tune and then one for Joseph as well?"

Kate flushed and glanced down at her hand. "It's difficult . . . but given those conditions, your Honor, I'll play and sing and dance as well."

In Kate's heart, the only tune she heard was a funeral dirge.

The first contractions of Brigit's labor began just after midnight. Joseph, who slept on a cot at the foot of her bed, heard her cry weakly for help. He ran to the corridor and called for Dr. Mahony, who bustled into the room and ordered Joseph out while he examined her.

Minutes passed like hours until the physician opened the door.

"The child'll wait no longer for her to gain her strength. I was hopin' we'd have another week."

"But she'll be all right?" Joseph questioned.

"I'll do what I can. The rest is in God's hands. Send my man for the priest." He passed a scribbled note with an address to Joseph. "Whatever comes, Brigit will not have the strength to feed the baby. Here's the address of a Quaker couple. They've brought an American Negro, a freedwoman, here to Dublin as wet nurse to their baby. The child is nearly weaned. Enough so we can pay the freedwoman to feed this infant if it lives. Send for her. We'll need her by mornin'."

The summons was sent, and within an hour, priest and nurse arrived. The woman, lean and with ebony eyes that carried great sorrow, aided the doctor. Her soothing, melodic voice was the only sound that penetrated the door.

Taking Joseph by the arm, the priest led him into the study where the two prayed and paced in turn.

It was near dawn when Dr. Mahony reentered the room.

"I have done what I could, Burke."

"The baby?"

"She has nothin' left. No strength. I explained to you. . . ."

"Brigit's dyin'?"

"She is."

The priest followed Joseph into the sickroom. The nurse, stroking Brigit's head, glanced up, and the inevitable was in her expression. Standing up quickly, the woman whispered softly, "You doin' good, honey. Yo' man be here now."

Brigit's eyes snapped open. Her hair was soaked with perspiration, and her luminous blue eyes shone too brightly.

"Joseph . . ." She breathed his name. "I've tried. . . ."

Kissing her on the brow, he smoothed back the damp curls. "You mustn't give up now. We're so close. . . ."

"You've led me home. I'm grateful. . . ."

"We'll go home together. The three of us."

She shook her head. "I wanted to hold him once."

"You'll hold him."

"I can't." She closed her eyes. "But take him to Da for me. Lay the baby in my father's arms and say how much I loved him."

"Brigit . . . ," he pleaded. "You'll do it yourself."

"Stop, Joseph." A contraction seized her, wrenched her, and then began to ease. "I know. You must . . . let me go now. . . Promise . . . and then dear Kate. She's been mother to us all, and no child of her own. . . . Promise."

"I promise," he said, choking. Tears stung his eyes. How he had wanted to bring her to Ballynockanor in joy and health and life! Could it be that his prayers were not to be answered?

"Take . . . me . . . home. Plant me in the soil of Saint John's, and there I'll bloom with the roses till Christ wakes me. Promise."

"I promise."

The priest stepped forward to take a place beside Joseph. Dr. Mahony hovered behind them as the sacraments were given.

"In the name of the Father and the Son and the Holy Spirit . . ."

"Joseph!" she said, sighing. "Love our baby well and tell him . . . I'll be watchin'. Lovin'." Her gaze fixed on the pastel sky beyond the panes of glass. Her expression filled with peace and joy. "Mother, I've missed you. Do you see we've got a baby?" She whispered, exhaled long and slow, and with that breath, her life ended.

"Brigit!" Joseph cried. "Not yet!" He dropped to his knees. "The baby! The baby!"

Dr. Mahony grasped Joseph's shoulder and pulled him away. "She's gone. Grieve later. No time for that now if you want the child to live!" Rolling up his sleeves, Mahony hefted his medical bag onto the night table. "Father! Get him out of here! Every moment counts!"

With a strong grip, the priest pulled Joseph to his feet and led him from the room.

With one final, horrified look back through the portal, Joseph saw Dr. Mahony, scalpel poised, throw back the blankets to expose Brigit's rounded belly.

The door slammed shut in his face. With a groan Joseph leaned against the panel. "I've lost even this battle."

The priest replied, "You led her home to her Savior's arms. She loved you for it and died a peaceful death. Saint Joseph, the patron saint of a happy death, could do no more. What else can you accomplish?"

"I'll keep my word to her and to her family. Sure, and I'll take her home to Ballynockanor."

∞

The trial of Kevin Donovan had already occupied several frosty December days. It was all a bitter disappointment to those who hoped for a surprise ending. There had been no impassioned orations from Daniel O'Connell and no call for bloody revolution. Kevin's life hung only by the thin thread of formality; he was as good as dead already. This was the consensus of all of Connemara on the night before the last day of the trial.

It was not that Constable Carroll was opposed to drinking in Joe Watty's pub; he just never felt welcome there.

But when Daniel O'Connell, the Daniel O'Connell, the Liberator, hailed him from across Castletown's Main Street and invited him to share a pint, how could he refuse?

There were more than a few nudges and wry comments when this unlikely duo entered the tavern and made their way to the dim, dark table known as "the snug." "Will y'look at that now," piped Clooney to Watty. "It's himself and the darkest spawn of a turncoat Satan ever begot. What d'ya make of it?"

Watty nodded knowingly. "Carroll is a great traitor to be certain but he's an even bigger fool. He does not have much worth takin', but whatever it is, the Liberator will pick him clean before the second pint goes down that gapin' gullet."

In the shadowy recess O'Connell was saying, "There is no reason for us to be adversaries. After all, we are both officers of the court, are we not?"

Carroll could not help smiling at this honor. He felt that

O'Connell was making a display of sportsmanship to the winning side. He crowed, "It's me as should be buyin'. Young Donovan's guilty as sin and will swing for it."

Daniel O'Connell frowned into his Guinness and muttered, "Ah, well, honest men can only do their best. Besides, it was not Kevin Donovan I was minded of just now."

Constable Carroll made, what was for him, a rapid mental connection. "I catch your drift," he said. "The delay of the trial may have slowed things some, but it will not save the Donovan cottage from tossin' nor themselves from eviction. I know 'twas Martin Donovan helped waylay me upon the road. Once his brother is convicted, the rest of the family must pay the penalty."

"How true it is, what the Scripture says," O'Connell said darkly.

"Eh? What's that supposed to mean?"

"Can a man take fire into his bosom and not be burned? You are so positive about the identity of Martin Donovan . . . just like another man who knows absolutely that an officer of the court, a certain constable as it were, is guilty of assault and attempted rape."

At these words, Carroll started upright, banged his head into a low beam, swore coarsely, and sat back down abruptly, holding his hand to the back of his skull.

"Is that the same place that got tapped during the rape?" O'Connell asked innocently.

"Yes! I mean, no! I mean, there was no rape."

"Lower your voice, man," O'Connell cautioned. "D'ya want to have your throat slit before the night is out?" Carroll, throwing anxious looks all around, subsided onto the bench. "Now, hear me," O'Connell warned sternly. "The same man who gave you that lump on your thick skull can and will testify at your trial for rape. That is, if ever you live that long."

"No," Carroll begged. "I was drunk! Nothin' happened, I swear."

" 'Tis well, or you'd be dead already, I think. Calm down and listen. All I'm suggestin' is that you are not so sure about the wee lad upon the road as you once thought . . . are you?"

"No," Carroll said eagerly. "His face was muddied, and I did not get a good look at him. I don't really know who it was."

"I thought as much," O'Connell agreed. He looked up toward the door as the mantel clock chimed eight. At the window beside the door, John Stone pressed the tip of his thin nose against the outside of the pane.

O'Connell smiled to himself. He withdrew a thin sheet of paper from inside his coat and unfolded it. "This is a deposition that states you cannot say with any assurance who it was you met on the highway. Sign here."

$$\infty$$

Spotting the stock-thin figure of John Stone was not easy in the cloud-shrouded darkness, but Daniel O'Connell located him at last under the portico of Castletown's courthouse.

"All right," Stone said acidly. "I'm here. And I played your game 'I spy.' What next? A few spindles of sally rod to pass the time? The bog-trotters may be impressed by your name, but I'm not."

"That's well said," O'Connell noted. "It will make our business easier to transact, man to man."

"What business could I possibly have with you?"

"It is my understandin' that you say Kevin Donovan fired treacherously, before Young Marlowe was set . . . clearly murder, if true."

"Every word of it," Stone said archly. "You may have managed to ring in a Dublin justice who will be sympathetic to your pleading, but even that will not change the facts."

"The facts?" murmured O'Connell, holding up a folded scrap of paper. "Did y'remark Constable Carroll takin' pen in hand to this very page?"

"What of it?"

"In it, he says that you caused the death of one Liam the porter."

This was so unexpected that Stone staggered away from a pillar and into the street. "That was fifteen years ago," he said. "No one can prove anything."

Daniel O'Connell's dark mane of hair shook ponderously. Over the heads of the two men, there was just enough light to make out the steel cage of the gibbet where the dead bodies of hanged criminals were displayed. O'Connell pointedly stared upward until Stone followed his gaze. "Men of lesser character than you," O'Connell said, "men like Constable Carroll, for instance, might sell out their friends to save themselves. It seems that Carroll also accuses you of the attempted rape of a certain local lass."

"Me!" Stone exploded. "He . . . I . . ." He shut his mouth suddenly on the string of pronouns.

"Now I admit that it would just be his word against yours," O'Connell noted. "But such a debate cannot do either of your . . . reputations . . . any good, eh?"

"Then what is it you want?"

Raising one hand, O'Connell mimed warding off the oppressive nearness of the gibbet. Then the Liberator placed his other hand on Stone's back and pulled the steward close enough to whisper in his ear.

December rains drenched the black plumes of the horses pulling Brigit's hearse. The Irish sky, as if in sympathy, wept on the land and upon the thousands of people who lined the streets of Dublin to watch her coffin pass by.

Was there anyone in all of Ireland who had not heard the story of the young woman wronged and abandoned? And what of the brother defending her honor who would now surely be hung?

Though his coach followed behind and he might have taken shelter in it, Joseph Connor Burke walked on through the storm with his hand never leaving her coffin.

The whispered word swept ahead through villages and towns as the procession approached.

Is the story of Brigit and Kevin Donovan not the story of Ireland? Could the poor girl not be my daughter or yours? Could young Kevin not be our son waitin' for the gallows? Aye, and the son of The Burke himself marryin' her to redeem her honor. And now Tom Donovan losin' two children in the same week. Too much to bear, it is.

From county to county people packed the roads and doffed their caps in the downpour.

In County Kildare the cry was raised that rallied the first hundred mourners to accompany the funeral procession bound for Bally-nockanor.

Sure, and it isn't a proper Irish wake a'tall. Not in the least! Come on, then! We'll walk the poor girl home together so the lad's not grievin' the whole long way alone!

It began with only those hundred. The numbers grew and with them grew The Legend.

∽

The morning of the last day of Kevin's trial dawned clear, crisp, and cold. The steps of the courthouse were three deep with soldiers and a ring of blue-coated policemen encircled the entire building.

The street was packed with onlookers. All of Ballynockanor was there, but then, so too were all the sheep farmers from Allintober, the peat-cutters from Lough Ballydoo, the fisherfolk from Lough Corrib's north shore, and a smattering of others from as far away as Clonbur and Tuam. Most were there to catch a glimpse of the Liberator, even in what was sure to be a defeat. Others had heard that Kevin's hanging would immediately follow his sentence; ginger-bread in the shape of a gibbet was sold in the market square.

Inside the courtroom, the gallery was likewise packed, but except for Tom Donovan and his family, no others from Ballynockanor were allowed. Those spectators permitted into the room were, like the members of the jury, known to be loyal Protestants. Even so, all were searched for weapons before being admitted.

In the center of the front row of the gallery sat Old Marlowe. Hunched and glowering, he glared like an angry spider at any who dared look at his bloated bulk.

Robed and bewigged, Justice Godwin entered from behind the bench to a call for silence in Her Majesty's court. To the surprise of all present, the prisoner was not brought into the courtroom, but remained in his cell, nor did Justice Godwin call the court to order. Instead he made the unusual announcement that Crown Prosecutor Stanley, Defense Counsel O'Connell, and two key witnesses, John Stone and Martin Donovan, were to join him in chambers.

Instantly the room was awash with speculation. All present knew that Godwin was not a virulent anti-Catholic like his predecessor, but even so, he had a reputation for coming down hard on terrorism and lawlessness. Perhaps he had gotten wind of a Ribbonman plot to disrupt the proceedings.

The rumor swept out-of-doors and into the street. Nervously eyeing the mob, the soldiers rapidly responded to an order to fix bayonets. Families were hustled into shop entrances to be out of harm's way; every man viewed unknown bystanders with suspicion.

Inside his oak-paneled office, Justice Godwin removed his wig and scratched his thin gray hair. Godwin invited Martin Donovan, Daniel O'Connell, and Prosecutor Stanley to sit. The judge very pointedly did not offer John Stone a chair and the storklike steward paced nervously near the window.

Searching the faces of all in the room, Justice Godwin observed, "This county is ready to explode. For that reason, it is important that every effort be made to preserve the peace while seein' that justice is done. Young man," he said to Martin, "would you please repeat to this group what you told me earlier today?"

Gulping, Martin stood beside his chair as if preparing for a recitation in school. He recounted truthfully Kevin's anger at the news of Brigit's ruin, the challenge, and the events on the morning of the duel. "But in the end it was an accident killed the young master," he concluded. "An accident caused by Steward Stone."

Stanley, the horse-faced prosecutor, objected, "This is preposterous! Steward Stone has made a sworn statement that it was perfidious murder committed by the accused. Isn't that right, Stone?"

Stone studied O'Connell, who sat with his head bowed as in deep thought. The steward mumbled, "Well, now . . ."

At the hesitation, O'Connell turned his face toward Stone. His eyes bored into the steward's. His steady gaze reminded Stone of the image of Liam the porter dead in a pool of his own blood.

His voice quaking, John Stone resumed, "Well, it is, and it isn't. It may have been an accident. . . ." The tone of his voice went up the scale toward a squeak. "But dueling is still illegal, and a dueling death is still murder, isn't it?"

"What?" Prosecutor Stanley exploded. "What is this? And why hasn't this boy come forward before?"

O'Connell rumbled, "Because of the law of family responsibility leading to eviction. He thought that merely being a witness would subject his da and his sisters to penalties."

Fumbling with his notepad, Stanley inquired, "And is there no charge of complicity against the boy?" The crown prosecutor shot angry looks at Stone. "Did he not aid his brother's escape attempt?"

Justice Godwin lifted a document from his desk. "Such was suggested by Constable Carroll, but the constable has withdrawn his accusation. Nor is there any evidence against the lad."

Prosecutor Stanley collapsed wearily back into his chair. "Then where are we?"

"If I may make a suggestion," said O'Connell. "But perhaps Steward Stone and Martin Donovan may be excused first?"

Kate gripped her father's hand tightly with her sound one, praying silently and fervently. All around her were the whispered rumors about what was taking place in Justice Godwin's chambers: Kevin had betrayed his Ribbonmen colleagues to save himself . . . the military had intervened and Kevin was going to be summarily executed as a terrorist . . . the whole case was too dangerous to conclude in Galway and was being moved to Dublin . . . on and on.

She saw Martin returned to the courtroom. He looked at her, but shrugged without expression. He did not know what was about to happen either.

Then everyone stood as Justice Godwin strode in again. His scarlet robe swung around him, and his face was set and severe. He looked like the angel of death.

When Prosecutor Stanley and Defense Counsel O'Connell were in their places, Kevin was brought in to stand next to the Liberator. Kevin's face registered fear and confusion. Kate saw O'Connell put his arm around Kevin's shoulders.

"Certain key facts in this case," Justice Godwin commenced, "are not as originally represented. Mister Stanley, I believe the Crown wishes to amend its charge?"

The only noise in the courtroom was a sharp intake of breath into hundreds of lungs . . . punctuated by the rattling hiss of alarmed inhalation from Old Marlowe.

"Correct, mi'lord," Stanley agreed. "Upon examination, the Crown finds that the actual circumstances of the death of Viscount Marlowe are shown to be accidental."

The crowd in the gallery clattered with confusion. The word *accidental* was passed back and back until it bounced into the street outside. As if a bomb had exploded when the news reached the open air, a cheer swelled from hundreds of throats.

Justice Godwin demanded silence, which the onlookers reluctantly gave. The cries of amazement and delight from the street did not falter, however, but grew until Prosecutor Stanley had to shout to be heard. "Dueling that results in a death is still a capital crime," he said, at which Kate's heart sank again. "However," he continued, "in this case there are sufficient extenuating matters for the Crown to recommend clemency. The proposed penalty is transportation."

"Kevin Donovan," Justice Godwin intoned gravely. "The charge is dueling. The penalty is transportation. How do you plead?"

There was an instant's pause during which Kevin searched O'Connell's face, and the big man nodded.

"Guilty, mi'lord."

Bang came the seal of office upon the desktop. "Kevin Donovan you are sentenced to transportation. Rather than Australia, Lord Mayor O'Connell has offered to be your surety that you will, within two months' time, remove to America, never to return to Ireland. The jury is thanked and discharged . . . court is adjourned."

Old Marlowe hopped up and down, waving his arms. "This is impossible! My son is dead! How can his murderer be allowed to live?" His face inflated with dark blood, and the veins in his neck bulged and pulsed visibly. "I'll tear it all down!" he vowed. "Destruction to everything. In two months all of you will be leaving for America, because none of your homes will be standing! Tomorrow it will begin! Tomorrow, you'll see!"

"Out! I want them all out, I say!" The corners of Old Marlowe's mouth were flecked with foam as he raged against the people of Ballynockanor. Stone, Vicar Hodge, and Constable Carroll were with him in his study as Marlowe hammered his fist on his desk.

"And so they will all be tossed," John Stone said soothingly, giving a cautioning look to the policeman. In the landlord's frenzy, no attempt to make him see reason would work. Better to humor him and hope for calmer days ahead.

Vicar Hodge did not pick up on Stone's warning, however. "Dear me," he dithered, smoothing an errant strand of hair over his balding pate. "Surely you do not mean to evict them all at once? I mean, won't that cause rioting?"

Marlowe stormed, "What of it? Unless everyone is as useless as you three, we have men enough to put down a rebellion by these wretches . . . shoot them all if need be! My son is dead while his murderer goes free? Never! We'll burn their hovels and heap the ashes over William's grave!"

The steward tried to catch the parson's eye, failed, and nodded for Carroll to shut Hodge up any way at all. Driver Stone and the constable knew how much they were in danger of Old Marlowe's wrath. Their only preservation lay in the fact that the trial proceedings had been concluded behind closed doors, and the blame could be laid squarely on O'Connell. Even so, every effort must be made to get back into the master's good graces.

"Absolutely!" Stone responded to the landlord. "We'll show the whole country how to properly deal with criminals . . . how can there be rebellion where there are no rebels?"

The constable had interposed his bulk between Hodge and Marlowe and was backing the parson toward the door. Even this was not accomplished quickly enough to cut off the flow of Hodge's fretting. "There have always been tenants on Burke Land . . . I mean Marlowe, of course, but Burke for generations before. Some of the Ballynockanor tenancy agreements go right the way back centuries. Why, the first Burke allowed their chapel to be free of rent as long as it was used for worship, and every Burke after reconfirmed . . ."

"Stop!" Old Marlowe roared, making John Stone flinch at a shower of spittle. Constable Carroll broke into a sudden acrid sweat. "What's that you say? The papist chapel is on my land and has been paying no rent for centuries?"

Hodge's babbling stopped abruptly, but too late. The damage was already done. "Er, yes," he agreed reluctantly.

Swinging around toward the window with a look of depraved delight on his contorted features, Old Marlowe pointed out the window with a knotted finger. "Tear it down! At once, do you hear? No chapel means no village . . . the total end of Ballynockanor!"

The celebration supper for Kevin Donovan was in full cry. The schoolhouse bubbled with laughter, merriment, and congratulations. Never in the history of Connemara, so far as any could remember, had a man received an American wake after coming so close to a real one.

Kevin danced with Mary Elizabeth. "Is it a great long way to America?" she asked.

"Not so far as heaven," he replied. "Don't fuss, Mary Elizabeth. We will write to you, and you shall write back, and perhaps you'll come there yourself one day."

"Who's we?" she inquired suspiciously.

"Me and Jane and all your little nieces and nephews!" He laughed, swinging her around with her feet inscribing a great circle in the air. "Now go and dance with Mister O'Connell. It's thanks to him that your brother is home for Christmas!"

Mary Elizabeth, commission firmly in mind, arrowed across the dance floor toward the Liberator, who had surely re-earned his title by that day's work.

Capering past, Mad Molly exclaimed to Kevin, "It's in the grave, you know!"

"Aye, Molly!" Kevin grinned back. "But I'm not!"

"Just remember the babe," she cackled, twirling away with an invisible partner.

Kevin stood looking after her. Kate approached and took him by the elbow.

"Kate," Kevin said abruptly, waving Martin toward him. The boy's hands were behind his back. "Will y'not play on the fiddle for me?"

"That I will," Kate agreed. "Only it is not here."

"Oh, yes it is," her brother corrected, taking the instrument from his younger brother. "I sent Martin back for it."

Smiling at the trick, Kate plucked and tightened the strings to proper pitch. With newly rosined bow, she tucked the fiddle under her chin. The first vibrant notes of "The Gray Cock" leaped into the dancing air.

Feet stamping on the floor in time to the tune masked the first few knocks of a fist pounding on the door, but the entrance of Constable Carroll made all the merrymaking stop. Kate's bow swept upward, but the note died in the sudden chill let in with the policeman. "God bless all here," he bawled.

Kevin stiffened, and several of his friends and neighbors interposed themselves between him and the constable. Seeing the motion, Carroll laughed. "No, no! 'Tis not young Donovan concerns me. He's leavin' anyway. It's the rest of you whose departure I have the honor to announce."

"What d'ya mean?" Tom Donovan menaced. "If you've but come to darken our festivity, then be off wi'ye."

"But it's official, Tom." Carroll chuckled. "Oh, aye! Ballynocka-nor to be cleared, startin' tomorrow. The church, it seems, is on Marlowe land . . . and the master will have his own again. Good-night, all."

In the uproar of questions that followed Carroll's departure, the arrival of Jack the coachman went almost unremarked.

Kate was standing near her father when the driver of the Galway mail coach approached him. "Tom," he said, "they told me in town where to find you. It's glad I am to hear your son is spared."

"Aye, thank you," Tom Donovan said, still puzzling over the announcement about the chapel. "Did y'say y'were in search of me?"

"That I did, and sorry I am for to come this night in the midst of your celebration."

"Out with it, man!" Tom demanded. "There's too many playin' at word games!"

"Then straight out, here it is," the coachman said to a silent and attentive audience. "Brigit is dead. Joseph Burke, your son-in-law, says to tell you he's bringin' her home at last . . . I . . ."

"Enough," Tom Donovan said. "Saints preserve us, could we not have even one night? Is all to be swept away?"

Kate took him gently by the arm. Tears stood in her eyes, but she said quietly, "Maybe we'll all be off to America with Kev. Come on, Da. Let's be goin' home."

It was early morning on the Eve of the Nativity, but no hymns were being practiced in the choir of St. John the Evangelist. No festive wreaths decorated the aisles. All one hundred thirty people from Ballynockanor stood in the churchyard, but they were not speaking about lighting candles to guide the Holy Family or what treats were planned to grace their table before the midnight mass.

Instead, they gathered in little knots of three or four to speculate on whether there would even be a midnight mass, since by then there would be no church.

Father O'Bannon did his best to comfort his little flock. "Be of good cheer," he said. "Men of evil intent did not welcome Lord Jesus at His birth; why should we, who are merely His followers, expect to have an easy time of it?"

"But *where* will we worship, Father?" Clooney inquired.

"Tut, man!" O'Bannon chided. "Where did the blessed Patrick preach to our heathen fathers? In a great hall or out on the stony hillside? 'Tis not the bad old days of the last century come again. They cannot forbid us to worship if we've a mind to, though it be in a stable."

Mad Molly capered in and out among the clusters of worried villagers. "Sure, and it's the miracle, Father! Joseph and Mary and all the saints! It's comin', Father! And the babe! In my porridge and in my potato . . . and the grave. Don't forget the grave!"

Father O'Bannon kindly but firmly insisted that Molly's daughter take the old woman inside the chapel. "The excitement is too much for her," he said.

Kate, Kevin, Mary Elizabeth, Martin, and Tom Donovan stood with their friends and their neighbors. Kate thought how Father O'Bannon was right, but how sad and how hard the thought that this was the end of the church. It was the end of Ballynockanor as well. It had been one year exactly since Joseph Connor had come to Ballynockanor. It might take six months or even as much as another year, but all the cottages would be razed, and only the mournful wind would sigh over the place.

From the road toward Castletown came the tramp of feet and the rattle of drums. Two columns of marching men appeared, Her Majesty's soldiers. The sight made Kevin and other young men burn with anger. "Look, Da!" Kevin said. "The English have come to tear down our church."

This was not correct. Though the soldiers paraded up to the gate of the churchyard and halted, forming an aisle of gleaming muskets and polished buttons, they did not advance into the sacred ground.

Martin tugged at his da's sleeve. "They have no rope or hammers," he observed. "They cannot be here to toss the chapel."

The captain of the detachment approached Father O'Bannon and saluted. In a voice loud enough to be heard by all he announced, "What I am about to say gives me no pleasure, Your Honor. It has been proven to the satisfaction of the magistrate that this building stands on land belonging to Lord Marlowe. No rents having been paid; he intends to tear down this structure and reclaim his property. He has the right."

"And will you be a party to this outrage, my son?"

"Not I, Father, nor my men. But we are ordered to see that no interference takes place. Will you order your people to step aside?"

Kate heard the drunken shouts of the destructives before she saw them. No marching order there, but a rabble of men carrying axes and spades and toting bottles from which they drank freely. A mob of the worst scum scraped together from Galway City bumbled up the road. Laughing, cursing, and telling coarse jokes, they swarmed toward the chapel. In the center of the horde was Old Marlowe's carriage and with him were John Stone and Constable Carroll.

"Look," Kevin remarked bitterly. "See what the dung beetles are rolling up to the churchyard."

When the coach reached the lane leading to the church door it stopped, and Old Marlowe stood up. "Clear off," he yelled. "This is my land. Clear off, I say. Captain, will you disperse these trespassers?"

The captain looked grieved, but he did not argue. Turning to Father O'Bannon, he said quietly, "Will you ask your people to leave, Father? I want no bloodshed here."

Nodding sadly, Father O'Bannon gently urged his people away from the door. Stone and Carroll organized the destructives into gangs with hammers and crews with axes.

"Why don't' we fight?" Kevin demanded. "What's the good of me livin' if I must run like a whipped pup? What must the Liberator think of us?"

"Where *is* O'Connell?" Da mused aloud to no one in particular.

"I saw him walkin' off east before daybreak," Martin remarked. "Maybe Kevin's right: he did not wish to stay and see our shame."

"Then let's fight them!" Kevin said again, clenching his fists.

O'Bannon and Tom Donovan backed Kevin toward the grave of The Burke. "D'ye count your life so cheap that it is returned to you on one day and thrown away the next?" O'Bannon admonished. "Think, man. There are forty men of Ballynockanor here and at least that many hoodlums beholden to Marlowe. Even if we could hold them off, what about the guns and the bayonets of the soldiers? Back up I say. Back up, all of you."

From off east, down the highway leading to Tuam and the post road that went clear to Dublin, came a sound like the growl of thunder. Kate looked up with surprise. It was a perfectly cloudless sky. There was not even a hint of a storm over the mountains in the direction of the low-roaring noise.

"Up to the roof," Stone ordered crisply, anxious to redeem himself with Marlowe. "Tear off those slates and get lines around the beam." Several of the mercenary wrecking crew obliged.

Kate shook her head with a sad memory: no angels danced on the gables, but Marlowe's demons instead. No miracle was going to save Ballynockanor.

The demolition crew did not begin their ruinous work at once. Instead they looked off toward the peak of Ben Levy that pointed the way toward Tuam. "Get to work!" Stone demanded. The men on the gable ignored him. Instead they stared and talked among themselves.

"What is that noise, sister?" Mary Elizabeth asked. "It sounds like a river or sea waves crashin'." Kate could not answer her, but the deep rumble was growing louder.

Martin pointed to where the view of the eastern hills was darkening into obscurity, the color turning from dark green to a hazy gray. "Sure, and somethin' is raisin' a mighty cloud of dust away there," he said.

"It's an army!" one of the men on the rooftop shouted. "Thousands and thousands! They are all comin' this way!"

The captain of the soldiers yelled up to the destructives, "Hold right where you are. Don't touch a single stone of the chapel."

Several minutes passed in silent consternation.

Then the first surge of an approaching multitude arrived in Ballynockanor. Moments later, a flood tide of men, women, and children swirled up the track toward the church of St. John. Overflowing the banks of the road, wave after human wave poured across the churchyard, the fields, the bog, and the meadows. They surrounded Father O'Bannon's cottage, clambered over the stone fences, split and coalesced and pooled. They perched on headstones and on tree stumps. They surrounded the church twenty, fifty, a hundred bodies deep.

Confused and uncertain, Stone ordered his men back from the building, despite Marlowe's oaths and threats. Overwhelmed in numbers, now it was the company of soldiers and housewreckers who looked forlorn and pitiful.

"But what is this?" Kate said. "Who are all these people?" It seemed as if the whole province of Connaught was traveling to Ballynockanor.

The answer to the riddle was not long in coming. Just ahead of a low ebony wagon drawn by a horse with muffled harness, two men approached down the center of the road. One of them was Daniel O'Connell. Beside him, dressed in black with a silk mourning ribbon around his top hat, strode Joseph Connor Burke. He looked at Kate and her heart jumped, but he did not speak to her.

Joseph went directly to Tom Donovan, as if there were no other people or any other concerns that day. "I'm sorry I could not return her to you alive," he said. "But I have brought Brigit home, as I promised." He gestured over his shoulder toward the hearse bearing a dark-red wooden coffin. "And," he added, summoning a black woman who carried a small bundle wrapped in a white shawl, "here is your grandson . . . may he be the first of many!" Tom Donovan's face softened with tears as the nurse laid little Thomas Connor Burke in his arms. "And all these," he added, waving his arm around at the throng. "They have heard Brigit's story and come with me . . . some of them for a hundred miles . . . to honor her."

The gathered horde of onlookers viewed the scene with silent reverence, till the spell was broken by angry, wheezing curses. Old Marlowe hobbled through the crowd, shoving people out of his way. "Get off!" he said. "This chapel is coming down. Stone, Carroll, get it done, I say!"

Kate saw Constable Carroll and John Stone look nervously around. Surrounded completely by the band of thousands that had accompanied Joseph and Daniel O'Connell, Marlowe's henchmen could not even see those they had hired to tear down the chapel. The destructives had melted into the crowd.

"Captain!" Marlowe demanded of the soldier. "Disperse these . . ."

"Mister O'Connell," the captain interrupted smoothly. "How many people would you say you have with you?"

O'Connell smiled. "Twenty thousand, more or less."

"And is your intention peaceful?"

O'Connell looked offended. "Captain, I do not allow even the suggestion of violence amongst my followers. Our intention is to hold a peaceful rally here in support of repeal."

"No! No!" Marlowe screamed. "Shoot them! They are blocking my rights."

The captain studied Marlowe's flailing arms and spittle-flecked lips. "There is nothing to be done," he said. "As you can see, it is impossible for my small force to disperse twenty thousand without resorting to bloodshed, which I am specifically ordered to prevent, not to cause. Company, atten-shut! About-turn! For-ward, march!"

The last command was drowned out by the cheering from twenty thousand throats as the soldiers left the churchyard to march back toward Castletown.

Old Marlowe shook his fist under O'Connell's nose. "You can't stay here forever," he warned. "Food, shelter, winter coming on. All these people will have to leave, and then this chapel will come down, just as I swore. You can't stop it; you can only delay it!"

"It may be so," Tom Donovan growled fiercely, clutching his grandbaby to his chest. "But today we will lay my daughter to rest in holiness and reverence. There'll be no chapel-tossin' this day!"

Marlowe was not used to being ignored, but such was exactly what happened as Brigit's coffin was lifted from the wagon and passed over the heads of the mourners. Like a frail ship in sight of a safe harbor, the wooden box bobbed and rose over the human wave till settling in front of the stone monument to The Burke. "With your permission," Joseph said to his father-in-law, "we'll lay my wife, your daughter, to rest in the tomb of my father for now."

Tom Donovan squeezed Joseph about the neck with the baby between them. The child squawked once and then subsided, secure in his grandfather's embrace. Father O'Bannon approached the grate that barred the entrance to the tomb of the Burkes. He thoughtfully patted the pockets of his cassock and said to Martin; "Run, lad, and fetch the great ring of keys from inside the cupboard beside the bellpull."

When Martin returned a moment later, he was not alone. Mad Molly, screeching and dragging her daughter and son-in-law bodily after her, approached the tomb. "I'm sorry, Father," Molly's daughter apologized. "But she would not be denied."

No sooner had O'Bannon unlocked the entry and opened the iron bars with a squeal of disused hinges than Molly broke free of her keepers and plunged into the tomb. "It's in the grave!" she shouted. "Joseph and Mary. Merrow. Marlowe. My porridge. It's in the grave." Babbling, confused excitement coursed through the crowd.

In consternation, Father O'Bannon went in after her, to be almost bowled over when she emerged again at once. "It's here!" she exulted, waving something overhead.

It was Martin who first made out the nature of the object. "It's nought but an empty oat sack . . . a porridge sack," he announced.

During the byplay with the old woman, Old Marlowe had crept, spiderlike, up to the tomb. "It's in her porridge," he chortled. "There's your miracle! It's in her porridge!" He babbled wildly as the throng of onlookers groaned.

But Mad Molly had not ceased to exult. Ripping open the cord that bound the sack closed, she upended the cloth bag on the ground and out dumped a small, brass-bound casket. "It's in my porridge," she proclaimed triumphantly. "Merrow Marlowe shall not have it. Here," she said, thrusting the box into Joseph's hands. "For little Connor, from his father, The Burke. Keep it safe, he said. Don't let Marlowe or Stone know of it, he said. Hide the key, he said. The key!" Molly jumped straight up in the air as though launched from a bow. "Mary Elizabeth, where's the key?"

"I'll fetch it," Martin shouted, and back into the church he dashed, returning a moment later with the key from beneath the feet of Christ.

When Joseph applied pressure to turn the key in the lock, he feared at first that it would break. Then slowly, with an audible click, the lock turned, and the lid of the chest opened. On top of a stack of papers was a single folded sheet. On it, Joseph read, "For my own, true son, Joseph Connor Burke, from his father. In these papers is my last will and testament, no matter what other forgeries may have been presented. Also, though I am already too weak to prevent it, contained here are proofs that my brother-in-law, William Marlowe, and my steward, John Stone, have conspired to poison me."

The reading got no farther, because John Stone and Constable Carroll, who had been backing toward the edge of the crowd, chose that moment to turn and flee.

"Seize them!" Daniel O'Connell bellowed. "By order of The Burke of Connaught!"

Kevin looked around, ready to pounce on Old Marlowe himself. But Marlowe had not moved. He was slumped beneath the stone carving of Joseph's tribute to this father. He was mumbling, "It's in my porridge . . . it's in your potato . . . it's in my grave. . . ."

∽ Epilogue ∾

And so the promised Christmas miracle came at last to Bally-nockanor.

Stone and Carroll were so busy laying the blame upon each other that Vicar Hodge's evidence, given freely out of a deeply stricken conscience, was scarcely needed to send both driver and constable off to prison.

Old Marlowe would have been imprisoned or hanged, but because of his insanity, was committed instead to the lunatic asylum in Galway City.

Daniel O'Connell returned to Dublin. The first "monster" meeting, set in motion by the pilgrimage that followed Brigit's body home, was judged to be the harbinger of a great wave of public support for repeal. Eighteen forty-three would be a momentous year for Ireland.

After all reminders of the Marlowes and Stone had been removed from the manor house, Joseph reoccupied the home of his birth. A Burke again lived in Burke Park and he set about redressing the ills of rack rent and tithe collection.

Before the New Year was fully one month old, a grand reception was held in the Great Hall. And as Da dandled little Thomas upon his knee, to be fought over by Martin and Mary Elizabeth, Molly Fahey promised to all, that within a year she would dance at the wedding of Kate Donovan and Joseph Connor Burke.

About the Authors

With twenty-four novels to their credit, over six million books in print and seven ECPA gold Medallion awards, Bodie and Brock Thoene have taken their works of historical fiction to the top of the best-seller charts and to the hearts of their readers.

Bodie is the storyteller, weaving plotlines and characters into stunning re-creations of bygone eras.

Brock provides the foundation for Bodie's tales. His meticulous research and attention to historical detail ensure that the books are both informative and entertaining.

The Thoenes' collaboration receives critical acclaim as well as high praise from their appreciative audience.

LOOK FOR THESE OTHER BESTSELLING NOVELS FROM BODIE AND BROCK THOENE.

Shiloh Autumn
A Novel

The most heartfelt book the Thoenes have written, this novel is a compelling portrait of an American dustbowl family going through the heartbreak and struggle of the Great Depression. Based on Bodie's own grandparents' lives, *Shiloh Autumn* takes readers back to experience Depression-era life, from possum hunts to mass migration, Penny Auctions to the Veteran's March on Washington. Another Thoene novel destined to become a classic.

0-7852-8066-9 • 480 pages • Hardcover
0-7852-7134-1 • 480 pages • Trade Paperback
0-7852-7273-9 • Audio

The Twilight of Courage
A Novel

An award-winning World War II epic, *The Twilight of Courage* is an extensively researched and beautifully crafted glimpse into the most terrifying era of recent history. With drama and detail, the Thoenes have brought to life the men and women living their lives in the face of danger during the early days of the war. Readers are transported into hope, loss, and passion via the Thoenes' visual and engaging writing style.

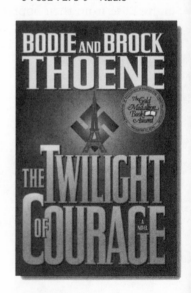

0-7852-8196-7 • 626 pages • Hardcover
0-7852-7596-7 • 524 pages • Trade Paperback

THOMAS NELSON PUBLISHERS
For every chapter of your life.